Forget Me Not

by
Jacqueline Falcomer

Print Edition ISBN 978-0-620-64538-6

Jacqueline Falcomer

www.jacquelinefalcomer.com

Cover design by Derek Murphy, *www.creativindie.com*

Editing & interior design of print edition by Fifth Street Design, *www.fifthstreet.com*

eBook conversion and publishing by David Henderson, *www.myebook.co.za*

Disclaimer. *With the exception of some historical events and public figures, this is a work of fiction. All characters appearing in this work are fictitious. Any resemblance to real persons, living or dead, is purely coincidental.*

Reviews

"*Chiropractic? Bulls? Life, death, ghosts and all kinds of love. There is something for everyone in this marvelously narrated story. It's perfectly delightful. Next book?*"

— Jane, London, England

"*Love that dog! The vivid narrative left me cringing in one moment, roaring with approval then crying my eyes out in the next. Unspeakable things. Betrayal. Unrequited love. I could not put it down.*"

— Franca, Tuscany, Italy

"*First of all, let me just say that I loved* Forget Me Not, *and I was not prepared to enjoy it because magic realism has never been one of my favorite genres — with one exception: Laura Esquivel's* Like Water for Chocolate. *Forget Me Not has the same marvelous cinematic quality as* LWfC, *and I found myself seeing* FMN *as a movie as I read.*"

— Joan, San Francisco, USA

"*You sure can paint the picture! It should be in braille . . . It is a page-turner with paragraphs of such poetic description that need revisiting, sometimes chapters later . . . The backdrop to the narrative is a visual and emotional experience. The interwoven detail of the characters is matched by the tapestry of history and events. Wait a moment while I linger in the place and live the writing . . . It has introduced me to things I have never known before and places I have not seen before and left me wanting more. You have a gift!*"

— Kathi, Cape Town, South Africa

"*Love, love, love the book. Could not put it down!*"

— Deb, South Carolina, USA

About *Forget Me Not*

Alejandro, or Alex as he is more often called, unfurls the multicolored banner that is his family history in *Forget Me Not*. In vivid and rich narration, from his grandfather's bull fighting ranch in Mexico, his father's chiropractic education in Iowa, to his own search for self and the woman he cannot forget, Alex is both guide and lost soul. Through three generations and across four continents, this is a multi-layered tale of all kinds of love, and of loss, hope, forgiveness, and, ultimately, redemption. And fear of being remembered for the wrong things. Or worse, simply forgotten. This lyrically-written story will grab and yank you through turmoil, depravity, tenderness, and awakening. A late-night page turner, this is not a book you will soon forget.

Dedication

To those whose nurturance
and generosity of spirit
coax even the most fragile wings to soar.

Personal Thanks

My thanks to all family and friends who journeyed with me until the end. Your unstinting support and kind words spurred me on.

Special thanks go to: Marie Louise Nykamp, who has supported every endeavor I have ever undertaken, this may have been the best; to Meriby Sweet, who was willing to read the book several times, looking for misplaced oddities and turns of phrase; and James Thayer (www.jamesthayer.com), who provided encouragement to write with my own voice. To each of you, I am vastly grateful.

To my first readers, Barbara Hodgkins, Kathy and Klaus Weixelbaumer, Joan More, Simona Berretti, and Deb Schwarz — you were very brave to take this on. Your feedback and enthusiasm to forge onward from chapter one helped me make the leap into this full-blown tale. I have immense appreciation for your patience.

Foreword

Miss Falcomer's novel, *Forget Me Not*, took me into another world and time: of bullfights, compelling exotic characters, orphanages, houses of ill repute, and high and low society.

Buoyed by lyrically-crafted sentences and phrase-making magnified by her powerful observations, her authoritative voice made this fictional saga credible and a delight to read. It gave me something new to look at and wonder about, something different from ordinary lives.

— **James Thayer**
Author of *White Star* and other
critically-acclaimed novels

WHAT YOU ARE NOW,
WE USED TO BE.

WHAT WE ARE NOW,
YOU WILL BE.

Inscription on Capuchin Crypt,
Church of the Immaculate, Rome, Italy.

W
hat is about to happen is no small matter. Vaporous and spectral, family members, friends, and others gather. Some sit, some stand. All are waiting to hear and bear witness to the account of their lives to be told for the first time.

This story has taken a while to piece together. Some may complain too long a while. But it has resulted in a densely woven chronicle that requires careful reading — I pray I am up to the task — and equally, it deserves attentive listening.

My name is Alejandro Salazar Herrera. But everyone, for ease of pronunciation, calls me Alex. Also, it avoids confusion, as my mother and I share the same first name but for the last letter. Hers ends in an 'a' and mine in an 'o'.

After an absence, I'm in my family home, in the market town of Medina del Campo, Valladolid, Spain, and seated at the desk that was once my father's, but which I now claim. My knees have begun to ache, a reminder I have sat too long.

On the desk are two piles of papers. One being the fragile letters exchanged half a century ago between my father and his mother. The other, a recently completed, typed manuscript in which are their stories and mine; the secret stories of those I never knew for the longest time; stories of those I loved and lost; stories of those I did not realize I loved and almost came to losing, too.

In a row in front of the two piles are five recently received, soft grey metal canisters with screw-on lids. These contain the ashes of my paternal grandparents, my father, my first lover, and a dog.

In a little while, once the sun has warmed the ramparts of the medieval fortress, La Mota — which keeps watch over our town — the ashes will be tossed to the wind. Wherever the wind wills, ash will fly and then settle.

Today is Sunday, November 2, 1980. As is the custom in Latin countries, *Día de Muertos*, the Day of the Dead, is being celebrated. In keeping with tradition, the deceased are remembered, their life stories recounted and — wholly dependent upon the teller — embellished or reduced.

By contrast, this story is as authentic as it possibly can be. And for the ease of simplicity, I'll start reading in chronological order the oldest story first starting here in Medina del Campo in the year 1900.

------------ ◆ ------------

It was also a Sunday, nearing the end of a late summer afternoon. My paternal grandfather, Felipe Salazar, just twenty-three years old was dressed in the *vaquero*, cowboy clothes of his time. On his head was his Sunday sombrero. It had a tall pointy crown and wide flat brim. It concealed the scrunched up space between his eyebrows as he focused on the bull upon which all his hopes were pinned. Around my grandfather, the fans who packed the bullring were assessing the third and final phase in the last bullfight of that day. Fizzy copper tangs wafting overhead cut through the thick smell of fresh blood from earlier fights.

The matador invited the bull to perform the paso-doble, double-step, better known in bullfighting culture as *Danza de la Muerte*, the Dance of Death. He swirled the magenta and gold cape inches from the bull's nose. All held their breaths. The bull's hooves slipped. In the next beat, he righted himself, then entered the dance.

In a cacophony of calls, hand claps, and foot stomps, fans demanded the courageous bull's reprieve from death.

The matador and his crew withdrew to a safer distance. The bull stood rock still. Alone. A wisp of a breeze rattled the long spears, and fluttered cheerful little paper flags attached to the barbed sticks protruding from his blood-slicked hide.

A hush descended upon the crowd. All eyes looked for the twitch of *el Presidente's, the President's*, little finger granting the reprieve. The fans whistled and whooped, but none louder than my grandfather.

The bull's prize was to be turned out to pasture, free to cover as many cows as possible. And my grandfather's prize was that his dream of riches would turn into real riches few *toreros,* bull handlers, ever achieved. For in meeting the requirements of the centuries-old practice, fighting bulls would be sold for a hefty price. And bullfighting requires a lot of bulls.

Like poor farmers before them, Felipe Salazar and his new wife, Maria Guadalupe Moreno, went in search of a better life.

She was short, dark, had a round cheerful face, was full breasted and blessed with broad hips. He was tall, fair, had a chiseled face, lean limbs, and blessed with agile litheness. But just like the Universe teaches, opposites attract and together they formed a perfectly matched whole.

The couple left Spain for Mexico, having heard Mexico needed a new seed line. Their honeymoon was an unconventional journey with the reprieved and crated seed bull in tow. Weeks and several near mishaps later, he was let loose in the corral distant from the patched adobe house my grandparents used as their new home.

As a *torero,* Felipe Salazar had raised and worked with bulls all his life. He would have told you bulls are aggressive, to be avoided at any cost. That there is an old ploy to moving bulls safely. If honored, the task can be accomplished with neither bloodshed nor loss of life. A bull needs to be moved while surrounded by his herd of females. Ideally, a barrier should separate beast from man. And the *torero* is responsible for an unhurried relocation best unnoticed by the bull.

On an afternoon two years later, the cows, tantalized by the smell of new shoots in the adjoining corral, moved forward more quickly than usual. Heavy and slow the bull, unimaginatively nicknamed *Toro de Semillas,* found himself alone.

In his peripheral vision, he must have caught sight of a moving shadow. His muscled mass swung round. He would defend his cows until death.

In the quiet time between two heartbeats Felipe Salazar found himself beneath the enraged bull.

A few days from giving birth to my father, my grandmother, Maria Guadalupe Moreno, heard her husband's cries through the ranch dogs' frenzied barks. She picked up her skirts and ran. He lay silenced. Curled in a fetal ball under the bull's belly, his clothes shredded. Miniature geysers spurted red, one from each wound.

Maria Guadalupe Moreno tore a sapling from the ground, the kind she wove into baskets. Gripping the frayed root ball she flicked the flexible end, stinging the lead cow's hindquarters. The cow turned back towards the bull. The others followed.

The bull looked at his arriving herd. Flanked by bobbing hips and swinging tails, he ambled through the open gate into the adjoining corral. He and his cows set about foraging the newly sprung grass.

With maniacal strength, Maria Guadalupe Moreno heaved and dragged her husband to the other side of the corral fence. His face was white with agony or loss of blood.

The long-legged ranch dogs, which normally dashed about like spritely shadows, halted. Heads and tails held low, they formed a semicircle a few feet from their leader's body.

Consuelo, the scrawny yellow bitch who produced litters of indefatigable hunters, sank down. With her nose pressed forward, she belly-crawled to the unconscious body. She lapped up the blood in search of its sources. When she found it, she settled into a licking rhythm until there was no more blood.

A gust of wind swept Maria Guadalupe Moreno into the house, the soles of her feet skimming the dusty ground. Passing through the kitchen, she raised one arm. From the top shelf — normally, she could reach it only by standing on a chair — she grabbed a clay pot. It was filled with a salve of crushed tobacco leaves. Had there been a clock, the second hand would have shown hardly a moment had passed before she was back, kneeling beside her husband and the licking bitch.

As the gored wounds emerged pink and clean, Maria Guadalupe Moreno plugged them with the tobacco salve. With her teeth, she tore her apron into strips and bound each injury. At the last binding, barely visible in the setting sun, she felt the first violent spasm. My father, José Salazar Moreno, was ready to enter the world.

My grandmother laboured. Her fingers scrabbled in the dirt with every contraction as she half lay, half sat beside her unconscious husband. Around them, the dogs inched closer.

At first starlight, the smallest of owls emerged from abandoned woodpecker holes in the trunks of cacti. Under their gaze, my father slipped out of the birth canal. His warm body hit the cold air, creating little clouds of rising steam.

With the newborn between her thighs, Maria Guadalupe Moreno tied two knots in the length of the cord. Unsnapping the metal button on the leather sheath on her husband's belt, she withdrew the Bowie knife. She sliced through the space between the knots.

By the glow of the gibbous moon, she noticed that the child's tiny left foot was smaller than the other. But there was another matter at hand. The placenta emerged. With the swishing sound of rippling silk, it slipped smoothly from her fingers as she threw it in an arc to just beyond the circle of dogs. Consuelo growled low. Two of her pregnant daughters jumped. In mid-air, they fought for a share of it.

With the newborn wrapped like a tortilla in one of her bloodied skirts, his pinched face barely visible in the crook of her arm, Maria Guadalupe Moreno lay down alongside her unconscious husband.

A torrent of emotions clamored for attention. Of these, she isolated three. Joy for the bundle she cradled in her arms, for which she thanked the Universe. Hate for the bull that had so injured her husband, for which she cursed the Universe. Frustration because there would be no reason offered for the difference in her child's feet. And for this, she ignored the Universe.

Under morning light, she would explore the child's feet and decide her own answer. It was the first step towards changing the course of her son's future from what was already written in *The Logbook of Futures Foretold*.

The pack drew together. They pressed their boney rumps up against each other and along the length of my grandparents' bodies. Their heads faced outwards resting upon their paws, ears swiveling, alert to any sound.

The owls yipped their calls, to which, if you listened hard enough, you may have heard the unborn pups in Consuelo's daughters' bellies respond. Thus, under a star speckled sky, they all passed the night.

At dawn, Maria Guadalupe Moreno awoke to see her husband's eyes open. Vacant. She raised their newborn close to his face. She placed kisses on her husband's forehead. The pressure of her lips increased imparting her urgent need for him.

A pinprick of light started to gleam. Coming closer it grew brighter and stronger then flooded his eyes reflecting Felipe Salazar's awed joy at his first sight of the new life.

The bull and his cows moved back to the fence. Through the spaces between the horizontal corral poles, they watched the life-overcome-death tussle play out before them.

Before the sun climbed a quarter arc, Felipe Salazar began the return journey to the house. He crawled and then fainted with the pain from his injuries, his progress monitored by Consuelo and her daughters. Each time he fainted, the bitches lay down beside him. Then, judging it was time to try again, Consuelo thrust her wet nose into his face. Past noon, he collapsed onto a makeshift pallet on the kitchen floor.

With her son tied to her by a woven sling, Maria Guadalupe Moreno never left her husband's side. Within hours of each other, Consuelo's daughters whelped in two large boxes, one on either side of the stove. Newborn suckling sounds filled the kitchen soon turning into strident yells or yelps, all eager for life.

Consuelo remained at the foot of the pallet, one eye on Felipe Salazar and the other on everything else.

The rest of the pack remained outdoors. When not hunting, they slept. Paws together, backs arched, each curled nose to tail. And, in a corkscrew spiral, each sank into their hollowed-out dustbowl. Furry-mounded sentinels, indistinguishable one from the other, dotted the yard.

Each morning, rabbits, birds, rodents, and once a Mexican hog lay dead at the kitchen door. My grandmother used what she needed from these kills, throwing the remainder to the dogs.

My grandfather's first meal was the blood of the Mexican hog, boiled, mixed with crumbled bread, and sprinkled with vinegar and cumin. It was also his second and third meal. By the fourth, he'd had enough. He asked for something else. My grandmother barely managed to contain the flash of a quick grin. And with her raisin-dark eyes dancing with mirth, she gave thanks to the Universe. Her husband was on the road to recovery.

The now-proven antibacterial enzyme lysozyme, found in the saliva of dogs was perhaps why my grandfather's wounds did not become infected. Or it was the unproven curative powers of tobacco salve on open wounds. His healed scars became soft and supple thanks to wild olive oil smoothed into them.

Felipe Salazar got back on his feet. But his original strength and mobility did not return. He was unable to stand upright. Each year, his upper spine curved more, forcing his head to drop forward. He could see to the right all the time. When he wanted to see to the left, he had to turn at a forty-five degree angle. His hunch became noticeable. He had to sleep on his stomach with his head turned to the right. He suffered blinding headaches and deadness in his arms.

Yet my grandparents remained on the ranch. They raised my father, Consuelo's extended line of hunting dogs, and their herd of cattle destined for the *abattoir*. And they raised the most aggressive and physically correct fighting bulls for the *Luis Longoria Plaza de Toros* bullring on Sundays and feast days.

While beef cattle prices fluctuated, there was no haggling over the price of a fighting bull. The more aggression and courage shown, the higher the price. By raising bulls destined for the bullring, my grandparents amassed more money than they needed for the simple life-style they led.

When *Toro de Semillas* died, they did not weep. Yet when Consuelo the bitch died, they mourned and wept enough to fill the cattle water troughs. Each year thereafter, upon the Day of the Dead they celebrated her life. And wept a little more, causing troughs to spill their brims.

Even in death, she remained true to the meaning of her name, bringing them comfort and solace. Of all the dogs, only Consuelo was buried under a home-fashioned cross in the area reserved for future members of the Salazar Moreno family. She was never forgotten. And once my grandparents died, there were three wrought iron crosses in the graveyard; theirs and Consuelo's.

The ranch spread over a few hundred acres. One side was bounded by the Rio Bravo, which the Texans on the opposite side called the Rio Grande. My grandfather managed it alone. Each dawn, he rode out with a team of horses. He returned home when chickens took to their roosts.

Several times a year, roaming ranch workers and their families stopped by. They would help mend fences, brand stock, and cut back dry and inedible brush, which around midday was prone to spontaneous combustion. It was then the companionless life my father led would be broken.

But his father had such a distorted physique, that, upon seeing him, children would run for their mothers screaming. So he'd go to their camps if he wanted to mix with others of his age.

To this, my grandmother was not inclined. For, from the night after his birth, she negotiated with the Universe much higher stakes for her son than the daughter of a roaming ranch worker.

When my father turned eighteen — standing nearly as tall as his father (his face by then had taken on his father's chiseled look) — my grandfather fell from a makeshift ladder. It was hardly a fall. His foot slipped from the first rung. But he landed at an awkward angle — on something blunt. He said it set off a ripple wave along his spine.

Each ripple was punctuated by loud popping like pulled bottled corks in choreographed timing, one after the other. He had drunk fizzy wine once. He felt as if a gallon of it had been poured down the length of his spine. All was a-tingle, light and bubbly, and his head felt aerated and bright. Fused colors became sharp and in needle point focus.

The subterranean land of the ranch was crisscrossed with the empty connected tunnels and dens of long extinct marsupials. A den just below the surface of the ground upon which my grandfather landed had collapsed. It reverberated along the network of tunnels reaching the town fourteen kilometres away. It carried such a loud and rumbling vibration, it was assumed by the townspeople they were experiencing an earth tremor.

He motioned to his son to let him be. A river of warmth flooded him. It reached parts that in former years had been tormented with hot or cold pins and needles. Or more worrying, tormented with no feeling at all.

With exquisite sensation, he felt the tip of the longest strand of hair on his head all the way down through to the end of his shortest toenail. He felt so well he dared not move. He did not want the glorious fountain of aerated bubbles bathing him from the inside out to stop. He lay there until the shimmering dust particles settling all around and upon him faded.

Mother and son stood alongside each other. Maria Guadalupe Moreno recognized they were in the presence of something inexplicable and unexplainable. But which, she knew, only the Universe would ever understand.

My grandfather rolled over to one side, bent his knees, and raised himself onto all fours. Hoisting himself up from the ground, he stood upright. As minutes passed, the crook between his shoulders straightened. He assumed the height of his youth.

His head adjusted and sat squarely upon his shoulders. He could see his wife and son in aligned focus from both eyes.

With the first step forward, his body moved smoothly. Joints worked as though oiled, all in sync, and with full range of motion.

Alert to change, the dogs sprang up. Testing, my grandfather first hopped, jumped, and skipped like a kid playing hopscotch. Then he sprinted in a straight line and ended in a victory lap. For every step he took, the dogs quadrupled, blurring the air in a mad whirl of exhilarating movement.

The chains choking his muscles and bones for near on eighteen years, fell away. He was restored to his former youthful and energetic body.

'A miracle,' the family's physician, Dr Raul Perez exclaimed peering over the rims of the pince-nez glasses perched on the bridge of his nose. He was still perplexed by the earth tremor he'd experienced in his consulting room the day before. Now even more so, given the time of José's fall and the vibration of the earth coincided.

Years earlier, he'd run out of herbal poultice recipes, scientific and quack medications, mud baths, and hot thermal spring suggestions to ease my grandfather's discomfort. Traditional, but open minded, he had listened to my grandfather's description of the ripples accompanied by a series of cracks and pops along his spine. He deduced that it was similar to the new-fangled cure from across the border.

The hands-only cure claim was bandied about as a breakthrough, ridding ailments of all sorts, real and imagined. This phenomenon was occurring regularly, without the aid of a single pill. Until then, it was unproven, but success stories were pouring into newspaper offices. Pages of testimonials were read and shared. There were skeptics who made sure their opinions were heard.

Nevertheless, standing before him was irrefutable proof that spinal adjustments worked. And could also cause the earth to move.

While the Salazar Moreno family was happy to accept a miracle verdict, my grandfather began to press the doctor for copies of recent articles on the new drug-free cure, "Chiropractic".

My father, too, got caught up in the feverish curiosity heightened by hearing his father laugh for the first time, throw back his head face up to the warm sun, and walk tall and proud with a spring in his step. And change did not stop there.

Light points flamed and danced in the centre of his mother's pupils. Conjugal rights had resumed with ardor, making up for the lost years. Their bodies spooned together, bones melded as one. Their weights rested, balanced against each other afterwards. Just as it was meant to be.

My grandmother's relationship with the Universe intensified. She now dispensed loud thanks several times a day for the return of her husband as she had known him. But, in silence, she continued the tricky business of negotiating the future for her son.

I t was a late afternoon in April, 1922. José Salazar Moreno, aged twenty-three, was almost ready to leave his family home in Nuevo Laredo, Mexico. For days prior, he had moved around the ranch saying goodbye to all that was dear to him. He did not know then it would be the first and last time.

But his sixth sense knew. It instructed his memory to record everything for which the first five senses were responsible. So in the future, when summoned, perfectly preserved memories would enter on cue.

In the final hour, he sat at the kitchen table. His mother stood at the opposite end. Words were not necessary — all telling was done.

Despite the gruelling hardship of raising cattle and fighting bulls, time had been kind to Maria Guadalupe Moreno. Her raisin-dark eyes remained bright, often dancing with merriment. Though her dark hair was beginning to fleck grey, and she'd lost her womanly bosom and ample hips — physical labour had seen to that — she stood upright and strong. Only her hands, and in particular her knuckles, showed her unending labour.

While she prepared and packed into a clean cloth as many tortillas as she could, José watched his mother's roughened hands that had separated him from her in the first hour after his birth. But immediately upon which, a new link forged, tying each to the other in ways far stronger than life's first cord. Their intuit was, even when apart, they would share the other's joys and sorrows.

Twenty years later, the strongest connection of all was their last. José dreamt of his mother who, upon waking, found herself trapped in her dead husband's stiffening arms. As she struggled to free herself, the last grains of sand in the hourglass that was her life, trickled out. When realizing the dream had turned into a portal through which he traversed, entering his parents' reality, José stopped fighting and embraced them instead.

Holding one naked and dead, and one naked and dying parent caused the death page in *The Logbook of Futures Foretold* to turn. Too late, the guardian slammed the book shut. José saw inscribed in faded ink the year of his passing.

Some dreams, try as hard as one might, are never remembered. But that dream he never forgot. No matter the highs and lows, twists and turns, the train that was his life, inexorably chugged on — the appointed year of his passing getting closer each day. All during which he never forgot his mother's last whisper-soft breath against his cheek kissing him goodbye.

Watching his mother in the kitchen, José was unaware there was a *Logbook of Futures Foretold* and all it had in store for him.

His father rode out with him to Laredo, Texas, the sister town to Nuevo Laredo, Mexico. Sleek dogs, all of which were Consuelo's offspring, loped alongside the horses. They darted off to flush quail, returned, and took up their flanking positions again.

At the invisible line separating the ranch from no-man's land, they halted. A single word, and the dogs settled. Father and son moved forward, entering the land no one could claim their own.

Daily life in the mesquite shrubs and trees dotted about the dusty landscape began to ease off. Bees returned to their hives, leaving hummingbirds to complete the day's nectar gathering. In their hives, the nectar would turn into a clear, bright yellow honey — José's favourite childhood food.

In times yet to come, when there was no possibility of acquiring this honey, he would be driven crazy with the memory of its taste. And as in the natural order of life, where one thing follows another, so too did the memory of its taste evoke perfectly preserved memories — of the ranch, his parents, and everything he loved that he had left behind.

Barring few past and future events, he shared all his memories with one other — his yet-to-be-born son. In hope that should his memory fail, Alex would remember it for him.

Behind Felipe and his son José, a vermillion sun began its climb down from sky to earth's crust. Long diffused rays highlighted the clouds of departing bees. Hummingbirds hovered dead centre to flower heads irrespective of the direction a breeze might move them. They glowed bright orange in the weakened sunlight.

The town of Laredo edged into view across from the Rio Bravo, or the Rio Grande dependent upon which side of the river one lived. As a new bridge (the old one had burned down) was still under construction, father and son dismounted. They walked their horses over the temporary wooden pontoon, remounted, and headed to the train station. Ninety years later, there would be five bridges connecting the two sides of the river.

They purchased a one-way ticket on the Sunshine Special, a passenger train run by the Missouri Pacific Railroad Company. To José, the name the Sunshine Special was a misnomer given it departed at night. It was scheduled to arrive in St. Louis, Missouri, on the second morning. Mental arithmetic told José he had neither enough tortillas to see him through to St. Louis nor his final destination, Davenport, Iowa.

In silence, Felipe Salazar slipped his parting gift into José's left boot. After embracing his son, he turned the horses and headed back over the border.

Shading his eyes, José watched his father ride into the dying sun. For the first time, he realized that except for his age and the two inches his father had on him, they were mirror images of each other.

They were lean limbed and broad shouldered. Taller and fairer than all their Mexican neighbours, and as tall and as fair as any of their Texan neighbours.

Both wore their hair long, parted in the middle, and tied back into a tail ending below their shoulder blades. They had the same blue eyes. They passed well for good looking. But because of their height, they were impressive.

Men and women crowded the platform. They sized José up calculating the weight of their limbs against his. Men assumed defensive stances. They flexed their muscles under the cloth of their jacket sleeves. Women's fans fluttered a little more, wrist and throat buttons loosening.

While José stood on the platform in the gathering dusk, men, perhaps realizing he was no threat, let go their posturing. But the women's interest must have held out much longer. Under the cover of their lashes and advancing darkness, their eyes swallowed José. Only when they lowered their sights was he released.

Urged on by the conductor's calls he boarded the train. After two long whistle blasts, the brakes were released. Steel wheels glided on tracks pulled by a steam locomotive fuelled by oil. It was José's first train journey. It heralded new beginnings and the first obstacle.

Tucked in the inside pocket of his leather jacket was a well-thumbed Spanish-English dictionary. It was a farewell gift from the visually impaired Dr Raul Perez whose name was inked on the inside cover. The dictionary would be the only way José could communicate until he learned to speak English.

Without Dr Perez's help, José would not have found himself on the train headed to a new country, life, and career. The thought crossed his mind that he should have been the one to give Dr Perez a gift.

Unknown to him, already written in *The Logbook of Futures Foretold*, he would return an even greater gift to Dr Perez in an extraordinary, twice removed way.

Tired from weeks of nervous anticipation, clothed and with his boots still on, he fell onto the ready made-up sleeper. Despite a variety of piercing whistles he slept throughout the night.

It was the first time he'd go to sleep and wake up knowing no one to whom to say good night or good morning. He felt alone. Like an unwelcomed guest, this feeling would turn up, even when surrounded by those he loved and those he thought loved him.

He woke eager to see the changed scenery rushing by. Although it was spring, it was colder with every mile northeast the train had travelled. José was not used to such cool weather. He was grateful for the steam pipes throughout the passenger cars that radiated heat.

Before breakfast, train staff, using an ingenious mechanism, turned his sleeping berth back into a broad, well-upholstered chair.

Upon discovering meals were included in the price of his one-way first class ticket, he pressed his mother's cloth of wrapped tortillas into the train staffs' reluctant hands. He was ready to try all that was new including on-board meals.

At the sound of each meal's gong, passengers made their way to the dining car. Too soon, he discovered he did not like the food. He was hardly able to swallow any of it. He regretted not keeping the soft and fragrant flour tortillas, especially as he never got to eat his mother's tortillas again.

He was the only non-English speaker on board. If there were Spanish-speaking passengers, they kept it to themselves. His attempts to engage the Mexican staff were rebuffed.

He heard his mother's voice cautioning him, 'Stay away from Mexicans. We are Spanish. We will only speak Castilian'. All her life, she insisted they speak in the tongue of their family origin.

If a snapshot could have been taken, it would be clear to see the reasons why José stood out from the rest of the passengers. Not only because of his impressive height and, as almost all women would have said, his chiselled good looks, but also because he was dressed in the common clothes of a working cowboy.

And when he got bored of the cold, flat Central Plains, he paged through the dictionary. He practiced rolling his tongue on the roof of his mouth trying to produce what sounds he thought were correct.

Passengers looked sideways at him and further separated themselves from him. For his tongue poked out. He licked his lips, grimaced, and snake-like hisses of spit sprayed the air.

Little did he know that one of the peculiarities of the English language is this: the spoken is often different from the written word. There are many words with silent letters and combinations of letters that have no audial relation to their sounds. Leaving the dictionary alone would have served him better.

The Sunshine Special announced its arrival in St. Louis, Missouri, with three short whistles. José got off to stretch his legs and to watch coaches being coupled to another train. At a blast of cold air, he turned up the collar of his fringed jacket. He was not wearing warm enough clothes. Nor did he have, he realized, enough warm clothes. His defective left foot soon lost all sensation. By the time he swung back up on board, he was frozen and limping.

He always forgot no one could see through his boots to the smaller foot. The toe-end of all his left boots were padded to take up the extra space. What he did not expect was catching a cold, making the last part of his journey flash by gripped by fever and the chills.

He fell asleep and his first visit to a bullfight, easily the worst nightmare of his childhood, returned.

------------- ◆ -------------

Carried into the bullring straddling his father's shoulders, his ankles held fast by Felipe Salazar's calloused hands, José always ducked his head for fear of hitting it against the Nuevo Laredo coat of arms.

The coat of arms for Nuevo Laredo has inscribed on it, 'City with Courage'. And his father believed the motto was not meant for the citizens of Nuevo Laredo, but for bulls and the cows that bore them.

Bulls inherit their courage and eyesight from their mothers. To test their courage, they are pricked three times by the *picador's*, lancer's, practice lance, no bigger than a small nail. If they return each time charging at the horse from where the prick is delivered, they are considered courageous.

And it is the distance over which they charge, having caught sight of a far off movement, that proves their eyesight. Contrary to popular belief, they do not see colour, only movement. The cape used in the professional bullring is dyed red, shielding the squeamish from the vast quantities of blood lost.

Before being put to the bull, a heifer's courage and eyesight are tested the way bulls are. If she passes the test, her reflexes and stamina are developed.

She faces matadors perfecting the art of the death dance in the practice bullring. She is encouraged to charge from the right-hand side to the left-hand side guided by the swinging cape.

Her reward: she is never killed in a ring. That pride of place is wholly reserved for her male offspring. When she is no longer of any use, she faces the mechanized killing machine of the slaughterhouse.

Courage Felipe Salazar understood well. For like his father, and his father's father, they had provided endless bulls to the crazed delight of bullfighting fans.

'But not only have bulls fought in this bullring,' he'd told José.

'In 1895, Daniel Boone, you know who Daniel Boone is, don't you son?'

'Yes, Papa.'

'Daniel Boone's great grandnephew threw his 550-pound African circus lion and a 700-pound American grizzly together in a specially-made steel cage.'

José's eyes grew wide. 'And?'

'The fight was a draw. But while the lion recovered from his wounds, a Mexican-bred bull — do you hear that, son? — a Mexican-bred bull was matched with the grizzly.'

'And then?'

'Of course the grizzly lost. A week later, Mexicans rooted for the bull and Americans from across the border rooted for the recovered lion. And then do you know what happened?'

'The Mexican-bred bull won again!'

'That's my boy.'

Father and son's attention turned to the beginning of the bullfight. Until José knew the order, the unwritten laws and technicalities of a bullfight by heart, Felipe Salazar continued to explain the three parts of a professional bullfight to him in minute detail.

Bulls have an inborn hatred of horses. Upon sight, they are driven to obliterate them from the earth. Horses have an inborn fear of bulls. At the merest sniff or sight of a bull, horses gallop away. Yet one without the other in the world of bullfighting is unthinkable.

Until the 1930s, more horses than bulls died in the bullring. Seeing horses trip up on their intestines trailing in the dirt proved distressing for bullfighting fans. So the centuries-old laws underwent a change. Horses were, and still are, required to be padded on one side in both practice and professional bullrings.

So when the first part — the salute parade — is over, two blindfolded horses trembling in fear, are held in check by the *picadors*. They are presented with their padded side to the charging bull. The solid wood panels of the ring protect the opposite unpadded and soft underbelly of the horse. All escape exits for both horse and bull are blocked.

In the second half, the *picadors* jam long lances into the bull's neck. Then *bandarillos*, flagmen, hook barbed sticks into the bull's shoulders. Lances, barbed sticks, internal injury to the bull's neck muscles, and the resulting blood loss, weaken the bull.

Last, shod in shocking pink socks and soft black velvet slippers, the matador engages the bull. He passes the cape several times in front of the bull, which, until that moment he has never seen.

From the bull's reaction to the passing of the cape, the matador learns which side the bull favours and tends to run. And it is this knowledge that the matador needs to bring the bull into the perfect position to end the dance.

A lot of factors have to line up for the perfect killing of a bull. And woe to the matador should he not deliver death to exact expectations. For fans' loud protests will be heard long after the bull has been dragged from the ring. Minus its ears and tail.

And the killing goes like this:

Front hooves together, the aligned horizontal shoulder blades' spread apart, transversing the elongated vertical spine. It forms the distinct shape of the cross on which Jesus died.

When the tortured neck muscles no longer hold up the bull's massive head, it dips. The treacherous horns drop out of the way offering a clear path to the sweet killing spot — the spot being the intersection of the cross.

It is the matador's first and the bull's last charge. The matador holds the sword in one hand and some claim the sword is guided by a different hand: that of an Angel of Mercy.

With the other, the matador makes the Roman Catholic sign of the cross. At the last moment he twists aside as the bull thunders by. The matador thrusts the sword with its downward curved tip, dead centre to the killing spot, right up to its hilt.

The blade punctures the heart or severs the aorta, causing instant death.

⸻ ◆ ⸻

José jerked awake, his vision blurred with the memory of slick blood pouring from the bull's nostrils as the train pulled into Rock Island Railroad Station, Davenport, Iowa. It was a cheery red brick building considered the heart of the city by the diverse nationalities who had walked through its doors. Years later, it would be flattened and today it is an asphalt car park.

Clutching a letter with his bag hoisted onto his shoulder, José left the station. He showed a cab driver the address. That it was his first ride in an automobile was lost on José. Within minutes, he was deposited at the kerbside opposite a small house. It would be his home for the next two years.

He pushed the gate open and stumbled up the straight and narrow path towards the front door. In a feverish haze, he stabbed at the doorbell several times before his finger made the connection. As the door opened, his world tilted. He crumpled onto the doorstep.

When piercing train whistles, disembowelled horses, and bulls thundering past pirouetting matadors punctuating his fevered sleep stopped, he re-entered consciousness.

José found himself in a bed and dressed in pyjamas that were not his own. He was barefoot. His first thought was that whoever undressed and re-dressed him had seen his foot. He was stricken with embarrassment. He almost never saw his naked foot as he always wore socks, even when asleep.

A woman's face swam into focus. It was Mrs Joan Smith, his hostess. Dr Raul Perez's introduction letter that he had clutched in his hand as though his life depended on it, lay smoothed, open on the bedside table.

'How are you feeling?'

He had no clue what had been said.

She tried again. 'I am Mrs Smith. You are ill.'

He stared without saying anything, but did wonder how this fragile woman could have lifted, dressed, and put him to bed.

Dressed in a French fishtail braided chignon, her dark hair made her skin appear paler. Bronze chips embedded in her green eyes framed by lush eyelashes, flashed like snapping castanets when caught in the right light. Or, as José would come to learn, when she silently set out to get her own way.

She wore a demure white cotton blouse with a high collar edged in lace. A row of precision-set-apart opalescent buttons ran from her throat, between her breasts and disappeared into a cinched in wasp-waist. Her dark heavy skirt ended where her ankle boots began.

'Do you speak English?'

This he understood, for Dr Perez had drilled this phrase into his head. He shook his head in the negative. And even if he had been able to respond, he could not. His swollen throat held his tongue fast. And, as everyone knows, speaking requires an infinitely agile and moist tongue.

'Don't worry. I'll teach you. But let's get you better first.'

His convalescence took longer than expected. Curiously, his genitalia appeared to sympathize with his infected throat by swelling and throbbing uncomfortably. Embarrassed, José ensured this grotesqueness remained well hidden from Mrs Smith and her doctor.

The doctor concluded — incorrectly — José was suffering from pneumonia, rather than mumps. He advised an extended period of convalescence. In this way, José missed the June start date to the Palmer School of Chiropractic where he had enrolled for the eighteen-month course. He was obliged, at the doctor's firm insistence, to wait until the third intake of that year.

As soon as his throat subsided to normal, Mrs Smith commenced teaching him English. She started with the NATO Phonetic Alphabet.

'Just in case,' she said, 'you ever get into trouble in a foreign country. Everyone knows how to spell using the North Atlantic Treaty Organization Phonetic Alphabet.'

Not so for José. He had no idea that there was a universal NATO Phonetic Alphabet. Like most school-going children, he had learned his country's alphabet. Spanish speaking countries use names and places for each letter. The letter A is remembered by the name Antonio and the letter B is remembered by the city Barcelona and so on. But the NATO Phonetic Alphabet was devised using a combination of words pronounced and understood by all sending and receiving voice messages by radio or telephone, irrespective of their native language.

It took him a moment to spell out his first name enunciating the first two words together, Johnnie-Orange, and then the words, Sugar-Edward. Once he got the measure of it, he began to spell out aloud every new word using the NATO Phonetic Alphabet. Using the correct stress and inflection took longer.

Mrs Smith was a junior schoolteacher. But first and foremost she was a dedicated taskmaster. As his recovery progressed, so she increased his studies. His real break in learning English came when Dr BJ Palmer, president of the Palmer School of Chiropractic started his own radio station, WOC.

While the Italian, Guglielmo Marconi, was credited for inventing radio transmission for the sole purpose of sending and receiving messages, it was BJ Palmer's idea to bring news and entertainment coming out of the air and into a box that sat in the parlour or on the kitchen table. WOC aired for the first time one Saturday in May, 1922.

Being entertained by a radio was a new concept. It spawned industries and changed the lives of millions forever.

WOC broadcast sports, news, weather, farm and stock information, live music, and church services. But mainly, it spread the Philosophy of Chiropractic extolling its drug-free health benefits.

Davenport households threw parties and those who could not afford to buy their own bulky radio set, went to neighbours who could. José, along with several others gathered around the RCA radio in Mrs Smith's home. The wooden box with separate earphone loudspeaker took pride of place on a table in her parlour.

Mrs Smith included another treat — a chocolate-covered vanilla ice cream bar on a wooden stick wrapped in foil. Her friends and neighbours were as interested in meeting José for the first time as they were listening to WOC's first broadcast and tasting their first Eskimo Pie, a recent invention by a local Iowan.

Many households in Davenport offered spare rooms to Palmer students, including foreign soldiers who had fought in WW1. But José was Palmer's first real *vaquero*, who did not speak English, and someone who took three months to recover 'from the flu'. Thus the label, 'greenhorn' was applied, if a little unkindly, to José by those who followed his recovery long before they got to meet him.

Mr John Smith had died fourteen months before José's arrival. It took only seconds for his former friends and neighbours to realize José was dressed in Mr Smith's sharply-creased dark wool trousers, herringbone jacket, and white starched shirt, the cuffs of which were modishly curved rather than straight-edged.

To the neighbourhood children's dismay, José's working cowboy clothes — being boots with silver spurs, fringed suede jacket, waistcoat, neck bandana, and broad brimmed sombrero that he'd arrived in — were nowhere to be seen.

A group of them had been walking home from school when they saw José collapse as Mrs Smith opened her front door.

'Come here boys,' she called out to them.

All four boys rushed through the gate set in the picket fence elbowing each other up the lavender lined path to arrive first.

'You and you,' she indicated to the two strongest looking boys, 'hook an arm around the inside of his thigh.' She demonstrated. 'And you two,' she inclined her head, 'link your arms together. Hold each other's wrists. Like this, see? On the count of three, when I lift his shoulders slip your hands under his back, link hands and support him. Got it?'

Wide-eyed, the boys nodded.

Mrs Smith tucked her arms under José's shoulders and counted to three. Between them, they manoeuvred José into the house and onto the guest bed.

The boys took turns in heaving José's boots off. This took longer than getting him into the house and onto the bed. And it was during this time the boys were able to admire José's cowboy attire.

They were further rewarded when on cue, loosened by the left boot wrestling, the snap button on the leather sheath came undone. A slender knife slid out. It clattered to the floor and came to rest between six pairs of boys' scuffed shoes. In dumbstruck silence, they passed it to each other, marveling at its balanced weight but more so its lethal blade.

'Hand it over,' Mrs Smith said and retrieved the knife from reluctant fingers. She ushered the boys out of the house.

For propriety's sake, she called upon a neighbour to help with the undressing of José. Protecting their sensibilities, both women averted their eyes and gazed unwaveringly at each other when it came to pulling off José's trousers and redressing him in a pair of loose pyjama bottoms. Thus they both missed witnessing José's painfully engorged genitalia — an un-contested symptom of mumps in adult males.

That Mr Smith's clothes fit José was a miracle and it was accepted that it was meant to be. Mrs Smith took comfort and pleasure in seeing her husband's clothes again. Later she would take equal comfort and pleasure in José whether he wore her dead husbands clothes or not.

WOC announced all programs on the second and listeners set their timepieces to its announcements. The first full phrase José learned to speak was announcing the time. It was also the beginning of his fascination with all things that sounded out the time.

Then WOC introduced a children's hour, "Sandman Visits" after the mythical figure who sprinkles a grain of magical sand into each child's eyes, bringing them good dreams after story time.

Children believed in the nocturnal visiting Sandman. For upon waking, they rubbed the grains of sand from their eyes. Stories were read from the six volume series, *My Book House* by Olive Beaupré Miller.

Parents rushed to buy the full set — for it was a cornucopia of real and imaginary tales with captivating illustrations — and if necessary paid it off in installments. Mrs Smith purchased a set outright and it was these stories that José first listened to and then read aloud many times over.

As soon as he was able, he wrote his parents. He explained he had been taken ill, but was now well. That in hindsight, falling ill had been a blessing. It had given him enough time to come to grips with the language.

He told them that his accommodation was good. The food was plentiful. But he let his mother know it was not as good as hers. Guilt tormented him when he thought of the cloth of squashed tortillas he'd given away.

He sang the praises of the cinema, which he attended each week on Sunday afternoons at the new and ornate Capitol Theatre located on the ground floor of The Kahl building.

The Kahl had ten storeys and was the tallest building José had ever been into. It's façade boasted stone and white terracotta cladding including classically-inspired moldings, floral panels, and caryatid-inspired pilasters.

The entrance to the theatre had a spacious cantilevered canopy at the top of which the name, Capitol, appeared in black script.

But it was really the inside of the luxurious cinema theatre that awed José. It was filled with gold leaf decoration and Chinese lantern style chandeliers. The two thousand five hundred seats were constructed in black wrought iron with wooden backs, cushioned in lush red velvet.

From the orchestra pit came the live music accompanying the silent films with the two grand pianos and a harp, all placed in their own alcoves. A Moeller pipe organ adorned one wall.

This form of entertainment was far from what he was used to in Nuevo Laredo. For by the end of each Sunday afternoon, the *Luis Longoria Plaza de Toros* bullring was awash with the blood of bulls descended from *Toro de Semillas.*

José did not tell them that after watching *The Sheik* starring Rudolf Valentino, he and Mrs Smith found themselves in their own silent discourse between her sheets.

At Mrs Smith's insistence, the lights remained off. Her bible and the framed picture taken on her wedding day stowed in her bedside drawer. With abandon, they did all that José's mother had tried to protect him from doing with the daughter of a roaming ranch worker. Nor did he mention Mrs Smith crying out to Mr Smith at the most delicate moments of their coupling.

Just to make sure his parents did not get the impression he was loafing, he also wrote about BJ Palmer. The amazing, practical, and sound discourse he offered on his evening talks via station WOC. This information was read with great interest and shared with Dr Raul Perez. And still today, recordings of BJ Palmer's succinct voice — a glorious resonant mix of Sir Winston Churchill and Alfred Hitchcock's voices — educating the public on the benefits of Chiropractic can be heard.

From then, the pattern set. Each week, mother and son exchanged letters. They would continue so for the next twenty years. At the end of each letter, they always wrote the same phrase. Maria Guadalupe Moreno wrote, 'never forget', and her son, José Salazar Moreno responded, 'never forgotten'. On either side of the Atlantic, each carefully filed the other's letters in date order, and bound them, a bundle for each year.

In September, José's life from being a convalescent changed. But his eager participation in carnal activities best left unspoken about did not change. He became a full time student of the Palmer School of Chiropractic.

He wore Mr Smith's dark trousers, jackets and white long-sleeved shirts, the dress code for all Palmer students. Each morning he walked up Brady Street Hill to school for the exercise instead of taking the tram.

The school was a mixture of buildings providing forty-two thousand square feet of teaching facilities. At the far end of the block was the WOC radio station tower. It was anchored to one of the Palmer school roofs and looked impressive at night, being illuminated by floodlights.

José was required to attend over four thousand hours of lectures in the eighteen month term. But the eighteen months were broken down into four sections, making it more manageable. Holding onto the saying that oaks start from acorns, José took courage. He immersed himself in self-explanatory subjects studied in the field of Chiropractic.

He remembered the first time he had walked into the Osteology Department. There were more than four thousand skeletons. Of those, more than half were human. The rest were the vertebra of exotic and local animals and birds.

The rufous hummingbird specimen caught his attention. It has a straight bill setting it apart from other hummingbirds whose bills are curved. Though it was now featherless, José knew that in the right light, males glowed like burning coals, bright orange with an iridescent darker orange throat.

The last time José saw this hummingbird was the late afternoon he left the ranch riding through no-man's land. Seeing the rufous hummingbird brought a smile to José's face. Not just because of his instant memory of their colourful splendour, but because they are feisty little fellows, chasing off much larger resident hummingbirds.

For study, students checked out skeletons from the Osteology Department, as one does books from a library. The first step, crucial to all adjustments, is to know which bone is married to which.

But before their first anatomy lesson, a hundred students assembled to pose for a Palmer School of Chiropractic publicity photo. The sight of so many skeletons outdoors incited an event never before seen in the gardens of the Chiropractic school.

'May I have this dance, milady?' a student asked his skeleton. He clutched the skeleton to his body and with his right arm outstretched waltzed around in circles, the skeleton's leg bones clacking against his.

The students laughed. Another student stepped up.

'You don't mind my cutting in, sir?'

'Be my guest,' and added in a stage whisper, 'But I warn you, she is a little on the thin side.'

The students swapped skeletons and went twirling off. Other students began to hum the melody to Johann Strauss' 'The Blue Danube'. They picked up their skeletons and began to waltz. Within minutes, the green lawn was a-swirl with luminous clacking skeletons and their human partners.

'Ouch,' cried one student remonstrating with his skeleton, 'that was my other toe.'

A female student kissed hers, like one does a lover. The skeleton's mouth remained in terrified rictus while its partner's tongue snuck between its teeth.

'That's enough,' cried the photographer. His face was red and his bow tie was crooked. 'Will you get serious? Get back in line. I have a job to do.'

In the resulting photo, live humans showed up grainy dark contrasting against their dead counterparts in ethereal white.

José decided to buy his own skeleton from a supplier in New York. The brochure boasted real Native American and Indian skeletons. He selected an Indian. Upon receipt, José discovered it was female. He was undecided. Would the mother of his newly acquired female skeleton consider her daughter blessed or cursed forced in death to live among the living?

One night while Mrs Smith slept moulded to his body, the skeleton called out to him. She demanded to be named.

Mrs Smith and the skeleton were both petite and equal in height and delicateness of bones. His nickname for Mrs Smith was 'Little Bones'. In Spanish little bones is *Huesitos*. After much research, the name, Little Bones, in Hindi, the most spoken Indian language translated into Chōtē haḍḍiyōṁ. José kept the grainy photograph close to Chōtē haḍḍiyōṁ. Just in case, he thought, she ever got lonely and needed the company of others like herself.

Splanchnology was a subject he was already familiar with. On the ranch, a Mexican veterinarian dissected dead livestock to see if the reason for death could be found in the organs. On occasion, cattle would die after suffering tremendous muscle tremors, sometimes from having ingested by mistake the pretty but poisonous plant, whitesnake root.

If the veterinarian confirmed the animal had died from ingesting the toxic plant identified by the fragmented mess of viscera, the dead animal would have to be burnt. And burnt as fast as possible before other carnivores, or worse, their dogs, got to it.

José's first task was to scrape out the intestines and soft tissue organs and burn them. Afterwards, he'd make a fire in the open cavity of the carcass and leave that to burn making sure that none of the remains were edible. He never became partial to grilled meat. The memory of the stench of charred hides, hooves, and horns polluted José's senses forever.

Then, he hunted even the smallest plant, pulled it up by the roots and burned it. Or, by the end of summer, its proliferation of seeds would scatter in the wind ready to sprout forth the following spring.

Of all the subjects studied, the most difficult and crucial was Adjusting Techniques. It is only with the correct adjustment facilitating the removal of nerve interference that restores the body to health.

The secret to successful adjustment techniques is based on two criteria; first isolating the diseased vertebra and then using lightening quick hand movements to thrust down onto the vertebra.

Simplified, it is like watching a cowboy at target practice. He takes up the correct stance. Swiftly reaches for his gun. Aims. Fires. Returns the gun to its holster. The entire movement flashes by in a blur.

Patients react in different ways the first time they undergo an adjustment. Some are stunned into silence. Some cry like the Niagara Falls just switched on. Others laugh. And it is not uncommon for first time patients to strike their chiropractor in swift retaliation to the shock. The body, inner and outer, reacts with the outer response visible for all to see.

The art of Chiropractic is knowing how much acceleration and mass are needed to produce the correct amount of force. The thrust on the vertebra causes it to move. Often times, a loud popping or cracking sound emanates from the spine. Contrary to popular belief, the louder the sound does not mean a better adjustment. Each person's body and sound reaction is different.

BJ Palmer stood in the centre of the classroom. He had piercing eyes under heavy eyebrows. He sported a Van Dyke beard, leaving the sides of his flat cheeks smooth.

He wore his dark hair combed back from a barely visible widow's peak. The length of his hair came to rest just below his shirt collar all at one length. He tucked his hair behind his ears causing them to look much larger than they were.

While BJ Palmer always arrived fully attired, it would not be long before he was jacketless. He often rolled up his long white shirtsleeves revealing bulging forearm muscles.

He was relentless in the practice of all adjustments. Students practiced thousands of times until the movements became second nature. He oversaw every student, ensuring they had the technique down before they were let loose on trying it out on each other.

A standard joke among students was, despite their initial perfect health, they would sooner or later suffer an inexperienced adjustment. This would leave them in desperate need of a correct one. It was a sure way of learning the correct adjustment technique.

José came to the Palmer School of Chiropractic already a believer. He had read all the brochures and articles Dr Raul Perez could get. He had witnessed his father's miraculous physical transformation years before. The impact of the fall occurred on the diseased vertebra, at the correct speed and angle necessary to produce an adjustment resulting in the re-alignment of his spine.

When he and his parents learned about Chiropractic, Maria Guadalupe Moreno claimed her son's future lay in this world. In this, José was a willing participant. But what he had not realized was, for reasons known only to her, his mother wanted José to return to her hometown in Spain to practice.

José was part of the largest intake of students for the Palmer School of Chiropractic until then. There were thirty-seven full time teachers for a total of three thousand, six hundred students that year. The split between male and female students was almost equal. There was plenty of opportunity to form relationships. But he was already well occupied at 22 Southside.

Recognizing that BJ Palmer was unique did not take long. One of his supreme skills lay in self-promotion. But to his credit, included in the variety of subjects taught, he instructed students how they could turn their future Chiropractic practices into successful money making businesses. He claimed that the school was founded on, 'We manufacture chiropractors. We teach them the idea and then we show them how to sell it'. This translated colloquially into one of BJ Palmer's favourite epigrams — 'Early to bed, early to rise, work like hell, and advertise — makes a man healthy, wealthy, and wise'.

The expectation was that all graduates would spread the word. This was his way of attracting new students to either the Davenport school or one of the many others that were opening across the country. But, more importantly, it was promoting awareness of healing ailments, without pills or surgical intervention.

Each student who graduated from the Palmer School of Chiropractic left with an arsenal of props. Props were crucial, according to BJ Palmer, for the success of their future careers as a DC, Doctor of Chiropractic. Weeks before graduation, they pored over the General Catalogue of Chiropractor Supplies. All items were sold directly to the students from the school.

When José came to leave, his packing trunks were loaded to their brims. A fourteen-volume set of Chiropractic reference books and boxes of patient cards for adjustment record keeping purposes took up one trunk. In another were two plaster cast bookends in the image of BJ Palmer and his wife, Mabel Palmer. Packed into the third were two wooden adjusting chairs, an adjusting table, and several posters showing views of the spine and step-by-step adjustment techniques. Soon, all of this equipment would go into furnishing his own new Chiropractic studio in Medina del Campo, Spain.

There are good chiropractors and then there are great chiropractors. Experience counts. But what sets chiropractors apart are those who have developed lightening quick reflexes. And those blessed with a heightened intuitive sensitivity.

When faced with a real patient for the first time, José closed himself off to all other external distractions. He focused like his father and other *toreros* did during a *sorteo*, the event where young bulls are selected for their fighting potential.

They noted whether the bull's shoulder blades and hindquarters were balanced, the length of the spine slicing between his shoulder blades, how close together the bull's front and back hooves stood together, and the angle of the turned-out hooves. José superimposed this image over the patient standing before him for additional detail.

In those first few moments of appearance assessment, the patient needs to relax. Having a relaxed patient is an important first step to a successful adjustment.

But the first time, he sensed he had changed — to be exact, metamorphosed — into an octopus and melded into the body of the patient, he gasped and withdrew from the dream-like state he had entered.

BJ Palmer stood to one side, his own antennae picking up on each student's personal manner and approach. He was watching José's turn at the patient assessment phase. He understood what had happened. When he caught José's eye, he said, 'Nothing to be afraid of. Take your time. Exploration is vital.'

Encouraged, José re-entered the patient's body. With octopus tentacles, he searched the patient's body picking up on the immediate and obvious problems. Others were coaxed and eased from their hiding places. Assessment over, José proceeded with the adjustment under BJ Palmer's critical eye.

Within seconds after the spinal adjustment, the patient rose from the table. He too was in a dream-like state. A river of nourishment sped throughout his nervous system tingling and vibrating with the sheer joy of body health.

Adjustments did not always happen like this. But when it did, there was no doubt that both patient and chiropractor were at one with the Universe.

It was an exquisite moment of purity and harmony in a perfectly ordered world. And it was at these moments when José came closest to accepting there is a gracious loving God after all. Not like the contrary Universe against which his mother waged war.

After José's first official patient assessment and adjustment, he found himself being singled out. He could not deny there were several other students whom teachers also singled out. He was pleased with their mark of recognition.

During José's eighteen months as a student, weeks had gone by when he almost forgot about the ranch and all that he held dear. The new world had gotten bigger. He had taken to town life almost as if he had known no other. Sometimes he glimpsed his cowboy clothes stored in the back of wardrobe. He struggled to make the connection from the new him to the old.

To Mrs Smith's credit, she urged José to move on with his life. Fulfill first his own, and then his parents' hopes and dreams. The closer he got to graduation the more intense and frequent became their non-verbal cleaving bodies.

José graduated in the autumn of 1924. Never were two lovers more relieved their affair was over.

What Mrs Smith had engaged in was taboo in her society. It went against all that she had been instructed in living a decent, God fearing life. She was eager to return to her former ways uncomplicated by nature's primal urges. Her Bible and wedding picture were soon to reclaim their permanent rightful place on her bedside table.

José was grateful to her, but also ready to move on. Chivalrously, he decided his relationship with Mrs Smith would remain his own business.

By then, Mr Smith's clothes had become his, and those which had worn through, Mrs Smith, on her own volition, replaced. He would leave Davenport, Iowa far better dressed than when he arrived. More importantly, he would leave with a diploma calling him Doctor of Chiropractic.

Maria Guadalupe Moreno's first wish, as negotiated with the Universe, of her son having nothing to do with bulls, had been realized. Her second, that José would become the first generation from both her and her husband's family to graduate, also had been realized. She had three more wishes that required skillful negotiation.

With José's trunks packed and not forgetting the glowing and delicate Chōṭē haḍḍiyōṁ, he was now ready to embark upon the next course of his life. On his wrist, by way of a farewell gift from Mrs Smith, was his first wristwatch, the first of many timepieces in his blossoming love affair that his son would inherit.

It was a Cartier Santos. It had an elegant square case, distinctive bezel, and a classic legible dial. That it had been the wedding gift from Mrs Smith to Mr Smith did not worry José. As fortunate as Mr Smith's clothes fitting him had been, so was the inscription. It was etched into the flat underside of the watch, matching his and Mrs Smith's initials. It read, *'To J S from J S with Love'*. Further below in a flourish of exaggerated swirls, *'Forget Me Not'*.

After graduating from the Palmer Chiropractic School, José Salazar Moreno aged twenty-five, left the United States for Spain. It took two weeks before he stood in the market square of Medina del Campo. In much less time, he emptied his crates and set up his studio. In the window, he placed a sign, 'Chiropractic — Natural Health'.

Spain, in 1925, had two types of medicine; battlefield and folklore. Battlefield surgical procedures were primarily limb amputations without the use of anaesthetic or antibiotics. Medicine focused on surgical infections, typhus, malaria, undernourishment, and sexually transmitted diseases. No matter the ailment, citizens of the market town resorted to Mother Nature's cures. These were garnered from common sense and generations worth of practical and shared experience.

Using natural cures for the folk of Medina del Campo was easy. They already farmed according to *Agricultura Luna*, Moon Farming, the belief being that the moon governs fertility, growth, and healing through moisture in the earth under the auspices of its four phases. They were not interested in the mystery of how the moon phases worked, but rather the results. And while Chiropractic had nothing to do with the moon, they placed José Salazar's bone popping and cracking into the same mystifying realm as moon farming.

Desperation overcame fear. First one, then another knocked at his door. No longer could women suffer pointed fingers accusing them of being barren. But without the presence of mothers or husbands, they could not be treated. And in the specific business of conception, husbands were obliged to avail themselves of Chiropractic treatment, too.

Awed by the sounds bones made, and encouraged by seeing their wives rise glowing from the adjustment table, husbands, too, abandoned themselves to José's magical hands. During their course of treatment, patients were instructed to walk twice a day, eat light meals, and sleep a minimum of eight hours. Heavy objects were not to be lifted and sexual abstinence for a while adhered to.

Many experienced immediate relief from physical ailments that had bothered them for years. In some cases, patients were freed from ailments they did not know they had until after the adjustment. For others, relief came over a few days. But for all, a profound sense of wellbeing prevailed.

Nothing is more powerful than the laudatory or denigrating voices of women. Good or bad, news spread like wildfire. With real or imagined ailments, and in some cases, none at all, the Medina del Campo folk wanted to experience the sound of their bones. Soon, a clear path was being beaten to José Salazar's door.

The health of Medina del Campo's citizens reached new levels. Free from aches and niggly pains, healthy bodies make happy people. Soon squirmy squalling babies were being born at an alarming rate. Shops opened vying to sell the best and most expensive confinement and newborn paraphernalia. Florists and jewellers along Padilla Street did brisk business, but none more so than the whorehouse. For a universal truth is — solicitous of their pregnant wives, husbands may seek home comforts elsewhere.

It was not in the least co-incidental then, the most prestigious jewellry store and whorehouse were owned by the sharp-witted and austere Madam of The House.

Madam was recognizable by three noticeable features. She was stick thin and her nondescript hair scraped back into a solid bun which from under the net holding it in place, not a single hair could stray.

She wore the same severely styled black dresses — she had dozens — the only hint of colour coming from a small jewelled brooch pinned to the collar of her dress. This ensemble she wore irrespective of the season and time of day or night.

And best or worst of all, no one could ever recall what she looked like. Like a chameleon she blended into surroundings through which she passed leaving no sense of her having being there. She rarely had conversations, but when she did, she focused wholly on the listener or speaker and was crystal clear in her communication.

The House was the name the locals called it, instead of the all too vulgar whorehouse. Despite the town's divisions, once men entered The House, political and social affiliations were abandoned and all were rendered equal.

At that time, political choices could only be one of two. Those who kept theirs to themselves managed to escape persecution from either the Red Terror, led by the Republicans, or the White Terror, led by the Nationalists.

The Spanish Civil War ended in 1939. But the winner, the Red Terror, continued its atrocities against the people for another fifty years in the form of mass executions. The execution of prisoners was official policy. This included socialists, homosexuals, anarchists, and anyone with money. Brutality was explained away as the means to unite the country.

So while husbands were occupied elsewhere, wives' climbing skills were put to test. Births, just as much as a death or wedding, was simply another means to legitimately enhance and elevate a family's social standing.

Pregnant eyes trawled through the region's centuries-old family pedigrees. Not knowing the sex of the still-to-be-born child, a selection of possible future matches were earmarked from an equal or better family.

And widows, or those likely to be, made lists of possible future husbands, whether they were, or were likely to be widowers.

The town's marriage broker, Guillermo Cabrera, (whose name translates directly into Billy Goat, looked with hardly a pinch of imagination just like his namesake, for he had pointy ears and walked — no, pranced — on the balls of his feet), professed political affiliation to both sides.

Maria Guadalupe Moreno, ignoring the broker's duality instructed him to find her son a life partner. A partner who would ratchet up her family's social standing by more than a notch or two. It was a tall order. The Salazar and Moreno family trees were not shining examples of families easily able to marry above their station.

And then there was the matter of José's foot, which the broker gently reminded Maria Guadalupe Moreno she had forgotten to mention. But not wishing to lose her as a client, he assured her in his next letter — *'José has many attributes to make up for his limp. He speaks American. He has lived and studied in America — achievements much admired and beyond the wildest dreams of most future mothers-in-law. His studio is well attended. Your son is respected more each day. He is quietly creating a name for himself'*.

The problem was getting José to consult with him. This he omitted telling Maria Guadalupe Moreno. The young man was more resilient than his limp had allowed the broker to believe. According to the town's mothers, the broker was beginning to sound like his namesake. They whispered loud enough for him to hear what he wanted kept secret: he was losing his brokering knack.

At first, José, engrossed with growing his Chiropractic practice, had no need of a wife. He refused all the marriage broker's tempting offers of introductions.

But mothers with marriageable, and more importantly, some not so marriageable, daughters were not as easily put off. They soon found their own ingenious way to José. As long as José remained single, he was considered fair game.

José's parents, their cattle farming and bull-raising lineage were clearly known to the whole town, for they had grown up together. Mothers' initial concern with José's limp faded as with every pop and crack adjustment, his future prospects increased.

Each thinking she was the only one to devise such a plan, mothers presented their daughters to José in the legitimacy of his studio.

———— ◆ ————

'Señora Crespo. Good Morning.'

'I present my eldest, ready-to-be-married daughter, Ona.'

'Señorita Ona. It is my pleasure. What seems the matter?'

Señora Crespo having previously instructed her daughter, indicated to behind the lattice screen where she was to undress down to her white undergarments.

'Ona suffers pains in her sleep. When she wakes she cannot rise. Her limbs are exhausted. She needs your special attention.'

Already familiar with such mother-daughter diagnoses, José repressed a sigh and fixed his inscrutable mask to his face.

'Señorita Ona, come forward please. Walk slowly towards me.'

Ona emerged from behind the screen. Her red face was in stark contrast to the virginal white undergarments threaded through with loose-ended dangling satin ribbons.

'Thank you. Stop. Turn slowly, face the wall. Now turn your head to the right. Look over your shoulder at me. Good. Now turn your head to the left. Look over your shoulder at me. Good.'

After a minute, during which Señora Crespo chewed her bottom lip, José presented his diagnosis.

'Señora Crespo, Ona looks very well. I cannot see any indication for her aching limbs. It's her diet perhaps?'

Señora Crespo drew herself up. 'Her diet? But Doctor, can you not see what a fine specimen she is? Look.' Señora Crespo hastened to her daughter and turned her around to face José. She grabbed a handful of her daughter's shift and pulled it to the side revealing Ona's lovely body outline under the sheer fabric.

'See. Is she not perfect?'

'Indeed, yes, Señora Crespo. And it is for this, I can see no reason for your daughter's aching limbs.'

But it was Señora Crespo's moment and she was going to make the most of it.

'Ona lie down on the Doctor's table,' she ordered her daughter. 'At least you can check if her legs are in equal length.' Then she bit her lip again realizing she'd come impolitely close to José's own impediment.

Ona lay down on the table. She shut her eyes. In another place, another time, Ona would have represented a sacrificial offering lying upon the altar.

To Señora Crespo's relief, José moved and stood at the foot of the examining table.

'Breathe, Ona,' she hissed. Two hard plum-like breasts rose and fell.

José placed his hands around Ona's ankles. Like a horse ridding itself of flies by vibrating its skin is what happened to Ona. A ripple ran up her legs, welled in her belly, travelled up her ribcage, nipped her rosebud nipples, tingled through her throat, and ended in a choked gasp coming from her opened mouth.

Señora Crespo was not exactly sure how that had happened. Then again decided perhaps it better that she did not know. For how to explain, if asked?

'I agree with you, Señora Crespo. Ona is in perfect, yet delicate health. I prescribe exercise.'

'Exercise?'

'Do you ride, Ona?' José asked.

'No,' she replied before her mother could do it for her.

'Señora Crespo, if you can, arrange horse riding lessons for Ona.'

While Ona re-dressed, José jotted down a list of well-to-do families with ready-for-marriage sons who rode and could be approached as horse riding instructors for Ona.

'Use my name by way of introduction,' answered José before Señora Crespo could ask the question.

'Would you attend the wedding?' whispered Señora Crespo.

'I'd be delighted,' came his whispered response.

'See you next spring then,' she said.

Señora Crespo and Señorita Ona left. They made an uncommonly attractive and desired marriageable pair. For every sensible man should know when he marries, he marries his wife's mother too.

A tap at the door announced the arrival of José's next appointment. This time, the daughter's buckteeth and squint eye disallowed her from place-ment anywhere near the top of the town's marriageable stakes.

——— ◆ ———

Three years, Maria Guadalupe Moreno thought, was time enough for her son to have settled into the market town and find himself a wife. She was frustrated by his reticence or recalcitrance — she could not decide which

— and the bleating goat broker's excuses. Most of all, she was frustrated with the Universe, which remained fixedly silent on the subject. Like the other mothers, she took matters into her own hands. She began communicating to José her urgent need for his marriage and her future grandchildren through the medium of dreams.

At the same time, the bleating broker, fearing the wholesale unleashing of mothers' tongues, took a detour to and from his office, stopping in at the church of San Antolín twice daily. Here he lit more candles than his *céntimos,* cents, allowed.

He knelt in spite of his cracking knees, clasped his hands, and tipped back his head. He gazed into the gentle eyes of the Holy Mother. With the smoke rising from the candles causing his eyes to cry he begged for her pity. José had to come and see him. Even if José refused the town's best, at least he would be seen to be doing his job. Or, he would soon be looking for a new one.

José was no longer able to withstand any more sleep-broken nights: his mother's intrusions upon his dreams, and candle smoke filled air which somehow found its way into his room. And he was desperate to be free of the daily pressures the town's mothers forced upon him in the form of their near naked daughters. He faced the inevitable.

Unannounced, he presented himself at the marriage broker's office. Disappointed, but relieved at the same time, he wrote his mother the truth. For upon formally meeting several marriageable young women, some of whom he'd had already seen nearly naked in his studio, his heart remained as solid as an unmovable boulder. This dilemma his mother understood.

When she and Felipe Salazar met, lightening cut the blue sky followed by an ear-deafening rumble of thunder. So great was the force, knees buckled and people everywhere crumpled to the earth. Then birds rained down upon them. Vast swathes of tall sunflowers bent in half.

Only Maria Guadalupe Moreno and Felipe Salazar stood upright. Over the wasteland of fallen people covered by fallen birds, their eyes locked upon the other's. Their hearts synchronized and from then beat as one.

Maria Guadalupe Moreno wrote to the broker again. She urged him to spread his net farther.

A few weeks later, José received a hand written note. He was to meet the broker that very evening. Suffering from lack of sleep and an annoying smoke induced cough made all the more annoying as he did not smoke, he limped into the broker's office. There was no lightening or thunder. Nor did the sky rain birds to the earth and sunflowers and humans everywhere remained upright. But like a sleeping tiger when upon waking finds itself caged, José's heart leapt and thrashed against the confines of his chest. He fell in love.

The same cannot be said for Alejandra Herrera. Love crept slowly upon her. When she realized she loved her husband — it took her twenty-five years, four months, and one day — it was too late.

José could not decide if it was her eye colour — a shade of blue for which he found no adjective — or her glossy black hair that he was sure when unpinned would fall like a curtain along the length of her sinuous spine to below her buttocks, that captivated him the most. She was just the right height for him, being taller than most Spanish women. And she was as slim as he was. He envisioned their twining around each other like supple vines.

José would learn however, being the partner of someone so incandescently exotic comes with a price.

In no time, paperwork completed, signatures blotted and red wax seals impressed with the official insignia from the Medina del Campo Town Hall, José Salazar Moreno and Alejandra Herrera were legally betrothed.

All over town, mothers folded their daughters' undergarments along their original crease lines. Layered between sheets of perfumed tissue, they were re-stowed in wedding drawers. Mothers' ulterior reasons for their artfully devised visits to the Chiropractic studio were erased. Overnight young women's health problems disappeared. Enthusiastic praise for Dr José Salazar Moreno and his magical adjustments were proclaimed. In private, each mother berated herself for her harebrained attempt to ensnare a husband for her daughter. In the next second, immediately after faithfully promising God not to resort to such schemes again, they returned once more to assess what other fish there were to be lured.

◆

Maria Guadalupe Moreno nudged her husband. 'Wake up.'

'But the cock's not yet crowed,' came his sleepy response.

'We need to pack. We're leaving for Spain.'

Felipe Salazar's eyes flew open and stared hard into the dark. He knew the determined sound of her voice. He was almost too afraid to ask why, but did, knowing she was impatiently waiting for him to do so.

'Why?'

'Our son is getting married.'

It was useless to argue with her. He rolled out of bed and mentally prepared himself to do her bidding.

'How do you know this?'

'From the dream that roared the news in my head last night.'

Maria Guadalupe Moreno trusted her dreams. They were always right. She had no need for a letter telling her to travel back to Spain.

Felipe Salazar asked the next question he also knew she would be expecting and already had the answer to.

'What are we going to wear?'

He lit the oil lamp, turned it up to its brightest and peered at the assorted cowboy clothes hanging on nails he'd hammered into the walls years ago.

'The clothes we got married in.'

'You've kept them all these years? Where?'

'Here.'

Maria Guadalupe Moreno rolled off her side of the bed. She went down onto her hands and knees. From under the metal-framed bed which stood high from the ground, she tugged at a wooden box.

'Help me.'

Felipe Salazar eased the box out. Together and naked — they had never slept any other way since Felipe Salazar's miraculous Chiropractic recovery — they lifted the lid.

'God protect us. What a smell,' he said making the sign of the cross as Maria Guadalupe Moreno pulled out a rolled up bundle.

It was the dress she'd worn as her going away outfit. It had not seen the light of day since the first and last time she had worn it. Next was the suit Felipe Salazar had worn at their wedding.

'Will it still fit?' he asked.

'Try.'

Felipe Salazar pulled on the trousers and jacket. They fit just as they had done decades before.

'Try yours.'

Maria Guadalupe Moreno was pleased. She only had to pull in her stomach a little for the dress to fit. But the short bolero jacket was perfect.

Felipe Salazar's nose wrinkled. 'And the smell. How to get rid of the smell?'

◆

Letters announcing the news of their son's wedding were in the mailbag arriving on the boat they were about to board.

The first came from the marriage broker, being his invoice. An amount larger than Maria Guadalupe Moreno had supposed. No doubt inflated, given her non-disclosure of José's limp. She hid the invoice from her husband, tucking it into the bottom of her bag along with their wedding gift, being all the money they had saved for this very occasion. For the first time, Maria Guadalupe Moreno thanked the Universe for *Toro de Semillas*, through whose dedicated mountings had produced many saleable fighting bulls. Her personal gift to her son was a crate packed with dozens of jars of the clear, bright yellow mesquite honey José adored. Simply from its smell, memories of his Mexican childhood flooded his senses with exquisite detail.

Upon reading the contents of the letter from his son, Felipe Salazar sighed with relief. He was not crossing the Atlantic Ocean for nothing. More to the point, his wife had not taken leave of her senses as he'd begun to fear.

Thus José's parents undertook their second sea voyage. The first, when they left Medina del Campo for Mexico in search of a better life with the crated thousand pound seed bull. And the second, returning years later to be present at their son's nuptials.

In response to her husband's concern about the smell, Maria Guadalupe Moreno lay their outfits side by side in the sun on the deck of the boat in hope the years-old musty smell would be replaced by fresh sea breezes.

During their return visit, both felt like the floundering fish the sailors had caught and left to flip-flop upon the wooden deck. Like most people who return to the place of their birth after an extended absence, there is a feeling of being part of, and apart from. Never was this truer than in their case. Medina del Campo had changed, and changed so much during their absence they felt out of place. All was familiar, yet all was different.

Meeting old childhood friends was galling. Despite the equal level of poverty in which they had all been raised, their childhood friends had become suave citizens of the world. Only Felipe Salazar and Maria Guadalupe Moreno had remained in their millennium-old, livestock-raising lives. But had their friends known how much money their bull-raising enterprise raked in, *they* would have felt inadequate. But money, like what went on between the bed sheets of others, was private: neither discussed nor shared.

José and Alejandra exchanged their vows before the sixteenth century, gothic-styled church of San Antolín on Sunday, July 25, 1937. The ornate altarpiece dwarfed all those who stood before it. Intricate gold leaf adornments glowed in reflection from the rising sun; its elongating rays of sparkling light encircled the couple.

Maria Guadalupe Moreno took the ring of light as a good omen even if it was not as dramatic as people falling to the ground, the sky spitting down birds, or sunflowers bending.

Though they married in church in the unseen presence of God, neither José nor Alejandra were religious. Together they would re-enter San Antolín once more at the baptism of their son.

Alone, Alejandra would re-enter San Antolín twice more. The first of which would be seventeen years later where she would sit before the glowing altarpiece under circumstances she would never have believed.

The bridal party celebrated with a modest meal in a restaurant facing the town square. A soldier driving the army-issued, Carro Blindado Bilbao vehicle, stopped at the town's communal fountain, in the centre of the square. Exhausted, he fell out of the truck. He crawled to the rim of the fountain.

Seeing the commotion from the restaurant window, the owner, also the waiter and cook, rushed out, abandoning the bridal party.

Weeks prior, Nationalist soldiers made up of Spanish, Mexican, and Moroccan troops travelled south towards Madrid. Medina del Campo's streets had rumbled with long lines of slow-moving military vehicles. Each truck was filled with soldiers staring at the silent Medina del Campo citizens watching them pass through.

The driver sputtered the news between mouthfuls of water, drinking from the spigot. News of the Republican defeat and Nationalist victory, at the Battle of Brunete with a loss of twenty thousand men, flashed through the town.

The reaction to both pieces of information was silence. This way, citizens of Medina del Campo could not denounce their neighbours for their political beliefs because no one knew for sure who supported which political party. Thus, under the watchful eye of La Mota, the town's crenulated fortress, harmony prevailed as it had done from centuries before.

But it was too much for José's parents. Their secret was, they were Republican supporters. They did not want to become another Nationalist statistic.

Maria Guadalupe Moreno nudged her husband. Felipe Salazar coughed, then taking his son and daughter-in-law's hands in his own, said, 'We need to leave on the next boat back for Mexico.'

'But Papa,' José protested loudly, 'You've not been here for two days.'

'I know. I know,' Felipe Salazar said. 'But things here are, you know, different. Too dangerous for us.'

Alejandra murmured sympathetic acknowledgement.

Maria Guadalupe Moreno clasped Alejandra in a close embrace. She held on to her daughter-in-law trying to convey to her, her warm acceptance of the lovely young woman. Then Maria Guadalupe Moreno felt it. There was no mistaking the rhythmic double tap that beat under Alejandra's ribcage. Maria Guadalupe Moreno's heart burst with joy. But looking deeply into Alejandra's eyes, she realized Alejandra was unaware of the new life already begun. She kept quiet. She would grudgingly share this news only with the Universe.

And when she received José's letter, she and Felipe would share the happy news together.

With her bag relieved of its money load, no longer lugging the crate of mesquite honey, and wearing their oldest clothes, Felipe Salazar and Maria Guadalupe Moreno appeared as simple farmers dodging victorious army columns on the move.

They took the first boat back to their beloved ranch, horses, Consuelo, and *Toro de Semillas'* long line of offspring. They overcame their feeling of inadequacy, for they — and it was Maria Guadalupe Moreno in particular — were well satisfied with the new union. It took her a while, but she thanked the Universe for the second time. Her son had married and a child was to be born. Although some would be heard later to say, born almost too soon.

Upon their return, Maria Guadalupe Moreno began dialogue again with the Universe. Like Consuelo's offspring's dedication to bone gnawing, she badgered night and day to make sure the Universe would not forget to grant her final wish.

My grandmother's final wish was granted — I, Alejandro Salazar Herrera was born with no physical defect.

A midwife selected by my father attended my birth. She was to monitor the event in his absence. For then, fathers did not accompany their wives during the birthing process. And birthing, he told my mother, often foretold what medical complications could arise later.

But unknown to her, he had instructed the midwife to watch out for a possible weakness in either of my feet. He had also engaged the services of a military surgeon. The surgeon was to remain on standby should the need arise for intervention. This my father was prepared to do with neither my mother's knowledge nor consent.

My father's foot had been left untreated in the hope that time and or Mother Nature would resolve the condition. But both failed him. All his life he was ashamed of his impediment. He concealed it by stuffing the toe of his left shoe tight with a wad of newspaper to support his smaller foot. I never saw him barefoot or wearing anything but closed shoes. He never looked at his foot, always keeping it covered with a sock including while bathing.

Defect or not, I adored my father. He might as well have been the Greek hero, Achilles, who also had a weak foot, a weak heel to be exact. Despite his defect, my father was tall and, sadly, just like Achilles, destined to die young — in the year revealed to him during the dream when he held his dead father and dying mother in his arms.

For my birth, and more to the point, for my complete wholeness he presented my mother with a piece of jewellry. Thereafter, every so often, not necessarily on a celebratory occasion, my father would present my mother with another jewelled token. These she never wore outside our home. When she did, it was always the same piece, thus ensuring gossiping neighbours were not able to attribute any more wealth to us than they had. Or attribute more wealth to us than we already had.

Although it was my mother's money, for she brought with her a large and independent fortune upon their marriage, my father ordered that we never hint at, or allow others the tiniest glimpse of our wealth. All the years I grew up in my family home, my father insisted that we live well below what we could easily afford.

My mother shared the hospital room with a new arrival to our town: Viola Flores, wife to Dr Jerardo Rivas, from Bilbao, a town located on the north coastline. Viola Flores gave birth a day later to a son, Diego Rivas Flores.

Diego and I remained single children born into well-off unions and were accorded privileges available within the small tier of our elevated social station. We became best friends and brothers-in-arms. Or, as our mothers with loving indulgence, would later say, terrors-in-arms.

Our mothers too became best friends — in reality, life sisters. They bonded to each other through the miracle of childbirth, supported each other by sharing in the joy and pain, trials and tribulations of women and mother-hood. Their husbands had no choice but to follow in the steps of their wives' friendship.

Their friendship was at odds from the start. Dr Rivas was a medical doctor. He held no belief in Chiropractic. Yet, as the years passed, patients found success with my father more than with Dr Rivas.

While my father's patients increased and his reputation grew, he did not always receive payment, for more than half of his patients could not afford the fee. Given my mother's independent income, nor did he ask for payment.

Eternally grateful, patients tried pressing upon him a key tool from their trade, a prize winning fighting cock, and a pair of matched plough horses. And once, a litter of pygmy piglets, so small they each fit in the daintiest of teacups, all of which he refused. Instead, he took up teaching Chiropractic to a few selected paying students.

My mother dedicated herself to my upbringing, and my father's and my wellbeing. She tried her hand at painting and played cards twice a week.

When my parents travelled to a different European city every year, my father allowed everyone to believe she was accompanying him to Chiropractic seminars. He did not consider this a lie but rather a fib. He explained the difference to me as fibbing being a softer version of an outright lie. And thus while still not right, a fib was better.

But the truth was, my mother suffered from wanderlust. She wanted to experience everything not possible in our agricultural town.

During their travels, my mother left nothing unseen or not done. She dragged my father to the opera, museums, and dress shops. They would return with my mother flushed with the success of the trip looking more beautiful than ever, while my father returned ragged and limping.

A few weeks later, a wooden crate would be delivered. Nosy patients satisfied their curiosity by exclaiming over the new, better treatment table or chair supposed to have come from the crate. Hoping to give further credence to his fib, my father secretly made changes to his treatment tables and chairs.

Over the following months, my mother would unpack her crate of delights. Decorative household articles would appear filling up our home, except for the visitors' room and en-suite powder room, which remained plain and unchanged in keeping with the rest of our neighbours' houses where social calls were conducted.

All new linen, chandeliers, antique mirrors so old the glass had de-natured, books, clocks, small pieces of furniture, carpets, and clothes, remained well out of sight behind the closed doors.

My mother wore the best and most fashionable clothes at night during our family evening dinners at home. It was a torment for her, but she followed my father's rule of not displaying our good fortune.

We had two servants, a married couple, Inés and Tomás. Inés arrived within days after my birth. I adored her. My mother's jealousy soon taught me to curb running to Inés or laugh when she was around. But Inés and I understood each other well. More importantly, we both understood not to vex my mother.

When I turned four, Inés married Tomás. My father thought it a good idea to have him live with Inés at the top of our house, so they both could be on call day or night. Thus, Tomás joined our family unit. He did the heavy and dirty work around the house, remaining responsible to my father. Neither employer nor employee knew the others' true political leanings. And it was better it remained so.

One day, when I was about six-years old, I lifted the silver beaten frame from a side table and held it in both my hands.

'Mama, who is this?'

My mother crouched down beside me. 'This,' she said, using a meticulously manicured finger pointed to my father, 'is Papa. Isn't he handsome?'

'Yes.'

'And this is me, your Mama. Don't I look just like a princess?'

I shook my head. 'No, Mama. Not a princess. An angel.'

It was no wonder I thought of her as an angel. Even though it was black and white, my mother's beauty radiated right out of the photograph. She stood tall and serene alongside my proud father who never stood taller or looked more handsome.

'Where am I?'

'You weren't born yet.'

'Where is *Abuela* and *Abuelo*?'

I knew my father's parents lived in Mexico, each night he told me stories — sometimes outrageous ones — of his life growing up with them. And I knew my mother's parents were dead, but somehow still lived in a place called heaven which no one could see. Because she cried each time I asked her about them, I had come to the conclusion heaven was a very sad place. I did not want to be responsible for making my Mama cry, thus destroying her coloured eyes — my father had suggested this — so I gave up asking.

'Here they are. See.' She pointed once again to the picture using her perfect manicured nail.

'No, Mama. That's not *Abuela* and *Abuelo*. That's Inés and Tomás.'

'That's not possible. We did not know Inés and Tomás when Mama and Papa got married.'

Just like I could see my mother as an angel, I could see Inés and Tomás as clear as anything. I was quite sure of it. After all, I knew who they were — I saw them every day. And I had never met my father's parents.

'No, Mama. You are wrong. It's Inés and Tomás,' and used my index finger to push my mother's finger out of the way.

My mother peered closely. Inés could easily pass for her mother-in-law. And then it dawned on her. It was for their similarities my father had employed Inés in the first place. To be close to the woman he adored as if he were still a child.

Inés was shorter than my grandmother, but had the same raisin eyes which flashed with mirth or blazed with adoration when her gaze fell upon Tomás, my father or me. She was dark, warm, and her bosom — which I often rested my head upon — was very comfortable.

Tomás was taller than Inés, not as tall as my father or as tall as my grandfather. Nevertheless, he had similar chiselled features, though he had much deeper crevices etched in a long line on either side of his mouth. This was especially advantageous when he pulled faces, either scaring me half to death or causing me to laugh until I got the hiccups.

The next time I wanted to look at the wedding picture, I found the photograph had been changed. I never saw that particular photograph again.

I was to find out many years later Inés and Tomás had two sons. The first was named after my father and the second, after me.

From that afternoon, Inés was further subjected to my mother's whims and fancies. She was questioned and contradicted on her method of keeping house. And as everyone knows, casting doubt on the ability of the proud and perfectly capable housekeeper can be likened to harvesting honey without smoking the bees first.

But it was Tomás who behind closed doors suffered the sting of Inés' laments. But whatever sufferances she was subjected to, and by default Tomás, they were loyal. Being paid above the going rate may have had some influence too. But mainly it was for my father that Inés bore her suffering. She and Tomás adored my father, as did half of our town, often provoking my mother to make jealous and ungracious comments.

Despite my mother's best efforts to prove the opposite, Inés and Tomás ensured our household was methodically organized. All manner of clocks, my father's sole collecting passion, were dusted with exaggerated care. They respected my father's rule and never moved or touched a single piece of mechanism. Thus the clocks struck and chimed on and in time.

Great attention was paid to the preparation of our meals. For not only was the quality of prime importance, so were portion sizes. And the season and the vagaries of each day's weather were taken into consideration.

Our household was noted for its healthy cuisine, but compared to our neighbours and certainly to Diego's household, our meals were considered frugal.

Ignoring protests, my father drilled his students and patients on his 'Less is Better' credo. Over time they came to accept it as their way of life too. And when they lapsed, they soon found themselves back at my father's studio for re-adjustment.

Beginning in our seventeenth year, Diego's mother and mine began to toy with the idea of finding suitable future wives for us. It soon turned into a full-scale project. It resulted in The Night That Changed Everything.

Our regions' family pedigrees were pored over and taken apart. Best-kept secrets were uncovered. And even some secrets families did not even know they had surfaced. Over the following months, entire families were scored from our mothers' lists and further reduced as they uncovered yet more irregularities of all sorts.

The task consumed our mothers' every waking moments. They neglected our fathers, us, and the daily running of their households like never before.

Diego and I revelled in the freedom and took advantage of not being the constant focus of our mothers' attention. And, it would later come to light, our fathers took equal advantage of their wives' relaxed scrutiny.

Diego and I were said to be possessors of top-notch marriage prospects. It was surmised we stood to inherit well. Our teachers praised our scholastic abilities. Lofty ideas for our futures were bandied about. Only our physical appearances set us apart.

I had the physique of a slender athlete while Diego never grew out of his childhood chubbiness. I had inherited much of my mother's stunning good looks.

Like hers, I had long hair which I wore tied back. Unlike her intense blue eyes, I had brown eyes, but her dark long lashes. I had a strong jaw line and well defined mouth. My nose was quite different from hers and my father's too, for that matter. It had a straight bridge ending in well-shaped nostrils.

Diego inherited his mother's confluent eyebrows and abundant hair. In addition, his hair — unless regularly trimmed — poked from his nostrils and ears.

There was one more difference between us. Although witnessed only once, our penises were vastly different. Mine appeared to conform in ratio portion to the size of my body. Diego's did not. It was a puny little thing — a flap of skin attached to two quail egg sized balls. As my mother would go on to say, 'Nothing at all to write home about'.

But what Diego lacked between his thighs, he made up for between his ears. He was by far smarter, and as I would come to learn, foxier and meaner than the foxiest and meanest fox of all.

Those who are sought out for money, social standing, looks, or intelligence are blessed. They have a lot less to worry about while maintaining position on the all important and fickle popularity stakes ladder.

Penis differences aside, Diego and I did have one particular mutual worry — getting between the sheets of a nubile and experienced woman. Coming from a society where girls had no option but to be virgins on their wedding night, made it difficult for youths like us to get any practice at all. We deliberated the dilemma for countless hours. Like the saying of best-laid plans, ours did go astray. Until the day my father introduced a girl-woman to his Chiropractic students.

Rosa was a year younger than me. If compared to my mother, she could not be called beautiful — no one came close to my mother's famed beauty — but more likely plain. She had an untamed mop of fudge coloured curls that framed a sweet elfin face. A strip of almost imperceptible freckles dotted her cheekbones and nose. She had brown eyes that appeared like deep pools given their darkness.

Yet to me, she was the most beautiful creature on earth. She appeared worldly wise. And I was not wrong. For in a short while, I was to learn she worked at The House. She was in need of a pelvic adjustment. With natural ease that comes with regular practice, she undressed down to her silk sheath and lay upon the examining table.

Her slim legs were outlined, ending at the beginning of the cleft of her *mons pubis* rising in a slight arch like an inverted sickle moon. Her belly lay flat. Her breasts splayed outwards pulling the silk taut across deep brown *areolae* in the middle of which her nipples puckered upright. This was as close as I had ever been to an almost nude woman. My wildest expectations were exceeded.

In between school, along with several male students of varying ages, I attended my father's Chiropractic lectures. It had been inferred I might follow in his footsteps.

Usually, therapies were conducted clothed, minus jackets and coats. But my father explained, seeing the body as near naked as possible for initial assessment purposes was better. As one, we cast our eyes, none more reverent than mine, upon the sumptuous landscaped beauty of valleys, peaks, and plains lying before us.

My father's voice took on a solicitous affectation, one I had never heard him use before. Instinctively, I knew the tone of my father's voice would have caused my mother to take note. But at that moment, all I consciously registered was the beauty before us, and my fear was everyone would hear the audible thumping inside my chest.

Asked to stand, the thin straps slipped off her shoulders. My father pointed out their imbalance but I could not stop my eyes focusing on her cleavage. She turned gracefully. Through the fabric hugging her buttocks, my father pointed to her left hip.

The treatment over in a blur, she dressed and left. On a pretext, I scoured my father's appointment book and adjustment cards for her details. There were none. But Lady Luck had not deserted me.

I saw Rosa three days later walking along Padilla Street where Medina del Campo's famous jewellry shops were located. Her eyes were steady as she nodded in recognition. As she passed me, her skirts brushed against my trousered legs. Electrical charges rushed to my groin. I did what I had to. I followed her. She entered The House with an air of belonging.

I related the whole account to Diego. He clapped me on the back. Another plan was hatched.

Each Wednesday evening, my parents left for their dinner arrangement with his parents. Diego slipped in the back door the moment my parents left through the front door.

'Did you find out?'

'Course. What did you think?' He searched and emptied his pockets spilling handfuls of new aluminium-bronze pesetas bearing the portrait of Francisco Franco onto the table.

'How much?' I reached for my wallet.

'Two hundred pesetas.'

I selected a hundred pesetas note bearing the image of my mother's favourite artist, Julio Romero de Torres. On the flip side of the note was a portrait of his muse, Maria Teresa Lopez González. That there is an uncanny similarity between the beauty of my mother and Maria Teresa Lopez González is coincidental. But if anyone wanted to know what my mother looked like, I would pull out a hundred pesetas note and show them the image of Maria Teresa Lopez González. I placed it on the table.

'What's that?' enquired Diego.

'My share.'

'No way,' he grunted. 'It's two hundred pesetas each.'

My eyes widened.

'I told the fat woman we didn't want to buy them. Just fuck them,' he said with bolshie bravado. 'And she said, "That's the price. Take it or leave it".'

I looked at him steadily.

'I took it. That'll give us an hour.'

I began to float like a hot air balloon. A whole hour with Rosa. I slipped out another hundred pesetas note, my entire month's allowance. Diego, as usual, did not have enough on him, so the last spare fifty-peseta note I had in my kid-lined wallet went onto the table mixed in with Diego's never-ending cache of coins.

We arrived breathless. The single lamp when on indicating they were open for business was off. Diego rang the bell several times. We wanted to enter the house as fast as possible should anyone see us from the street.

In her absence and, never knowing Madam to turn business away, a plump woman, with a braid of blond hair twisted around her head like a crown, who had earlier advised Diego on the cost, opened the door.

'One ring is enough,' she said as we squashed through the doorway, got stuck, and then wasted time extricating ourselves.

'I am . . . ,' I began to introduce myself.

'I know who you are, Señor Alejandro Salazar Herrera. And you, Señor Diego Rivas Flores.'

I looked at Diego enquiringly.

Diego shrugged his shoulders. Clearly, introductions were unnecessary. Our very presence spoke the reason for us being there. We'd meet Berta weekly thereafter for a year. On The Night That Changed Everything, I met her under different circumstances. As hard as I have tried to forget it, the memory has stubbornly remained.

She showed us into the salon, furnished to my surprise much like my home's living room.

Berta shook her head at Diego's number of loose coins. But after counting out our money, she admitted us into the inner workings of the house. A long passage with closed doors faced us.

'Any door,' she said. 'You choose.'

There were no names on the doors. How to find Rosa? My throat contracted and out squeaked a sound reminiscent of when my voice underwent the pubescent voice change.

'Third on the right.'

Diego dashed for the first door on the left.

I raised my hand to knock. A desire to run overwhelmed me. I hesitated. I stepped away from the door. A new, much stronger, desire rose up. I stepped back to the door. Once again I raised my hand. This time I knocked. Then knocked again. Getting no response and contrary to my mother's rules, I opened the door and entered.

The largest piece of furniture in the room was the bed. It stood high off the ground on thin iron legs with a headboard of intricate wrought iron winged angels. The mattress was covered with many pillows of assorted sizes. It would always be made up with clean, and always white linen, as was the matching white coverlet, but which never remained for long in its place on top of the bed.

Above the headboard nailed to the wall was a plain wooden crucifix such as one would find in a nun's cell. In one corner, stood a small wardrobe with double doors that sported long mirrors — cracked and silver-shadowed with age. But which when correctly angled — I would come to learn — reflected wavy coupling images that stretched into blissful infinity.

The window overlooking the main street below was hung with white, hand-pulled lace curtains through which street lamplight gleamed.

On a small dressing table, stood a pitcher of water and washbowl. Next to that was a bar of floral scented soap and a vase of fresh flowers, which for a split second reminded me of my mother's dressing table. And on the dressing table was a hairbrush, a far cry from the ornate one my mother used. A chair stood beside the dressing table. The room was clean, plain and functional. The sole decoration — Rosa.

Lace-filtered streetlight played over her perfect body reclining naked on the bed supported by the multitude of pillows.

Nothing existed from that moment on. Just Rosa and I. And after, I could not say for sure, but I almost believed it was Rosa's first time too.

From Diego's detailed telling later on, he had a vastly different experience to mine. The only similarity was we both overran the allotted hour.

'Compliments of The House,' Madam murmured. She arrived just as we were about to take our leave. 'Be sure I see you two boys again and very soon.'

And so she did, every week for nearly a year on Wednesdays while our parents dined together. We lived for those Wednesdays. We became model sons. We worked hard. Our study doors remained open at all times. We were determined not to do anything to upset our parents. As this could well result in a punishment, halting the single secret hour a week available to us in our disciplined routine. As our school grades improved, our rewards, slipped to us by our fathers, passed directly to Madam.

Diego worked his way up and down the passage of doors several times over, but he never had an hour with Rosa. That was my agreement with him. I could not bring myself to go with anyone else. Each time Rosa and I were together, it got better. Deep down, a connection began to grow, and when it materialized and knocked me in the heart and head, it was too late.

Sometimes Rosa would relax and like the teenagers we were, we'd romp and frolic a while before she'd conclude business within the allotted time.

But Diego and I overplayed our hand.

———— ◆ ————

One night, as my parents and I were sitting down to dinner, my mother appeared brighter-eyed than usual. I always took this as a sign of the beginning of an interrogation and wondered who my mother would be lining up in her sights. It could only be my father or myself. I ran through a mental list of any possible misdemeanors my mother could have stumbled upon.

'Alejandro,' she began. My heart sank. She usually only called me by my given name when she was in a serious mood.

'Yes, Mama.'

'You were seen walking along Padilla Street this afternoon.'

My mind raced back. Had I been anywhere near Padilla Street? No. I had not. I was safe. I breathed a sigh of relief.

'Nope. Whoever told you that made a mistake. I was at Diego's house all afternoon studying. Scouts' Honor.' I raised my right hand in the traditional scout salute.

My father sat at the head of the table. For reasons of his own, he too gave a relieved sigh.

'Ah. Diego's house. Studying,' she said. Her eyes narrowed. I realized then things were more serious. My relief had been short lived.

'You are always at Diego's house. What is it that attracts you so much to Diego? I can't remember the last time I saw you out and about with a girl.'

Aha, so that's what this is all about I thought: the same old story of girls versus boys, or, to be more explicit, me versus girls.

'Mama, my attraction as you put it is simply this. Diego is a good student. We study. I'm hoping that some of it rubs off.'

'Surely there are girls you could study with?' My mother began to fiddle with the most recent jewelled pin my father had presented her with. It was attached to her left shoulder.

I shot a glance at my father. For someone who was not particularly keen on food, he suddenly seemed extremely interested in what was on his plate. Clearly I was not going to get any help from him.

'I don't know any girls who are as clever as Diego.'

'Are you saying all girls are stupid?'

The conversation was taking a dangerous turn.

'Of course not. I just said I don't know any girls . . . ;'

'Very well. I shall introduce you to some.'

My father's shaggy eyebrows — in contrast to his almost bald pate — rose sharply.

'Who?' he managed to mumble.

'Why Maria Galvez of course. She is as sharp as a knife. She would inspire Alejandro. And best of all, she is an absolute stunner. What do you say?' She turned her attention back to me.

I waved my fork around in the air indicating I could not talk with my full mouth, just as she had drummed into me for years. My mother was always very particular about table manners. She said people's breeding was instantly apparent when they ate. Patiently, she waited. I could no longer extend my chewing. I swallowed the last mouthful of food, reached for and lifted the cut crystal glass of water to my mouth. My mother's patience was wearing thin. Her eyes had narrowed again. I had pushed this out far too long.

'Say about what?'

'About her good looks, of course.'

'But I thought you were talking about intelligence.'

'Alejandro, don't play the fool with me,' she snapped. 'You know exactly what I am talking about.'

My father began to cough into his linen table napkin. As mine and my mother's were, it had his initials embroidered into one corner.

I shook my head. My mother bristled and if it were possible it appeared my father had melted into and became part of his chair.

'I need to know. This is important. Alejandro do you prefer girls or boys?'

My father choked and his face turned puce.

'I suppose so,' I said.

'Suppose so what? Girls or boys? Answer me.'

'Well what do you really think?' I feigned anger trying to cover my fear. The last thing I needed was my mother interrogating me about what kind of girls I liked, when my every waking moment (and most sleeping moments) danced with sumptuous visions of Rosa. I threw down my own initials' embroidered table napkin, stood up, and excused myself from the table.

———— ◆ ————

Confused more than ever, my mother believed I was dangerously close to the brink of homosexuality. Homosexuals, along with a few other miscreants, were on the Nationalist list for execution by gunshot. It took only a hint before soldiers paid a call.

Overnight, Diego and I were obliged to attend our parents' Wednesday night dinner dates. These now included parents and daughters from the families spared from our mothers' lists. We were intensely scrutinized. Every word, breath and movement in reaction to an endless array of delightful young girls was analysed. We protested. We refused to attend any further dinners using our studies as our excuse. Our mothers stood firm. Tensions heightened. Drastic measures were called for.

Diego and I turned in several consecutive abysmal homework assignments. Our teachers contacted our mothers inquiring what the matter was. As Diego was interrogated by his mother in their home, so too was I by my mother in our home.

'Well Mama, what do you think the matter is?' I shot back at her. 'All I ever hear from you is that I must do well in my exams. Then you deliberately set me up with all those girls. Of course I'm losing my concentration. Who wouldn't?'

My mother sighed with grateful relief. 'So you're telling me . . . ;'

'. . . that I am attracted to girls.' I finished her sentence for her. 'I confess. Yes, I am. And it's not helping me at all with my schoolwork. If I fail, it'll be thanks to you.'

This was the excuse Diego and I had hoped would halt Wednesday night dinners. Out of sight and sound we celebrated. We hollered and jigged in the tight circle of a powwow dance. But our win was short lived. Our mothers engaged private tutors taking up Wednesday evenings.

Diego and I continued to spend hours studying together, either at his, or my home. But in truth, we discussed The House, and how to re-commence our visits without alerting our parents. The agonizing weeks we were unable to visit The House, had a serious effect on our bodies. We felt lethargic and super-charged at the same time. Concentrating was difficult and sleep impossible. I lost weight. Diego said he'd lost some too, but it was difficult to see as he was always heavy.

To counter the negative effects of not visiting The House, Diego claimed to have taken up self-pleasuring. Leaving him, as the Catholic priests from whom we had taken our religious instruction had warned, feeling worse. I chose not to. Instead, I trod the tightrope between succumbing and holding onto self-discipline and felt worse for it, too. Either way, we both suffered.

Our mothers' foreheads creased with perplexity. Once again, the question of our sexual preference raised its head. My mother accused me of making her look older before her time. When she saw me, she drummed home her message by using the tips of her fingers to smooth out imagined facial lines.

This time our fathers were alerted. Fears were whispered behind cupped palms. The problem was handed over. Diego and I accompanied our fathers to an 'all boys' dinner. What we did not know, our dinner was to be concluded with a late night visit to The House.

She had not been forewarned, and to her credit, Madam's stiff countenance slipped only for a moment. Never was invisibility so earnestly wished for. Neither Diego nor I could look Madam, or each other, in the eye. Worse followed.

'*Buenos, amigos. Bienvenida.* Good fellows. Welcome.' A chorus of male voices called out. The salon was filled with the fathers of our school friends, a relation or two, and other town professionals, many of whom had sat around our family dinner tables in the company of their wives, daughters, and our mothers.

'*Qué tenemos aquí?* What do we have here?' said the town's apothecary, whose own ministrations had not resolved his pustulous face.

'*Nuevos Polluelos.* New Chicks. Come to try out your wings?'

Our presence was greeted with hoots, hollers, and lewd guffaws. Our fathers' chests puffed out. They strutted, blew great plumes of cigar smoke, and chucked back tumblers of whisky.

'Here chicks, drink this. It will help your wings to fly.'

Two tumblers were thrust into our hands. To the great hilarity of all, we gagged on the contents we were encouraged to drink down-in-one accompanied by the noise of their own empty tumblers banging on the tabletops.

'José. Jerardo. If you run out of money for your boy chicks, let us know. We'll pay.' The men roared with laughter.

Like circus buffoons, our fathers emptied their wallets with great show, and handed over the money for an hour each. After back slapping us and each other we were shown into the inner workings of the house.

The long passage with closed doors faced us. Why was I surprised when my father made for the third door on the right? He did not knock. He walked straight in. Rosa squealed with delight. The same welcome she'd assured me in our most ardent moments was reserved just for me.

Diego's father flung open the first door on the left. This being the first and thereafter most entered by Diego during our year of Wednesday visits. He'd begun to realize what benefits were to be had coupling with the same partner.

We stared at each other.

'The apple . . . ,' he began to quote in a futile attempt to cover his own disillusionment. I could not utter a word. Like spotlight caught rabbits, we stood rooted to the floor. Madam appeared.

'Gentlemen, this way please.' She guided us to a door each and ushered us in.

Diego experienced a new arrival whose expertise focused on the clinical. It was over, with more than half an hour to spare. True to his nature, he set about making use of the remaining time. And this is the memory that refused to be forgotten.

———— ◆ ————

Berta stripped off her gown revealing herself to be Brunhilde, the Wagnerian Valkyrie. Her long blonde hair was braided and wound around her head. She was encased in an all-in-one boned girdle. Her breasts jutted out like two ice-cream cones intent on puncturing anything that got in their way.

She fussed and clucked like a broody hen, and I found myself stripped in half the time I could manage it on my own. When there was no physical sign of what was expected, Berta's clucking and fussing turned into forceful pulling and painful tweaking. Still, nothing happened.

She strong-armed me down onto the bed face up. Sensing a game about to begin, my member, like a puppy eagerly pulling at its restraining leash, headed off to the playground. For Berta had buried her face between my thighs, a sure-fire way to get my member's instant attention.

Minutes later, with a long yodelling whoop, reminiscent of a sound I'd heard somewhere before, Berta leaped onto the bed straddling and pinning me between her thighs. Crazed with delight, my member in a single stroke, snuck in.

She leaned forward, a hand on either side of my shoulders. The ice-cream cones poked at my eyes. Within moments the bed began to undulate punctuated by ramming thrusts causing the bedsprings to squeak in earnest.

Then she changed stride riding me at a canter. Her braid slipped out of its serpent coil and a curtain of hair rolled down surrounding my head. It was difficult to breathe anyhow, and now hair clogged my mouth.

Dodging the cones, I began to choke. Concentrating on not suffocating and keeping my eyes intact, I relinquished all control.

Brunhilde grabbed me by the shoulders and wrenched me upright. She clutched me to her armoured bosom. I was no viking to Brunhilde. My arms dangled, flopping with every thrust. The cartilage in my nose bent at a ninety-degree angle, squashed against her plated chest bone.

The ice-cream cones provided immovable supports to either side of my head. Each thrust chaffed my ears until they burned red hot. Before I could protest, Brunhilde went into full gallop.

Disregarding my life-threatening situation, and intent on satisfying its own mad desire, my member joined the race. Just when I thought I would explode from suffocation, the desired result came to a momentous end. Johnny Weismuller's victory jungle cry whooped once more drowning my feeble whimper.

She released me and I fell backwards, my chest heaving out and caving in, desperate for the life saving air I was now free to breathe.

Still straddling me, I vomited all over Berta. Her chest, long curtains of hair and ice-cream cones dripped with slimy whiskey dotted with food particles pooling between the thick blonde thatch between her thighs and my stomach. The nightmare did not stop there.

How were they to assure their wives that their sons were not homosexual as feared, without incriminating themselves in regards to the visit to The House? In contrast to our loud arrival, we quietly separated. Each father and son pair walked home in silence. I knew my father well. He brooded over the answer to this dilemma. I felt a twinge of joyful revenge at his discomfort. But the tables soon turned.

Try as I might, I could not get to sleep for hearing Rosa's girlish squeals of welcoming delight. It reverberated around the inside of my skull and not even trying to asphyxiate myself with the pillow clenched around my head could stop it.

All my senses revolted and refused point blank to entertain the vision of my father and Rosa together, no doubt doing all that we had done.

What had passed between Berta and myself, I forced into the deepest recess of my memory. Although I never voluntarily re-visit that event, under times of stress it tends to repeat, no different to a needle stuck in the groove of a vinyl record. I have never watched another Tarzan film with its signature jungle call.

The next morning, the clocks did not chime. My father had forgotten to set them before going to sleep. This was an unprecedented break in his ritual.

Worse, neither parent arrived for breakfast. I could not eat for the gaping hole that had gnawed its way into the pit of my stomach. Inés' face remained unreadable as she returned the untouched food to the kitchen. And the same happened at lunchtime. No one appeared and my parents' standoff continued through Wednesday.

Our respective parents did not get together for their standard dinner date. I remained in my study now with my door closed. I imagined that Diego might, too, be in a similar situation.

My father and I never spoke of the visit to The House. From that night, the relationship between my parents changed. The extent of which I was still to discover. Their relationship with me changed too. A mantle — a subtle mix of not quite identifiable blame, responsibility and guilt settled around my shoulders.

On the other hand, both mothers were heartened by the news that we were not homosexual. They redoubled their efforts to find us suitable future marriage partners.

Given there were not enough young women of equal or better standing left in our community, they both decided upon the same girl. This was the direct cause that our mothers' lifelong friendship soon lay in tatters, from which neither recovered. Never to be thwarted, my mother vowed to extend her search to foreign countries.

With the real excuse of final exams becoming a reality, Diego and I saw less of each other. On the afternoon I finished writing my final exams, I returned home to find Inés and Tomás gone. My mother had dismissed them. Not only did they leave our employ, but they left the region. I never heard from Inés again.

I retired to my room. This time, I locked my door. With my elbows bent, the palms of my hands resting on the wall I banged my forehead hard. One bang for the loss of Inés and Tomás. One bang for the relief that the stress of exams was over. One bang for the frustration of not having been able to see Rosa. A bang for the tension that permeated my parents' relationship that somehow had a direct bearing on me. And, finally, a bang for the loss of my friendship with Diego.

For he had not greeted me as we settled down at our wooden desks placed ridiculously far apart at exam writing time. And, unlike past times when we waited for the other in the school quadrant to go over the test questions, which his memory recalled with photographic precision, he was not there.

During the following months, we exchanged birthday greetings given we were a day apart, and Christmas tidings. Thereafter I received nothing, and by return, sent nothing. Communication lost its meaning. We were living very different lives.

The next morning, to our neighbours' disapproval and my father's angst, my mother departed for foreign countries alone. She was going, she claimed, in search of a suitable future wife for me.

My father and I were alone. We made a miserable pair: both unhappy, lonely, and bewildered. My father would not disclose his reasons for his state. I certainly would not disclose mine.

Upon my mother's return, and to my enormous relief, without a prospective bride in tow, my parents withdrew into two distinct parts of the house. In retaliation for his participation at The House, she meted out the most cruel of punishments. While she could not consider divorce, she did the next best thing. She cut herself off from him. She extinguished their past life together like snuffing out a candle flame. For two years thereafter, I moved between my parents, and no amount of begging on my part shifted my mother from her stance.

The clocks chimed discordantly and then stopped. My father aged to the point where he became a shell of his former self. He limped all the time. He became melancholic and spoke to me about his parents, the ranch, his youth and wild fantastical stories of adjustments causing earth tremors. He gave me a sealed envelope and said, 'Promise me you will not open this until after I am dead.'

I promised. I slid the envelope into one of my old schoolbooks gathering dust on the shelf. Fearful of the letter's contents, I all too soon forgot about it.

And each time I looked at my father, I saw Rosa's light nut-brown body tinged with rosy hues, her unruly mop of curls dancing around her face and her naked limbs entwined with his. I tried to separate the two of them, but could not. I spent as many hours out of our home as I could.

My mother turned from a beautiful glowing woman into a beautiful brittle woman. She withdrew from society. She no longer played cards. Her brushes and canvases stood gathering dust. Her box of bejewelled trinkets, stood open on her dressing table. I often found her running her fingers over them. I could never forget the dripping blood from the pricks where she had forced the sharp safety pins into her fingertips.

On Sunday, September 3, 1939, the only Spanish newspaper allowed to operate, the national right wing ABC, carried an article and picture of Albert Forster. He was making excuses for the German invasion of Poland. At 11.15 a.m., the British nation tuned in to hear Prime Minister Neville Chamberlain announce their country was at war with Germany.

But shortly before the sun rose on that summer's morning, a young mother eased herself up. Her long skirt was cumbersome being wet with heavy dew. She stepped out from under the fruit tree where she had huddled all night. Holding her six-week-old child to her chest, she walked towards the arched gate of the Capuchin Convent located in rural Nava del Rey, northwest Spain.

Tied around the newborn's neck was a bit of string. Attached to that, a torn off piece of card on which the mother had already written her baby's name, RosaMina, in a steady and well-curved hand. Checking that the card was still in place, she kissed her baby for the last time. She laid the child directly on the ground in the centre of the gate. She withdrew to behind the fruit tree. Church bells tolled. On the sixth, the convent's heavy door swung open.

A novice nun stepped out. She immediately saw the small bundle. She hastened across the chequered forecourt to the gate, unlocked, and pulled it open. She glanced left and right. Not seeing anyone, but knowing the mother was somewhere near, she bent down and picked up the baby. She relocked the gate and in less than a minute the convent door thudded closed.

'We are blessed. A child . . . ,' she called out.

The drum of footsteps sounded from around the convent. Nuns dressed in black habits gathered around the novice and peered at the sleeping baby.

'A child of God,' said one.

'An earthly angel,' said another.

Heavy slower footsteps getting louder announced Mother Superior's arrival.

'Show me,' she said.

The novice held out the child. Crippled with age, Mother Superior's hand looking like a bird's frozen claw, scrabbled about the baby's neck and pulled off the card.

'Read it.'

'The mother requests the child be baptised with the name RosaMina.'

'Bah,' said Mother Superior. Her lips curled back revealing a small black hole where an eye tooth should have been. 'Did the mother not write the day of birth?'

The novice turned over the card. On the reverse side was written, *21 de Julio, 1939.*

'July 21,' she read aloud.

'Money for the child's upkeep?' asked the Mother Superior.

The novice loosened the shawl the child was wrapped in. Several coins were lodged in the folds.

'Yes.'

'Very well. Just this once. But use the surname.'

The novice's eyes sparkled. A child with a different name rather than the default name — Maria — given to all girls whose names and birthdates were not known.

As the card requested, the novice registered the baby at the births, marriages, and deaths office in the Town Hall as RosaMina. Rosa meaning rose, Mina meaning love. And exactly as Mother Superior ordered, the child was given the surname Expósito meaning exposed.

All the children in the orphanage where RosaMina grew up had the same surname, making them one big family. But no one could claim the same first name.

Over the next twelve years, and barring a few events, RosaMina did not remember much about the orphanage. There was the constant cacophony of shouts, screams, and cries of rarely less than forty female children ranging from a few days to fourteen years old. Loosely sorted into age groups, older children were assigned younger ones to take care of. So, they remained a mishmash of lost children trying to take care of and be cared for by each other. In spite of this, RosaMina never developed an attachment to anyone — neither to the older child in charge of her, nor the younger child who was her charge.

The children spent their days circling around the inside of the convent's rectangular courtyard where grass had long been trodden into dust. A carved white marble fountain dominated the courtyard. The wall forming the pool's wide circumference was low, and provided a seating ledge. It had a tiered centrepiece made of two bowls, the smaller placed above the larger, supported by a central spindle. When empty, the fountain was used as a jungle gym as found in children's playgrounds. One day a week during summer it was filled. The children bathed in it with their clothes on. To dry off they either ran around or lay down, face up to the sun.

When RosaMina lay on the ground looking up, she wondered where the moving clouds had come from, where they were going. Sometimes they were in a hurry and other times not. And sometimes, they visited each other, stopped right above her. When the sky was blue, she knew the clouds had found their destination. They would just be taking a rest before starting new journeys, once again passing directly above her head.

Orphans' nights were spent in the adjacent arched corridors surrounding the courtyard on four sides. They started off sleeping head to toe on cotton pallets laid out in neat rows. By morning they resembled a jumbled nest of newborn mice.

Meals were unvarying. Each day vegetables were cooked in the black iron pot. It always surprised RosaMina that the smell proved better than the taste. Breakfast consisted of a bowl of milk and bread. Lunch, the main meal of the day, was an oat gruel mixed with vegetables thickened with cornstarch. Dinner was oat gruel leftovers cut into wedges. She developed a dislike for eating. By the time she turned twelve, RosaMina still looked like a seven-year-old.

The orphans' education focused on the purity of Mary the Immaculate, mother of the baby Jesus. Unlike their own mothers, the baby Jesus' mother never left his side. The nuns assured them this meant their abandonment was wholly complete. It would never change.

After Mass on the last Sunday of each month, the children gathered in a smaller courtyard. The public stood squashed together on the narrow balcony at mezzanine level overlooking the courtyard and the children within it. From there, they saw to what good use their pennies thrown into the collection box was put.

The Ramírez Espina family regularly appeared. The father, Juan Ramírez, was tall and stooped. His face was permanently creased into a mask of resignation. He gripped the handrail and bent over as far as he possibly could in an effort to see all the orphans below.

'What more can we do for these poor children,' he'd ask no one in particular. His question faded before it reached their ears.

'Be careful Juan,' his wife, Teresa Espina said her voice rising. 'You don't want to go falling, break your neck, and kill these children.'

A sea of gaunt, raggedy and barefoot girls clearly heard the last three high-pitched words. Like the tide rushing out, they retreated their backs pressing up against the chests of those behind them. The girls in the last row had their backs pressed up against the wall, trapped. Teresa Espina, a dumpling in too small clothes called out, 'Don't be afraid. Come back. We just want to see you.'

She reached into her bag. The orphans thinking sweets were about to be tossed to them, moved forward, this time like the tide rushing in.

Instead, her left hand emerged holding her handkerchief. Her right hand curled into a fist and rested over her heart. With a theatre's sense of tragedy, she whispered loud enough for all to hear, 'Poor lambs. God have mercy.' She recited the phrase, dabbed the corners of her eyes, knocked her fist against her heart, and rocked on her heels, all in a syncopated chant.

Their eight-year-old son, Miguel Ramírez Espina and ten-year-old daughter, Valeria Ramírez Espina were clones of their parents.

The tall-for-his-age boy cocked his head and eyed the orphans below him. He worked his tongue around his mouth storing up saliva. When he had enough, he'd bend his head over the rail and spit down on the orphans. If lucky, his saliva would land with a splat and meld with the snot often running from the victim's nostrils.

His older and fat sister, Valeria, not being tall enough, pulled strange faces through the vertical bars of the railing. She stuck out her tongue, stretched the corners of her mouth horizontally with hooked index fingers. Her eyes crisscrossed and then rolled backwards until opaque.

The orphans spent hours entertaining each other by trying to copy her. As there were no mirrors, they relied upon the increasingly terrified screams of the younger children of their progress.

On this day, Miguel Ramírez Espina pulled out his penis. The first the orphans had seen.

'Watch out,' he called to them, 'it's beginning to rain.' He waved his penis from side to side to maximize its spread and urinated upon them. The orphans froze in shock. Then they began to laugh, even if splattered by the hot jet stream coming from what appeared to be another eye.

Alerted by the orphans' laughter, Juan Ramírez looked down from searching the sky for rain clouds and witnessed the event.

'Are you mad?' he asked his son. 'Don't you know God sees everything?' He dealt a swift clip to the back of his son's head.

Miguel Ramírez Espina's face screwed up as he erupted into wails. The orphans laughed harder. Without yet knowing why, but indignant at being jolted from her hypnotic incantations, Teresa Espina also clipped the back of the boy's head. For the sake of expediency, together, the parents clipped the back of the girl's head too. She gasped, glared at both parents, and then let loose a caterwauling of shrill howls.

Like battleships advancing upon tugboats, the parents bore down upon their children. They each fixed a thumb and forefinger to a child's ear. No different to tail clutching circus elephants, the father led them, squeezing sideways through the balcony door. The boy's penis poked meekly from his fly. Throughout this event the orphans noted, the eye had not blinked once.

Couples contemplating adoption would gaze down upon the orphans' upturned faces gazing back at them. At these times, bar an infant's cry, a cough or sneeze, the orphans were silent. And the clear sweet bird song from the orchard on the other side of the vast protective wall — twenty-four feet high surrounding the entire convent — could be heard.

Of the orchard, the orphans never laid eyes upon it. Nor did they eat its fruit, or play upon the soft green carpet of grass mixed with daisies.

Without exception, couples turned away from the sea of upturned faces. If still courageous enough, they would choose instead a foundling, swaddled in a cotton wrap. And so, to RosaMina's surprise, she was adopted.

The day the stick woman stood on the balcony, the sun was at its highest. Blinding light filled the courtyard and, try with their collective might, the orphans struggled to make out the solitary figure blanked out of all colour. It was a wonder the woman saw anything either. But it did not matter whether she saw them or not, for her choice had long been made.

A nun pushed her way through the orphans, calling RosaMina. She knew her name. But so infrequently was it called, it took her a while to make the connection. Shaking her head and muttering with the effort of being forced to fetch her, the nun pounced upon RosaMina. A path in the sea of orphaned children opened before nun and child. Her forearm in an iron grip, RosaMina was dragged out of the courtyard.

The moment RosaMina was the chosen one, each child suffered acute pain, struck by the pendulum of hope and anguish. It swung from one side, hope, there would be a next time, and then to the opposite side, anguish, because it was not this time. For the rest of RosaMina's life, that pendulum held her captive to its endless swings between hope and anguish.

The woman was her new employer. RosaMina had forgotten that between the ages of twelve and fourteen, orphans were sent out to work. Thereafter, many orphans would return — only to place at the gate of the Capuchin Convent, their newborn daughters. Some had a bit of string tied around their necks with the name the mother wished their child to be called written upon the attached piece of card. Some with the date of the child's birth, and some not.

A taxi waited outside. RosaMina left the orphanage in the only dress she had. It was an hour's drive to the town of Medina del Campo. She was overwhelmed. It was the first time she'd seen a car much less been in one. The countryside slid by. With the intense midday heat, she fell into a deep sleep.

Berta, a natural blonde and buxom young woman, carried the sleeping child from the taxi. She placed her in a single bed alongside her own. RosaMina would share Berta's bedroom for the next two years.

She awoke in the late evening. For a moment, she believed she was on the inside of a white cloud. The walls glowed white, the curtain at the window was white. The cotton sheets and bed cover were white, too. A tray covered with a white cloth was placed on the table separating the beds. On it stood a glass of honey-sweetened milk and a small plate of *mantecados*, madeleine biscuits. The room was small and tidy.

RosaMina had to urinate. She slipped off the bed, the first she'd ever slept in, and walked to the door. It opened out onto a passageway, off of which, on either side, were other doors. There was no indication of a place to be used for ablutions. A door, several along, opened.

A tall man with erect bearing dressed in a wool coat, holding a pair of leather gloves in one hand and a hat in his other emerged. The stick woman whom RosaMina would come to call Madam materialized. Another door opened. A short round man emerged dressed in similar clothes.

In a low voice Madam called out, 'Berta, the child.'

Berta rescued RosaMina while Madam led both men away. She showed RosaMina into a warm well-lit bathroom decorated in clinical white. On the wall was a long mirror. RosaMina stood rooted to the floor forgetting her urgent need to urinate. It was the first time she had seen herself. She was thin. Her skin from being outdoors was light nut-brown. Like all the orphans, her hair (curly and an uncommon fudge colour), had been hacked short. Peering closer she saw her eyes were brown. A smattering of pale freckles looked like golden sugar sprinkled across the bridge of her nose.

Berta ran a steaming bath. She gave RosaMina a bag holding a toothbrush and a tube of cleaning gel, her own facecloth, a towel, and a small pot of face cream. She was instructed how to use the toothbrush.

'Twice a day,' Berta said.

RosaMina's gums tingled. Getting submerged, scrubbed, and rubbed dry did not feel unpleasant either. But best of all, she was dressed in her first pair of pyjamas. Berta tried brushing RosaMina's unruly hair. Her tongue clicked with disapproval as each curl defied straightening and ruffled up again.

'Don't worry. After it's grown, we'll get it cut properly,' she said.

Returning to the bedroom, RosaMina swallowed the sweetened milk in between nibbles of biscuits. She stretched out, feeling the perimeter of the mattress with her fingers and toes — imprinting how much space there was available before rolling off onto the floor. With her head supported by a soft white pillow, she slept again. Like the clouds that used to pass over her head going to new places, she too had been transported to a new world.

Early the following morning, the house was quiet. Except for Berta. She was already up and dressed. Her blonde hair had been plaited and wound around the top of her head like a coiled snake. From the wardrobe, she selected a plain, but new, cotton dress for RosaMina along with cotton panties and a pair of leather strap sandals. By midmorning came the audible sounds of rising occupants. The door to the bathroom opened and shut time and again.

Berta bustled about in the kitchen preparing breakfast. Into bowls of fresh-diced fruit, she added a careful measure of powder from a bottle labelled *Cohosh Azul*, Blue Cohosh. A place was laid for each girl at the large table, which stood in the centre of the room. In a corner, stood a sofa and several odd chairs surrounding a low table.

The first girl arrived freshly bathed and wrapped in a morning gown. It was by the head of bright bronze hair that fizzed out down to her shoulders that RosaMina recognized her. She had been one of the orphans, but several years older than her. Her eyebrows were tweaked into two thin half moon arcs. Her eyes were red rimmed.

'So this is my replacement,' she said, giving RosaMina a passing glance. She did not remember RosaMina. Or, if she did, she chose not to.

'Shh! Be quiet,' said Berta. 'She's only a child.'

'Hah. She'd better make the most of it. Not long now.' She turned her back to RosaMina, sat down and began her breakfast.

Berta threw RosaMina a quick soft smile. The kitchen door swung open. In ones and twos the rest of the girls shuffled in, yawning and rubbing the sleep from their eyes. At once, the air was filled with gales of laughter punctuated by contemplative pauses. A tiny vertical crease between RosaMina's eyebrows appeared. She hardly understood anything they said. Silence fell when Madam arrived.

'Good morning, Madam,' the girls chorused.

Madam sat at the head of the table. She opened a notebook and glanced down at a column of jotted numbers.

'Rubí,' she said looking directly at the girl with bronze hair. 'You had a good night. But tonight should be busier. Rest this afternoon.'

RosaMina's crease dissolved. Madam spoke clearly and plainly.

Rubí nodded. She took the folded piece of paper Madam slid over the table towards her. Without opening it, Rubí tucked the paper between her morning gown and her bosom. She'd read it in the privacy of her room and then add the paper to a growing collection in her bedside drawer.

The same pattern followed until all accounts had been settled and during which the tiny vertical crease between RosaMina's eyebrows reappeared. RosaMina had never heard such names before.

The pale blonde girl alongside Rubí was called Cristal. The girl next to her with café au lait skin was, Ámbar. And next to Ámbar sat Nácar, whose teeth did look like white pearls. Last, was Berta.

'Berta, you will be required this evening,' said Madam, 'we're overbooked.'

Berta dipped her head in acknowledgement.

'There has been a request for the corset. Wear it.'

Berta's head dipped again.

'Any questions? Problems?' she asked looking directly into each girl's face.

Nácar's voice squeaked, 'I have a doctor's appointment this afternoon.'

'Yes. At three.'

'Am, I to . . . ?'

'If he requests your services afterward, oblige him.'

Nácar managed a tiny flash of those pearly white teeth.

'When can we expect the order of lingerie?' asked Cristal, her hand straying to her hair. It looked like it could do with a good brushing. But RosaMina would come to learn that this untidy fly-away hair was Cristal's permanent hairstyle. Only the colour changed on a regular basis.

Madam looked at Berta who consulted her own notebook.

'Delivery is expected tomorrow.'

The girls sighed. New lingerie was always something to look forward to.

'Please don't put any more of those small white flowers in my room. I've suffered such an attack of the sneezes,' said Ámbar.

Again Madam looked enquiringly at Berta.

'Those are the tiny white lily-of-the-valley flowers the florist delivered last week.'

'They are beautiful,' Cristal said.

'Not if anyone has an allergy to them. Cancel the next order,' said Madam.

'Anything else?' Madam looked at each girl once more. 'No?' She paused and then said, 'This is Rosa.'

Rosa's vertical crease deepened. Only the first half of her name, she realized, was to be used.

The girls stared her up and down. Finally they chorused, 'Hello, Rosa.'

As they left the kitchen, they each, bar Rubí, hugged her or touched her on the cheek.

———————— ✦ ————————

Berta and Rosa sat opposite each other to eat their lunch. Berta spooned the tiniest portion of pork and bean stew into a bowl and set it in front of Rosa. The rising smells were delicious. Even better, there was not a vegetable in sight. Rosa tried the stew cautiously.

Berta finished her larger portion and said nothing about the food left in Rosa's bowl. She whisked it away replacing it with a custard tartlet.

Rosa had never seen anything like it. It was beautiful. Was it really to be eaten, she wondered. Sweet warm cinnamon and nutmeg tantalized her nostrils. Watching Berta wolf hers down whole, Rosa could no longer hold out. With caution, she lifted the tartlet to her mouth and nibbled. Then bit into the crisp pastry filled with cream custard. Finally, she pushed the whole thing into her mouth. Just as she had seen Berta do.

At the moment while RosaMina's cheeks bulged, Madam entered. She and Berta exchanged glances. As Madam left, Rosa swallowed the custard tartlet. She could not drag her eyes from the tray where the rest of them sat. But she was not offered another.

Each day, she'd try something new. If she did not like it, Rosa was not forced to eat it, but then there was no dessert. Soon Rosa began to eat everything placed in front of her while keeping one eye on whatever dessert was available that day. And so her education in eating came into being.

The routine in The House was the same each day. The girls got up late, ate breakfast at lunchtime, and lunch before the evening's events got underway. Rosa ate dinner and went to bed long before the front door opened and closed with regular monotony until the small hours. From the remnants of meals, Berta cleared up each morning, it was clear that the girls snacked before going to sleep — just as the sun was about to rise.

Each morning, deliverymen arrived bringing boxes of tissue-wrapped gowns and multi-coloured lingerie, cigars, food, wine, books, fresh flowers, and other goods via the tradesmen's entrance. One of Madam's notebooks listed all the expected items. Individual costs were written in her distinctive handwriting. Berta paid out the exact amounts owing. Madam's rule of equality for all tolerated neither ribald humour nor wisecrack jokes. A generous set tip for each deliveryman made sure of that.

Rosa took up the task of arranging fresh flowers for the salon. With Berta's help, she placed filled vases on tabletops interspersed between numerous two-seater sofas. The largest vase was reserved for the *faux* marble mantelpiece over the fireplace. Rosa did not like the salon. It was dark and the air stank of stale cigars. But when the side lamps were lit, light moved through the chandeliers' crystal drops reflecting off the wallpaper with the classic floral design etched in gold. Then the room was bathed in a warm welcoming glow. It was in this light the girls were shown off to their best advantage.

The tops of the tables were covered with hundreds of circles made from the wet bases of liquor glasses. Beeswax rubbed into the tops made little difference. Rosa soon recognized the smaller rings being those from champagne flutes, the larger from whiskey tumblers.

One afternoon while the girls were resting, Madam entered the kitchen.

'Rosa, come. Sit beside me.'

Dutifully, Rosa scooted along the bench until she was alongside her.
'Do you know what this is?'

Rosa shook her head.

'It's a children's story book.'

It was tattered. On the front cover was a picture of a little girl wearing a red cape.

'Open it.'

Rosa's eyes were first drawn to the faded coloured pictures telling the story in ordered sequence under which were sentences explaining each event.

Madam picked up a pencil. 'Look, this is how you hold a pencil. Here try.' She handed it to Rosa.

Rosa gripped the pencil as though her hand had turned into a paw.

'Only with these three fingers.'

Rosa felt Madam's cold hand as the tip of her thumb, index, and middle finger of her right hand were pressed together to hold the pencil.

'Relax your hand. Let this part rest here.' Madam ran the tip of her finger along the fold of skin between Rosa's thumb and index finger. 'Yes. Much better. Now see the first word. The first word in the title of this story is 'Little'. Copy the word over and over in this notebook.' Madam opened a new notebook to the first page and placed it in front of Rosa. 'When you can write this word easily and uniformly, move onto the next word.'

Thereafter Rosa sat at the kitchen table each afternoon. Her hand eventually found its own uniform style. She guessed the story from the pictures, but still did not understand the meaning of the words.

Six months later, Madam sat down with Rosa again. This time she read the book to her. Rosa followed each word with Madam's pointed index finger moving over the page. The written story was revealed. After Madam had read the book to her several times, she said, 'Now you read.'

Why Rosa struggled was not clear at first. Was it shyness at reading aloud from a book for the first time? Or hearing the sound of her voice? For until that moment, she'd had never spoken. With hesitant lisps and stop-start stutter, she managed to string together the first four words in the opening sentence of the classic children's tale.

Berta stood up and applauded.

Madam chucked Rosa under her chin.

Praise. Rosa's eyes pricked, releasing first teardrops. She read the book many times over until her voice settled into its own pitch and rhythm. And she began to respond in monosyllables when asked a question. Then, an unexpected event forced her to utter her first spoken phrase.

◆

She had risen after Berta and gone to use the bathroom. There was a strict rotational order in the house to use the bathroom. Knowing it was her turn, she entered and gasped.

'Help me,' whispered the morning-gowned body — unrecognizable but for the copper hair — lying on the floor in a pool of blood.

Rosa turned and ran. Her heart bumped with each step. Berta was not in the kitchen. She hesitated. She'd not been through the doorway leading to Madam's rooms. But she entered and found herself in a glass-fronted shop. The room was full of upright cabinets displaying glittering pieces of jewellry.

Madam was talking to a bearded man. His sideburns had been allowed to grow so long they formed two ringlets which danced on either side of his thin and fully-bearded face. A tall black hat sat upon his head. Both he and Madam turned and looked at Rosa in startled surprise. Rosa was paler than a ghost.

'Come quickly,' she blurted and retraced her steps.

The girls were solemn during their breakfast at lunchtime meal. Although Rubí had had the best room, for it faced the morning sun and overlooked the street, it remained unoccupied. Later, there were low grumbles, but no one dared ask Madam if they could move into the best room of the house.

Decorators arrived and painted the walls. The furniture got moved around and new lace curtains Madam had ordered were hung. A matching coverlet was placed over the large bed.

On Fridays, Rosa placed a vase of fresh flowers in each girl's room, including the still unoccupied, newly decorated room.

All trace of Rubí had been erased. Except for the pink stain on the white ceramic bathroom floor where her blood had seeped into the soft cracks between the tiles. No amount of scrubbing got rid of that.

From then on, Rosa had no excuse not to speak. Still, she spoke only when spoken to. It would be a while longer before she spoke unprompted.

As Berta had promised, her hair grew. And sticking to her promise, Berta and Cristal — who'd been a hairdresser in former times — armed with a pair of dangerously sharp scissors set about cutting Rosa's hair.

Rosa realized hedge clippers, not scissors had previously been used to cut her hair. With Berta acting as assistant Cristal snipped and shaped her curls.

'Ooh, don't you look lovely,' said Berta.

'Mmm . . . just a little more here,' said Cristal. 'Oops, don't move. Another minute.' She fluffed out Rosa's hair and then ran the hot tongs through each curl framing Rosa's face. 'Sorry Rosa. Did I burn you?' she asked as Rosa flinched pulling her head away from the smoking hot tongs. The air filled with the smell of singed hair. 'Last curl. Then it's all over.'

'You can look now,' said Berta. She held up a large hand-held mirror twisting it from side to side so Rosa could see her new hair cut from every angle.

She could not see much of a difference. But what she did see, her hair colour had changed to warm golden fudge matching the freckles on her nose.

Thanks to the improved meals, she had grown a couple of centimetres. Her legs had filled out. No longer did her knees knock together when she walked. Her dresses had tightened. She looked again. Two small bulges pushed out from her chest.

A few weeks later, she entered womanhood. Her relief was enormous, especially so, when month after month, nothing like what happened to Rubí, happened to her.

Soon after, Madam chose to celebrate Rosa's birthday. She had turned fifteen. It was her first birthday celebration and the day upon which she first came to know the date of her birth, July 21, 1939. Though how Madam knew this, left RosaMina perplexed.

Berta prepared a tray of snacks and Madam popped open a bottle of champagne. With all of them gathered in the salon at lunchtime, they toasted Rosa and sang Happy Birthday. Each girl gave her a small gift. Rosa was deeply affected. She felt a profound sense of gratitude. She had no control over her tears. Madam's gift was Rubí's old room. She cried even harder. Not in gratitude, but because her time to pay Madam back was approaching.

Now being so close to the working rooms, she lay awake at night. Her hearing caught sounds coming from the girls and their clients. She distinguished murmured words of encouragement and in the beginning clapped her hands over her ears at piercing shrieks addressed to God. She wondered what the nuns would have thought of God being addressed so often and with such fervour. Surely, they and He would be pleased? After a while, she sensed what was going on. How, still remained a mystery. But soon all became clear — vividly so.

———— ◆ ————

One midmorning, Rosa accompanied Madam into her bedroom. She removed a framed picture from the wall where a mirror was revealed. And then she switched on all the lights in the room although it was daylight outside. Madam motioned Rosa closer to the mirror.

Cristal was lying in bed under a twisted mound of sheets. Clothing was strewn on the floor. Two glasses, one half full, stood on her bedside table. An empty champagne bottle rested on its side under the bed. The vase of flowers which Rosa had arranged lay upturned. Flowers were scattered everywhere — some caught fast in Cristal's fly-away hair, which looked more rumpled than her bed.

She began to stir. Sat up, stretched, yawned, rubbed the sleep from her eyes, and pulled at the flowers caught in her hair.

'She can't see or hear you,' Madam said. 'From tonight, come into this room. Sit in this chair. Watch everything.'

Each night for a week, Rosa sat horrified and then mesmerized by the goings-on in that bed. Never had the differences in humans become so apparent. Yet, by the end of it all, they were all the same. And for sure, neither nuns nor God would be pleased.

The following week, Madam took Rosa to the walk-in linen wardrobe. She'd been into it many times but never noticed the square of mirror. It became obvious once the wardrobe light was switched on. Here she had an exact view of Ámbar's room. The same procedure followed.

The one-way mirror to Nácar's room was located in the passage, which meant every time Rosa heard a door about to open, she slipped into her own bedroom so as not to be seen. And when she entered, she had to fight off the overwhelming desire to lie down upon her bed and sleep, carried far away on the inside of a white cloud. But she could not. For surely Madam would see.

Sleep would have been a blissful alternative to watching the repeated frantic grapplings played out before her. It was a wonder, she thought, the girls were not completely bored with the same old merry-go-round repeated several times each night.

After hearing Nácar's door open and close for the fourth time that evening, she slipped back out into the passage and stood in front of the mirror set between two matching wall sconces. Her eyelids drooped. She was tired but more important, numbed.

Without realizing it, a barrier had grown separating and inuring her to the events she had witnessed. She alternately shifted her weight from one foot to the other, rested her forehead against the mirror, shut her eyes and slept standing up.

From her vantage point, Madam watched with satisfaction. This part of RosaMina's desensitizing education was complete.

RosaMina now rose in time with the girls and ate breakfast at lunch-time. There was no longer misunderstanding on Rosa's part. She knew what she too would be doing. Only, she had to wait until Madam deemed the day. She had long given up wondering what the nuns or God might think.

On the surface, Rosa remained a nonentity in the other girls' eyes. She was not included in their chatter. But she came to understand there was to be an auction. An auction meant a big boost to The House's coffers.

The girls discussed their anticipated share of the financial benefit. Acceptance of their share meant Madam secured their collusion in the event.

Rosa realized it was she who was to be auctioned. Unlike the girls, she would not receive a share of the auction's income but a prize of another sort. She'd be available exclusively to her buyer for a whole year.

Rosa listened to the girls relate their experiences of how much easier it was with one man for a year. An array of bosoms rose and fell as they all sighed wistfully at the telling. And what a rude shock it was thereafter, when the season opened and they became fair game to all. Those bosoms rose and fell once more as they all sighed exhaustedly at their collective memories. For better or worse, open seasons were all memorable.

As Ámbar recalled, her purchaser's friends were all eager to see what different delights her café au lait skin offered compared to their fair-skinned wives. Generously, her purchaser gifted each friend a turn with her before the exclusive year ended. This equated to an alarming loss of future earnings. For when her open season started, there was not a long line of men waiting their turn for which they would pay. They would already have had theirs. And for free. A collective sigh of sympathy rose up at this telling.

While open season was always discussed, their first time was never spoken about. And it was this Rosa desperately wanted to know.

She had become intimately familiar with The House's clients through the one-way mirrors. For new clients, variety was fun. But most men quickly settled on a girl that suited their predilections. This suited the girls, too. They knew what to expect. They got the job done within the allotted time, efficiently but satisfactorily enough, to keep the client coming back for more.

The tall, erect, and well-dressed Dr José Salazar, with his shorter, round, but equally well-dressed friend, Dr Jerardo Rivas, were late Wednesday night regulars. Dr Rivas, true to gluttonous form, tried all the girls. He'd settled on one for a while, then go back to the others. Dr Salazar stuck to Cristal but found it increasingly difficult to satisfy his particular fantasy. To complicate matters, Dr Rivas sometimes arrived alone.

'Cristal,' he would say to Madam. 'I want Cristal. But no telling Dr Salazar.' He wagged a monitory finger in the air. 'It will be our little secret. Now promise me. All of you. You, too, Berta.'

'We promise.'

But Dr Salazar suspected and alluded to this on more than one occasion. Discretion being the law of The House, Cristal denied it. But Madam knew it was Dr Rivas whose aptitude for insidious conniving fed hints of this information to his friend, Dr Salazar. It had to do with the competitive spirit that simmered under their façade of camaraderie. Everything with them was a game of one-upmanship. And Madam suspected Dr Rivas held the lead with Dr Salazar trailing way behind.

Madam knew everything and planned for everything far in advance. She instructed Cristal to 'fail' with Dr Salazar.

Cristal had to pretend to be an innocent — quiet and passive. This was the illusion he required for his manhood to function. All would go well until, lost in the moment, or so she would claim, she'd cry out his name too early. And more than once, adding to his misery, (as instructed by Madam), she cried out the name of another. Either way, the illusion evaporated. The man's nerves were so ragged by the end of each session, Rosa began to feel sorry for him.

———— ◆ ————

One late Wednesday evening, sensing it the right moment to strike, Madam made her move.

'Dr Salazar, please come with me.'

He immediately wondered which of the girls was in need of his Chiropractic attention. Madam led him into her private rooms. None of the girls were to be seen.

Dr Salazar puffed his chest. He had been singled out. To his knowledge no client had ever seen the inside of Madam's private quarters. For a moment he wondered if she intended to offer herself to him. When he saw there was no bed he gave thanks. Madam was definitely not his sort.

She motioned that he be seated in one of the two wingback chairs placed intimately close together in front of a comforting fire.

'You are my most valuable client,' Madam started off saying. 'We've been together for a number of years.' She handed him a glass of bone-dry, clear Almacenista Manzanilla Pasada. A sherry that took seven years to mature, was difficult to obtain, and beyond the reach of most pockets. Though Dr Salazar rarely drank, it was his favourite.

Dr Salazar first eyed then sniffed the sherry. His nose tingled. Taste buds alerted, his mouth filled with saliva. Shutting his eyes, he took a goodly sip. Using his tongue, he ran the liquid around his mouth making sure it got to every part, under his tongue, and every nook and cranny between his teeth. Controlling his throat, he swallowed the mouthful. Warmth glowed in his belly.

He opened his eyes. 'Excellent,' he said twirling the glass.

Madam made a mental note to send six bottles over to his studio the next day. It would be expensive, but if things went how she'd planned, it would be a small investment for a much bigger return. She sat down in the opposite wingback chair.

'Dr Salazar, you know you can count on me, don't you?'

Dr Salazar nodded. 'Your discretion has been unimpeachable.'

'And I am known to be fair. Am I not?'

'Yes.'

It was true, Dr Salazar thought, no one knew how better to manage her girls more fairly than Madam. The House was much desired from afar — not only by clients, but by women, too. For Madam let her girls leave when they had learned all they needed and helped them set up in other towns. The most recent being the copper-haired girl. His brow furrowed. But the girl's name did not come to him. Nevertheless, she was an example of what a generous and goodhearted woman Madam was. Even though from her cold physical appearance one might be led to believe otherwise.

'Dr Salazar, I'm sharing this with you this in strict confidence.'

Almost a question mark formed between Dr Salazar's shaggy eyebrows. 'Madam, I am at your service. If there is anything I can do . . . .'

Oh, yes. You shall be at my service, thought Madam, though her face showed nothing of it as she gazed steadily into Dr Salazar's eyes. She leaned in towards Dr Salazar. Not being able to help himself he too leaned towards her.

Madam spoke quietly. He strained to hear her.

'I have, under this very roof, a virgin.'

'A what?' he whispered back.

'A virgin.'

No sooner had his brain made the connection, desperate desire like a starving trout rose in Dr Salazar. But as skittery as an old trout can be, Dr Salazar had to be further enticed.

He took a deep drink from his glass and swallowed. This time without the bother of tasting it.

'I see.'

'But there is a problem, Dr Salazar.'

Madam knew one of the differences between men and women was women discussed problems. Men solved them.

Dr Salazar's shaggy eyebrows rose.

'I want you to have her.'

'You are very kind,' said Dr Salazar. He chucked back the rest of the sherry.

'She comes at a very high price.'

'How high?'

Madam wrote a sum on a piece of paper. She folded it and slipped it across the small side table towards him. Dr Salazar received, opened, and read it. His face was inscrutable. Only a pulse that throbbed at the side of his neck just above his sharp collar showed his internal reaction.

'The problem?'

Madam appealed to that ridiculous or infantile — she could not decide which — competitive spirit that pervaded his relationship with Dr Rivas.

'Dr Rivas has already put in his bid.'

He bit down onto the hook. 'His price?'

'Half again.'

'Will half again secure my bid?'

'Yes. Cash up front.'

———— ◆ ————

There was no surprise when, after slicing open hopeful bidders' envelopes, Rosa became Dr Salazar's purchase.

To her relief, he did not exercise his right that night. Nor did he for the whole of the following month. He had gone to a convention in a foreign country with his wife.

But on her bedside table lay a box in which nestled a jewelled pin in the form of a hummingbird crusted in bright orange sapphires surrounded by white diamonds and a darker orange sapphire at its throat.

And when the event occurred, it was wonderful and terrible.

Wonderful — the dreadful anticipation had come to the end. Terrible — she was forced to deny her body's urges and become a lifeless doll. Passive. Silent. Until instructed to call out his name.

One year later, they parted. Dr Salazar, in bitterness. Rosa, in sweetness. For despite the ridiculous habit of keeping his socks on while naked, Rosa found him gentle and kind, even if he was also a little foolish. She was obliged to let him believe she thought of him as her lover. In reality, he came close to the father she never had. And this sentiment she valued far more than his being her first lover.

Open season was declared. Rosa's second client was none other than Dr Rivas. Like before, he wagged his finger in the air and made Madam and now her, swear they would not tell Dr Salazar. Cristal said this was something all men did — like dogs' scent marking their territory. Only some men were more covert than others.

If cannibalism were legal, she would have been devoured. Rosa struggled to hide her disgust. Madam kept a close watch through the one-way mirror into Rosa's room. She remonstrated and ordered Rosa to hide her squeamishness. It served Rosa well. She soon learnt the more resistance shown for an act, the more it would be tried. The more she was in control of a distasteful act, the easier it would be for her.

A succession filed through the door. After a busy evening, she felt her movement blocked. Berta called Madam. Seeing the pain she was in and listening to her symptom description, Madam sent for Dr Salazar.

In the year they had together, Rosa thought him a general practitioner. But he was not. He was a chiropractor. He performed a series of movements on her bones that made them click and pop. Minutes later she stood up and walked. The restriction was gone and the relief was immediate. Her fondness of him increased ten fold.

'And,' he continued, ignoring Madam's unfathomable look, 'Rosa is to take a week's rest. Go for brisk walks twice a day,' he said, 'and return to my studio on Saturday.'

She chose to walk early morning while everyone in The House still slept, and shopkeepers and townspeople were beginning to go about their business. She also walked after lunch when the town shut down and everyone took an afternoon siesta. It was the first time she experienced the freedom of being alone. And for this she would have traded one of the jewelled trinkets in her drawer.

As instructed, she went to his studio. Rosa discovered herself to be used as a model for his students. She saw a mass of faces trying hard to look detached and professional gazing down at her while listening to Dr Salazar's theorizing. What they could not pop and click, he did. She returned the next Saturday.

This time among the mass, she saw a new young man closest to her age. Although he was shorter, he was, she assumed by their mutual affection and close bond, Dr Salazar's son. And Alex Salazar was the most handsome boy-man that ever was.

Her heart underwent a change. From shadow, it moved into light, split open, and turned inside out.

On a practical level, Rosa saw she and Alex Salazar held the others' missing pieces. Like two matching halves, they slotted together. They formed a perfect whole. And it was in this way Rosa fell in love. The kind, if fortunate, happens at least once. If lucky, is reciprocated. And if blessed, lasts.

At the end of the adjustment session, she got dressed and left as fast as possible. Her world stopped. She clung for life to the pendulum of hope and anguish. It swung from one side; hope, she would see him again, and then to the other side; anguish, because even if she did get to see him again, to what point?

Still relieved from her duties, she walked twice a day. She prayed hard to the mother who never left her son's side, she would see Alex again. And so she did. Before he saw her.

Her heart thrummed in coded signals as they walked towards each other. At the last moment, she tilted up her head searching his eyes for a matching response. She was not disappointed.

As they passed, Rosa twitched her skirts, catching the cuff of his trouser leg. Electrical charges shot to parts of her body, which had yet to be thrilled. Every fibre in her being, exhilarated to the point of exploding, urged him to follow her. She slowed her pace. Reaching The House, she entered by the front door. She did not have to look back. Humming currents broadcast he was close behind.

The following Wednesday, she heard the first hesitant knock on her door. He had come. She took a moment to breathe whipped off her chemise and arranged herself upon the pillows of her bed. After the second knock, the door opened. He entered.

Clock hands whirred backwards. Her past erased. They were equal innocents together.

Madam was not present, having gone out on an errand. This gave Rosa the immeasurable gift of privacy. No one would be watching through the one-way mirror.

Her body's natural responses sprang free joining her true voice in perfect rhythm and harmony. This memory she protected. Stored perfectly intact in her heart.

—— ✦ ——

Open season still being underway, Rosa continued to get her fair share of clients. But she lived for early Wednesday evenings when Alex paid her a call. That his father called upon her much later did not worry her at all.

Rosa and Alex had the natural inquisitiveness of new lovers. Old or young, it is always the same. Only time was restricted. Her business had to be concluded meeting Madam's strict criteria.

During their ardent couplings, or simply lying together spent afterwards, she'd whisper in his ear the diminutive of his real name Alejandro, being Álejo. Although which, when further Anglo-Saxonized, turned into Alex. She was tempted, but she never told Alex her real first name. That was against house rules. But he arrived at his own love name for her. *Pequeña Morena* meaning Little Brunette. She was never sure if it was in direct reference to her head of fudge-coloured curly hair or matching colour pubic hair. Both of which he took great pleasure in running his fingers through or stroking.

Her hope was that their paths would not cross, but continue travelling on the same trajectory. Only she had no idea how. Once again, she appealed to the mother who never left her son's side for help. That prayer was answered in an unexpected way.

For years, apart, and unknown to either of them, Rosa and Alex breathed in the mixed particles of their combined breath transported by their travelling family members and loved ones.

On the day she told him her surname, he pulled back from her, their slick bodies sucking apart.

'Expósito! You're an abandoned illegitimate.'

She was shocked seeing distaste pulling down the corners of his mouth. 'No. I'm an orphan.'

'Who was your mother?'

The knife, resting in the shadow of her heart rose up.

She took a while to reply. 'I don't know.'

'Who is your father?'

The knife tip dipped, poised to strike.

'I don't know.'

'Do you know anything at all about your history?'

'No.'

The knife plunged dead centre into her heart.

'So both parents relinquished all interest and claim over you.'

The knife sliced back up poised to strike again.

'Neither of them wanted you then. Nor did they ever intend resuming their claim of you in the future.'

The knife plunged down.

'So, therefore according to the law, you are abandoned.'

Back up came the knife.

'And if you don't know who either of your parents are, then you are illegitimate.'

This time the knife ran down to its handle. And stuck.

'But being orphaned is another whole thing,' he continued as if he were lecturing a group of students not much different to how his father lectured his group of Chiropractic students. He'd risen from the bed and began to pull on his clothes. 'And by far better and easily forgivable.' He buttoned his shirt. 'Orphaned,' he said, 'means you have history.' He shrugged on his jacket. 'You would know who your parents are.' He tied his shoes laces. 'But, you. You, are an abandoned illegitimate.'

The knife handle twisted.

He left the room.

She shut her eyes against the acute pain drowning her rose heart.

The barrage of slick words put her in her place. She had nothing. She was nothing. She was worthless.

Roused by Berta's urgent knock on the door she pulled herself together. She faced her next client.

For the rest of the week, her brain turned into a roulette wheel. Alex's words rolled around her head like the ball spinning in the opposite direction to the turning wheel. Bumping and jumping from one landing pocket to another, but it never came to rest. Exhausted, she rationalized away her pain. She made excuses for Alex. She concluded his belief towards illegitimate and abandoned children was one pressed upon him by others. While he was right in that many children came from unsanctified unions, there was worse.

The country's general and dictator Francisco Franco's strategy was to *limpieza*, meaning cleanse anyone who supported the Republican political party — to eradicate left wing thinking throughout Spain. Hundreds of people were executed daily from 1936 to 1939. And the executions continued for many more years.

In an attempt to protect their offspring, parents who had the means shipped their children out of the country by train. If not, they abandoned their children in the middle of staunch Nationalist dominated areas in hope of luring away suspicion. The region in which the orphanage she came from was just such an area.

Children were instructed to claim themselves as abandoned illegitimates. It was safer than admitting their parents had been killed for their political views. But even denying ones' known parentage did not always guarantee survival.

For soldiers would burst through the convent doors. A hastily scratched up list was presented. All names were the same. Only ages according to each soldier's preference varied. Against the nuns' futile attempts, girls were hauled out into the night. With dawn came gunshots — one for each Maria Expósito taken.

Rosa wanted to believe she may be one of those brave children, who to secure their survival, denied their parentage. But it rang false. She simply had no parents to deny. Alex was right. As her surname made clear, she had been exposed. She had nothing. She was nothing. She was worthless.

It was her first salutary lesson in understanding bitter and unfair double standard principles that prevail in life.

From one Wednesday to the next Alex did not appear. Thrown into torment, she realized there was no one to ask. Certainly not Dr Salazar, nor Madam even though she knew everything.

As Rosa's physical disposition was well recovered there was no longer an excuse for her to take a walk. Nonetheless she dressed for outdoors. She selected the first jewelled gift she'd received from Dr Salazar as the sole decoration to her plain dress. She stepped out into the street.

With no destination in mind she set off. She gazed into the window of a woman's clothing shop. Looking at leather gloves on display she realized she had left The House not wearing any. She entered intent on purchasing a pair.

An elegant woman was just leaving. They stopped a pace apart. Each waited for the other to negotiate a pass.

The woman had wondrous blue eyes framed by long black lashes. Above that, perfectly arched eyebrows. She wore a hint of red on her lips, Her skin was flawless and pale. Her thick glossy hair was styled in looping waves on either side of her face, caught at the nape of her neck and rolled into a low bun secured by a hairnet. This style revealed her married status — plaits being worn by girls and unmarried women. She wore a fiery orange sapphire and diamond-encrusted hummingbird pin attached in the same place to her dress as was Rosa's.

There was no mistaking the women's surprised looks as they each glanced at the other's hummingbird. In mirror image, they touched their own ensuring theirs remained secure.

A shadow crossed the face of the woman. She made the first move to step aside and passed Rosa.

It took Rosa mere seconds to conclude the woman was the wife of the man who'd had exclusive use of her for a year. And, mother to the boy-man with whom Rosa had fallen in love.

She left the store without new gloves and returned to The House. Opening her bedside drawer, she pulled out the box of trinkets Dr Salazar had showered upon her. One for each of the twelve months she had been his exclusive purchase.

With painstaking care Dr Salazar had made sure she understood his sentiments attached to the gifts — their uniqueness and monetary value. And each one he told her, represented a treasured memory from his youth.

She liked them all. But her favourites were the hummingbird, an owl, a cactus, a dog in a basket with a litter of pups and, a delicate human skeleton whose dangling limbs danced. She was quite sure that Alejandra Herrera had a similar collection of jewelled trinkets. One for each month of the year that Dr Salazar did not take up his rightful conjugal position with her.

Relieved she had been a diligent pupil, she scoured Madam's record books. They were hidden in a secret compartment and listed the names of the buyers and their purchases. Her hunch proved correct. Dr Salazar had ordered two of everything, one for his wife and one for her.

———— ◆ ————

As was already written in *The Logbook of Futures Foretold*, Alex's friend Diego arrived unannounced. No different than his father, he paid for the pleasure of Rosa's company with the strict proviso it be kept secret from

Alex. The pendulum swung from anguish to hope. She would ask Diego of Alex's whereabouts.

Being an enthusiastic *bon vivant* like his father, Diego had already run to adult fat. Knowing not to resist anything she found distasteful, she adopted the punishment and reward method. She controlled Diego's discovery around her body. He left well satisfied.

'Rosa, Diego Rivas has become his father's contender,' said Madam consulting her notebook. 'Soon he will overtake his father's time spent with you.'

Rosa held the pendulum back from swinging towards anguish which would reveal her stress. Not even the tiny vertical crease appeared between her eyebrows.

Madam's eyes glinted. It was the closest she ever came to congratulating any of the girls.

To Madam's further approval, Diego returned daily. Rosa wanted to ask him about Alex. But did not. Instead, it was he who was full of questions.

'Rosa, tell me. Do I give you pleasure?'

'Of course,' came her mechanical response.

'Does everyone give you pleasure?'

'Of course not.'

'Who gives you pleasure?'

'That's not fair. I wouldn't ask you that.'

'I'm telling you to ask. Go on. Ask me — out of all the girls, who gives me the most pleasure.'

'Out of all the girls who gives you the most pleasure?'

'You do.'

Rosa's heart dropped. She knew exactly what was coming next.

'It's my turn now. I get to ask. And you have to answer truthfully. Say, "cross my heart and hope to die".'

She nodded.

'Say it.'

'Cross my heart and hope to die.'

'Who gives you the most pleasure?'

'I'll tell you next time.'

'*Puta-zorra*, vixen-whore,' he yelled as she pushed him out of the door.

A bell rang in the back of her head. Like his father's jealousy of Dr Salazar, so too was Diego jealous of Alex. If she were ever to receive information regarding Alex, she realized then it would not come from Diego.

She returned to the roulette wheel. Had something happened to him? Unlikely. For news would spread if he'd met with an accident.

She knew Alex and Diego were soon to write their final school exams. It was a difficult time for both of them. But how, she asked herself a thousand times, was Diego able to call upon her almost every day and not Alex? Did it really boil down to a surname?

With the knife twisting away she accepted that he could not bear to be with her. She had been abandoned. Again, her heart transitioned. It turned outside in back to its original position. It began to close. Light faded to dark.

And then, something else written in *The Logbook of Futures Foretold* came to pass. The extract of Blue Cohosh failed. She was pregnant.

The pendulum of hope and anguish swung wildly. Hope shimmered like bright sunrays dancing upon the surface of calm water. In her imagination, she gathered her child into her arms and walked protected from harm into a new and free life. Anguish raised visions of Rubí lying in the growing pool of blood. She knew as certain as night follows day, her child's life would be halted.

A primeval feeling of protection, that only mothers know, coursed through her being. She made her first clear decision. She would keep the child and raise it herself. With care, she traced through her appointment book trying to determine who the most likely father could be. She laid her plans carefully.

Alex still did not return on early Wednesday evenings. Diego continued to arrive at all impossible hours.

Each time, he pressed harder determined to get an answer to his question. Rosa prepared herself. She reached down in the depths of her heart where the perfect memory had been securely stored. To her memory, she whispered, 'Please forgive me.'

The next time, before Diego could ask the question, she looked him steadily in his eyes. She prayed her plan would not backfire.

'Diego, you are a fool.'

Diego's jaw dropped. 'What the hell. No one calls me a fool.'

'Well, I am. If you can't understand that it is I who has stopped Madam from sending others to me because of how I feel about you, then you are a fool. And stupid to boot.'

Diego's mouth fell open.

While he was still recovering from the insult, she appealed to his appetite for the uncommon and took him on a journey to places he'd not yet dreamed of.

After, thrilled and exhausted, Diego gathered Rosa close to him.

'I'm going to miss you. A lot.'

'Going somewhere?'

'I'm leaving for London after I've completed my exam.'

'When's that?'

'Two weeks' time.'

'Pity.'

'Why?'

'We were just getting started.' She knew she had his attention. She snuggled into him. 'I'm going to miss you awfully too. How far away is London?'

The baited hook dangled. He remained silent.

'If you like, I can go to London, too. We'd be free,' she murmured. 'Free to be together, exclusively, anytime you choose.'

Temptation rose. He pondered the offering, but maintained his silence.

The following few days were crucial. As she anticipated, a new question Diego was desperate to have answered was asked.

'I vow on all that's holy,' she said, 'Alex comes nowhere near your prowess.'

Diego's mouth split into a wide grin. He was spurred to greater excesses. All of which she choreographed with enthusiasm dredged from the darkest parts of her core. Artfully, she ran through the gamut of her repertoire. Something he had begged her to contrive she kept until last: the whip's leather handle, well anointed with gel, inserted into his anus.

As he was rewarded, so was she ten days later. With a well-aimed fling of Diego's trousers, she covered the one-way mirror until they were done and an envelope safely stowed under her mattress. In the envelope, was her first passport, travel documents, and cash. If Madam had noticed the obscured view, she said nothing. The day of Rosa's departure was determined upon an opportunity to riffle through Madam's papers. For hidden among those papers, was something of hers. Something she wanted.

A small bit of string that was attached to a piece of card. Her name, RosaMina, was written in a steady and well-curved hand. On the reverse was the date of her birth. The writing on the card matched that of Madam's. But not one fibre of her being, responded to this evidence of Madam being her mother. Rosa's heart softened and warmed, her skin jumped and tingled a thousand fold more when she amused herself with the cat and her kittens in a basket on the kitchen floor.

Without a backward glance, Rosa walked out of Madam's house. In the clothes she stood up in, string and card, jewelled trinkets, money, travel documents, and Diego's address tucked into her small bag looking to all the world as though as she was going out for a walk.

6

When RosaMina did not return from her walk, Madam did not go in search of her. She knew RosaMina had run away.

The unexpected always split Madam's psyche in two: Reason and Mercy. Reason being as natural as breathing. Mercy, by contrast, being as unnatural as is taking a breath under water. She avoided the emotional roll-ercoaster of Mercy at any cost. For the ride forced open the bars to her heart. Freed, her heart hurtled out of control. Thus Mercy terrified her. With the upheaval of RosaMina's running away, Reason took precedence.

She had been in RosaMina's shoes years ago. But not having the freedom of choice money brings, she could not run away. She was forced to remain and do the best she could. To give her strength, she turned the betrayals and deceits she'd suffered into pillared reminders why she would, above all, become self-reliant. She utilized the skill nature had given her. Talents inherent in every woman developed more or less as survival required. To her credit, unlike those who had abused her she made a decision to be fair in her dealings with everyone.

Alone in the privacy of her rooms, Madam raised her hands over her head and twirled. RosaMina was keeping her child. After all, it was what she too had decided when pregnant with RosaMina. She was going to be a grandmother.

She stopped twirling. What was the point of being a grandmother if her grandchild would be nowhere to be seen, she thought to herself. Then she realized, RosaMina's running away stung her in more ways than she cared to admit. For once, she was grateful she had no one to tell her, 'serves you right'.

She poured herself a glass of sherry and sat in one of the two floral, upholstered wingback chairs that faced each other. The chair's wings were meant to trap heat from a roaring fire around the sitter, while blocking cold drafts. Though there was no draft — Madam made sure of that, her bones would not stand it — there was a crackling fire burning in the grate. Rarely did she permit herself to think of her past. But now, her thoughts turned to events leading up to the most joyful period of her life.

--- ♦ ---

Abandoned at birth, Madam was brought up in a convent orphanage run by the Capuchin nuns. By age fourteen, all girl orphans, ready or not, were sent out to work and fend for themselves. A man who frequented the orphanage selected Madam as his next employee. She soon found herself accompanying the travelling salesman both in and out of bed. Within months she was pregnant.

'Aw, that's wonderful,' he had said while she threw up into a basin. He retrieved his wallet from the inside pocket of his overcoat and pulled out a single large bank note. 'Here go at once and purchase some baby clothes. Pay the innkeeper. Pack up. I'll be back at noon. We're leaving for the next town.'

He kissed her on her clammy forehead and left.

Madam arranged their matching cases and set them at the door. She struggled into her clothes, rinsed her mouth picked up the note and made her way down to the innkeeper's desk.

'I don't have change,' he told Madam as she proffered the large note. 'The bank at the end of the street will exchange it for smaller notes.'

Madam entered the bank and approached the counter. It had a shiny brass grill separating the public from staff.

'Can you change this into smaller notes please?'

The clerk looked up from his ledger his ear alerted to the sound of the young voice. He saw a pale-faced young girl with such large dark eyes that not only could he see himself in their reflection but felt he was drowning in them. He tore his eyes away from looking into hers and focused instead on her mouth. Raw flesh was visible between the splits in her thin lips to which tiny flakes of dry skin were still attached. Her coat was too big for her.

Still unused to dressing her hair in a low bun caught at the nape of her neck, the mismatched hat sat awkwardly upon her head. She had no ring on her finger to confirm her married status as purported by the messy bun.

'A moment', he said. Seizing the opportunity of protecting the bank from a suspicious transaction such as this — thus ensuring his own promotion — the clerk alerted his superior.

Madam watched him walk over to and confer with an older man. The clerk spoke urgently. Both men turned and looked at Madam. At that moment, a cold draft from nowhere caught her in its path freezing her to the floor.

The salesman, having waited on the landing on the floor above, returned to their room. He packed up his samples, picked up both cases and left. He held a mental picture of Madam's height and weight. The next girl he'd pick up from a convent in another area would more or less fit the clothes of the last one.

Within the hour, Madam was taken into custody. Her court appearance happened that afternoon. Having no documents or fixed address she was given the maximum six months sentence for vagrancy and theft. By evening, she was locked in a single cell away from the rest of the prisoners. A prison officer showed her into the cell.

'Will I get my money back?' she asked.

There being no female prison officers in the town's jail, the male prison officer said, 'If you are friendly, you'll get it back.'

Without delay, he taught her a lesson in the art of being friendly. Several hours, later she realized how busy being friendly she was going to be. The prison had three shift changes in a twenty-four period. Four prison officers were in each shift.

Soon on, she took the initiative inviting the officers in one after the other at the beginning of each shift. After which, they left her alone. Without those few free hours where no one pawed or suffocated her, she believed she would have lost her mind.

When her expanding belly made full frontal coupling impossible, the reverse position was adopted. Her swollen breasts were clutched at, used as support grips. All the while, she held onto the hope that the bank note would be returned to her. It was a lesson in the futility of wishful thinking.

When her water broke, she was pushed through a side door out into the street. She tumbled to the dirt, a handful of coins spinning after her. She came to rest at the feet of a vegetable seller.

'God have mercy what's this?' said the vegetable seller almost trampling upon her. Filthy hands helped Madam to her feet. But, wracked by a pain threatening to split her belly apart, Madam collapsed to the ground.

'Get up,' urged the vegetable seller. Once again she pulled Madam to her feet. This time she had her vegetable barrow positioned.

'Ease back into the barrow.'

Dazzled by pain, Madam sank down. Her legs from her knees down flopped over the edge of the barrow. Her hands grasped its sides. The barrow was too short to support Madam's head. But the next contraction saw to it that Madam's neck muscles standing out like rigid ropes supported her head.

From her, Madam learnt her first lesson in Mercy. The vegetable seller had gathered the scattered coins and pressed them into Madam's palm. Then she trundled Madam into her tiny house.

Without a minute to spare, she gave birth on the floor among baskets and boxes filled with produce in varying forms of decay. The vegetable seller assisted the birthing. Her five-year-old daughter, Berta, brought cloths and bowls of water.

The baby emerged wrinkled and red. Within hours her little body turned creamy pastel pink. She had a dark fuzzy patch on the top of her head, a sweet nub of a nose and rosebud mouth. Her eyes remained closed behind two puffy slits. Her tiny hands were clasped into fists with dimples where one day her knuckles would be. Only when Madam gently unfolded each hand did she see perfectly formed fingers at the end of which were perfectly formed nails.

The rest of her resembled a plump ball with her elbows bent, knees flexed, and arms and legs held close to her body. Swaddled, she fit the crook of her mother's arm. Stimulated by the scent of milk, the baby nuzzled and sought out a nipple.

Madam cupped her palm around her baby's head. Palm and head fit perfectly. Together, they entered that blissful space only for nursing mothers and babies, and found nowhere else on earth.

Madam spent the next six weeks with her defenceless newborn, never leaving her once. While the baby slept and nursed, and slept and nursed, over and over again, Madam's body underwent it's own recovery. Not only from the birth, which was surprisingly quick and easy, but from the accumulation of years-old stress starting with her own conception, being not much different from her baby's.

And it was those six weeks that had been the best and most joyous time of her life.

Madam wished she could remain in that place forever — time never moving on. But it did, and as each week passed, the cache of coins diminished.

And then Madam learned another lesson — money was everything. For her vegetable seller saviour would allow her to stay only for as long as the coins lasted.

With her newborn in her arms, Madam returned to the Capuchin Convent. All night, she kept her child warm to her chest, huddled under a tree in the orchard. It was just on the other side of the wall of the enclosed court-yard where she had grown up.

Before dawn, she placed the six-week-old at the entrance of the con-vent. She tied a card by means of string around her neck. Written on the card was the name and birthdate of the child. Madam retreated behind a tree.

At the strike of the first of six bells, the convent door opened. A nun stepped out, picked up her child and withdrew into the convent. Madam's first task was done. She set off back to town ready to implement the next step in her return years later to claim her child.

Prison had been her period of schooling. Free copulation had the offi-cers assemble in haste as though called to arms. Single-minded, each satisfied nature's primeval call. No sooner was the act over, then all memory of it was forgotten. After a few calculations, she came to a simple decision. And with it, her name, Maria Expósito changed to Madam.

In the same plains town where she had been imprisoned, she lingered at the prison's side door. At the time of shift change, she serviced those who had used her for several months at will. It was an easy transaction. She knew each man's wants.

Her face held no interest for them. She was plain looking, blending well into the background. And it would have been a surprise had any of the prison officers recognized her. For when they had used her, they never looked at her face. More to the point, further into her pregnancy, she was obliged to face the floor or wall.

Grateful for being serviced between shift changes, officers going on duty arrived early and lined up. Officers going off duty, hastened to take their turn before going home. No matter how quirky the request, she always obliged for a previously agreed price. She never short-changed them. They left satisfied with promises of future delights buzzing in their heads.

Then she rented the vegetable seller's spare room. Madam's business transaction with the vegetable seller was no different to the model for her clients. She gave added value by paying the vegetable seller more than the going rate and in advance.

By turn, the vegetable seller introduced Madam to an extract of Blue Cohosh. A plant whose roots, when dried, grated into powder, and sprinkled over a bowl of cut fruit, brought about menses. Madam grew to be sure of many things. The first was she never wanted another child. The second was she vowed to spare her child her experiences.

Berta, the vegetable seller's chubby sweet daughter, made herself useful during the hours her mother was away at market. As she'd done once before, she brought Madam rags and bowls of water. Mercy ensured Madam took care Berta would not see what went on behind the closed door. She took time and taught Berta how to read and write.

All men were the same to her. As long as they had the money, she would provide her service. But she began tipping the scales in her favour. She increased her prices. She made herself available to fewer men. She changed accommodation and returned to the inn.

And just as it had been written in *The Logbook of Futures Foretold*, the room was the one she'd once occupied with the travelling salesman.

The keeper did not recognize her. He was pleased to earn a coin ensuring clients did not meet leaving or entering Madam's room. Every so often, when he'd saved up sufficient coins, the keeper would avail himself of her services, too.

Madam never turned business away. Nor did she provide her services for nothing. But the keeper received a discount. In more ways than he ever knew, he received payment tenfold for the accommodation not paid for by Madam two years earlier.

Over time, she built up an understanding of each client's likes. And how much money they were prepared to part with satisfying their desires. Matching these pieces of information was key to her success. Later, to the keeper's protestations, Madam left.

With the help of a client, Jacob the Jeweller, she rented her own space. It was a house with a large downstairs salon and kitchen. At the back of the salon was a concealed door opening into a small antechamber with two facing doors. One door led into a suite of private rooms, which became Madam's office. The other led into the back of the jewellry store.

Upstairs was a long corridor with several bedrooms and a bathroom. Jacob the Jeweller owned both the store and the house.

'Madam,' said Jacob the Jeweller one day, his sideburn ringlets bouncing around his face, 'I believe we can be better business partners.'

Inwardly, Madam heaved a sigh of relief. She'd planted the seeds of change several weeks before.

'How so?' she asked though she already knew.

'I have clients. You have clients. Let's share them.'

Jacob the Jeweller paused. He thought Madam needed some moments to absorb his idea. Then he continued. 'I'll inform mine of the fleshy delights to be had. For a discounted price, they can discreetly enter through the secret door.'

'And, I'll inform my clients that if they buy a piece of jewellry and mention my name, they'll be guaranteed a discount,' said Madam.

'And the differences we'll . . . '

'Split,' said Madam finishing his sentence for him.

Jacob the Jeweller was pleased his suggestion had been so easily understood and cemented their new agreement on a handshake.

Easing their guilt, old and new clients found themselves purchasing an abundance of jewelled trinkets. Overnight, Madam and Jacob the Jeweller's businesses grew. Everyone was pleased. But none more so than those wives whose suspicions, if they had any, diminished upon receipt of a jewelled gift.

Jacob the Jeweller had a predilection for pubescence. By now, Madam had several girls working the rooms upstairs. None of the girls fit his criteria.

Berta, the vegetable seller's daughter arrived in a bewildered state at the tradesmen's door carrying her belongings in a sheet with the four corners tied into a knot. She handed Madam a note. It said, 'Take care of her.'

The vegetable seller had already passed by the time Berta reached Madam. Before the rollercoaster, Mercy had a chance to break open the bars to her heart, Reason appeared. Madam took Berta in.

Still encased in puppy fat, Berta was just what Jacob the Jeweller wanted. He paid Madam well, boosting her coffers. To halt any objections, Madam's girls got a fair share of the fee. Realizing the same fantasy for others would become a profitable business.

Madam returned to the orphanage, the source of a never-ending supply of girls. She stood on the balcony selecting one she thought appropriate.

Then she'd search out her own child among the sea of lost and abandoned children. For as long as possible, she'd fix her eyes to her child, imprinting the vision to her memory. Too soon, Mother Superior would make a noise in her throat bringing Madam's time on the balcony to a close.

The selected child was taken to The House, and once menses had set in, was auctioned off.

Each time she returned to the orphanage, she donated a large sum with promises of more as long as her child was not adopted. Madam watched RosaMina closely. She despaired. Her child hardly grew. Madam was told she ate little. She was not surprised, given her memory of the awful food.

With one eye on her earnings building up, the other on clients and girls, Madam willed the time to pass. She wanted to claim her child and bring her home. She prayed that when the time came, her child would still be there. That is to say, her daughter would still be alive.

Madam maximized her earnings at every opportunity. She exploited her clients' weaknesses. She pit them against each other. Best temptations were reserved for last and awarded only to the highest bidder.

Some girls took to life in The House as though they had been born into it. Berta was not one of them. After her yearlong exclusivity with Jacob the Jeweller came to an end, she was drained of all energy. She mechanically performed her services during the open season. It was a great disappointment to all clients, and a great irritation to Madam. But still honouring the vegetable seller's request, Madam kept her.

With additional reading, writing, and arithmetic, Berta became far more suited and valuable keeping house. She became Madam's ears and eyes. Only when The House was overly extended, Berta helped the girls out.

The time came sooner than Madam had expected to collect her daughter.

---- ◆ ----

'I'm moving to London,' said Jacob the Jeweller. 'I've got a job designing with a jewellry manufacturer.'

It was already written in *The Logbook of Futures Foretold*, that Jacob the Jeweller would become sought after by royalty, the rich, and famous. In the future, books filled with glossy photographs of his iconic designs would grace coffee tables around the world.

'Congratulations,' said Madam. 'You'll still supply me with jewellry won't you?'

'Yes.'

'Sell me your house and the jewellry store.'

'Of course,' he said and shook Madam's hand so vigorously his side-burn ringlets danced madly.

Jacob the Jeweller sold Madam his house, shop, and all its stock for a price higher than the market value. He knew no one in town would allow Madam to become a property owner. Not because she was a whore, but because she was a woman. Sentiment played no part in Jacob the Jeweller and Madam's transaction. She agreed to pay his too high asking price. She used all her savings, but came up short.

'An announcement,' said Madam to the girls at their breakfast at lunchtime meal. 'From tonight, request a token of remembrance from each of your clients. Say that in this way you will never forget him and always hold him dear to you.'

The girls looked at each other in confusion.

'A token of remembrance?' said Cristal her hand straying to her untidy hair.

'This is what I mean.' Madam pulled open a velvet drawstring bag and turned it upside down. An array of jewelled pins rained down onto the table.

'May I?' asked Cristal, her hand now hovering over one of the pins.

'Yes.'

Each girl selected a pin. Soon the air was filled with intakes of breaths punctuated with soft sighs.

'Are they real?' asked Ámbar, her eyes widening as she turned a pin around, looking at it from all angles.

'Yes.'

Madam gave the girls time to thoroughly examine all the pins. 'Choose six. Tonight show a different one to each client. Ask him to purchase it for you. And then tell him if he buys two, one for you and one for his wife, he will get a discount.'

'We'll have the same pin?' asked Nácar her forehead crinkling.

'We don't mind if the wife has the same pin as ours do we?' asked Cristal looking at the other girls.

'Hell no,' they chorused.

Convinced, Nácar's forehead returned to smoothness.

The next day, each girl called out her clients' names and the jewelled pins of which they had ordered two.

A month later, the pins arrived. At the same time, Madam increased the girls' prices. Now only the wealthy could afford to frequent The House.

Money breeds excess. Excess results in jaded appetites. The cure — a return to the pure and innocent. To keep the aura of exclusivity, Madam kept auctions down to one every two years.

Between the doctors, two judges, (including the one who passed a six-month sentence on her more than a decade before), and several other wealthy men, the next auction would be the biggest. She was still in need of the final payment owing to Jacob the Jeweller making her sole owner of the house and store. Only then, fourteen-years later, at the age of thirty would she fulfill her promise to herself and become self-reliant. Then, she'd bring RosaMina home.

Rarely did Madam allow herself to indulge in fantasies. For fantasies are worthless unless made true. Nevertheless, in one of them RosaMina would take over the businesses from her. In another, she'd sell everything and move to the seaside. RosaMina would marry. Madam would become a grandmother. This particular fantasy gave her special delight. But *The Logbook of Futures Foretold* had other plans in mind.

She had missed holding the last auction. The girl she'd selected did not work out. Madam had let her go soon into the grooming stage. There was no point wasting her time or efforts. No auction had worked to her advantage. The men were howling like dogs to a full moon.

The girl she'd let go returned to the Capuchin Convent. She told the nuns the fate all girls faced when adopted by Madam. The nuns refused to allow Madam to adopt another. Hurts Madam thought long forgotten rose up threatening to choke her. She accused the nuns of false virtue. For they well knew her fate when allowing a man to employ her twelve years before. From the look on one of their faces, Madam knew she had struck a chord. But the rest stood resolute. Worse followed.

'God will not allow me to release your daughter to you,' said Mother Superior whose other eye tooth, had long since fallen out including a front tooth. A great wave of ice washed over Madam. She froze. By contrast her belly burst into a ball of red-hot fire. Her eyes glittered.

Mother Superior had had to face far more dangerous threats than Madam's eyes. She was not afraid. For this time, there were no soldiers' guns being brandished about.

'Give me my daughter.'

'No,' she said defiantly, perhaps trusting God's invisible shield protected her.

Madam turned into a snarling lioness. Claws unsheathed she sprang. She broke through the invisible shield and struck Mother Superior. She scratched her in the face with such force her last front tooth — which Mother Superior had been praying would last a little longer — flew out of her mouth and bounced across the well-polished floor. Mother Superior fell to the ground. Her wimple had wrapped itself askew around her head blinding her.

'My daughter. Now. Or I expose this house. Even if it means exposing myself.'

Unused to such violence a new nun — one who, judging by the bright gold wedding band on her finger, had recently married God — rushed for the door leading to the courtyard where the orphans spent their days milling around. Other nuns gathered around the Mother Superior.

Madam made her own way to the balcony. The rollercoaster Mercy started up. She witnessed her daughter being hauled out from the milieu of children. Seeing the look of hopelessness cross each abandoned child's face the bars to her heart opened.

She exited the balcony for the last time and went to meet her daughter. She passed the Mother Superior still on the floor, but sitting up, her legs shaped like a vee in front of her. Her wimple had been righted. Her cheeks bore the marks of Madam's raking nails. Her mouth was bloodied.

When denied her child, Madam thought to hold onto the bag of money she'd brought with her. It was heavier than usual. But the bars to her heart remained open.

'Get those children some decent food. And your teeth fixed,' she said calmly and tossed the bag to her. Despite her injuries and age, Mother Superior deftly caught it and slid it between the folds of her habit.

In the taxi on the way back to The House, her child slept in the heat of the midday sun. Madam had come to a decision. Because of the pressure of the expectation of a new auction, she would present RosaMina for the next one. There would be a further delay but she'd turn that to her advantage.

Madam touched her child for the last time. She placed her hand over RosaMina's while she slept.

———— ◆ ————

adam remained sitting in the wingback chair, watching the embers alternately glow and fade. She did not need the rollercoaster Mercy to break
open the bars to her heart. They opened unaided exposing all her life's sorrows
crying out piteously for acknowledgement and solace.

She grieved for herself and her child. For what had been. For what
could have been. For what was lost and for what they would never find. Madam
pushed her memories back into the past where they belonged. She closed the
bars to her heart. She made another vow. This vow she would keep.

RosaMina would know one day she had never been forgotten, nor
would she ever be forgotten. And what she could not do right by her daughter,
she would do right, by her grandchild.

Madam raised her glass in a toast towards the empty wingback
chair opposite her. She sipped the liquid and waited for the warmth to flood
her insides.

When Alejandra Herrera bumped into Rosa, whose name she later learned was RosaMina, the walls she'd erected separating her from her past collapsed. She fled home. Her head buzzed with responses to the chance encounter, giving her an instant thumping headache. Alejandra curled up on her bed. She pulled on her eye mask. In a moment, she was asleep. Demons long denied clamoured for attention. She slipped into the mashing jaws of the nightmare that was her past.

———— ◆ ————

It was 1925. Where the light-dappled alleyways of the Medina stop and Jemaa el-Fnaa, the wide open market square of Marrakesh, starts. Looking like bundles of bones covered in rags, Alejandra and her mother squatted on their haunches. They watched the arrival of an early morning caravan. The loaded camels bent their front legs, tipped forward, rolled backward and sank to the ground. Within the hour, a mesmerizing array of goods for sale sprang up.

Ten paces away, a market trader negotiated with a man whose belly stretched the intricate fabric of his *jalabiya* to popping point. Having reached a price, the trader's fast-moving hands slowed. He motioned towards mother and child.

'Go,' hissed her mother through broken teeth. She shoved Alejandra forward, tugging at the scarf covering her head.

The child's face screwed up tighter with each step. Earlier, when the sun took its first place in the sky, her leather sandals were exchanged for two glasses of hot tea. Now her bare feet were being razor sliced by sharp edged stones. With dough-soft hands, the fat man drew the scarf away from her forehead. He tipped back her head.

'Ai . . . ,' came the satisfied murmur of a woman's voice. 'She has the eyes as you say.'

Hands above Alejandra's head exchanged money. She looked for her mother. But she'd disappeared into the labyrinth of the Medina's alleys.

'I am your mother now.'

She fainted. Either from fright or hunger she did not know which.

She woke lying against the belly of the fat man from whose throat came the voice of a woman. The smell of mint funnelled through her nostrils, setting her stomach to growl. Sensing the child had woken, Abd-al-Aziz, servant of the most powerful, raised a small glass of tea to her lips. Followed by a chewy almond macaroon. Before long, with the horizon dipping and tilting in rhythm to the camel's plod, the five-year-old fell back to sleep.

During the following scorching days and freezing nights, she never left Abd-al-Aziz's side. Not because of the enforced proximity of riding the same camel for hours, or sleeping tucked in Abd-al-Aziz's cloak, but for all the reasons a newborn monkey clings to its mother — to survive and for comfort.

Four days later, the caravan approached a desert compound in Ouarzazate, one-hundred and twenty-six kilometres southeast of Marrakesh. Welcoming ululations drew them into the safety of the mud-brick compound. As the last camel entered, heavy doors shut, closing out the rest of the world.

The compound was built around precious desert water seeping through cracks in an outcrop of rocks. Channelled and then heated, it provided the steam required for a *hammam*.

Her eyes wide, Alejandra clung to Abd-al-Aziz — a mountain of fleshy handholds — until pinching, slapping strangers prized her from him, one finger at a time. Multi-skinned eunuchs blocked her attempts to squirm from their grasps. She was stripped, scrubbed and steamed, and scrubbed and steamed again. Her emaciated body slumped. She gave up the fight before the last bucket of water was poured over her.

A few feet away, a group of twelve boys aged between five and seven years of age underwent the same process. But so intent on surviving her own ordeal, she had no eyes or ears for their fear-filled screams as each boy in turn, underwent lightening quick castration.

Pinned down on their backs, legs spread, Abd-al-Aziz gathered and held each boy's scrotum between his curved index finger and thumb. He pulled down hard with a deft twist of his wrist. In less time than a sharp intake of breath, the sliced off penis and scrotum came away intact. A quill was inserted deep into each boy's urinary canal to prevent it from healing closed. Hot sesame seed oil was poured over the wound, searing it, creating a seal and staunching the blood flow. Standing upright, the boys were buried up to their necks in the desert sand. There they remained for three days and nights.

The weight of the Sahara sand kept the boys immobile, preventing them from frantically tearing out their quill as their bodies raged hotter than the desert. By the end of the first night their screams of pain, interspersed with calls to their mothers, diminished into whimpers.

'*Hooyo*,' cried one in Somali.

'*Maman*,' cried others in French.

'*Iya*,' cried the youngest boy in Yoruba.

By the end of the second night, barely audible breaths escaped them. By morning after the third, all were silent. Those who were alive were dug up. The dead had several buckets of sand dumped over their heads.

When the caring winds blew, head mounds were swallowed by the changing desert dunes. When the heartless wind blew, it uncovered the centuries-old desert graveyard of skeletons standing upright.

Of the twelve boys, five were dug up. By two moons past, three miraculously survived.

Around a campfire, a feast held in celebration of their lives continued. Each boy was presented with a gift — his sundried and shriveled genitalia wrapped in a piece of cloth. For as long as they lived, it would become their dearest treasure.

The dead boys' treasures were ceremoniously buried around the roots of an orange tree. An inordinately large and prolific fruiting tree due, no doubt, to being fed by the desert waters and the nutrient-rich compost of rotting genitalia.

While the boys were being castrated, Alejandra's hair was shorn and her skull shaved. Sores and patches of discoloured skin were exposed for the first time. Her head scabs fell off long before the boys' scabs did. She was relieved when the sharp prickles of new hair growth emerged. But not as much as the boys, when they began to urinate freely and the last of the infected heat left their bodies. They and Alejandra would consider these events as their rebirth.

Several years on, deep purple-black hair, much the colour of the Damson plum, cascaded below her waist. It was cared for and well-anointed with extracts of essential oils by Abd-al-Aziz.

'We'll make a princess out of you yet,' he said, his dough-soft hands brushing her tresses for the second time in a day. 'And it won't be because of your hair. But your eyes.'

In Muslim culture, the third eye symbolically wards off evil. It protects against bad luck and is depicted in blue. Thus anyone with blue eyes is revered and sought after as the ultimate good luck talisman. The eunuchs spent hours trying to decide the precise colour of her eyes, which, dependent upon light, and her mood swings, would change.

'Cobalt.'
'Sapphire.'
'No, cornflower.'
'Lapis lazuli.'
The colour of cyan,' another would say.

As she had arrived, Alejandra left her desert home by camel eight years later. When the last beast made its way under the archway, the iron-studded wooden door thudded closed. The crash set the mud-brick walls trembling and lizards from their crevices scattering. Eunuchs' good luck ululations rose up and over the walls sending her back across the sea of golden sand.

Abd-al-Aziz presented her to court. Not to the Sultan's court but his sister's who was in need of all the good luck charms and talismans with which she could surround herself.

The walls and floors of the royal princess Marrakesh's *riad* were covered with dazzling hand-painted tiles. Large rooms opened onto cool, airy courtyards with tinkling fountains. Cages, dotted everywhere, were filled with exotic animals and birds.

It took only a moment for the royal princess to verify Alejandra's unique eye colour. In order for her never to be traded again, Alejandra was adopted as the princess's ward.

After signing several weighty scrolls and an exchange of gold, the transaction was complete. Just as Abd-al-Aziz had planned, she was now a princess.

'Aziz,' she whispered using the diminutive of his name. She held herself up with grace just like the desert eunuchs had taught her. 'Please don't forget me.'

'Forget you? Never!' he said, his sagging cheeks and double chin rolls wobbling. 'But watch your feisty temper. Make me proud. Be a good princess. Remember all I have taught you.'

Alejandra's indulgent idyll lasted three years. The royal princess's new secret lover was an English diplomat years younger than she. He had watched Alejandra from the moment of his arrival. The time came when he could no longer contain himself. During the minutes guards exchanged sentry posts, he left the bed of the sleeping royal princess and padded into Alejandra's adjoining room.

She woke with the weight of his body covering hers. One hand clamped her mouth shut. As the sun climbed into the morning sky, caged birds opened their throats and trilled their dawn chorus.

When the princess discovered her young lover's early morning visit to Alejandra's bed, the need for protection rose above petty jealous sentiments. And beyond that, superstition held sway.

The colour of Alejandra's eyes saved her. Not even under the threat of death would anyone harm her. Notwithstanding, punishment of those eunuch-guards was immediate. Their beheadings were carried out within the walls of the *riad* dangerously close to the lions' cages. Alejandra's punishment was also immediate: banishment.

Within hours, she was accompanied by a group of the princess's older eunuch-guards to the middle of the Spanish plains. Alejandra cried throughout the first day of the journey. Her wails for Abd-al-Aziz were in vain. Unknown to her, Abd-al-Aziz had died.

Within the walls of the desert compound and in the manner of all Muslims, he had been buried in a hole dug much larger than normal to fit his body. He lay on his right side, perpendicular to Mecca, with a clod of earth supporting his head.

But at his request, his grave was located close to the orange tree under which countless treasures had been buried. Thus, his favourite fragrance accompanied him into the afterlife. Buried treasures, long disintegrated between the roots of the tree, served to remind God that after death, Abd-al-Aziz's genitalia were to be fully and gloriously restored.

As he had promised, Alejandra was not forgotten. Knowing all too well how life's fickle paths change — in less time than a sharp intake of breath — he had negotiated a clause in her adoption. Should banishment occur, Alejandra would be taken care of financially until her death. An advisor countered the clause with an addendum to protect the princess. All events leading to banishment would have to remain secret.

On the second day, Alejandra set aside her tears. She followed Abd-al-Aziz's lesson on keeping her wits about her — turning a difficult situation to her advantage. On the fourth day, she was deposited in the home of a marriage broker.

Guillermo Cabrera restlessly moved about on the balls of his feet looking as if he was about to spring upon the furniture.

Alejandra, travel weary and dirty, nonetheless exotic looking — for she wore the rich clothes of a princess coming out of the Arabian Nights tales — sat still and silent. Not being accustomed to dealing with a minion and despite speaking fluent Moroccan Arabic, Spanish, French, and English, she would not answer any of the broker's questions. Instead, using sign language she referred him to a well-stamped, silk-wrapped document. As his eyes ran down the Moroccan Arabic script, punctuated with words from Berber, French, and Spanish, his face flushed red. All his immediate problems, he probably thought, were about to be solved.

The doorbell rang and after a few moments José Salazar Moreno entered.

Do all the central Spanish plainsmen have foot problems, Alejandra wondered? For though she immediately liked José Salazar Moreno, it was clear he too suffered from an obvious foot impediment. But even if he had been a dwarf hunchback, she would have married him — in this, she had no choice. Her contract included leaving Morocco and starting a new life as a married woman within the month.

José bent low over her delicate proffered hand. Her touch radiated heat. His was light and cool.

Alejandra could not help but notice José was tall, almost as tall as the royal princess' lover. As far as looks went, José was handsome. His long fair hair was clean and neatly tied back. Though when he'd bent over her hand, Alejandra noticed he had the beginnings of a bald patch. She reckoned he was more than a few years older than she. He had clear blue eyes and a chiselled face — two etched lines highlighted his mouth.

She summoned up all the artifice she had learned from the eunuchs, using her eyes and hair to ensnare her future husband. It was unnecessary.

Deafened by the roaring of his heart, his eyes blinded by love, José skimmed over Alejandra's family lineage the marriage broker had hastily cobbled together, bolstered by a document wrapped in silk. The document was covered in all manners of wax seals rendering it illegible, but nevertheless lending it an air of importance.

After a four-week engagement, they married. It was a simple religious ceremony during which Alejandra met José's parents for the first and last time. They were country bumpkins — cattle farmers from Mexico, with their family origins from Medina del Campo, the plains town, which was now to become her home.

Something her mother-in-law had said, Alejandra forgot as quickly as she heard it. And the meaning of which would only come to be understood years later.

'Daughter-in-law,' Maria Guadalupe Moreno said embracing Alejandra in a farewell hug, 'may the Universe be with you and yours.'

Hints of rotten fish, which seeped from her mother-in-law's dress, made Alejandra feel sick to her stomach. She fled to the bathroom and threw up.

During the four-week engagement Alejandra had risked a gamble. She had acted on Abd-al-Aziz's shrewd words of, 'Always put others into one's debt'. Contrary to all social etiquette, she had lain with José once before their marriage.

José had been sweet and kind. The earth trembled for him, yet he hardly made a sound. Nothing happened to make the earth tremble for her. Not wishing to offend him, she followed his example and made even less sound. That seemed to please him. She noticed he had left his socks on. This was to irritate her for the rest of their married life.

Well after the birth of their son, and setting her irritation with José's socks aside, she began to be inquisitive about the conjugal rights of married women. All the silent groping felt unnatural. Yet she bore it and took from it what she wanted.

The royal princess honoured the clause Abd-al-Aziz had included. She held to the belief that Alejandra had the power to protect her. And equally, if thwarted, had the power to cast evil her way. She paid Alejandra an extravagant amount of money once a year. It was delivered by hand around the date of her English lover's early morning visit to Alejandra's bed, serving as a reminder the reason for the agreement.

Thereafter, once a year, a trusted servant appeared, whom Alejandra would see for as long as it took to pass a bundle of what looked like books wrapped in brown paper.

'Abd . . . ,' she would start to say. But before she could complete the question, the servant vanished.

After their marriage, and long before they had begun to settle down into domesticity, there was a surprise.

'Alejandra, you don't look well.' José touched her forehead. It was clammy and hot. 'Go back to bed, I'll bring you some tea and toast.'

At the mention of tea and toast, Alejandra's stomach heaved and she barely made it to the bathroom in time. She locked the door behind her. José stood on the other side.

'Alejandra, let me help you,' he begged. He was met with the sounds of retching. His face changed from concern to growing amazement.

'Alejandra, let me in. I know what's wrong with you.'

'You do?' Her voice was muffled and weak.

'Yes. You're pregnant.'

'I am?' sounded her disbelieving voice, followed by another round of retching.

Her early pregnancy was met with extreme happiness. José strutted about and told everyone. His patients, the flower seller — for he now filled the house with flowers until Alejandra begged him to stop — the vegetable and fruit seller, the butcher and the townspeople. His joy was so infectious it rubbed off on everyone. Soon the whole town began to count down the days to the child's birth.

And Alejandra began to like her husband even more because of his genuine happiness at her state. And more so, when from the moment of clapping his eyes on the swaddled newborn, José adored the child. She was perplexed that José was capable of such openly displayed sensitivity towards their son. It was in complete contrast to the cool closed-ness he offered her between their bed sheets.

Being a mother did not come naturally to her. She was grateful that José did a far better job of caring for the child than she, though she would never admit it. Affection turned to care. But it was a slow process. Only after it was too late, did Alejandra realize she did not care for him, but . . . loved him deeply.

For years, they watched over their son Alex with all the intensity of parents guarding the single most precious valuable in their lives. José took an active part in Alex's growing up right from the first burp. He encouraged and joined him in play. Later, he kept close watch over Alex in his studies, all the while never letting Alex forget just how much he was loved.

Alex inherited Alejandra's looks. As he grew, he displayed the same sensitive soul and mannerisms that were José's.

Alejandra made few friends. Her haughty airs separated her from others. But Viola Flores, whom Alejandra deemed to be closest to her own self-perceived lofty station, became her best friend. They met in hospital where they gave birth to their sons. Viola's son, Diego, was born one day after Alex. Like them, their boys became firm childhood friends, whose friendship lasted until their life's separate callings forced them apart.

One of her greatest regrets was falling out with Viola. It was over a local girl whom they had selected, each believing the girl would make the ideal wife for her son. Alejandra put down her irrationality with Viola to the period in which, at her insistence, José accompanied Alex to the whorehouse.

The visit to the whorehouse was presented as the occasion for the boy to have his first sexual experience. But above all, it was for the knowledge to be made public that their son was not homosexual. Alejandra wanted to prevent army men from knocking at their door in the middle of the night. For suspected homosexuals were hauled from their beds and shot.

———— ♦ ————

'José,' said Alejandra, 'it's time for Alex.'

José was re-setting the kitchen's cuckoo clock whose pine-cone weights had descended and hung parallel to each other suspended just above the floor.

'José?'

'Sorry, what did you say?' He had finished pulling the chains to raise the weights.

'It's time for Alex.'

'Time for Alex? What do you mean?'

'You know. For Alex to experience a woman.'

The corners of José's mouth turned down.

Alejandra ignored her husband's face. 'Have you seen Alex show any interest in women?'

José coughed, removed his handkerchief, and then blew his nose. Alejandra's eyes narrowed. 'Stop trying to divert attention. This is serious. Well, have you?'

José replaced his handkerchief. 'The boy's only seventeen,' he said. 'After all I was . . . ,' here José almost slipped up. As quickly as Mrs Smith appeared in his mind's eye, he closed the memory. 'Let me see . . . thirty.' He had lied, but as only he knew it, it did not, in his opinion, count.

'Yes. But that was years ago and in a different time. You know the government rule on homosexuality.'

'Alejandra, relax. Give the boy some time. He's studying for exams. His brain is exactly where it should be.'

'No. I want this problem resolved and resolved soon.'

'What do you propose?' Almost as soon as the words were out of José's mouth, he regretted it. He knew what Alejandra was going to say.

'He needs to visit the whorehouse.'

'Well, how are you going to arrange that?' he asked.

'I'm not. You are.'

What did not occur to Alejandra was that her husband would benefit from the visit too.

Their intimacies had come to an end more than a year before. José used his age as his excuse being years older than she. And he led Alejandra to believe he was no longer capable despite his recent surge in robustness.

―――― ◆ ――――

The front door closed quietly behind the returning father and son. Alejandra was sitting up in bed. They were later than she'd expected. She heard their muffled goodnights to each other and Alex's footsteps head towards his bedroom. She prepared to wait a few minutes longer for José to pass her bedroom door. He always checked each clock's timekeeping before going to bed. But that night he did not. Limping heavily, which indicated stress, he headed straight for his bedroom, passing Alejandra's door.

She got out of bed and without slipping her feet into slippers — this was unheard of, for, since childhood, she never went barefoot — she dashed across to her bedroom door and opened it. She called José.

By his miserable face, she knew something had gone wrong. Her heart contracted. Alarm bells jangled. Oh God, please no. Alex was homosexual after all, she thought.

José entered Alejandra's bedroom.

'Well? Did it happen?'

José hesitated in his response. Alejandra's alarm bells turned into sirens.

'Yes,' he mumbled.

'Oh, thank God. Did you make sure everyone knew?'

'Yes.'

'Well what else happened? Why are you so upset?'

José did not answer for the longest time. He looked down at his feet.

The sirens in Alejandra's head had lessened. She began to think clearly. Then like a bolt of lightening it struck her.

'You also . . . ?' She could not bring herself to complete the sentence. José's head hung further down.

'No,' she cried, 'that's not possible. You can't. Or can you? Did you?'

Before long she was in possession of the facts. José admitted he had tried one of the girls. The event he claimed, was so inconsequential, he could not recall what she looked like. Nor her name. It had, he assured Alejandra, been a dismal and embarrassing failure. And, if she really wanted the truth, Alejandra was to blame. For during the loveless episode, José could think only of her.

Like eons of women before her, she bought the excuse, albeit for a little while.

Then when she met RosaMina, two events happened.

She instantly recognized the hummingbird pin attached to RosaMina's dress. So clearly her pin was not unique as José had claimed, she thought. It was the first of twelve he had gifted her at the time when he took to sleeping in the guest room. She did not bother to wonder about the uniqueness of the other eleven.

Although she was not the perfect example of motherhood, like her mother-in-law, Alejandra was blessed with an innate sense of a pregnancy already begun. Moreover, she accurately predicted the sex of the unborn.

And so the second thing she realized — the child RosaMina was carrying, was a girl.

During her years in the eunuchs' desert compound, Alejandra was the only female. Each time Abd-al-Aziz returned from his trading ventures, he brought her a new doll. She spent endless hours playing with her dolls. The eunuch's spent endless hours hand stitching an enviable wardrobe of matching clothes. It was through them Alejandra developed her love for clothes and particularly for the rich but understated style.

While dressing her dolls, she fantasized having a real dress-up daughter one day. The clothes she'd put her in and the jewels she would adorn her with — for her daughter would be a miniature version of herself. And together, they would make a great mother and daughter pair.

Each time Alejandra changed Alex's clothes, those dreams re-emerged. She had hoped to provide José with the daughter he much longed for. But she never fell pregnant again. She believed the fault lay with José, given his age, rather than with her.

◆

She woke with a start and pulled off the eye mask. Abd-al-Aziz's words rang clear — be in possession of all information, good or bad. Rising from her bed, her headache gone, she knew what she had to do. She secured the services of a short and chubby detective. She paid dearly for his results, and in more ways than just money. His thorough report arrived a few days later. Puzzle pieces materialized and slotted together.

José had been with RosaMina during the year from when he'd absented himself from their bed. A year later, Alex, too, (thus, she learned her persuasion for the arranged whorehouse visit had been needless) had enjoyed what pleasures RosaMina offered.

And not only had she paid for her husband's year long exclusive pleasures with RosaMina, but also the duplicate jewelled trinkets he'd bestowed upon the two of them. This stung her, she found to her surprise, more than anything else. The careless duplication meant she was no better than RosaMina, or RosaMina was considered as good as she.

She learned Viola's husband Jerardo, and their son Diego, had also been regular RosaMina visitors. But the report did not hazard a guess as to whom the father of RosaMina's girl-child was. Nor could Alejandra. Her pregnancy intuition did not stretch that far.

But looking through the notebook the detective had purchased, with neatly entered dates and names, it was clear that based only on frequency, Viola's son Diego was the strongest contender. Then Viola's husband, Jerardo. After, came José and half a dozen townsmen. And last of all, Alex. For he'd visited RosaMina the least.

But Alejandra knew that pregnancy was not a result of frequency. But rather, the single collision of two stars forming three, as only the heavens can conspire.

She came to a decision. If she could help it, no one besides RosaMina and herself would know about the child. She did not care who the father might be. Even if the child's father was her son.

Alex was about to write his all-important exams. For his sake, she reined in her emotions, which alternated between calm clarity and terrifying turbulence. Abd-al-Aziz would have been proud. Long ago lessons she had learned on thinking before acting came to the fore.

On the day of Alex's final exams, she dismissed Inés and Tomás. She gave them a cash-stuffed envelope, told them to pack their belongings and move out. Within hours, their rooms at the top of the house stood empty.

As most evenings, when José returned home, he presented her with a single fragrant bloom. Alejandra first regarded it as touching but over the years felt stifled with the on-going gift. Then, it irritated her. Within the last year, she accepted the offering with less and less grace. That evening was no different. Except José limped more visibly. His mouth turned down and his eyes were clouded.

'Darling,' he said his voice lower than usual. He presented her the bloom and at the same time popped a chaste kiss in the middle of her forehead.

'I have news . . . my parents . . . ,'

Alejandra was not interested in his news, even if it were about his parents. She had her own that needed immediate voicing. She cut through him.

'So, why don't you tell me about your whore?'

At that moment, the world stopped turning. The silence was so loud she thought her eardrums would burst.

'Darling? What are you talking about?'

'Don't pretend. You know who and what I mean.'

'Alejandra, are you not feeling well?'

He moved to place the back of his hand on her forehead.

'Stop.' Her voice went up an octave. 'Answer me. I want to know every-thing about you and her.'

'Darling . . . ,'

'Don't call me that. I'm no longer your darling. You have another!' she yelled.

Just as Abd-al-Aziz had taught her, she shut her eyes, counted to ten and released a long, slow breath, deflating her ribcage. She opened her eyes again.

'I know everything,' she said waving to the closed file on the table. 'But I want you to tell me in your own words. I want to know — why did you chose her over me?'

'Alejandra, this has nothing to do with you.'

By the look on her face, he probably realized there was no escape.

'It was just sex. And anyhow, it's over.'

As the words left his lips, his face flushed. Alejandra's heart contracted so hard it cracked audibly.

'It wasn't just for sex. You are in love with that girl.'

'No . . . no it's not like that.'

She grabbed the single bloom and whacked him across his face. 'Well then tell me . . . tell me!' she yelled venting her hurt, rage, and jealousy.

The petals fell to the floor and she was left holding a broken stem. She balled her fists, then grabbed the file, and yanked it open. The pages of the report, released like white doves, flew into the air. A valuable vase smashed into the smoky antique Venetian mirror. Now, just like her life had been shattered, so too did the mirror explode into a million glass shards.

Still not finished, she ripped the jewelled hummingbird pin from her dress. She threw it at him. With surprising accuracy the straight and sharp bill hit him in the middle of his forehead. Only then, did she emerge from the black place she'd been in. He'd remained unflinching throughout.

'So tell me,' she whispered.

'You'd never understand,' he said as a single rivulet of blood travelled down between his eyes and along the bridge of his nose. He limped out.

She stood in the centre of the chaos she had deliberately created. Things would be different from then on. She knew that. And she was terrified. And in her terror, she completely forgot that he had news too.

———— ◆ ————

The next day Alejandra was writing a note to RosaMina, telling her where and when to meet. Before she could send it, she received RosaMina's note asking for a private meeting. Her shock from the night before had lessened. But now she was furious the little upstart had beaten her to it. For what it really meant was RosaMina had a thought-through plan of her own.

Alejandra arrived early. She sat in the front pew facing the ornate golden altarpiece of San Antolín's church in front of which she and José had been married seventeen years before. While she waited, a silent film of her life reeled through her head. Clips she still did not want to see, she skipped.

She felt the swoosh of air as RosaMina made the sign of the cross, knelt, interlaced her fingers, and bowed her head, as if in prayer, in the pew behind her.

'Alejandra,' she said in a low voice.

Alejandra swallowed hard. How dare she call her by her name. She pressed her lips shut tight knowing that she had to let RosaMina do all the talking.

'I am so sorry for all the hardship you have suffered.'

Again, Alejandra was caught unawares. She would never have guessed RosaMina's opening gambit would be an apology. She pressed her lips even more tightly.

'I am pregnant. It is not José's child. It is Alex's,' she whispered forcing Alejandra to strain her ears. 'It's best for everyone, that I leave. As I . . . I can't, I won't give up this baby,' RosaMina said firmly.

Silence lay between the women. They both may have known what was coming.

'You have my word,' RosaMina continued, 'I won't ever contact Alex. Or José.'

A variation of what Abd-al-Aziz had written into Alejandra's adoption contract re-surfaced but slid from RosaMina's lips.

'To keep this between us, I need help.'

Alejandra was amazed that this young girl, an Expósito at that, could have such clarity in what she needed to keep her child. Like it or not, a skipped clip began to reel through her head. Of how her own mother relinquished her, rather than fiercely fighting to keep her child, as RosaMina was doing.

Reined-in tears spilled from Alejandra's eyes. She dared not turn her head, lest RosaMina should see. Following the self-protecting actions of the royal princess, she formed her decision. By helping RosaMina, she would save her family by separating them from RosaMina and her girl-child. Even a pea-brain, she rationalized, knew no father and son's relationship would hold together, knowing each was desperately in love with the same woman. Let alone that the son had fathered a much wanted girl child. That, she knew, would tear them apart.

To further protect the relationship between father and son, she would have to destroy the relationship between herself and her husband.

In exchange for never contacting José or Alex, Alejandra agreed to settle money upfront and thereafter monthly. Nothing but their word held the two women in agreement. Relieved both women left the church, one after the other.

Overnight, Alejandra built an impenetrable wall separating herself from her husband. Thus protecting him from any future, unwitting words she might let fly in anger that would devastate the father-son relationship.

But life was not going to let Alejandra off so easily — her relief was short lived. She found her thoughts constantly wandering to the unborn girl-child. This wondering increased after RosaMina gave birth — and Alex left home.

Alejandra and José continued to live separate lives in the same house. The status quo remained in place for the following five years during which she often travelled alone, leaving and returning without communicating her whereabouts to José. Weeks might pass when he hardly heard or saw her.

The townsfolk of Medina del Campo shook their heads. They treated José with even more respect than before. All wondered where this state of affairs would lead. For, to be sure, it would not be a good outcome. As they predicted, good did not come. José died. And for the first time in her life Alejandra found herself physically alone.

During the year of required grieving she had had plenty of time to review the film clips of her life. Particularly those she had skipped. These provided her with new and unexpected insights. Now that she could no longer hurt José by mistakenly let slip information best left buried, she broke her part of the agreement with RosaMina.

I t was Monday afternoon, March 17, 1954. Dr Giulia Hernandez, a family therapist, aged fifty-five, was going home. Her strawberry blonde hair was lighter than when she had left thirty years before. Silver-white strands threaded through the plait, though its tip still reached her waist.

She had a smooth broad forehead, warm brown eyes, and a generous curved mouth. When she smiled, dimples appeared in her cheeks. Her fondness for oversized earrings had led to an enviable collection. On that day, large silver hoops dangled from her ears.

She wore a pair of high-waisted apple-green, three-quarter length slacks which Europeans called Capri pants (named after the Italian isle from where they rose to popularity in the 1950s) and Americans called pedal pushers. A blouse imprinted with tiny green and black geometric squares, and over this a black vinyl-treated cotton raincoat. On her feet, a pair of flat espadrilles, and a soft leather bag slung over her shoulder. Her only concession to paring down her high fashion ensemble in preparation for the journey, and the dust she was sure to encounter, was a black handkerchief scarf tied around her hair, upon which rested her oversized sunglasses.

She sat in the passenger seat of a small truck, squeezed in by packets of last minute items, and a possession or two that required hand holding. The back of the truck bore the bulk of her life in Madrid.

The driver, a chain-smoking, large-girthed man, normally talkative, drove in silence listening to the World Cup qualifying play-off between Spain and Turkey. This left Giulia to her own thoughts.

Retiring, leaving Madrid, and returning to Medina del Campo, her family's hometown, was not easy. For years, she had vicariously lived through all the melodramatic heartbreaks and joys of her fellow Spaniards lives. Leaving meant she had to let go all that gave purpose and value to her own life, including her married lover and colleague of thirty years. And who, without a hint of protest or regret, returned to the welcoming arms of his forgiving wife.

A therapist should know better, she berated herself possibly for the hundredth time. But, in her defence, as life teaches, many are left hapless and helpless when it comes to *Los caprichos del amor*. Given that she too had fallen victim to the vagaries of love meant she empathized well with her patients, rendering her an effective therapist.

During the hours-long journey, she resigned herself to living out the rest of her years alone.

Just as the driver drove the truck through the town square, the game blaring out from the vehicle's radio came to an end. With no penalty-kick provision in place at the time, the winning team was decided by the toss of a coin, with the Turks calling correctly.

Spaniards around the world sighed with heartfelt disappointment. Though she had no interest in the game, Giulia sighed, too. In her work, and way before others in her field, she had identified several facts about soccer results.

A lost match was usually accompanied by a surge in domestic violence, heart attacks, and even suicide. A won match seemed to boost self-esteem and generated higher levels of tolerance and love.

But matches, lost or won, resulted in a spike of births nine months or so after the event. Lost matches in children conceived by rape, and won matches in children conceived through genuine celebration.

The town's soccer supporters, who had packed the square's bar, streamed out. Their interest switched to the truck pulled up in front of the Hernandez family home. It had been closed since the last member had died fifteen years before.

Giulia noticed little had changed but for the town's communal water fountain. It had been restored and then resplendent, stood proud in the centre of the square.

Shutter slats were adjusted, and, through the opened cracks, women neighbours too watched the truck's arrival. Before Giulia or the driver could exit the truck, they were surrounded by Medina del Campo's disappointed soccer supporters.

'*Imbéciles malditos*, Goddamn morons,' the driver muttered while reaching into the door pocket. His fingers closed around an iron monkey wrench. Giulia placed a light hand on his forearm. Together they stared at the group staring silently back at them through the windscreen.

'Giulia?' called out a voice. A woman wearing slippers, an apron over her dress, and a large scarf tied around her hair hurried down the steps of her home.

'Giulia Hernandez, is that you?' she queried again. The men opened a path to her elbowing and let her through.

Giulia's face lit up, her dimples imploding her cheeks.

'It's okay,' she said to the driver. She leaned forward — her earring hoops spinning — and opened the passenger door.

As soon as her identity was established, memories re-ignited and the townspeople warmly welcomed her home.

As easily as the neighbour had remembered her name, she recalled many of theirs. In a moment, the air crackled with question and answer exchanges. It was as if it were only yesterday since they had last seen and spoken.

Directing more helping hands than necessary, the driver soon had the truck unloaded. Giulia's goods were placed at the foot of the steps to her home. Mopping his brow in relief rather than effort, he started the engine. As if it were thumbing its nose at the earlier threatening townsmen, the truck backfired, and in a cloud of belched smoke, rumbled off.

Home was a two-storey house with a turreted tower creating a third level, which an ancestor in good times had commissioned an architect to add.

A medieval fortress, La Mota, overlooks the town of Medina del Campo. Its fine, turreted Keep tower is over one hundred and thirty feet high.

A scaled down copy of the tower had been added to the house, making it far more prosperous and important then than was true.

The addition commanded a fine view of the town and outlying grazing plains, caught the evening breezes during the hot summer months, and provided an inescapable, albeit sore-thumb landmark for all newcomers.

Giulia brought out a large heavy key from the bottom of her bag. Despite age, the lock turned.

The rush of air passing through the opened door disturbed spiders and mice. As she had feared, everything was shrouded in tanged cobwebs. Just like her neighbour, she'd soon tie a large scarf around her head, don an apron, and swap her espadrilles for a pair of house slippers.

Furniture required a good deal of dusting and waxing, and most carpets were thrown away, as they disintegrated upon lifting.

Once the furniture had been reorganized, Giulia found herself in the front room. It looked comfortingly similar to her old office in Madrid.

She had placed her desk in front of the large window overlooking the square and communal fountain. The swivel wooden chair on wheels was placed at the centre of the desk. On the right-hand side of the room was a seamless chrome chaise lounge with separate matching leg rest covered in ivory pigskin. In some places, her patients' bodies over the years had worn the leather down to a dull grey mass.

The shelves on the opposite side of the room held her collection of bright-jacketed books alongside her ancestors' dark leather-bound ones.

A silver-faced clock with contrasting gold bars in place of numerals, and slender gold hands, was fixed to the wall to the right-hand side of the door. As before, she would use this to see when a patient's time was up.

A plush Persian rug with a central medallion repeated on its outer edges in red and gold lay on the wooden floor. A floor lamp stood to one side of her desk and two sconces on either side of the chrome chaise lounge provided additional lighting.

She wholly embraced it as a sign her therapy days were not yet over. Before long, she began to receive new patients. They came because they were curious. Giulia was the first therapist in town.

If she thought the *Madrileños* of Madrid held the monopoly rights to melodrama, she was wrong. Nothing could have prepared her for the intrigues of the small agricultural town. Everyone knows there are three sides to a story. That is to say, hers, his, and what really happened. In Medina del Campo, it was the three sides, and then everybody else's version, which at best, included half the town. At worst, the whole town.

First up was José Salazar Moreno. Like her being the town's only therapist, he was the town's only chiropractor. He came limping in under the old fashioned pretence, well meaning though it was, of welcoming her. But in truth, it was to establish if she could help him escape the dark place in which he'd found himself.

———— ◆ ————

'Tell me about Alejandra.'

'She was, and still is, the most beautiful creature on earth. I could not believe my good luck. My heart exploded. The air I breathed turned into champagne. I walked on clouds. You name it, I felt it all,' he said.

'Did she feel the same way about you?'

'I thought so.'

'How soon on did you marry?'

'Within weeks.' Then he paused.

Giulia waited, listening to the shipwreck of his life creak and groan as it pulled free from the seabed.

'Ma'am, t'was the fastest wedding in the west, minus the shotgun,' he said, imitating a Texan cowboy twang in a feeble attempt at humour.

'When did you discover Alex was not your son?'

'Jesús Cristo. You know how to pack a punch.'

She mouthed, "Sorry".

He took a minute to compose himself. 'One doesn't need Einstein's brain.'

As her head dipped forward, inviting explanation, her earrings — on that day she wore an elaborate pair of wire-beaded chandeliers — caught the light and flashed.

'It's simple. I've blue eyes. Alejandra has the most unique blue eye colour in the world. And what does our son have? Brown.' His voice raised and then he shouted more in despair than rage, 'Fuck it. The boy goes and gets brown eyes.' He paused, caught his breath then continued. 'Every eye genetic book told me the same thing, more or less. Two blue-eyed parents can have a brown-eyed child. But it is uncommon. When Alejandra could not fall pregnant . . .'

'You both desired another child?'

'Yes. No question.'

'And then?'

'I thought the fault may be with me. I had my friend Dr Rivas run a check.'

The wreck cranked its way towards the surface.

'That's when I realized for sure Alex is not my son. What little sperm I produce is infertile.'

Giulia did not miss a beat. She got the next question out while José Salazar was at his most vulnerable.

'Did that change anything for you with Alex?'

'I loved him all the more.'

'And Alejandra?'

His chest collapsed expelling air sounding like a freight train's dying whistle. He could not answer.

Giulia changed tack. 'Tell me about Rosa.'

'I wanted a shot. A chance to experience first time love and Cristal . . .'

Giulia's chandelier earrings flashed again.

'One of the girls whom I regularly went with. Bless her. She tried hard to create the perfect illusion. But it wasn't working. She couldn't give me what I needed.'

'What did you need?'

The wreck inched closer.

'Innocence.'

'Virginal?'

'Sure. Then Madam produced Rosa at an extravagant price and it was all over for us.'

'Us?'

'I gave up on my wife. I traded Alejandra for Rosa.'

'So you bought your illusion.'

He winced.

'And did you achieve it?'

'She was a virgin.'

'Did she love you the way you needed?'

'Well as you put it, I bought my illusion. So she was paid to love me in the way I needed.' His head bowed.

Giulia's chandelier earrings stilled as she held back her surprise at José's clear understanding of his situation with Rosa. Then she pressed on.

'Given the chance, would you do it again?'

José glanced down at his wristwatch. He checked the time and compared its time to her wall clock. The slender gold hands on the wall clock ticked a full minute before he responded.

'Yes.'

'Would you use your wife's money again?'

'I'd have to,' he replied with a nonchalant shrug. 'I make a fair living, but I've never had the financial means Alejandra has.'

'Do you resent that?'

'Not in the beginning. But later it got me mad. Especially as I had asked Alejandra to come clean with me about the money.'

Giulia's earrings flashed. 'You asked her about the money rather than who Alex's father was?'

'Yes.'

'Why?'

'I felt the answer to the money issue would prompt her to tell the truth about Alex's father.'

'Where did Alejandra say the money had come from?'

'She never did. When I asked, she flew into violent rages. Broke things. Apologized afterwards. But then it would happen again.'

'What would?'

'The money would arrive. Just like it does every year.' José tugged at a bag from which he produced a torn brown paper wrapping. 'It arrives in this looking just like a small parcel of books. Here's the string it gets tied with.'

Giulia lifted the paper to her nose. Golden yellow sand grains of the Sahara rained down from the creased folds. It reeked of fat mixed with cumin and mint.

'I saved the last one. I knew you would not believe me.'

'Who delivers it?'

'No idea. Just every year, around Alex's birthday, Alejandra has new piles of cash tucked away in the back of her dressing table drawer.'

'What really stopped you asking her outright about Alex's father?'

José fiddled with his wristwatch.

'José, its time for you to face that which has been making you miserable.'

José raised his head and looked into her eyes. 'It will kill me.'

She leaned over and touched his tightly clasped hands. Her earrings flashed. 'I'm here.'

José's gaze returned to his wristwatch.

'What really stopped you asking Alejandra outright about Alex's father?'

The wreck hovered beneath the surface.

'I . . . I was afraid to hear her say she loved him.'

The shipwreck rose breaking through the surface.

Next Giulia planted the seeds she hoped would take root and grow into José Salazar's consciousness.

'Are you sure Alex's conception was by mutual consent?'

The clock's ticking was loud in José Salazar's stunned silence.

'Did it ever occur to you Alejandra is not at liberty to tell the truth?'

The ticking got louder and longer.

'Never crossed my mind.'

Their session was up. But Giulia waited. In her experience the last few minutes always yielded something important.

'I will die in 1967. I will be 64 years old.'

'How do you know?'

'Because it is written in *The Logbook of Futures Foretold*.'

Giulia, familiar with *The Logbook of Futures Foretold*, knew immediately he had seen it in a dream. It is the only way information in each person's *Logbook* can be revealed. But just to make sure, she stated, 'You saw it. In a dream.'

José exhaled. His hands released and uncurled. 'Yes, but only the year. Not the date.'

'When did you have the dream?'

'In the early hours of the morning when my parents, one after the other, died.'

'Who else did you tell?'

'I planned to tell Alejandra. To get things sorted. Wills and suchlike. But she beat me to it. She had her own bad news, you know . . . the night she confronted me about Rosa.'

Giulia's earrings flashed in time to her nod.

'Of course my news was inconsequential to hers.' His voice hinted at self-depreciation.

Giulia reached over and this time held his hands. Once again he had been short-changed — prevented from dealing with issues important to him. She could not make up her mind whether life, or death, had cheated him.

And, *Los caprichos del amor* was still not finished with José Salazar. Just like life, death, too, can be full of startling revelations. For it was only after he died that Alejandra Herrera discovered her love for her husband.

After José Salazar's passing, in the year as foretold by his life's *Logbook*, Giulia had all the scandalmongers in town call upon her to malign Alejandra Herrera. They bayed for her blood, given the unproven circumstances of her husband's death. While Alejandra was regarded as the "royalty" of the town, based on her beauty and perceived wealth, her husband was the revered person. He was beloved by all for his gentleness, discretion and lightening quick healing hands, not forgetting curing their ailments without payment.

———— ◆ ————

Next up was Maria Expósito. She arrived looking like the least likely brothel owner or jeweller. She was thin, lack-lustre, and austere. Her story was a continuum of grey grimness except for a single light filled blip: giving birth and being a mother for six weeks. That ray of light matched an exquisite multi-coloured pin attached to her dress.

By contrast to José Salazar, she was strong and clear in understanding and the acceptance of her life, past and present. She blamed no one. She had no misgivings. No recriminations or remorse. Therapist and patient got down to the basics.

'Would you have forced Rosa to abort?'

'No. And her name is RosaMina. It means Rose Love.'

That day, Giulia wore a pair of earrings fashioned after a flamenco dancer's opened fan. One side was coloured bright red spotted with white polka dots the other side coloured with the inverse — white and spotted with bright red polka dots. Anyone looking at them for too long might have begun to feel dizzy. The fans slid smoothly forward and then backward caressing Giulia's cheeks as she nodded, acknowledging the change to Rosa's name.

Maria Expósito had to glance away for a second relieving her eyes of the blurring dots. Then she continued, 'Because when I learned from Berta that RosaMina had not had her menses . . . ,'

'Who is Berta?'

'Berta manages everything, including doing all the girls' personal washing.'

'So she knew that RosaMina had not had her monthly cycle?'

'Yes, and of course Berta told me.'

'RosaMina is your biological daughter.'

Maria Expósito never twitched a muscle as this secret transitioned out into the open.

'Yes.'

'How did you feel about RosaMina being pregnant?'

'It was a divine gift. My opportunity to set things right.'

'So, that's why you would not have enforced an abortion?'

'Yes. And for a while I allowed myself to dream I could be a surrogate grandmother to the child, given I was not able to mother RosaMina. But then, through the missing birth tag from my drawer, I realized she'd discovered before I could tell her, I'm her mother. This, and her possible fear of an enforced abortion, no doubt caused her to run away.'

'How did you feel about that?'

'Disappointed. But I understood her reasons.'

'So what would you like to do now?' Giulia asked, unsure of where all of this was leading. Maria Expósito was one of the better-balanced people she'd encountered in a long time.

'I want to find RosaMina. I want to help my daughter and my grandchild.'

It was one of the few times in her career Giulia had been caught off guard in a good way.

'The problem is,' Maria Expósito continued, 'RosaMina is in England. I have never been abroad. Nor do I speak English. Will you help me?'

—————— ◆ ——————

Giulia was pleased one evening to welcome Fausto Casales, a childhood school friend. She'd invited him as she'd learnt he'd done Alejandra Herrera's snooping work for her. Now that Maria Expósito had asked her to help locate RosaMina in England, he was the person she thought of.

Within seconds of opening the door, she was transported back in time. The most prominent memory being the painful pulling of her pigtail by Fausto Casales, which set her scalp tingling. He'd sat behind her all through their junior school years.

To their teachers' angst, he'd been blessed with the gift of mimicry and could be relied upon to disrupt their classes. Their revenge: rapping his knuckles until the skin split and bled or the ruler broke.

'Fausto. Welcome,' she said, noting he'd changed little but for several more kilos. He had also always been on the short side. Now it was clear he was never meant to grow much taller. Despite the warm weather, he wore a cotton dustcoat, the kind a factory supervisor might. Three pens in a row, blue, black and red poked out from the top of the left hand chest pocket. With old-fashioned manners, he pressed his lips to her hand.

'Giulia. It's been way too long.'

Lifting his head, she saw a spark of the old mischief.

'May I?' He grasped the tail end of her silver threaded plait and gave it a tug. More than just her scalp tingled.

They went up to the turreted tower where Giulia spent her evenings listening to music, catching the breeze, eating her solitary dinner, and emptying her head of the day's therapy sessions.

They fell into warm easy companionship. She told him of her doomed thirty-year relationship, interminable dinners, and holidays spent alone.

He filled in the years after middle school. Having never mastered writing or reading, he'd left school to work the family farm. But with his ability to observe and recall in detailed colour pictures, and by using the process of elimination, he became adept at solving mysteries of all sorts. His detection abilities soon had him invited to other towns. He made a decent living. He'd never married or had any children — to the best of his knowledge.

Giulia had not had so much fun in years and was disappointed when their first evening came to an end. But she was to give him English lessons, for she spoke English well enough, as she'd travelled to the United Kingdom on many short breaks away during her Madrid years. They agreed to meet several times a week with Maria Expósito paying for the lessons in preparation for his travel to the U.K.

Giulia was not at all surprised that Fausto was a quick learner. He had a good ear for language. Which meant he also had a good ear for rhythm. Soon on, (though it took longer for him to remove his dustcoat), they fell into the habit of playing scratchy old vinyl records — the music of their childhood, 'La cumparsita'.

During festivals their families and townspeople would dance the Tango around the square under glowing lanterns until dawn. On the edges of the square, out of harm's way, children, including Fausto and Giulia, attempted copying the kicking up of feet, stiff quick walking, and fast twists. Now almost forty-five years later, together they pieced from memory the multiple step combinations.

They made a strange dance couple. Giulia stood a head taller than Fausto. They were both larger around the waist than they should have been.

But aside from this, they attacked, repelled, and enticed each other and tangoed with vigour within the square of the turreted tower.

Giulia made a note to remove her earrings the next time — for they prevented her feeling the whole of Fausto's cheek against hers.

A flame began to glimmer. With growing and girlish delight that was, Giulia thought, unbecoming for a woman of her age, she moved forward into the beginning of a new phase of her life. She was not to spend the rest of her years alone after all.

———— ◆ ————

The third person in the RosaMina triangle was Alex Salazar Herrera. When he arrived in her front room she was obliged to busy herself at her desk, hiding her blushing face from him. He wore his blond wavy hair long like a woman's, tied back in a thick ponytail. His skin was clear. It glowed with the freshness of youthful health.

As José Salazar had told her, Alex Salazar Herrera had brown eyes, but he sported the longest eyelashes she'd ever seen on a man. He was tallish and athletic. His jeans clung to lean legs. He did not have José Salazar's chiselled face (indeed it would have been quite improbable), but rather a smooth-planed one. The bridge of his nose was straight and long, and ended in well-defined nostrils, which flared when he felt strong emotion. Under his shirt, she envisaged a flat belly and strong torso.

To her, he represented a centaur, the mythological creature with the head, arms, and torso of a human and the body and legs of a horse.

Giulia surprised herself. She wanted to take him into her arms and nurse him from her breast. Then desired to feel the throb of him between her legs so much, she had to cross them and press her thighs together. It was clear that for the rest of his life, women would fly to him like bees to honey. She feared for the young man sitting before her. Women of all ages would attempt to tame him or desire to be tamed by him. This was not a foretelling of happy future relationships.

Most strange of all, Alex Salazar Herrera was devoid of vanity. He was blind to the fact he was beautiful. His mother, Giulia had heard, knew how beautiful she was. But he appeared to have no sense of the effect he had on others. But like José Salazar, Alex Salazar Herrera was afflicted by raging conflicting emotions and was almost at breaking point.

Giulia had high hopes when patients arrived in her office in such despair. They were easier to work with — their defences down. They were in so much pain they would do anything to be free of it. And so it was in Alex Salazar Herrera's case. Recognition and understanding arrived fast — like a camera stuck on automatic shutter mode.

———— ◆ ————

'Your parents' relationship is their relationship. What happens between them is their business. You are their child.' Giulia's pink dancing flamingo earrings started to swivel.

His nostrils flared.

'Oh come on, Alex. You know what I mean. You're a man but you are still their child. Will always be.'

'Then how come I'm in the middle of it all?'

'Because you put yourself there.'

Shutter click.

Then his nostrils flared again.

'So, you're saying I should remove myself.'

'Yup. It's as simple as that. Let me add that you being in the middle has delayed them from dealing with their own issues with each other.'

Shutter click.

'If I'm not there, they'll deal with it?'

'One way or another. But the important thing is that this is their conflict. Whatever solution they arrive at will be theirs alone. And if it works, great; and if it doesn't, that's their problem, not yours.'

Shutter click.

'My mother might kill my father in the process,' he said with the flash of a wry grin.

'Maybe. But not your problem.'

Alex wrestled a while with his saviour-of-his-parents attitude. Wanting to be a super-hero was hard to let go. But when he did, relief flooded his eyes. What came next was far more difficult.

'Alex, think about it.' The flamingoes had reached their maximum point of torque. 'How could Rosa (she could not disclose RosaMina's real name) tell you that she had been servicing your father? Remember it was her job. And just like what you tell me is confidential, Rosa was not at liberty to tell you anything at all about any of her clients.'

'She wasn't?'

'No.'

Shutter click.

The flamingoes turned, waited.

Alex paused. Then his nostrils flared wide with effort — for he had his own shipwreck to haul to the surface.

As expected, *Los caprichos del amor* came calling, complicating matters.

'But Giulia, we fell in love. We truly fell in love,' he repeated.

'Falling in love does not mean exclusive ownership, or rights, over the other person.'

The flamingoes appeared to concur and began their spiral descent in earnest.

Alex shifted his gaze and stared at the static bookshelves opposite him.

'And, it's ridiculous to think that people are not allowed to have a past. Everyone has a past,' she emphasized.

Shutter click.

'You're right. You're right,' he said.

Giulia was prepared for the next question.

'But, how did she feel knowing that she had slept with my father. For God's sake, he's an old man.'

'You'll never know how she felt. And moreover that's none of your business. She was doing her job.'

Shutter click.

'But how do I know for sure that what I thought we had was for real?'

Los caprichos del amor was overstaying its welcome.

'Trust your gut, Alex. What did it feel like to you?'

'Real.'

'So, what's the problem?' she asked, though she well knew the answer.

'The problem? She's gone. I've begged everyone at The House but nobody will tell me anything. Only Cristal. And what she told me I did not want to know.'

'Did it occur to you they really don't know where she is?'

Shutter click.

'It didn't.'

'I've been thinking Alex. It's time you left the nest.'

He nodded. 'Funny. I've been thinking along those lines. Getting my own apartment.'

'No, I mean leave Spain. Go abroad. Get qualified. Take off a year — go exploring.'

'You think?'

'I think.'

Shutter click.

Having reached the end, the pink flamingoes stopped twisting.

---------- ◆ ----------

Alex walked into Giulia's front room office the following week.

'I did it,' he said with a grin so gorgeous her heart beat faster. 'I told my parents. I'm leaving this afternoon. This is our last session.'

Giulia's cheeks dimpled.

'Thanks for everything,' he said.

'You know where I am if you need me.'

'So you won't forget me?'

'Forget you? No Alex. I won't forget you.'

They hugged. She closed her eyes and deeply inhaled the smell of his youthfulness — and castigated herself for thinking too-young thoughts for her old body. They said goodbye. From the bottom of her heart, she wished him the very best.

---------- ◆ ----------

The centaur left, leaving Achilles and Maria Expósito behind.

The Salazar Herrera family story was not difficult to piece together. Having more knowledge than the trio put out — thanks to Fausto Casales — Giulia kept one step ahead. But even with her additional insight, it was not easy.

Giulia could use only one word to sum up Maria Expósito: tenacious. And her tenacity paid off. Pea brains could not have missed from reviewing her girls' chronicled client list, that of all, Diego Rivas was RosaMina's most frequent visitor leading up to her disappearance. All possible avenues leading to her discovery pointed to him.

Maria Expósito instructed Cristal, Dr Jerado Rivas' favourite girl, to extract the whereabouts of his son, Diego Rivas. Months later, Fausto Casales set off for London. Diego Rivas' address had been carefully written down. But Giulia had described in vivid detail and drew in colour (using his blue, black, and red pens) exactly how he was to find his way about London. Maria Expósito had told Fausto Casales not to come back until he had concrete proof of her daughter and grandchild's whereabouts.

And Maria Expósito decided to sell up and move on. She'd earned enough to live on for the rest of her life. She would take Berta with her. She planned to retire to the coastal town of Havea, one hundred kilometres south of Valencia. There she'd walk the curving promenade feeling the sun and a sea breeze on her face. Years later, when she could no longer walk, Berta pushed her in her wheelchair. But before she sold up, she paid for each of her then current girls to go to Giulia as patients.

Giulia listened over and over again to the same litany each with a slight variation on a theme. She put it to Maria Expósito that if she wanted to gift her girls with anything, it should be education. Again, Maria Expósito surprised her by immediately setting up a fund calling it The Rose Love Education Fund. From it, the girls would be able to use funds for the strict purpose of education, either for themselves or their children.

'With education,' said Maria Expósito matter of factly, 'comes money. And money provides choices.'

What she did not say was, this way they could be spared the lives they had all lived until then.

The townswomen of Medina del Campo were not sorry to see the back of Maria Expósito. But soon after when it dawned on them that gifts of jewellry had come to a halt they began to wonder if they had not been premature in saying farewell so heartily. And when their middle- and old-aged husbands returned to the conjugal bed demanding their rights, a few were pleased, but most not — and it was those who began to wish Maria Expósito had never left.

Maria Expósito would never how much she was missed. In how many ways and by more people she could ever have imagined. Thus Maria Expósito was not in the least forgotten.

Giulia continued to listen to the symphony of cranking shipwrecks that passed through her front room office. When their sounds quietened, she noted their positions and kept watch for the slightest movement indicating their readiness to move towards the surface.

I experienced a deep sense of relief when I realized the unnecessary role I had played in the on-going battle between my parents. More to the point, my mother's relentless on-going battle against my father. Where my mother fought viciously and tenaciously, my father never defended himself. He absorbed all her aggrieved rage raining down upon him like a curled-up dog taking a beating.

One morning, I woke with a clear plan. I arose with purpose. With my bag packed, containing bare necessities, I went in search of my father. He was at his usual early morning place.

'Morning, Papa.'

He folded the paper and set it back on the table alongside the last bottle of his favourite childhood mesquite honey. Agonizing for others to watch, he'd unscrew the lid and sniff its fragrance, rather than smear a knife full of honey onto his toast and eat it.

'How are you this morning my son?' His blue eyes scrutinized my face.

'Good. You?'

'Much the same. Your Mama . . . ,'

Before he could start his sad lament about the state of their relationship, I interrupted him.

'Papa, I have news.'

It was the quaint opening my father always utilized to get my and my mother's attention. And it always followed the same format. This piqued his interest and he drew himself up.

'Good news?'

'Yes.'

His face lit up.

'And, no.'

His face dimmed. He glanced down and checked his wristwatch, a Cartier Santos, the first ever mass-produced timepiece. It was the oldest of all his wristwatches and its age showed for the black leather strap was well worn, frayed, and greyed at the edges. Then he looked up and compared its time to the ornate wooden cuckoo clock mounted on the wall opposite him.

One of three (the other two were located elsewhere in the house), it was his favourite. It had a blue-painted door through which the head of a cheerful miniature red cuckoo popped out when announcing the time on the hour by issuing forth two short, medium-pitched whistles. Alongside that stood a long case clock from France called a Morbier, distinct from other freestanding grandfather clocks because of its potbelly. While the cuckoo clock announced the hour, the Morbier announced every quarter hour in a high pitched reverberating metal tone that sounded throughout the house. I knew better than to rush my father. He devoted thirty minutes twice a day to his collection of clocks and watches, winding and checking their timekeeping. After a minute and a half, he turned his attention back to me.

'So give me the good news first. It will help the bad go down.'

'The London College of Chiropractic has accepted my application.'

He was not surprised. My father held an ironclad belief in my ability as a chiropractor.

'Because,' he'd often say in happier times, 'you learned everything from this old dog.'

The truth was that my father had taken Chiropractic to an art form, whereas I practiced it as a craft. I had long ago given up trying to match him. He had an innate sense, a superior touch. Because of his gentleness, his patients trusted him and relaxed immediately. All of which are necessary primary steps for the conclusion of a successful adjustment. Yet he believed I was better — I put this down to fatherly pride.

'And the bad?'

'I'm leaving today.'

A breath escaped him, causing his chest to contract. At the same time, he touched the purple bruise on his forehead. A sympathetic charge coursed through me, seeing him wince in pain. Two days before, my mother had thrown a book at him. He had once again crossed the invisible line delineating her part of the house from his. He had hoped his most pathetic implorations would bring her round to talk with him, at least. For this, he had been attacked.

Once again, I explained I needed a certificate and license. Then I would be entitled to work as a qualified chiropractor anywhere within Europe. I had given up trying to make him understand the world had changed, none more so than the world of Chiropractic medicine.

He finally nodded. 'Okay my son. Go. Show them what stuff we're made of.'

He made an attempt to shake my hand. I stood up, drew him up too, and clasped him in a bear hug. The never-let-you-go kind he gave me when I was child. While the clocks ticked around us, we held each other. I was the first to let go. His fingers reluctantly slid down my jacket sleeve.

My mother's place opposite his was laid, as it was by him for each meal. And each day, he placed a single bloom across her plate. But she'd not joined him since her return from her European holiday a year before.

And after my mother had dismissed Inés and Tomás, my father prepared breakfast and most often dinner, which he ate alone. A new cleaning woman arrived to rid the house of the gathering dust. Things were falling into a state of disrepair, none of which my father could see. Somehow my mother, who had never done housework, managed to keep that section of the house she claimed in good order. I wondered what state of mind I would find her in, what her reaction would be to my decision.

A year before, I spilled the secrets of my parents' behaviour and the causes I thought were to be the reason, to the town's newest medical addition, Dr Giulia Hernandez. She listened carefully. She asked few, but insightful questions, aiming at the very core of the issue. She was attentive to my story about Rosa.

'So you are upset your father had sex with Rosa.'

It was blunt. I floundered in the tangle of writhing serpents.

She tried again.

'Rosa was paid to provide sex.'

It was cold comfort. I understood and accepted Rosa had been with many men. But I could not understand my father and I physically sharing and enjoying the same woman. It was just too close and damned uncomfortable. God knows how my father would have reacted had he known.

Dr Hernandez was patient. I realized she wanted me to change my way of thinking about it. But I was not ready to relinquish my tenacious grip on the violent sea of misery and pain that held me fast.

'Alex, I believe you are suffering from the green-eyed monster.'

Jealousy. There it was. Laid bare.

'Do you know what the remedy is?'

I shook my head.

'Simple. Get over yourself.'

The writhing serpents went into a frenzy. My hands fastened around the seat of the chair. Others before me had done the same — the leather had worn through in places right down to the cold chrome.

On an intellectual level, what she said was right, but it was not what I wanted to hear.

In much less time, however she managed to educate me in understanding my mother's fury at my father's indiscretion with Rosa. The fact that for the year he'd been with her, he claimed he was unable to maintain his intimacy with his wife because of his approaching older years. Unbeknownst to him, my mother had consulted her doctor who acknowledged such flagging of the libido was normal. A treatment of long established herbal preparations was suggested.

With marked determination, my mother set about feeding my father, without his knowledge, the precise quantity of the prescribed remedy, including it in his food or liquids.

My father responded quickly. He developed a twinkle in his eye, and what was left of his hair shone. He lost weight. He had taken to going for brisk walks after dinner — to aid his digestion, he had claimed.

Yet still, there was no sign of resuming their intimate activities. My mother had no idea that the results of her ministrations were being put into practice with someone else. My mother was old-fashioned and traditional. She believed that what passed between a husband and wife was not to be shared with another. Later she underwent a complete change. Her old-fashioned beliefs and behaviour disappeared.

Meanwhile, bewildered, my mother began to take stock of herself. She tried to improve what was already close to perfection. During this period she increased their social engagements. It was an attempt to catch my father's eye by showing herself off in a new light. They were both in great demand at dinner tables around our town. They provided something special to be gazed upon given both were tall, slim, and my mother's beauty quite mesmerizing.

My father, normally by far the quieter one, became an avid conversationalist and entertainer. Hosts insisted he tell of his early days studying in America. They always pressed him to pronounce phrases in American English. Everyone was enthralled with his mimicry of the diverse accents found in the great United States of America, especially the Texan drawl. The Texan drawl was incomprehensible to most, bar Texans. The Iowan accent by contrast was considered television English, and commonly understood by all Americans.

He indulged his wife in their busier than usual social calendar, and, encouraged her with largesse. He showered my mother with all the love niceties of a courting couple, including fresh bouquets and generous and beautiful gifts. On the pretext of not sleeping well because of increased social activities, over indulgence, and not wishing to disturb his wife, he took to sleeping in a guest bedroom. Overnight, it seemed, the guest bedroom became his domain. With enough of his personal effects around, it appeared that he was there to stay for good.

One may wonder how a seventeen-year-old knows all of these intimate intricacies ostensibly shared only between parents. Both wished to exonerate themselves in my eyes, though neither would ever say precisely what they had done to fall foul of the other. Each pressured me into taking sides letting slip more information that I ever wanted to know. And it was this pressure that sent me to seek, unbeknownst to either parent, the services of Dr Giulia Hernandez.

My mother discovered the full extent of my father's betrayal through the detective she'd hired after The Night that Changed Everything. She blamed herself and meted out her own punishment. She pricked her fingertips with the twelve jewelled pins my father had given her, one for each month he'd been with Rosa. To add insult to injury, she discovered my father had bestowed upon Rosa the identical gifts. By comparison to my mother's stunning beauty, anyone at all faded into insignificance, Rosa included. Yet my father found that Rosa was worthy of the same gifts as my mother.

While I could or would not recognize jealousy in myself — of my father — I had recognized it in my mother — of Rosa.

I believed my mother was jealous he would consider Rosa her equal. But when the truth aired, what mattered most to my mother, or so she claimed, was that Rosa was a mere child. This I thought ridiculous. Because if Rosa was a child at sixteen, then she must have considered me as one too at age seventeen. I did not attempt to dissuade my mother of her opinion. For it would further complicate and worsen matters, should she know I, too, had engaged with Rosa.

What I did not know was, my mother did know. But for her own very good reasons, which I was again to learn only in the far distant future, she chose not to make the slightest inference she had known about Rosa and me.

I told Dr Hernandez of the last time Rosa and I were together. That I'd come to the conclusion, too late, something I'd said about her surname had offended her. Other than wanting to hold her in my arms and lose myself in hers, I wanted most of all to apologize. Apologize to her for the slow deep hurt that crossed her face. To erase the haunted shadows that hung like sad moons in her eyes after I expressed my distaste at hearing her surname.

In Dr Hernandez's office, and despite their painful piercings, I refused my tears their release. Instead I dug into the carefully placed box of tissues. Drawing out a handful I blew my nose several times over.

Thanks to Dr Giulia Hernandez, I had begun to see things more clearly. With relief, I understood my parents' relationship was theirs alone to manage. I needed to move on with my own life. Having said goodbye to my father I was now facing the same task with my mother. With firm intention I first knocked, waited for a response, and then entered my mother's bedroom.

The unexpected is always exactly that — unexpected. My mother froze with her hand raised, about to repeat the downward movement of brushing her heavy waist-length hair. Hair, which remained blue-black, compared to my father's almost bald pate, and what sparse hairs were left, were silver.

'Why London? Aren't there other schools in Europe where you can complete your studies?'

'There are. But London has the best. Everyone goes there if they can get in.'

'You won't survive the English food.' For a second her nose wrinkled.

'I'm not going for the food.'

'The streets are dirty. And the weather abominable.' Her voice ended on a high note.

'I'm only going for six weeks. Then I plan to do some travelling.'

Like a flipped light switch turning dark into light, she changed.

'A splendid idea,' she crooned. 'I plan to travel again soon. We'll meet up.'

She pulled open her dressing table drawer and from the back of it, drew out a brick of cash. I gasped.

'Alex, here, this is for you. Go to London. Do well in your exams. And most importantly, have fun.'

My eyes grew larger. Lodged in the back of the drawer were several more brick stacks.

'But Mama,' I protested.

'This money is yours, too,' she said.

Years later, I would find out what she meant.

'You deserve it,' she said, interrupting my next protest. 'And, Alex, let me say this now. I apologize unreservedly for the trauma which we have all been embroiled in over the last year.'

This was unheard of. My mother never apologized for anything. Throughout my life, I sometimes thought maybe she had been a princess in a past life. From my childhood I recalled her saying on several occasions, 'A princess never apologizes'.

To my further shock, she continued.

'That you have been brought into it, has been wrong. The problem remains your father's and mine. It has nothing to do with you.'

I wondered if someone could pinch me awake. At that moment, I was almost convinced my mother had also been to see Dr Hernandez. I froze at the very thought. Just as I would have, had I known then that, like me, my father was a regular client of Dr Hernandez. Though Dr Hernandez's neighbours knew — their shutter slats adjusted in time to the arrival and departure of each patient.

'Alex, do you understand me?'

I nodded, looking down at the weighty wad of cash in my hand.

'I mean, do you understand me?' she repeated, tugging at my sleeve to get my absolute attention.

My mother could be alarmingly forceful at times and then just when you least expected it, the most understanding and gracious, too. Her mercurial manner kept many chasing to keep up or running away from her.

'I understand.'

She jumped up with the exuberance of women half her age. She hugged and held me close, enveloping me in perfume, a new light English floral fragrance; a mixture of rose and geranium.

She murmured in my ear the diminutive of my name, Álejo, the name only she called me when I was a child. And Rosa had called me, lying in my arms.

With my pockets bulging, and my bag packed, I entered the taxi and settled back for the long drive to the airport.

The route out of town took me past The House. Thanks to the traffic, I was able to look up at the window of the room where I had so enjoyed Rosa. My heart beat against my chest but I turned those thoughts off and closed the door to that part of my life.

———— ♦ ————

Upon arriving in London, I realized I would have to continue using my abbreviated name. The English could not get the back of their throats closed enough to sound out the correct pronunciation of my name. Everyone's attempts grated in my ears. Alejandro, is the male form of my mother's name, Alejandra. When broken down, it results in the Anglo-Saxon, Alex. This, the English had no problem at all pronouncing. So I continued with the name Alex and it became the name I was to be called for the rest of my life.

I had written to Diego at the address he'd provided, but not yet received a reply. As I had left abruptly, it was possible his reply and I crossed mid-air. At the first opportunity, I set off in search of him.

Several tube rides and many direction questions later, all of which I bungled in my broken English complicated by my Spanish accent, I arrived at the address. I stabbed the bell, one of many, alongside which written on a scrap of sticky paper was the surname Rivas. I rang twice again. As I was about to turn from the door, I heard Diego's voice, cracked with sleep.

'Diego, it's me, Alex.'

Dead silence and then, '*Mierda*, shit. Wait, I'm coming.'

I stepped back down the grimy grey steps and waited on the grimier grey pavement. Diego, whom I had not seen in two years, opened the door. He waddled down the steps, kilos heavier, trying to button his shirt over his jellyroll belly and stuff it into his trousers. His jacket swung behind him with one arm anchored in a sleeve. His hair stood up and he had sleep in his eyes, nightshade stubble, and a bad case of halitosis.

'Hell,' he said. 'Why didn't you let me know before.'

'Hello and nice to see you too,' I responded.

He clasped me in a bear hug, all of his personal hygiene enfolding me too.

We headed down to a café. We drank coffee. He got stuck into a mess of English breakfast. He vacuumed up his food, calling for more oil crisped bacon and doorstop slices of fried bread.

He related, between mouthfuls, his experiences at the local hospital where he worked part time and attended medical school full time. It was a hectic schedule. There was no time off for life's delights he assured me. Just by his appearance, I did not envy him. I hoped that my new schedule over the next six weeks would nowhere near affect me in the way to which he had been reduced.

We walked back to his apartment.

'I'd invite you up,' he said. 'But it's an unGodly mess. Too many bodies and not enough space.'

But he fished around in his pockets and came up with a pencil stub and a piece of paper.

'Here, this is my number. It's a messaging service. I'll get back to you.' He handed the scrap to me.

'Yours?'

'I don't have one yet.'

'Okay when you do, let me have it. We'll get together my next weekend off . . . visit a few pubs.'

I retraced my steps to the underground station leaving Diego to go back to bed. Not one meaningful word had passed between us about our earlier shared lives. We had both skirted around our sets of parents, giving nothing of note away. I was not going to elaborate upon the dire state of affairs between my parents. That was their business. Either on purpose, or by sheer omission, neither of us mentioned The House. A palpable weight lodged between us.

Nine months before, the last time I had gone in search of Rosa, Cristal instead of Berta opened the door.

'Cristal, please I beg of you, tell me where Rosa is.'

She raised her hand to her hair pinned into an unkempt nest on the top of her head.

'Alex I truly don't know.'

She threw a quick look over her shoulder and took a step beyond the door. She leaned in towards me.

'I suggest,' she said in a lowered voice, 'you take a look closer to home.'

My face flamed red.

'No, silly. Not your father. Ask Diego. He may know. After all he was Rosa's most regular visitor right up to when she left.'

From nowhere, came the mule kick to my belly. While trying to recover, Cristal continued in her lowered voice and I further learned Diego's frequency of visits in the two-month pressure cooker time leading up to our exams almost exceeded the number of times I had been with her over a year of Wednesdays. Cristal went to great pains to point this out — in fact, she repeated it twice.

I stumbled down the steps while the door closed softly behind me.

I had worked with Dr Hernandez on trying to figure out, of the two, which was more painful. Diego's blatant disregard for our agreement, or the number of times he'd been with Rosa versus the number of times I had. Still I had not come to a conclusion. So no longer did I only have the visions of my father's long thin limbs entwined with hers, but Diego's much shorter, fatter ones, too. Images of his penis also entered my brain, and though I kept swatting at it like a pesky fly in order to make them go away, they did not.

I had planned to call him on the issue of our agreement, and ask the question outright. Why did you break our agreement and go with RosaMina? But, I kidded myself, given the way things turned out, I let it go, promising myself I would save it for another time. It proved to be a missed opportunity. And I never did get to ask the question. Years later, I realized I did not ask, because I did not want to hear his answer.

Monday arrived, and for the next week I worked in what seemed to be permanent night. I rose and returned to my small rented apartment in darkness. Soon I understood my mother's dire warnings of the British weather. In a day, one could experience all four seasons. My negative mood was further aggravated in that Sunday was the only free day.

Exhausted and lonely, which added up to depression, I slept every spare hour I could. Those hours that I could not sleep, I listened to the radio. My father told me he'd learned English in America by listening to children's stories on the radio. I also tuned into the cartoons on television.

I was bored at the Chiropractic college. Even the most difficult techniques were pedestrian to me. I could not generate any enthusiasm for the group of students with whom I worked. While I understood everything being said and what I read in English, I had very little practice speaking. Such was my state of mind that I had no energy or wish to put communication into practice.

The girls in my group watched me from the corners of their eyes. They pounced at any opportunity to engage me even on the flimsiest excuses. When they did, the guys bristled, eyeing me up and down, waiting for a chink in my armour to show. But I ignored them all.

Then the road split. And until recently, I could not help thinking 'what if' had I chosen the other path.

The following Sunday, I ventured into Kew Gardens. My mother's vivid description had been accurate. Great swathes of soft green grass. Cultivated flower beds that drew the eye like the butterfly's random lift-and-land-flutter from flower to flower. Oaks standing tall and stately, and other trees, their shapes and colours to be believed only by seeing. And most impressive of all — glass panes set between painted white iron supports — tropical houses whose ceilings soared skyward like cathedrals, and where my mother had warmed herself.

Upon entering, a blast of warm, moist air hit me. For the first time since my arrival, I thawed and my blood flowed. I found a Victorian wrought iron bench hidden under the mighty fronds of an exotic tree fern. I sat down. Shutting my eyes I breathed deeply, filling my lungs with the moist air. As if waiting on cue, Rosa entered my head.

She was as warm and alive as the warm air I was breathing. I felt my body fill up with hers. Our limbs entwined like the twisting trunks of another tree before me. She could not be closer to me and yet she was nowhere. Pain pierced my eyelids. Despite my will, tears filled my eyes.

'Rosa,' I whispered with a shuddering gulp for the millionth time. 'Where are you?'

At that moment, a child's pushchair stopped feet away from me. A toddler dressed in pink looked at me. She had deep brown pools for eyes. She raised one little fist and clenched her fingers open and closed, in what I imagined to be a newly learned greeting. Embarrassed to be caught crying by anyone, even if it was a cute little girl saying hello, I vacated the bench, ducked under the fronds, and walked away in the opposite direction.

Once outside The Palm House, I took the Broad Walk and entered The Orangery where there was a marble sculpture exhibition. It was less than an hour before closing time. The last of the late winter afternoon's low grey skies had turned black; the marble life-sized naked human statues in a variety of poses and abstract pieces glowed luminously. The sculptors were a mixed bunch. I wondered how I could find the model of the supine headless sculpture.

She had long slim legs ending at the beginning of the cleft of her mons pubis rising in a slight arch like inverted sickle moon. Her belly lay flat. Her breasts splayed slightly outwards with nipples puckered upright.

For the second time in less than ten minutes, my world stopped turning. I choked. And I failed my very best intention of keeping the door to my heart, upon which Rosa's name was etched, closed. A tsunami caught me up. Helpless, I tossed and tumbled in a vortex of swirling memories.

I cannot say how long I stood there for. Then a tug at my jacket sleeve with the words, 'Sir, it's time. We're closing,' dumped me back down onto earth.

'Where can I find the model or the sculptor?' I spluttered. The woman, with a moon face, cheeks like the broad, flat side of a leg of pork, unplucked eyebrows, a wobbling turkey wattle, and wispy nondescript brown hair that was in desperate need of attention, responded, 'It's all here. Sir, now if you don't mind.'

She handed me a brochure publicizing the exhibition and led me to the half-shut, large, arched glass door. Her voluminous thighs rubbed together through her shiny nylon trousers.

I left Kew Gardens taking the Broad Walk towards the Victoria Gate exit. I crossed the busy Kew Road and entered a traditional English teahouse. Not for tea, but because I had to sit down under bright light to scour the brochure I held. But I did order tea and one of the house specialities, a Maids of Honour tartlet. I unfolded the brochure, spreading it flat on the table before me.

'Which did you prefer?' asked a voice. A woman, close to my mother's age, dressed like an Indian maharani, minus the turban, sat close to me. On the table was her tray of tea and a ladened three-tiered cake tower. Soft leather gloves, placed one upon the other on an expensive leather bag, all of which my mother would have approved.

'Well?' she asked again waiting for my response.

She had clear intelligent brown eyes, generous shapely lips, good skin and long straight blond hair strands of which had slipped from the tie at the nape of her neck and fell across her face. She lifted a hand to brush it all aside. Although her nails were short and clean, it was a rough hand with largish knuckles.

'It goes with the territory,' she said, apparently noticing my eyes follow her hand movement. 'Manuella Balducci.'

She extended a warm hand, which also had a very firm grip, something of which my mother would not have approved.

'Alejandro Salazar Herrera. But call me Alex,' I added, seeing her slight quizzical look at hearing my formal name.

'Alex.'

My tea tray with the single Maids of Honour tartlet arrived. Manuella motioned to the server to place the tray at her table. I joined her.

'You're Italian,' I indicated at the brochure listing the sculptors and their nationalities, 'but you speak English fluently.'

'My mother was English.'

'And you came to be a sculptor ... er ... sculptress ... ,'

'Sculptor is good,' she said.

'A sculptor because ....' I suddenly had a vision of my father speaking similar words when he engaged a new patient in divergent conversation just before he commenced an adjustment. This invariably threw the patient off-guard and relaxed them, which is what a chiropractor needs to do to facilitate a positive adjustment.

'I can't help myself. And besides, sculpting runs in both sides of my family.'

The tea was hot. I added sugar and milk in the English way and bit into the Maids of Honour. I wanted to dispense with social etiquette and ask the question outright. Who and where is your model of the sickle moon mons pubis? Just like before, I let the opportunity go, promising — though later I realized I was kidding — myself I would, at another time. And of course, I never did.

'Great, isn't it?' she said.

I nodded, turning my attention to the moist, petal soft custard encased in a feathery light crust. She pushed her three-tiered cake tower towards me.

'Please,' she said. 'Help yourself.'

A few moments elapsed while I absorbed the tartlet and she looked at me keenly. Or, more to the point, scrutinized me. I felt I was a prized specimen being examined under a magnifying glass. It was not an uncomfortable feeling. I did help myself to more tartlets.

'Which sculpture did you like the most?'

I could not bring myself to tell the truth. The vision of Rosa was still too present. So I chose instead an obscure androgynous form which morphed into a nothingness ball but somehow reminded me of my father taking an emotional beating from my mother. Miss Balducci (I assumed, as I had noticed she was not wearing a wedding band) looked at me sharply but said nothing. She likely knew I was not telling the truth.

Yet she invited me home. She lived alone not much further down the road from The Maids of Honour. It was a large stand-alone Edwardian house filled with her and her mother's sculptures.

She prepared a plate of *Puttanesca*, whore's pasta, a dish from the south of Italy.

'It's in complete contrast to the virginal Maids of Honour,' she explained with a laugh, while buzzing about in her kitchen — which could have been used to prepare a meal for a hundred or more.

The bottle of wine was great, as was her large comfortable bed in which, along with her, I lost something of my old self and found something new in myself.

The weather no longer bothered me. The last few weeks at the college came to a swift end. There was a graduation party of sorts. Manuella was my guest, as my messages via Diego's messaging service had all gone unanswered. My fellow graduates looked at me askance. It was clear they thought the age difference between us ludicrous. I did not care. Nevertheless, caution aught to have prevailed. I should have heeded, the small warning.

The rented apartment I saw once more, when handing in my keys and chucking out weeks-old milk, which had the place stinking of overripe cheese. With my clothes shoved into my bag, I joined Manuella on her return trip to her father's hometown. The sculpture Mecca of all aspiring, or already famous, sculptors, located on the coastline at the top end of Tuscany. The flight to Pisa was short. A friend of hers, who was also one of two taxi drivers in Pietrasanta — the town known since 1841, as the City of Art to which we were heading — collected us.

Marco, on the far side of middle-age, spoke English with an Italian/ Irish accent. Barely eighteen, he had followed an Irish tourist back to her home country and married her there. They had several kids and ran a fish and chips shop. When he decided to return to Italy, he gave his wife five years notice. But she and the family stayed in Ireland. He never saw any of them again. His voice cracked and when I glanced up, I saw tears roll down his face in the reflection of his rear view mirror. Manuella assured me later, he repeated this story word for word to every new fare, and to those he'd thought he'd not told before. His well of tears never dried up.

As a welcome to Tuscany, Manuella instructed Marco to drive by the Leaning Tower of Pisa. It was springtime — the early morning sun beginning to warm *Campo di Miracoli,* the Square of Miracles. And the ivory-white tower was exactly that: part of a miraculous and beautiful formation of buildings rising from the deepest meadow-green grass contrasted against a cloudless blue sky.

Other than vendors opening their stalls, there was not a tourist in sight. I came to learn to avoid at all costs the very same place in the height of the season when tourists swarmed and heaved like army ants between those medieval buildings.

Manuella led a sedate life in London, but that was not the case in Pietrasanta. From the moment we arrived at her small, humble hilltop house — complete with stunning sea views — nestled among fruit and olive trees, within walking distance of 'The People's Restaurant' that served the best *tordelli* (similar to ravioli) in the whole of Tuscany, the phone did not stop ringing. The locals, all of whom looked dirt poor — I was assured that was just the way they looked — flocked up the hill to greet her. Over several bottles of homemade wine, all caught up on the latest news. Like the fact that the local mayor, who had just been cleared of suspicion of various nefarious deeds, returned to his mayoral office, honour-bound to complete his term of duty.

As my mother's paella pan was always ready at hand, so too was Manuella's pasta pot in which only water for pasta was ever boiled. Within an hour, the pot was in use. Everyone had brought something to share. We ate a feast. Not once did my father's 'Less is Better' credo enter my head or spoil my appetite.

Manuella transformed herself from a sophisticated city woman into one of the locals. She put away her smart clothes and changed into worn trousers and manlike shirts, rolled up the sleeves, wore desert boots with a pair of thick socks. Irrespective of the season, she tied a cotton bandana around her head. She introduced me to the marble studio where she worked. Then I could understand the reason for the dress code. Marble dust was everywhere and if mixed with water, clogged up everything.

I saw her in a different light. I liked what I saw even if it were a more comfortable side to the sophisticated one I'd seen during our time in London. She introduced me to her fellow sculptors, who came from all corners of the globe, with English as the common language. In addition to improving my grasp of English, I began to pick up and speak Italian.

Before long, I had a number of artists first, then locals, come to me for adjustments. I have to thank Manuella for that. She was unstinting in her praise of my abilities. She proclaimed I had worked magic on her. The proof could be seen in her hands. The swelling had disappeared, her shoulders squared off and arm lengths were equal, all of which she showed off. So sculptors working with heavy machinery, in many cases with repetitive movements, were relieved from their aches and pains by my own craft.

When my patients heard their bones popping and cracking, and feeling better almost immediately, they put it down to magic. I got paid in cash, or I was offered by way of exchange my choice of a sculpture, free dental cleaning, homemade goat cheese, several litres of olive oil or wine, all of which I accepted. Except on one occasion: I declined a quick roll in the hay.

A group of us were on the lower slopes of Mount Sagro, a mountain easily identifiable from the beaches of Tuscany as it has, by contrast to other spiked mountaintops, a gently curved one.

We were enjoying a picnic Tuscan style. A barn used for overwintering a small herd of white cattle stood close by. Bales of leftover hay, piled up high to the chestnut beams, offered the perfect place for a quick private romp. But I had seen what faithlessness had done to my parents. I'd promised myself I would be faithful to Manuella. Indeed I wanted to be faithful to her. While she was older than me in chronological years, she had a vivacity and adventurous streak, with which sometimes I struggled to keep up. She was also my steady ship, navigating me to calm waters, opening up a whole new social life far different to that in Spain. And in a more immediate familial sense, a life far different to that I had so far experienced in my family.

My thoughts turned to my parents. My mother in particular, who had written saying she would join me in Pisa in a fortnight's time. I was at odds to know whether to invite her to Pietrasanta or not. There was no way of not introducing Manuella and my mother if she came to Pietrasanta. On one hand, I had no idea of what my mother would make of Manuella being a couple of years shy of her own age, or how Manuella would react to my mother's astonishing beauty.

I should not have bothered worrying. My mother solved it for me. She arrived unannounced three days later. She ensconced herself in the best hotel, whose every inch of inside walls were covered in muted, hand-painted frescoes. Like me, she fell in love with the square of Pietrasanta.

'It looks like a Hollywood film set,' she exclaimed, removing her sunglasses and then putting them back on again as if to get a better look and make sure her eyes were not deceiving her.

The square of Pietrasanta dates back to 1255. It forms a long rectangle running east to west and is dominated by several notable buildings: a red brick tower which stands thirty-six metres high, alongside is the elegant stone clad Cathedral of San Martino, next to it stands the Palazzo Moroni — a canary-yellow painted building with an elevated bridge staircase and which was once the city hall, ahead of these three edifices stands the façade of the Sant'Agostino church. Rising above and behind them all are the remains of a feudal fortification, accessible on foot up a panoramic path best described by the poet Giosue Carducci born in Pietrasanta in 1835 who thus wrote of his home town in a letter dated June 1877, '*I like Pietrasanta: a beautiful small city with a singular piazza, a cathedral worth of a great city, all against the back-ground of the Apuan Alps. And what a landscape all around! What mountains, what greenery, what shadows, what rivers, what cool streams running merrily under the chestnuts, olives, and orange tree, and the marble quarries flank the greenery on every side!*'

To beat the rising heat, my mother wore all white, even down to her sunglass frames. On top of her head, she wore a large and floppy straw-woven hat — and a white gauze cloth wrapped around its crown, which floated down the length of her back. Pearl and silver bracelets rattled at one wrist, while on the other she wore a large-faced wristwatch. Knowing her as I do, it was so she'd not have to squint or furrow her brow to see the time.

The locals fell in awe, dubbing her *la Sofia* of Sofia Loren fame, who at twenty-three was currently taking Hollywood by storm.

It was common for artists and sculptors to gather for an aperitif in the square before heading home for dinner. News soon got around that my mother, someone worthy to behold, had arrived. More than usual numbers of white-dusted artisans from the marble workshops tucked in between homes, galleries, clothing stores, bars, and restaurants, of which there are a surprisingly vast number, appeared.

To my astonished relief, Manuella and my mother took to each other. Within minutes, they formed a powerful bond respectful of each other's position in relation to me. Never once did either overstep the mark or tread upon the other's toes. Years later, when Manuella and I separated under less than pleasant circumstances, my mother wholly supported her even as each of Manuella's sins of omission were revealed.

For the week my mother remained, I acted as her tour guide. I took her to see the local Tuscan sights, all of which makes Pietrasanta such a desirable destination. We were invited out each night, as everyone wanted the honour of hosting my mother. I was surprised at my mother's energy. And, although I did not want to admit it, I saw more than just a few similarities between my mother and Manuella's personalities. I briefly wondered what Dr Giulia Hernandez would have made of that.

The more we did, the more my mother bloomed. I was exhausted and relieved when I dropped her off at Pisa airport. Only then I asked, 'Papa?'

'Everything remains the same,' she said her lovely mouth hardening into a thin line. And so the standoff remained. I thanked my lucky stars I was no longer involved with my parents' madness.

A couple of months later, after a middle of the night call — the one everyone fears — I flew to my father's side as he lay dying. He hung on until I arrived. I sat by his bedside holding his hand.

There were moments when I was not sure who comforted whom. Long silences were punctuated by condensed stories; some were fragments of other stories I'd heard before and had not taken much notice. They were spoken quickly, as if he was afraid they would run away before their ends. Those I remembered I helped him with, for he was getting the telling of them jumbled.

'Papa, the bull's name was *Toro de Semillas*.'

'Just checking, you haven't forgotten,' he said. 'And did I ever tell you about the most beautiful little bird in the world?'

I restrained a sigh and replied, 'No, Papa. Tell me about the most beautiful little bird in the world.'

He fell asleep before he began the story of the feisty hummingbird, which glowed like a burning coal and flew all the way from North America each winter to summer over in Mexico. I fell asleep with my head on the edge of the bed and awoke to his hand resting on my cheek.

'Alejandro. Are you asleep?'

'No, Papa.' I remained with my head on his bed.

'I have news.'

'Good news?'

'Yes and no.'

'So give me the good news first. It will help the bad go down.'

'I love you.'

'I love you too, Papa. And now the bad?'

'You are not my son.'

—————— ♦ ——————

The coroner could find no obvious reason for my father's passing. But the citizens of our town put his demise down to a broken heart. The blame for which they heaped at my mother's feet.

After his funeral, for which everyone turned out in their Sunday best, I went back to see Dr Hernandez. This time it was all about him and me. I celebrated that which we had had, wondered about what I thought we had had, and grieved for all that we clearly had not. During that hour, the only thing that appeared not to have shifted from its well-positioned place was the box of tissues.

And I recounted those last few hours during which my father made me promise I would not let my mother know that he knew I was not his son. He had known, he said, almost from the beginning. Words cannot describe my shock. First, I put it down to the meanderings of his mind. But such was his calm clarity, I had no reason to disbelieve him, though my face must have shown my incredulity.

'I never had a lot of, well . . . you know . . . .'

Although it was just the two of us, he lowered his voice, 'Sperm, and on top of that, I'm infertile,' he whispered.

We both needed a while to recover. With trembling fingers he removed his wristwatch.

'Tell me the time.'

'It is fifteen minutes past noon.'

'Or?' he said slipping back into how he taught me as a child to tell the time.

'It's twelve fifteen.'

'Good boy,' he said pressing the watch into my hand.

'It's yours. Take it.'

I did not argue. I turned the watch over and for the first time saw the faded inscription, *"To J A from J A with Love"* and further below in a flourish of exaggerated swirls, *"Forget Me Not"*.

The inscribed date was before my parents had met and married. Relieved to have something with which to change the subject, I asked, 'Who is the other J A?'

He did not answer. But said, 'Don't blame her. Forgive her. She gave birth to you. For that, I am eternally grateful. And, never forget, I love you as my own true son.'

'Write,' Dr Giulia Hernandez said. 'Write it all down. It will be cathartic. And let it be your legacy. Honour your past and that of your father's. Be proud of all the good things and the not so good things, too. It is what makes you who you are.'

———— ◆ ————

From the moment of my father's disclosure, his death, and during the funeral, I could not look at my mother or utter a civil word to her. She put it down to my grief. But creeping upon me, I began to understand something of what it meant to be an Expósito. Suspended before me were two haunted shadows that hung like sad moons.

Overnight, my mother turned frail. The first hint of silver threaded its way through her luxurious dark hair. Intent on punishing herself, she first revisited the minutiae of the wasted years she had held out on him, maintaining her ridiculous vengeful and unforgiving war. Second, she faced having to live on her own. And then, as it so often happens, the victim turns the villain into a saint. She deleted his indiscretions, placed him upon a pedestal and showered him with praise to all who would listen. Like Marco, the Pietrasanta taxi driver, my mother would repeat the same litany over again even to those who'd heard it all before. And neither did her well of tears dry up.

In accordance with society's expectation, my mother remained largely secluded in the family home. After a year, to the exact date of my father's death, she emerged. Wiser and quieter, with an air of sadness hovering around her, but ready to explore the new life widowhood offered. This included circling the world a couple of times in the company of several men. All appeared to be her lovers. Though some only slept beside her, grateful for the cover she provided, hiding the true nature of their sexuality.

And a fat man who tried to look like a man and in doing so all the more highlighted what he was: a eunuch. And it was with him, to my utter confusion, with whom she seemed to have the most deep-rooted relationship of all.

'He was a guard you know,' she'd say mysteriously, 'at a famous Moroccan princess's palace, many years ago.'

I questioned her on her choice of partners, lovers or not, and she put it to me one day saying, 'I don't want to be alone. I take what my money gets me.'

I had no idea of the value of my mother's wealth, but did know that she was a woman of independent means. The man I considered my father left the cattle ranch that he'd inherited from his parents to me. Since their deaths, no more bulls were raised. Its management as a beef-raising ranch was now part of a larger co-operative, which had required no assistance from him, and now, nor me.

Moreover, there was no need for fighting bulls. Though the bullfighting ring in Nuevo Laredo still stood, it had been closed. Rival gangs hijacked several Sunday afternoon bullfights. Not only did they shoot each other up, but shot the matador and his team. And the bulls, and the blindfolded horses too. I had considered going to see the ranch, but somehow life in Pietrasanta had a far stronger calling, as was my sudden and urgent need to write.

That my mother's lovers grew younger as she grew older, I could not comment upon. But I understood a little of the complications it brought about, as I too was living my life with someone, to put it baldly, quite older than me. And with each passing year, the difference became more noticeable.

I was at once hailed as the prodigal son returned and re-absorbed into the very fabric of the town of Pietrasanta, and especially by our hamlet neighbours. Manuella's humble house was a converted cow barn, with thick walls and small windows, meaning it remained cool in summer and warm in winter. I settled down into a routine that worked well for both of us.

Well before dawn, I'd ease out of bed, put on the coffee and sit down at the kitchen table to write. When I heard Manuella stir, I'd serve her coffee, get back into bed and lose myself in her warm slipperiness. By eight, she headed off to the sculpture studio, and I would prepare for my first clients of the morning. At noon, with the pasta pot on, she'd return, we'd have lunch, siesta and by four she headed back for the studio. I settled down to re-read and make changes to what I was writing.

It was not easy going. Many things were still so painful that I found myself writing about everything but the very things I should have been pouring out onto paper. Manuella never made an attempt to read what I was writing, but said, 'I'll read it the day it's a best seller'.

I was put out and took this as a mark of disinterest. It stung more than I cared to admit, as I'd engaged with her for endless hours, tracking her trials and tribulations with a new piece of problematic sculpture.

I would remember later, that it was the first crack that appeared in our relationship. Notwithstanding what I perceived to be a snub of sorts, I was relieved. I had decided to get over the sting of writing about the truths that still hurt. Finally they began to appear in black and white. Some truths long denied, I was to discover, were still best left unsaid.

Our winter evenings were spent in front of our, or friends' firesides. In summer, we barbequed, ate late, went for midnight swims in the sea. I would swim out, but for the reason of childhood fears, Manuella only paddled her feet in the lapping waves. When nature decided, we harvested grapes and collected olives, all of which, once processed, filled our bellies.

Manuella returned to London to check up on her house there and to make sure her and her mother's collection of sculptures remained intact. She used this time as her inspiration. She sketched ideas for future works and contracted new commissions. She caught up with her snobbish, and sometimes envious, English set of friends. They always showed surprise when discovering Manuella and I were still together.

I had forgotten almost all of my short stay in London — the grey clouds and cold weather had seen to that. Excepting for an obscure reason: my visit to the exotic glasshouses in Kew. This was a memory I treasured and often visited in my quieter moments. So, I remained quite content and alone in Pietrasanta. It gave us a break from each other, absence makes the heart grow fonder proving true in our case, but as time moved on, less so. I had a growing feeling that our relationship would have to end sometime. But like the proverbial frog in warming up water, I remained too comfortable to make the jump.

I never wanted to think of Diego. But the artists by whom I was now surrounded seemed to have unwittingly conspired against me. There was a larger than life size bronze statue created by Fernando Botero. He was a Columbian artist and regarded as a 'Son of Pietrasanta'. He had titled one of his bronze statues, 'The Warrior', which stood in its own mini island opposite Pietrasanta's Town Hall.

The Warrior was beyond chubby and his penis was tiny, disproportionate to the size of his body, serving to remind me, each time I passed it, of Diego.

Rosa was a different story. Not a day went by when I did not think about her and wonder where she was. Daily, my heart would involuntary clench in acute pain. I hoped with all my being that wherever she was, she would know that I had not forgotten her.

1929. It was a year filled with memorable events. The Vatican City became the smallest country in the world; Italian children were taught that loyalty to Fascism and God were one and the same; two hominid skulls with Neanderthal features were discovered outside Rome.

On the morning of March 29, another event would be added to this list. And for the Balducci family, their friends and neighbours in their medieval Tuscan hamlet, it would become the most remembered event of that year.

They were returning home from early morning Mass. Ignoring his mother's warnings, Giovanni Balducci sprang off the moving donkey drawn cart.

'Wait for me,' cried his sister Manuella as she scrambled after him when the cart came to a stop.

Guided by their grumbling bellies, they took a short cut to the kitchen's back door, passing under the arch, and entered the enclosed herb garden. Disappointment awaited them. Kitchen helpers flapped their aprons and cloths shooing them away. Not even the humble crusty heels of that morning's oven baked loaves were spared from a kitchen where the preparation of headier dishes were in hand. Mouth-watering aromas, intent on torture followed the siblings as they headed for the orchard.

Being a seven-year-old girl, Manuella was not the ideal playmate for her fourteen-year-old brother. But like an indelible shadow, she tagged after Giovanni never quite managing to catch up. Today was different. Not only did he slow down but reached for her hand. Despite his too-hot hand, she held on and they entered the orchard together.

Bee hums and bird songs filled the sun-warmed air. Spring blossoms smothered trees. Branches sprayed out, their tips touching, forming a dense canopy of pink and white. Standing tallest was the forbidden cherry tree.

Giovanni kicked off his sandals and shimmied up its trunk. He wedged his backside into the highest fork. Boughs lurched and cracked their protest under his weight. From previous attempts, resulting in scratched knees and palms, Manuella knew she could not follow him. She stood aside. In her sweetest voice she pleaded, 'Giovanni, please come down.'

'No. You climb up.'

'I can't. We shouldn't.'

'What are you afraid of — a little punishment?'

'Yes.'

'Baby.'

Her lips pursed. 'I'll tell on you,' she said. But the threat was met with silence.

She tried again. 'I'm counting. One . . . two . . . three.' Still there was silence.

Gazing up through massed clusters of blossom she could barely make out the soles of Giovanni's feet and gangly limbs disappearing into cotton shorts. Forlorn, she sat at the base of the tree. Then cheering herself up she began to fashion a bracelet of daisies — a peace offering to her brother.

A few disturbed blossoms drifted down. He called out in a lazy sing-song voice, 'Guess what I can see.'

'The sea,' she replied with a wistful sigh.

They lived only four miles from it, but she'd not yet seen the sea. The excuse was it had taken far too many — those who fished for a living and those unsuspecting of the dangers lurking beneath the surface, who paddled with pleasure at the waters edge.

'What does it look like?'

'An upside down, blue-side-up sky that moves.'

'Giovanni, Manuella,' one of their identical twin aunts called out.

Their aunts were their father's older spinster sisters, Carla and Marla. They could just as well have shared one name. For no matter whose name was called, both responded.

They were short and slim. They wore their hair scraped up and twisted into top knots held fast with an abundance of metal hair pins. Each twin had a spot — too large to be called a beauty spot — just above the top lip. As they grew older, the spots sprouted stiff grey hairs. When barely visible the twins tweezed the others' facial hairs with meticulous care.

Year round, they wore sensible, slightly too heavy lace up shoes, the style never changed. They favoured dark dresses over which they wore straight edged pinafores — a different colour for each day, except on Sundays and Feast days when they wore white.

From them, Manuella learned the reason why she had not yet been to the sea. There was nothing their aunts did not know.

'Dear Sweet, what are you doing?' one of the twin aunts asked helping her up from the grass and dusting off Manuella's short pink skirt covering a stiff tulle petticoat. 'Where is Giovanni?'

Manuella pressed a finger to her lips and pointed skywards with the other.

The twin aunt expelled an abrupt huff then yelled up into the white covered boughs, 'Giovanni, come down. You know you should not be in this tree.'

Their paternal grandfather who lived in heaven, had planted the only Morello in the orchard, marking his first son's birth. From it, the twin aunts made the region's best sour cherry preserve. These coveted bottles were traded for hard-to-come-by items. They were regularly counted and stored under their twin beds.

'I can't. I'm stuck.'

An aunt calculated the time before the family would gather for lunch. 'How are you stuck,' she yelled back.

Aunt and niece waited a few moments before Giovanni's voice floated down again.

'*Cara zia*, Dear aunt, 'it's bad. I don't feel well. I have a headache and I cannot move.'

With a click of her tongue she asked, 'Manuella, is this one of your brother's pranks?'

Manuella shrugged her shoulders to her ears and lifted her palms heavenwards. The aunt squinted at the sun's arc. It was almost dead centre to the intense blue sky. Her mouth hardened, but erring on the side of caution she said, 'Dear Sweet, go and find Pietro. Tell him to bring rope and a harvesting ladder . . . ,'

Before she could add 'quickly', Manuella had raced off.

Giovanni was rescued from the top of the cherry tree. Several field-workers' linked arms easily bore his weight. As they carried him into the house, Manuella trotted alongside, her face on the same level as his. They stared solemnly at each other.

Then unnoticed by the anxious women crowding the procession, he winked at her. It was their code: he *was* playing yet another prank.

Manuella was gripped in fearful awe; fearful of the punishment that would follow; awe for his disregard for the auspicious day — the day when the grown-up baby Jesus got nailed to the cross and died.

Reaching out, Manuella offered Giovanni the now crushed daisy chain. He took it, smiling his thanks. When laid on his bed his head skewered backwards. An attempt to move his head to a natural angle resulted in such a piercing scream of pain all hearts missed a beat.

The rabbits in their confined hutches scrambled over each other. The chained hunting dogs dropped back their heads and howled mournfully at the sun now past noon.

Preparations in the kitchen came to an abrupt halt. Platters of anti-pasti were hastily covered. Bundled mounds of hand-cut pasta would soon harden. The enormous pot of fragrant sauce, in its third hour of simmering was forgotten.

In the manner of the past, the doctor was summoned. His name was called passing from one household to another, until it reached his own.

With a still clean napkin tucked under his chin, he abandoned his lunch table. His moped — the only form of mechanical transport in the hamlet — coughed into life. He headed towards the Balducci family home; the loose exhaust alternated between splutters and explosions.

Padre Amadeo, having heard the doctor's name pass over his head, waited at the steps of the church. The doctor slowed, giving the priest just enough time to gather his clerical dress, execute a quick two-spring step and with a jump and twist of his lower body, land on the pillion seat.

The engine laboured up the winding dust road and stopped under the arched entrance to the stone house. The flock of chickens scattered, squawking and flapping their wings against a rainfall of pepper dust.

Manuella's parents remained with the doctor and priest in Giovanni's room. She knocked incessantly upon the locked door. The aunts each cupped one of Manuella's elbows and steered her to the hard bench in the gloomy passage. There they sat.

'It's just a joke,' she said. 'He told me so.'

Both aunts' fingers flew to Manuella's lips to silence her. During their wait the light darkened, blending sky and land into one. Rosaries appeared. Together, the aunts made the sign of the cross and intoned the words commencing the prayers of the holy rosary.

An uncommonly strong wind blew up. Shutters rattled, shook free from their latches and banged against the window frames. The first lightning cracked the sky open, releasing torrential rain. With equal force, the aunts' tears began to fall so hard to the marble floor they splashed back up. Before long, they were as sodden as the household washing flapping and tugging against the pegs secured to laundry lines. The storm lashed on. When it stopped, the church bell began to toll. By the end of the third toll, her aunts' well of tears dried up. A harrowing shriek was followed by a dull thud. Manuella's mother had fallen to the floor, bringing the net curtain surrounding Giovanni's bed down with her.

His spirit, Manuella's aunts told her, went straight to heaven, guided by angels and welcomed by the sound of heaven's trumpets.

'Did St. Peter really allow him into Heaven?' she asked.

'Yes,' replied one aunt.

'Even though he was sometimes naughty?'

'Yes,' replied the other.

'Does that mean I can be naughty sometimes too and still go to heaven?'

'No.'

'But . . . ,'

'*Basta*, enough of this conversation,' the aunts chorused.

She could not figure it. Everyone good went to heaven. Everyone bad went to hell. Giovanni had done bad things. And so had she. She was happy he was in heaven and not in hell. But she was happier he was not floating under an upside down, blue-side-up sky that moved.

Later, Manuella would suffer nightmares worrying that when she died St. Peter would forget to make the same mistake and send her to hell. Because if St. Peter did and sent her to hell where she rightly belonged, she'd be separated from her brother forever.

Holding a pot handle each, the aunts tipped the ruined Good Friday feast into the pigs eating trough. The pigs snuffled and snorted, and in an extraordinarily short time, the ruined feast, just like her brother, was gone.

Had anyone been outside at the moment of Giovanni's death, they would have seen the orchard vibrate to a single grief chord. Weakened by the torrential rainfall, spring blossoms dropped to the ground. No sour cherry preserve got bottled that year. The spaces under the twin beds went empty.

Giovanni's death changed everything. Her parents' relationship swung from a respectful one, the kind that comes with age and experience, to a tortured and pain-filled one. One night, Manuella woke to the sound of their raw and bitter argument raging back and forth.

'But I'm not able to bear any more children,' her mother cried.

'And I need an heir.'

'Manuella is your heir.'

'Only a male can inherit.'

'The law says the last surviving child, male or female inherits.'

'I don't care what the law says. I care about my family tradition. Only a male will inherit.'

Understanding the implication of the unspoken words, her mother cried, 'Get out.'

A week passed and one evening, after her mother had tucked her in, Manuella got out of her bed and crept to her parents' bedroom. She slipped into their large bed. When her mother came into the room, she did not have the heart to move her daughter back to hers. And in any case, she'd heard her husband's tread upon the landing. Quickly, she closed and locked the door.

Fed up with sleeping on a dusty sofa, he came to take up his rightful and comfortable place alongside his wife. He stood before the locked door.

He was dark, short, and wiry with a thick neck. A cigarette stuck out from the side of his mouth its pencil straight smoke trail rose up and dispersed against the faded frescoed ceiling.

'*Cara*, dear,' he said, 'Stop torturing me. You know I love you. From the moment I saw you. Please open the door.'

He was met with silence.

Manuella lay still pretending to be asleep. But through the forest of eyelashes obscuring her slit-open eyes, she watched her mother, willow tall and fair, rest her forehead and lay flattened palms — fingers spread — against the door to support her.

'Never has there been another,' came her father's voice muffled through the two-hundred-year-old chestnut wood.

Her mother's shoulders stiffened. She knew he'd had other women no different to his father. And both, more so when she and her mother-in-law had entered menopause.

This pattern of behaviour, Manuella's mother believed, was due to men's fear of bedding non-fertile women. That somehow it would affect them by reducing their own fertility, or, even more terrifying, render them wholly impotent.

But she'd been blessed. On the occasion of their last intimacy, a dream-like event, occurring whilst both still slept and more for the reason of familiar comfort rather than desire, Manuella had been conceived.

'*Cara*, please understand. This is something that must be done. Open the door. Let's discuss it.'

Her mother clenched and unclenched her hands to each of her husband's entreaties.

His implorations were still met with silence. He tried again, '*Cara*, in this matter my hands are tied. Can't you see this is not my choice but my duty?'

To his credit, as he craved his wife's understanding and blessing, he thought perhaps louder proclamations would soften her. Soon his nightly bellows resounded throughout the stone house and exhausting through the open slats of the night closed shutters, flowed over the gardens, breached the stone house's protective walls, rushed down the winding road, swirled around hamlet houses, and flooded the valley drowning out all other sounds with his voice, and he cared not who heard him embarrass himself so. But the silence continued. Loyalty to duty, greater than discretion and common sense, pressed him forward.

'My to-be-conceived son and his mother will live here. It's only natural for the boy to grow up in the home that he'll one day own. Surely,' he argued, 'you can at least understand that.' Message delivered, he turned away from the door.

Manuella's mother got into bed. She gathered her pretend-to-be-sleeping daughter into her arms.

Another week passed. His back and feet sore from too much standing, his voice hoarse and his patience spent, he declared, 'Okay that's it. Don't ever say I never warned you.'

His wife broke her silence. 'Then know this. I will leave. Manuella comes with me.'

Furious by his wife's intransigence to see his reason, and now, for the first time in their marriage, directly challenged, he called her bluff. His towering rage dwarfed her.

He yelled, 'Good. Go. Get the useless girl away from me.'

She was not fast enough. His words had sunk into Manuella's core long before she could clap her hands over her daughter's ears.

Manuella's father went ahead with his unilateral decision. As it was, he did not have to search long, hard, or far to find an unmarried woman.

───── ◆ ─────

Giovanni's passing had also paved the way for the elderly and infirm extended family members to let life go. Within a month of her brother's death, her paternal great uncle and two second cousins died. Rooms off the gloomy passage that had long been occupied emptied. Furniture was shrouded in dustsheets, shutters battened down, and doors locked.

'Dear Sweet,' one of the aunts assured Manuella, 'don't worry, the old people will take care of your brother. They now live all together in heaven.'

'In a house as big as ours?'

'Much bigger.'

Though she missed her brother dreadfully, she was not convinced of the benefits of living in heaven in even a bigger house than they had on earth. Now that she was an only child, she got to eat all the dessert she wanted.

She'd seen little of the nonagenarian members of her family confined to their bedrooms being mainly bedridden. But she accepted their full time carers as part of her extended family. Relieved of their duties, they returned to their own homes in hamlets close by. Of them, one returned the following morning with her unmarried niece in tow. Flaxen haired, rosy cheeked, and broad hipped.

Manuella's father lost no time. Like a rutting stag high on elevated levels of testosterone, he bedded the girl. The flesh-slapping sounds heard by all were loudest in her mother's ears. Almost to the date of the first anniversary of Giovanni's death, she gave birth to a stillborn boy. Within months, she was pregnant again, but miscarried.

Manuella's father could not believe his bad luck. His manhood was at stake and time nipped at his heels. Hedging his bets, he impregnated yet another young unmarried girl. This child too was lost. He blamed his wife. She maintained her silence.

Clearly possessed by the devil, with whom he accused her of being in cahoots, he re-doubled his efforts. He took to eating larger meals in hope of stemming his flagging energy. For by now a clear path had been beaten to the stone house. The news was official. The *'Padrone'*, Master, was in urgent need of a son.

Every self-respecting mother for miles around, eyes firmly fixed upon the stone house, brought their willing, coerced, or forced daughters to it. All trod carelessly through Manuella's mother's fragrant herb garden and arrived at the kitchen's back door. More often than not others were ahead of them. Face-offs culminating in caterwauling sent the semi-tame felines streaking for cover. Yet injuries were ignored. Spoils snared would be rich pickings indeed.

Manuella's father cursorily looked over the daughters. One, he self-righteously and promptly returned to her mother, reminding her of their own brief harvest encounter some sixteen years before. And then, even less cursorily, he put each applicant to the test.

The lean-to alongside the pigsty served as a repository for sacks of animal feed. Curious, the pigs turned their heads sideways and pressed a pink eye through what holes were to be found in the wooden panel separating them from the lean-to storage. They grunted in discordant rhythm to the staccato thumps upon the stacked and scratchy bags.

Manuella's mother removed herself as head of the household; she left her twin sisters-in-law in charge; she withdrew her wifely duties, and to a large extent the mothering of her daughter, too. Manuella and her new friend, Loneliness, drew closer.

Her mother was in equal measures heartbroken and angered by her husband's actions. That, and suffering the loss of her adored boy child — a suffering that would never end — she struggled from throwing herself into the deep well which beckoned, promising sweet oblivion from the madness of her life.

She took little comfort from Padre Amadeo, who refused to voice God's opinion, but whose lips pressed more tightly as the queue at the kitchen door got longer. The doctor, to whom she went in hope of receiving a tonic for her jangled nerves, had begun to make house calls in distant hamlets. He was not available unless it was an emergency and nerve tonics in his opinion did not qualify. The town's lawyer had yet to grant her an appointment. He could not find time to fit her into his suddenly busy schedule.

Turned away from holy, medical, and legal advice, her opinion cemented. Based on her husband's earnest yet less frequent roaring entreaties to the contrary — most likely due to physical exhaustion — she concluded she and her daughter had been rejected. It was simply a matter of time; they would be forgotten.

She went on to indoctrinate her daughter to expect that once a woman entered menopause, it was the end of her life as she had known it. Burdened with this knowledge, and even before she could celebrate her first menses, Manuella lived in fear of the day when she too would enter menopause. Worse, she accepted her fate that, one day she would be replaced by a younger child-bearing woman.

Under Italian law, a child born to a married union was acknowledged as being the husband's even though it was common knowledge the child had been fathered by another. Though no formal claim to the offender's family name and coffers could be made, informal compensation was negotiated. Land over money being the most requested settlement. Given this was the fastest way husbands could improve their lots, some coerced their wives into these acquisition-by-birth schemes.

So the peripheral edges of Manuella's family's large estates for generations had been nibbled down. It gave rise to a reduced shape on the land map housed at the local Town Hall.

Years later, when this devaluing system became clear to Manuella she raged against God and man. For money or land went only into the control of men.

Before Giovanni's death, attempts to conceal the fact that the Balducci siblings had several half siblings in their hamlet failed. A universal truth is that truth will out.

During harvest, all labourers were in the fields. If Manuella's father called out to her brother, several boys would respond, having the same name. Though firstborn sons were always named after their father, a later born son, as a mark of respect to their *Padrone* would be given his name. And it followed that sons fathered by the *Padrone*, were named after him too. So, it was understandable why a number of the hamlet's boys were called Giovanni.

Of course, not all born were sons. Daughters were called Giovanna. Thus ensuring, albeit an unofficial connection, firmly tied them all to Manuella's family tree.

True to her word, Manuella's mother left the family home for England whence she had originated. She bided her time until the next harvest season when all available hands, able or not, were well away from the immediate vicinity of the stone house.

Men with two trucks from the neighbouring town arrived. Well before the first of twelve bell tolls, furniture that had been sent by way of a dowry twenty-five years before, were lifted from their places. They left behind ingrained dust marks of their former positions.

Holding hands, mother and daughter walked down the gloomy passage made gloomier by the many closed doors. Under her breath Manuella recited the name of each person who had once lived in rooms behind those doors. When they passed Giovanni's room, she could not utter his name.

They were driven in one of the trucks to the port of La Spezia. Years later, during the Summer of 1945, when 23,000 Jewish displaced persons boarded ships, Israeli geographical maps would list La Spezia as *Shàar Zion* meaning Gateway to Zion.

Two hours later, mother and daughter boarded a cargo boat for England. In self-imposed exile from her marriage home, Manuella's mother returned to the place of her childhood home. She arrived with both children. One she led by hand. The other, she carried in her heart.

Her mother's family home was in Kew, the town in England famous for its Royal Botanical Gardens and stupendous Victorian glasshouses. They were greeted by a homecare nurse and led into her grandmother's bedroom. Manuella's mouth formed a little circle like a goldfish about to take a breath. She had never heard her mother speak English, and, until that moment, believed both maternal grandparents dead.

Her English grandmother did not recognize her only adult child. But upon seeing Manuella, a miniature version of her daughter, she screamed out Manuella's mother's name and collapsed. Her heels and elbows drummed against the floor. Her eyes rolled back showing white. The nurse hustled them out of the bedroom. The screaming stopped. That night, she died. Within days, all traces of the English grandmother, now truly dead, were removed.

After surreptitiously scattering her English grandmother's ashes over the roses at Kew Gardens, mother and daughter went to The Maids of Honour Tea House. Manuella experienced her first quintessential English afternoon tea. When they got home, they were in for a surprise. Their furniture from Italy had arrived.

From memory, Manuella's mother integrated the new with the old placing each piece of furniture in its original position. The house, nowhere near the size of their Italian home, was nevertheless, a large two storey, free standing Edwardian house. It had spacious and high-ceilinged rooms, and tall sash windows.

Once they settled into a routine, and after she began attending the local preparatory school, Manuella's mother, two years after the event everyone in the Tuscan hamlet would always remember, let go and grieved. She grieved for her golden boy child. She grieved for the man she still loved, but no longer recognized. And she grieved for the loss of her life as she'd once known it. In order never to forget any of it, she lived in the past, only stepping into the present to manage the most fundamental elements of everyday living.

By contrast, Manuella's old life was soon overtaken by her new one. She grew up fast, taking control of those things she should not have. She became adept at role reversal. In many ways, the mother-daughter couple appeared normal. Though Manuella's mother was labelled as an eccentric, returned home from an extended sojourn to foreign lands.

Later, Manuella concluded eccentricity was not to be lauded; it simply being a convenient excuse not to deal with the awkwardness of madness.

As the years rolled by, she thought less of her father, her identical twin spinster aunts, and the large stone house in Italy. On those few occasions when she bought their past life up, her mother reached for the gin bottle — never far from hands' reach. Thus Manuella gave up trying to revisit their past together. Her mother had assumed exclusive rights to their memories.

But each night, Manuella touched the framed sepia photograph of Giovanni on her bedside table and whispered, 'I'll never forget you.'

The rest of her childhood and teenage years were blurred. When Manuella graduated from art school her mother was into the final stages of alcohol addiction. There was no point in pretending to hide her problem anymore.

The day her mother died of mass organ failure, Manuella called her father. Upon hearing the phone being picked up she said, *'Babbo?'* using the Tuscan dialect for daddy, a word she'd not uttered aloud in more than seventeen years. One of her father's idiosyncrasies was he always waited for the other party to speak first irrespective of whether he'd made the call or was responding to an incoming call.

'Manuella,' his voice rasped. He was still smoking.

In spite of time lost, their shared DNA kicked in. It knocked them both hard in the chest. It took a while before either recovered enough to speak. In the ensuing silence, they listened with comfort to the familiar harmony of their breath. And with each breath, the long lost years fell away.

To her enormous disbelief, but equal relief, Italian first stuttered and then flowed smoothly from her mouth. She filled him in on his wife's passing. From him, she learnt the twin spinster aunts had died, too. In matching coffins, they were no longer not only indistinguishable, but unrecognizable — for their spots turned red, had grown, and covered most of their faces.

Her father was companion and servant-less, rattling around in the big house alone.

'*Cara mia, tornare a casa*, my dear, come home,' he said and put the phone down.

She carried her mother's ashes and a half life-size carving of Giovanni back to Italy. With her father — older, slighter than before, and a burning cigarette sticking out from the side of his mouth — they scattered her mother's ashes over Giovanni's grave. Her father laid claim to the sculpture. She let him live with Giovanni's uncanny likeness.

Manuella took stock. While the house remained large by most standards, it seemed to have shrunk in size. Broken or missing terracotta tiles caused the roof to leak; in one section, a chestnut beam finally succumbed to the wood-eating worm, and had cracked and sagged; copper drain pipe seams had split, permitting gushing rainwater to pour down and soak the walls through; missing window panes had been stuffed with wads of assorted cloths; shutters hung askew or had disappeared altogether.

The groves of unpruned olive trees closest to the house were disfigured with twisted branches. Wild, thorn-wielding brambles overwhelmed the orchard. The sour cherry tree was slowly being squeezed to death by rampant ivy reaching into its very top-most branches.

Glorious Tuscan sunshine highlighted the decay, including several feral felines whose poor physical condition caused her to weep. But her body joyfully responded to the sun and, taking its warmth and energy, she peeled off one English layer after another.

Manuella's return did not go unnoticed. Within hours, the large kitchen was filled with welcoming hamlet residents. Pietro was the first. She kept her mouth from falling open when she realized how similar he looked to her father, for they were after all, half brothers. With tears running down his weather beaten face, he clasped Manuella in a bear hug. He roughly kissed her cheeks and then kissed her again.

Later, a wafting aroma woke her childhood belly, caused it to grumble and drew her outside. At one end of the long table that once daily seated thirty, stood a dish of fragrant tordelli. Alongside, a half jug of cold *frizzante* wine and an oven-baked loaf of chewy bread. Hand-picked strawberries spilled from a cone twisted out of paper.

An ache, until then deeply buried, surfaced and knocked the breath out of her. She shut her eyes not so much for the loss of breath, but against this memory blazing brighter than the sun.

⸻ ❖ ⸻

Every day, drifting smells enticed Manuella and Giovanni's bellies with culinary inclinations of their own to return home. They rushed to be seated first at the table. The pecking order at mealtimes was this; those who sat closest to the top of the table got served first, those who finished first, were offered seconds first. And no excuse was accepted for a late arrival. Because, as their twin aunts said, 'If the sun always knows its place at midday, so should you.'

And to make sure they did not forget the time, the church bell announced midday with twelve tolls. That gave everyone enough time to be seated. As the sun took its seat in the sky, a steaming platter of tordelli was placed on the table. Unless of course, something out of the ordinary happened — like an earthquake or a death. At the mere hint of which, both aunts, in perfect synchronization, would make the sign of the holy cross.

Manuella opened her eyes. Her father appeared and just as the twelfth toll ended, they sat down at the table — she in her former place, her father, in his. And the ghosts from the past at theirs.

That afternoon, unbidden, women arrived armed with buckets, cloths and brooms. Within hours, years of dust got dusted away. What could be swept and polished was diligently swept and polished. Her childhood bedroom was aired and cleaned.

Linen from the deep wardrobe in which she and Giovanni hid in an attempt to escape Sunday Mass was retrieved. All was washed in the small stream flowing at the bottom of the long road leading to the stone house. For the rest of the afternoon, it dried in the sun draped over rosemary bushes imparting their natural scent into the fibre of the linen.

Pietro and a gang of former fieldworkers and their sons, some of whom were her half brothers, arrived. They hacked down lianas studded with vicious thorns and set alight piles of undergrowth debris. They crowned the olive trees. Relieved from the dead weight of too many and too heavy branches the trees breathed once more. Ivy tendrils as thick as a man's arm stifling the sour cherry tree were sawn through. Within days the ivy drooped and then died. The cherry tree lived on for another decade or so.

That night, disturbed by closed door hinges grating open, and floor-boards creaking, she left her room. Guided by unseen hands she walked along the pitch-black corridor, and missed knocking into the hard bench. The door to her parent's bedroom stood ajar. The light of a full moon slipped through the shutter slats. Her father lay on her mother's side of the bed. He cradled the stiff and cold sculpture whispering her mother's and brother's names. Caught in moonlight, silvery tears ran down his face, pooled in the hollows of Giovanni's eyes until, overfilled, ran down his marble face, too.

In seeing her father embrace the statue of Giovanni in the place where she had once slept cradled in her mother's arms, a truth was revealed. Her mother had given up her life in Italy to protect her. For within the invisible threads connecting the males in her family, there was no place for Manuella. That truth which her mother had tried to shield her from, now stared up at her.

By counting the number of steps (which were less than when she was a child), Manuella retraced the path to her childhood bedroom. On her bed, she curled herself into a ball. Her old friend, Loneliness, embraced and comforted her, while she accepted on a visceral level, it would have been better had she, and not Giovanni, died.

By the next morning, Manuella vowed she'd never permit this absurd patriarchal division between the sexes be visited upon her children — simply by not having any.

Despite her father's rejection of her, she took up her role of being a dutiful daughter — whether he had wanted and loved her as a daughter or not.

The rest of that year followed the same progress as a boat riding the waves of a stormy sea. Manuella's brain was crammed full of jumbled emotions, activities, and decisions to be taken. The hard part was understanding her father's finances. Stubborn and proud, he was reluctant to reveal the dire state of his affairs. Once she had convinced him to hand over the dusty ledgers, haphazardly entered since her and her mother's departure, she understood why. He was broke.

The marriage bed mattress in good years was always raised several inches higher than normal. This being the most common place where Italians then hid their money. But not only had the marital mattress returned to its normal height, it sank forlornly in the middle showing clearly there were no cash reserves to prop it up at all.

Several of Manuella's half siblings had leaned on her father to finance schemes, all of which had failed. Her father sheepishly alluded to women who also had managed to inveigle money from him. Worse, she learned that to keep her mother and herself in England, her father had sold off what land he could.

Each sale had cut his heart. Their family land dated back to the very first person to whom it had been presented as a gift for loyalty shown to the Medici family. They still had the original copy dated 1450.

But, her father tried to reassure her, his sorrow was because he had lost his wife and daughter, not because of the loss of the land. Manuella's lips flattened tight holding her tongue fast.

According to the lawyer, Manuella's father never did sire the son with a single woman, to whom he promised to recognize and leave everything. Thus Manuella, would still in the event of her father's death, inherit. But her inheritance would be an arm-long list of debts for which she would become solely responsible including what was left of the pitiful family lands and a large crumbling house that needed millions of lire to restore to its former glory. Against

Italians' ingrained belief of keeping property within the family at whatever cost, they sold.

An American, who had been one of the soldiers whose platoon had liberated Pietrasanta on May 2, 1945, returned to show his family the medieval town with which he'd fallen in love. When he retraced his steps along the route connecting one mountain top village to another, he was recognized and welcomed.

He and his family were pressed into drinking local wine and eating platters of home-bottled vegetables preserved under oil or vinegar and slices of home-cured wild boar. It was during his umpteenth glass of viscous lemon liqueur burning his throat that he heard the stone house was up for sale.

By the next afternoon, he had signed the 'promise to buy the house' document. A year later, the transaction was completed.

Manuella and her father kept a parcel of land upon which stood a former cow barn facing the sea. The barn, Manuella was informed, had been the hiding place of guns and ammunition during the war. After the war, it became the home of a local woman. She provided a service of a different sort.

Fed up by their husbands' nocturnal wanderings — who claimed their affliction of sleepwalking was caused by something in the mountain water that only affected men — the woman was run out of the hamlet. Wives chased her down the road their brooms held aloft. Their menfolk, sons included, downed tools and regretfully watched the fiasco wind out before them.

With the help of Pietro and several others, the barn was developed into a one-bedroom cottage with a deep, covered summer terrace for Manuella. They purchased a ground floor apartment in the old part of Pietrasanta for her father. From here, he could walk everywhere and take lunch at the local eatery whose prices were less than half for card-carrying members.

Her father whiled away his hours with friends over too many glasses of wine at their local bar. They played cards and argued about old times. His stalwart cronies were the lawyer who had had no time for Manuella's mother and the doctor who had diagnosed Giovanni's dying of meningitis and considered prescribing nerve tonic as a non-emergency.

Padre Amadeo was often seen crossing the town square of Pietrasanta. He still refused to voice God's opinion unless the sinner knelt within the confines of the holy confessional. For as long as he'd known Manuella's father, the lawyer, and the doctor, none had bent their knees for the reason of forgiveness in the last fifty years.

'Manuella, my child,' he said, his rheumy eyes lit up as he grasped her hands in his. Seeing the priest caused her memory bank to jolt. Out slipped the very best kind of memory — rainbow airy infused with bubbling innocence and joy. She shut her eyes. Giovanni materialized and stood alongside her and the priest. He placed his hands over theirs. Altogether they entered this memory.

◆

Some weeks before his passing, Giovanni had found an abandoned egg nestled in a tuft of grass.

'Phew,' cried Manuella pinching her nose. 'What is it?'

'Stay away,' Giovanni warned waving at his sister. Using a long stick, he poked and prodded further opening the cracked shell.

'Ow,' they cried in unison as defensive tears welled their eyes protecting them from the sulfur's sharp sting. In a fit of horrified giggles, they raced away to a point where they could inhale again and their eyes stopped weeping.

Spellbound they returned to assure themselves of the abominable stench.

'But what is it?' asked Manuella remaining on the outskirts of the invisible circle where the odour was just bearable.

A thoughtful look passed over Giovanni's face.

'Tell me.'

'Later.'

In the same week, the household turned upside down.

'Where is the darning needle?' asked a perplexed housemaid.

'In the mending basket where it always is,' replied one of the twin aunts.

Not wanting to contradict either twin — everyone knew they accessed extraordinary powers forbidden by God — the housemaid turned the basket upside down and emptied its contents onto the table.

'What are you doing?' cried an aunt. Thimbles and cotton reels scattered. 'It's in the basket. It's always in the basket.'

Her face paled. She whispered, 'Then, it's disappeared.'

Over the next few days there was a sharp decline of eggs from the flock of hens. The twin aunts' poultry knowledge was put to the test.

'What do you think?' asked one of the other while holding the best laying hen, plump and glossy feathered upon her forearm, her fingers curved around its scaly legs.

'She looks fine.'

'Then why has she stopped laying?'

The aunts' brows furrowed. Their common sense told them one thing. But nature was telling them another. They stared mournfully at the empty nest boxes. Ignoring their common sense, their oldest but still best laying hen did not escape having it's neck wrung. But not before they had hypnotized it into a state of complete relaxation. For good measure they selected and hypnotized a few more and wrung their necks too.

The aunts' worries did not stop there. Normally the carcasses were destined for the stockpot.

'But what if there is something else wrong?' asked one aunt. 'Something bad inside we can't see?'

Again they ignored their common sense. Instead of relegating the carcasses to the stockpot, they dug a deep hole and buried them. So not even the hunting dogs or semi tame felines benefitted.

Padre Amadeo visited the stone house far too often, according to Manuella's mother and aunts. Once a month he celebrated home Mass for the older members of her family who were unable to go to church on Sundays.

Days before his arrival, the sisters-in-law began to chafe with irritation. Home Mass broke into the tightly controlled day-to-day running of the large household.

Padre Amadeo brought with him a large amount of altar paraphernalia. A chalice, paten, candles and candlesticks, wooden cross, an assortment of cloths including the napkin used to wipe the lip of the chalice, a jug each for wine and water, a bowl to wash his hands, and vestments. All of which had to be unpacked. Then cleaned, polished, and re-packed by day's end.

He laid out the articles in order of use on a specially-provided table covered by a starched, hand-edged cloth. It was Manuella's task to pick flowers and arrange them in a vase as part of the altar table decoration.

First, the devil needed chasing. To purify the air, Padre Amadeo swung the thurible suspended from chains, in which incense burned. It created a pall of smoke which further blackened the faded frescoed ceilings. There the pall hung suspended until cross-breezes blew it away. Each time it happened, Manuella's mother and aunts vowed it would be the last.

But before Mass could be celebrated, the sins of the elderly had to be confessed and pardoned. Padre Amadeo sat behind a three-paneled lattice-work screen. A carer wheeled each family member one by one to the screen. Confession began.

Although they claimed deafness, at these times the elderly family members' hearing reversed.

Zio Angelo, (a paternal great uncle) began long before he was invited. 'Bless me Father for I have sinned . . . .'

After, followed a rapid-fire litany of sins, starting with the very first. Given he was ninety-two years old, it took a while before he finished.

Padre Amadeo interrupted. He'd explained to Zio Angelo his soul had already been cleansed of those ancient sins. Zio Angelo took no notice.

But when a family member interrupted saying it was another woman whom he'd bedded, and not the one he claimed, Zio Angelo argued back.

The elderly family members were anxious for their turn to recant and receive absolution for their sins. They were coming to the end of their race and knew they could not pass the finish line with a single stain on their souls. But eager to set the record straight, confession was put on hold while the facts got sorted. Disputes, settled or not, and some having no bearing on the argument to hand also got thrown in.

At these times, family secrets had a habit of sneaking into the open. Hopeful, they hung about waiting to be claimed. But like the smoke pall, they would get blown out of the opened windows only to reappear at the next month's confession. Occasionally, someone foolish enough would pipe up and acknowledge one as theirs. But most did not.

Confession would end just before lunch was served. After everyone napped and upon rising, took part in the home Mass. Once Mass was over Padre Amadeo needed to restore his energy.

He helped himself to a tray of the aunts' delicacies and several glasses of homemade wine. While Padre Amadeo fortified himself, mother and aunts radiating irritation, cleaned and re-packed the articles and vestments. When the last item was packed, and knowing it would be a month before the process would be repeated, they sighed with relief.

While the sisters-in-law saw to the repacking, Giovanni and Manuella spied on Padre Amadeo. They carefully counted the number of times he filled his glass. When he reached the tenth, the children were in for a treat.

He'd glance left and right making sure no one was around. He'd place his palms on the table to support himself. Leaning forward and then to the left, he'd raise his right buttock letting loose a trumpeting fart.

The sound never failed to thrill them. And the smell never failed to horrify them.

Whether it was the noise or the odious smell, the semi-tame felines would rise as one and slink away. But Padre Amadeo's nose would crinkle. Then his nostrils would flare open. He'd breath in his own gaseous fumes with great satisfaction.

With the daylong home Mass almost over, Giovanni slipped one of the needle punctured sun heated eggs under a cushion. It was the cushion upon which Padre Amadeo's ample buttocks would come to rest. Only this time, to the siblings' dismay, their mother and aunts having completed the repacking sooner than usual, joined him.

As Padre Amadeo sat down the eggshell cracked. Muffled under the cushion it sounded exactly like a single forceful fart. A sulfuric wave of tsunami proportions erupted from under Padre Amadeo. The semi-tame felines streaked off.

Mother and aunts jerked backwards with the force of the assault. Their eyes smarted producing instant waterfalls of tears. Blinded and unable to breathe, they clutched at their throats, rising from the table as one. They fell over each other, further tripping up on an upturned chair.

Terrorized by whatever had occurred under his buttocks, Padre Amadeo remained seated. His nostrils quivered but did not flare.

When he thought it safe, he eased himself away from the table. He left not having a single drop of wine. Nor one of the delicacies he could pop into his mouth faster than the aunts' remaining chickens could peck.

Holding his nose and daring not to breath, Giovanni rushed to remove the evidence from under the cushion.

Conjecture swung wildly. Soon, the aunts through the process of elimination and helped by the return of the yolk-encrusted darning needle, discovered the culprit. They set aside their remorse for their too-early killing of the oldest egg-laying hens. For the two-month home Mass reprieve, they slipped Giovanni a double portion of dessert.

'God Bless you my child,' said Padre Amadeo making the sign of Holy Cross above her head. He walked away, crossing the square. Manuella started her new canary-yellow Vespa motor-scooter and with a much lighter heart than she'd felt in years, her spectral brother riding pillion, she rode off. She wound her way up to the little house nestled between olive trees, which had a deep summer terrace with a lovely view of the Mediterranean sea.

Three years passed before Manuella was free to go in search of her dreams. Finding them was not difficult. They had been close by patiently waiting. And just as neither sibling ever forgot the other, she'd not forgotten her dreams — as they had not forgotten her.

RosaMina arrived in London on a Saturday and on the first full weekend Diego had free. It was also pouring rain. It did not take rocket science, or the fact that he was studying medicine, to figure that RosaMina running to the bathroom to throw up had nothing to do with anything she had eaten.

Diego surprised RosaMina with his calm acceptance of the fact that he was the likely father of the child and, less likely, his father. Immediately, he set about exploring every inch of her already changing body. He took great pleasure in her enlarged breasts and nipples. He sucked away at them almost as though he was the child.

RosaMina bore this as best as she could. Although in truth, she wanted to slap him away from her. Gritting her teeth, she held back. Plan A was successfully in place. But there still remained parts of Plan B, which unknown to Diego, required his participation to be completed. As if he were reading her mind, Diego caught RosaMina again by surprise.

'Don't worry,' he said. 'I'll arrange a blood test for all of us. The results will give you a reasonable idea. But RosaMina, whether I am the father or have a new half sibling, I am not taking responsibility. Nor will my parents ever know. Is that understood?'

RosaMina stared at him for a moment too long. He reached for her. She flinched waiting for the painful flick of his thumb and forefinger to land somewhere on her body. His preferred place was her left breast.

Diego quirkily wore his family signet ring on his index finger. It was heavy, in yellow gold, and studded with rubies where the band crossed through the shield. RosaMina believed he wore the ring on this finger deliberately — that the added weight gave his fingers more flicking power. When his fingers got too fat for the ring, he wore it on a chain around his neck. RosaMina's belief proved wrong. The forceful pain inflicted by the ring-less index finger, was not reduced.

She nodded and tried to hold back tears filling her eyes. Normally, he took pleasure in seeing her response to the pain inflicted upon her. But this time, he took her tears as gratitude. So he surprised her for the third time in the space of a few hours. Instead of a flick, he ran his hand over her buttocks in a caress.

'*Mi putita dulce,* my sweet little whore, don't worry. I will still take care of you,' he said with a tenderness she had never heard before.

'But . . . ,'

She sighed internally. It was inevitable. With Diego there was always a compromise. The outcome always weighed in his favour. He was like a bottomless pit. No matter how much was poured in, it remained empty.

He continued, ' . . . as long as you take care of me.'

She thanked him with feigned thanks. She had learned to do this well. If Diego did not hear a genuine ring of gratefulness in her voice, he'd fly into a rage resulting in more finger flicking or worse. To her relief, her thanks rang true to his ears. He was pleased. So pleased, it gave him cause, and these are his own words, 'to have another go again'.

In the beginning, RosaMina thought of Diego as an excited puppy only caring to play, eat, and sleep. But she was wrong. His immature façade hid a keen intelligence, with which, despite his short, stubby fingers, he achieved and was recognized early on for his exceptional surgical skill. Families with children born with deformities or, as a result of accidents, adored the young surgeon. He was their God. For he gave new life to their own.

But both his intelligence and skill concealed many of his insecurities. She had learned of the seven deadly sins and their counterbalances, the seven virtues, in the orphanage. Diego was afflicted with six of the seven deadly sins. For slothful he was not. Of six, his three constant sins were lust, envy, and gluttony.

Unbeknown to RosaMina, she was not the only recipient of his sexual advances. He was welcomed at several brothels and, in true Diego fashion, tried out all the girls several times over.

Envy still caused him to reference Alex during his intimate moments with RosaMina. It drove her first to distraction, then pity for him. His envy of all people and things permeated his every waking moment. It resulted in a relentless need to control everything and everyone around him. And for sure, if things were not carried out exactly to order, a punishment soon followed.

On one level, terror of the punishment conquered any possibility of RosaMina mentioning the puny size of his penis. Or the pleasure it was unable to provide. Yet, on another level, she foolishly challenged him. She thought she could play him at his game. But he was always way ahead of her. He had already figured the outcome, even before she left the starting line. He controlled RosaMina like a mere puppet. It took her years to realize she was no match for him.

In RosaMina's head, Diego was Plan B and as yet not complete. One way or another, she and her child were going to be okay. With each step taken forward, RosaMina feathered her nest. She kept her eye firmly fixed on her long-term goal. Had she known her mother's history, she would have realized that in this, she was no different from her mother's nest feathering.

The pendulum of hope and anguish stilled. It gave her a welcome break. She was able to focus on the last few months of her pregnancy. She watched the BBC children's programs and began to learn English. Soon she became mesmerized by the antics of Lucille Ball in the television show, 'I Love Lucy'. She simply had to know what Lucille Ball was saying to cause such a constant uproar and laughable consternation.

She realized her English had improved on the day she caught herself laughing out loud at Ms Ball. It was a sound so rare she stopped almost as soon as she started. Thinking about it, RosaMina could not recall a single time in her life when she had laughed. But alone, in the private confines of her apartment, she joined the river of clipped studio audience laughter.

When she was not watching Ms Ball, and weather permitting, RosaMina took to walking in Richmond Park. She never went without taking a bag of bread and fed the ducks at The Pond. Always remaining at a safe distance, she admired the herds of Red and Fallow deer that roamed free.

Through the windows of White Lodge, a Georgian house of grand proportions, she glimpsed young dancers practicing to the ballet piano melodies.

Wending her way through Richmond Gate, she passed The Royal Star and Garter, a home for injured soldiers. On sunny days, men sat in their wheelchairs, many with their war decorations pinned to their chests. Some chatted. Some sat apart and silent. Despite missing limbs, cheeky whistles erupted at the sight of any female. It was a great tonic for all women passing by, irrespective of age or beauty. As her belly grew, whistles stopped coming her way. All sorts of hats, caps, and berets were doffed instead.

The town of Richmond was a shopper's paradise. She purchased the minimum essentials she needed for herself and everything required for the child she was carrying. She had sworn to save money, ensuring the future financial safety and security of her child. In doing so, she became frugal regarding her own needs, almost to the point of neglect.

The Royal Botanical Gardens, Kew, one station stop away from Richmond, also became a favourite. Particularly the exotic Victorian metal and glass hot houses. The Palm House had just re-opened to the public, having undergone its first refurbishment since its construction. Each time she entered the curved wrought iron structure that soared to dizzying heights, she felt she had walked into a glass cathedral — but one which instead of God, paid homage to exotic palm trees of the world.

She discovered a well-camouflaged bench where she would sit hidden among the green foliage. Heat rose through the iron gratings underfoot, warming her. As she relaxed so too did the child in her belly. It was the most satisfying and peaceful period of her life. The only thing that marred this idyll was Diego. He came back to the apartment at all odd times. To coin his phrase, "can't fall pregnant again, now can you", and would, ignoring her increasing belly, be all over her.

Carmina's birth was easy. RosaMina was overwhelmed with amazement as she held her newborn daughter in her arms. For the first time, pure love made itself known to her, in great big solid dollops. She never doubted she had made the right decision. But now she was thrilled. RosaMina could not imagine not having her child in her arms.

Before Carmina's birth, RosaMina had sown some seeds. She was putting her final step of Plan B into place. She'd discovered Spain had passed a law allowing people with the surname Expósito to change it to anything they wanted, for free and no questions asked. She had mentioned this to Diego as a snippet of information she'd read. A few weeks later and right on cue, Diego suggested she change her surname. When she hinted she'd use his surname, he said, 'It's a free country. Use whatever name you must.'

But he had smiled. He took it as a mark of respect. And Diego liked to be shown a lot of respect. Thus she became known as RosaMina Rivas.

Being a single mother in England was frowned upon. But nothing like the frowns the small town of Medina del Campo would have produced. Moreover, if she had given birth in Spain as an unmarried mother, as a matter of course, her child would have been taken from her. On the birth register, she carefully wrote her daughter's name, Carmina Rivas.

The day came when Diego arranged for them to have blood samples taken. Their blood types were compared to see if there was a parental link between Diego and Carmina. Parents with both O blood type can only produce a child with an O blood type. Both Diego and RosaMina tested positive for B blood type. In this scenario a child can have either B or O. And Carmina's blood type was O. According to Diego, his father and mother were B. So Carmina's paternity remained questionable.

For a heart-stopping moment, RosaMina thought Diego would throw her out. That she would have to resort to living on Plan A only. But as promised, he did not. Catching her unawares, he asked, 'So who do you think Carmina's father could be?'

She made reference to one or two men.

'Is there a possibility Alex is Carmina's father?'

If she had seen the eerie, steady glint in his eye, she would have known something bigger was at stake. But she had not. She murmured there was a slight possibility. He continued to lead her down the path.

'Well, it can't be Alex's father. And this you should know.'

'What do you mean?'

'José produces little sperm.'

In a second, she was transported back to her first days in The House. Sperm quantity was not something one could see through the mirrors into each girl's room. When she became José Salazar's purchase, she had nothing to compare against José's. Each man's sperm, after José, was different. She had given no thought to the differences.

'And anyway, he is infertile.'

Her mind raced on. Both Madam and Berta must have been aware of José's condition. For Berta did not bother to give her a sprinkle of Blue Cohosh during the first year with José. When open season started, she had begun to take the powder. But not being fond of fruit, she ate hardly any of it. And then none at all.

'How do you know?'

'José consulted my father.'

'Whatever happened to doctor-patient confidentiality?'

'Bah,' Diego said, waving his hand in the air with a dismissive gesture.

The crease between her eyes appeared. But given Diego's closeness to his father, it was understandable that such private information could be easily gotten hold of, or shared. As soon as she thought of Diego's father, she had an unwelcome flashback — she'd momentarily forget who was on top of her — Dr Jerardo Rivas or his son Diego. For between the sheets, father and son were alike. The moment the Jerardo-Diego flashback entered her conscious mind, she deflected it back out into space. She had no time for such memories. The crease disappeared.

But she never had the same reaction to any flashback regarding José or Alex. That father and son pair was different. As were her memories of them. For each, she had a separate, special place in her heart. Then it hit her — and despite its enormity, no crease appeared at all; if José was infertile who was Alex's father? Was José aware that his son was not his son? And more to the point, was Alex aware that José was not his father? RosaMina dared not question Diego. She knew she would in turn suffer another tirade of ridiculous questions.

But the importance of the fact that Alex was possibly a half Expósito was not lost on her. Her immediate reaction was one of acute pain and extreme sadness for him.

RosaMina was pleased to know José Salazar was out of the running. And that now with the blood test results, both Rivases were almost out of the running, too. That left only a handful of men, and Alex.

She regretted having sold her notebook. A short and rotund detective had paid her a call. He came under the guise of being a new client. But quickly confessed he was looking for information on a suspected philandering husband. She had sold the notebook for a good price. But having the notebook to hand now would have helped her remember the names of other likely possible fathers.

As ever, the pendulum swung towards hope that the father of her child was Alex. If he was, RosaMina prayed the Gods would see fit and arrange, somehow, for Carmina to know her father.

But it was Diego who raised the odds against this probability. He did not care who Carmina's father was. He simply wanted to conjecture and assume that Carmina was his child. Not difficult, now they carried the same surname. But, more importantly, he wanted one other in particular to know that he, Diego Rivas, had had RosaMina. And all told, far more times than Alex ever had.

To this end, and not relying solely upon conjecture, he'd paid Cristal to let slip this information to Alex when he went to The House in search of RosaMina.

RosaMina and Diego settled into a routine. Diego came to visit at every opportunity between studying and writing exams. He lived in a shared student apartment close to the hospital and he still worked part time. He did not have to work, for his parents had more than sufficient means. But he did so in order to be better than everyone else.

Diego opened a joint account in 'their shared surname'. RosaMina could draw out the generous allowance and he never questioned what she spent it on. What Diego did not know was that RosaMina had a joint account in her and Carmina's names.

When Diego arrived, RosaMina was obliged to leave Carmina with a neighbour who took children in for a few hours. Carmina screamed and squirmed her little body like a worm. But RosaMina had no choice. All the while she serviced Diego, RosaMina forced her thoughts away from Carmina. She did not want anything but good and pure to enter her daughter's innocent life.

RosaMina saw no other men. She had no desire or need to. Her life revolved around Carmina and when Diego would put in an appearance. He came to RosaMina more tired and fatter than before. Should the time between his visits lengthen, RosaMina became anxious. And despite often wishing he would magically die, she was, to her disgust, relieved to see him.

A link far stronger than love held them captive and dependent upon the other. Twenty years later, psychologists would recognize a new disorder — Stockholm Syndrome — and as much of the criteria required to be labelled as such, RosaMina and Diego fit.

Although RosaMina viewed Diego as a child in an adult body, and in many ways treated him like one, she was interested in his work and studies. When he passed each exam, top of his class, they celebrated. Not out, in a restaurant, but in the apartment. For Diego would never be seen in public with RosaMina. And it was here that Diego's other vices, gluttony and lust took centre stage.

Only then did he stay overnight. She'd shop and prepare several of his favourite childhood dishes in large quantities; change the bed linen using older sheets and double layered them, and unpack the box of sex aids that Diego added to on most visits. She laid them out in a neat row.

After eating, Diego smeared the remains of the food over her body, particularly between her thighs and around her nipples. RosaMina performed all Diego demanded, saving his best for last: the handle of the whip shoved up his arse along with as much food as RosaMina could possibly stuff into it.

The day came when Diego made an announcement.

'I'm getting married.'

RosaMina's eyes widened. She had no idea where he would have found the time to go courting. Recalling his behaviour trying out all the women at The House, one after another, and then going back for more, it stood to reason.

He was a man who, in spite of his puny penis, was driven by lust. She returned to his marriage statement. Hope and anguish were about to gush right out of her.

Her bottom lip trembled. 'Are you and I finished?'

Diego looked at her over his hairy paunch. His mini penis and quail size balls stuck together, sticky with sperm.

'*Mi putita dulce*, I will never finish with you. Only when I am dead.'

Making sure she understood his meaning, he flicked her left breast. RosaMina choked. The pendulum did not swing. It remained stock-still, stuck in her throat. She reviewed her situation.

Thanks to Alejandra, who was Plan A, her secret account showed a healthy balance. Now that Carmina was older, she had a small support group of mothers around her. They offered friendship, which RosaMina accepted from a distance. She offered immediate help when needed, though never asked for theirs. RosaMina vowed to change her situation.

She weighed the pros and cons this announcement offered. She could threaten Diego with their truth to be 'discovered by his new wife'. As soon as this thought entered her head, she rejected it. There was no need to lure the monster from his lair, unless absolutely necessary. She had, after all, her daughter's safety to think about. No, she'd find a job and earn some money that way. And a job came sooner than she expected.

On those days when the sun shone and the sky was blue, RosaMina took Carmina out. She was beginning to walk. It was much easier for her little unsteady legs to walk on the pristine and soft green lawns of Kew Gardens rather than the rough uneven turf of Richmond Park.

A woman sitting under a tree with a sketchpad paused. She watched as RosaMina encouraged Carmina to get up from yet another tumble. Carmina managed five steps before falling onto her padded bottom. She had done well. And she knew it. She raised her little face to RosaMina full of smiles, gurgling with delight.

As it so often happens with English weather, a dark cloud cast its shadow. In less than a minute, mother and child were drenched. RosaMina grabbed Carmina and ran for the nearest tree. She was weighed down with

the blanket, pushchair, and general paraphernalia that goes with each toddler's outing.

The sketcher jumped up to help. Carmina forgot her tears from the
shock of the sudden downpour as she was transferred into the arms of the
woman dressed in an Indian outfit of trousers and flowing tunic. Carmina was
enthralled with the brightly coloured, hand-stitched tunic beads. Her little
fingers sought out and touched each, one by one.

RosaMina took up Manuella's offer of modelling. With Carmina she
went to Manuella's house on Kew Road. This became a practice for several
weeks, during which RosaMina learnt about Manuella. Of her past, RosaMina
revealed little. She said she'd had fallen pregnant with her first lover. Instead of
an abortion, she had chosen to live in England where unmarried mothers were
more readily accepted. Manuella was quite satisfied with the explanation. She
never pressed for further details.

Carmina adored Manuella. In between sketching, Manuella kept
her occupied while RosaMina remained as still as possible. She was never
asked, but it seemed natural to be naked rather than clothed. From the outset,
Manuella sketched RosaMina nude. Carmina was sketched too, when she fell
asleep. She rested on RosaMina's naked chest or curled up on a pile of blankets
on the floor.

The marble sculpture that Manuella created of RosaMina was headless.
Yet there could be no doubt that the supine body emerging from under her
hands was RosaMina's.

'Manuella, you are amazing.' Using a fingertip she traced the smooth
contours of her marble legs. 'You have made it so beautiful.'

Manuella looked directly at RosaMina, which could buckle even the
strongest knees.

'You are kidding, aren't you?'

RosaMina tried to figure out her meaning. 'I am not. You are an amazing, talented artist.'

'RosaMina, it is you that has the most beautiful body. One all figurative
sculptors would kill for. My rendering you in this manner is just what you are.
Perfect. Glorious.'

RosaMina was quiet. She never thought of her body. It did not belong to her. She'd done some reading on why she had separated herself mentally and physically. But it got complicated. It left her feeling breathless and light headed. So she'd given up and resigned herself to accept that it was enough she'd connected to her body the times she'd been with Alex and during her pregnancy and Carmina's birth.

'There is no art involved here. Just technique. Here, let me show you how this will turn into art.'

Manuella pulled out a handheld cine camera. She began filming RosaMina's reclining marble form and captured the room, its furniture, the modelling tables, tools, and the view out into the garden through the conservatory's glass walls. Then she moved stuff around the room and in some cases removed them altogether. She repeated the filming moving the camera in a clockwise circle. A few days later, after Manuella had developed the film and somehow had blanked out the images of RosaMina's reclining marble form, she showed RosaMina her intent.

She ran the silent film throwing its images up against a wall. It showed a full circle of the room and its contents coming to rest on the real sculpture, its form re-filling the cut out film space. The image repeated passing over the never changing marble form, but showing articles that had moved or had disappeared completely.

'See,' Manuella said, 'life moves on. It changes. But the sculpture is there, timeless. Always whole. Always complete. Always present.'

RosaMina could not say she understood. Nevertheless, she sensed the weight of Manuella's words. It was clear that Manuella was in control of change while she created it. And because change was Manuella's greatest fear, she had to keep creating it, so that she could control it.

'One day, RosaMina, I'll hold an exhibition in one of the most picturesque squares in all of Italy. You will be immortalized. And,' she continued scooping Carmina from her arms and doing a little twirl, 'you and Carmina will be the guests of honour. What do you think about that, little one?' Manuella blew noisy raspberry kisses on each of Carmina's cheeks. The child squealed her delight.

Manuella returned to Italy. RosaMina and Carmina continued going to Kew Gardens, walking right by Manuella's house.

Kew Gardens provided more than just manicured lawns on which Carmina could learn to walk. RosaMina entered the exotic glasshouses pushing Carmina in the pushchair. It was the perfect heating system for RosaMina during both summer and winter. With hardly any fat on her body RosaMina remained cold in all seasons. Carmina's well-padded baby sitter had suggested it was because she was so very slim. Bordering on skeletal.

The moment they entered the moist air of the glasshouses, Carmina quieted. RosaMina always headed for the bench she had found when pregnant. The New Zealand tree fern branches reached almost down to the floor. Sitting under it was like being in a secret tree house, well screened from everyone. Here RosaMina would feed Carmina a biscuit and give her a bottle of milk. Soon she'd fall asleep and RosaMina was free to open her box of memories tied with ribbons.

One morning, RosaMina woke feeling strange, a humming coursing lightly through her head. She wondered if it was because she'd not seen Diego for more than a fortnight. He was due back sometime soon from his honeymoon.

She lifted the receiver of the telephone. She held it to her ear. It was working. When she replaced the handset into the cradle, the humming sensation continued. She shook her head. Wiggled her fingers in her ears. But nothing dislodged the sound. She considered perhaps she was in for a cold. She was unable to concentrate. She felt drawn to staying in the apartment close to the telephone. At the same time, she felt the need to leave the apartment.

Though the previous Sunday, clocks had advanced one hour so that evenings had more daylight, it still felt like it was late winter, if one felt pessimistic, or very early spring, if one felt optimistic. Either way, on that day, Sunday, April 28, 1958, RosaMina's bones felt colder than usual.

Distracted, she completed a few household tasks while keeping Carmina occupied. Sensing her mother's anxiety, Carmina fussed. After lunch and an unsuccessful nap, RosaMina gathered what was needed. They headed out to Richmond Station.

The light humming, similar to the metal tracks vibration heralding the arrival of a train, increased.

One stop on, they got off at Kew and walked the four hundred metres to the Victoria Gate entrance to the gardens. Posters on either side of the gate advertised special exhibits and events. Once inside, RosaMina turned left along the path to the ten storey, octagonal, cherry red and gold Japanese Pagoda. It was a gentle stroll, and from there they looped back along Holly Walk. By the time they reached the Palm House, the hum had gotten louder.

They entered the Palm House and took the pathway to their favourite hidden spot. RosaMina was about to duck under the low hanging fronds — the humming was about to reach a crescendo — when she heard a different noise. A light muffled cry. It even caught Carmina's attention. She turned towards it looking under a frond that was just as high as her head. She stared and then raised one hand. With her palm facing her she flexed her fingers open and close, open and close. She had recently learned, after a fashion, how to wave hello.

RosaMina tried seeing through the fronds but they were too thick. Someone was occupying the bench. She was not going to disturb anyone, especially if crying. RosaMina continued along the iron-grated path out of the Palm House heading towards their next favourite, the Water Lily House. Carmina howled her disappointment, twisting in her seat. Her eyes remained fixed to the palm fronds. Through Carmina's noise, RosaMina deciphered something else in the humming that had begun to fade. She heard the words, 'Where are you?'

From an unknown depth, her heart responded, 'I am here'.

For a moment, RosaMina thought she was going mad. Was the voice Alex's? It could not be. But she walked back to the spot. The humming increased. She ducked under tree fronds. The space was empty. The humming stopped. Carmina's gurgles of pleasure filled the air.

On the bench was a scrunched entrance ticket. She smoothed it out. It was stamped with that day's date and the entrance time. An unseen force guided her hand. RosaMina placed the ticket in her pocket. She sat down on the still-warm bench. She could not pinpoint it, but it was a warmth reminiscent of one she'd experienced before. No words could describe how much she missed it.

Anticipating a bottle of milk, Carmina began to fret. She grasped the offered bottle with both hands, sucked hard, then finally succumbed to sleep, her eyelids drooping closed. RosaMina was free to review a turn of events.

Two days before Diego had taken off with his wife on their honeymoon, RosaMina received a letter. It was from Alejandra Herrera Salazar. What she wrote left RosaMina speechless. She had come to a decision. She was going to take an active interest in Carmina. But, the original agreement of RosaMina never to seek out and contact José or Alex, was to remain.

By way of a sweetener Alejandra had enclosed a copy of another bank transfer. It was for a much larger amount than usual. She further announced there was no need for RosaMina to write back. Alejandra would be in London the very next week. She would visit RosaMina and Carmina on the following Wednesday afternoon.

RosaMina was relieved Diego could not put in a surprise appearance as he was still on honeymoon. Alejandra arrived and caused a stir among RosaMina's elderly neighbours. They all thought she was a movie star. But their failing memories were unable to dredge up a name that fit.

RosaMina had seen Alejandra face-on just once. The second time, she saw only an obscured view of the side of her face. Alejandra appeared to have become even more beautiful with the passing years. And yet, it was as though Alex stood before her. RosaMina had been dreading the moment, but managed to hold her pendulum still. Alejandra graced through the front door, then gazed round at the surroundings.

'RosaMina,' she cried. 'You have done so well.'

RosaMina assumed Alejandra was complimenting the furnishings. And then Alejandra added, 'you have been thrifty.'

RosaMina was at a loss to know how Alejandra could miss the safe haven she had created for her child and herself. The furnishings were second hand, but good quality, chosen for their subdued colours, creating warmth and peace.

RosaMina bit her tongue from retorting. Instead, she thanked Alejandra for all the on-time bank transfers and the new increased sum. She did not permit Alejandra the embarrassment of asking if she had another man in her life. RosaMina told her point blank, there was no one, just Carmina and her.

But that did not stop Alejandra from looking in the bathroom cabinets for any sign of another man. RosaMina spied on her through the keyhole and congratulated herself for her forward thinking.

Prior to Alejandra's arrival, RosaMina removed the packet of condoms from the mirrored medicine cabinet. She hid it under Carmina's cot mattress where she lay sleeping.

Upon waking, Carmina was fallen in love with instantly. And because she was such a joyful trusting little bundle, she took to Alejandra. RosaMina knew Alejandra would instantly look for Alex's characteristics in Carmina. But there were none. For Carmina was wholly in her mother's image. Yet that did not stop Alejandra's emotional floodgates opening and pour out. Alejandra's whole body marshmallowed. Her lovely face softened and glowed. Once again, she could not keep back the tears, as she had once tried in the church of San Antolín.

Over Carmina's head, Alejandra lifted her eyes to RosaMina. 'Thank you,' she mouthed.

From then on, Alejandra visited several times a year, and Carmina grew up believing that Alejandra was her godmother.

Still, Diego did not call. Like a mother worrying about a late returning child, RosaMina phoned the hospital. She put on her old Spanish accent and asked to speak with him. RosaMina was referred to another doctor. He asked her with the correct tone, had she not read the article in the newspaper?

From the Richmond Library, RosaMina secreted a back-dated copy of the newspaper carrying the article. It was reported that recently graduated Dr Diego Rivas, had died in a drowning accident while on honeymoon in Jamaica. He was found floating just below the surface in the shallow waters of the Caribbean Sea by a lifeguard. His belly and other soft tissue parts, including his ears, nose, and lips had been destroyed, having been thoroughly nibbled off by a myriad of small fish.

RosaMina was surprised how calm she was. She left Carmina with the babysitter. On the way to the bank, she ditched the box of sex aids along with the last box of condoms into a bright yellow, builders' rubble dumpster. She withdrew what money was left in their joint account and closed it.

The one thing RosaMina had left connecting Diego Rivas to her and her daughter was the blood type report, which proved nothing, and Carmina's birth certificate, where the space for the father's name remained empty. This, along with the drawn out cash, RosaMina placed on top of the jewelled trinkets she was keeping, should the need arise to sell them one day. She included the crushed Kew Gardens entry ticket she'd found on the bench. The date of Diego's death as reported in the newspaper article and the entry ticket bore the same date. She relocked the box and placed the chain upon which the key was suspended back around her neck.

Only then did RosaMina rest. She lay down and folded her hands on her chest like those of a corpse in a coffin. Images sped backward to her first memories; watching puffy white clouds move above her head; the Maria Exposito's of the world, including the stick woman; the mother cat grooming her kittens in the basket on the kitchen floor; Berta and the girls; the light pink stains before, and those still to come on bathroom floors; José and his socks; Alex and the different parts they had once slotted with the other, making them whole; Diego, for what he had been, good and bad and for what he could have been; and at last she began to create a new image — her freedom — that now, with his passing, had finally been secured.

Several times a year, Manuella returned to her house in Kew for her quiet creative time. She'd call and the round of modelling would start up again. RosaMina got to see photos of Manuella's London sketches transformed into sculptures. RosaMina had no idea of what constituted good or bad art. She did not like the abstract pieces, but particularly liked the realistic ones. Of them, Manuella's first piece of her, remained her favourite. And despite Manuella's words, remained in awe of how Manuella managed to produce something so beautiful from her body.

Once, Manuella told her that the younger man, whom she had been sharing her life with in Italy, had begun to distance himself. She had been waiting a long time for it to happen.

'I am getting to the menopausal stage in life you know. It's natural that he should start looking around.'

RosaMina shook her head. 'What's menopause got to do with it? If two people love each other . . . .'

'Don't you know? All men seek out younger women when their partners hit menopause.'

RosaMina did not bother to offer her view on the subject. But she did say, 'Maybe Manuella, you have both come to a new set of crossroads. Not just him.'

The moment the words fell from her lips, RosaMina regretted it. Manuella's face cracked.

'Come here,' RosaMina mumured and gathered Manuella into her arms.

'I can't live without him.'

RosaMina held and rocked her. But not all the comfort in the world could have made a difference to Manuella at that moment.

RosaMina would have been equally bereft, had she known Manuella was grieving for the very same man who continued to fill her dreams. For, to be sure, not for a single moment had RosaMina forgotten Alex.

It was 6.15 a.m., Saturday, July 21, 1973, the day of RosaMina's (thirty-fourth) birthday.

Carmina had come to learn over the years that her mother did not appreciate any effort on her part to celebrate her birthday. But each year, she found herself asking, 'How old are you now?'

'Twenty-one,' RosaMina would always respond.

'Oh Mum, get serious. Tell me how old you are, please.'

'Fifty.'

'Stop teasing me. You could never be fifty. That's so old.' Carmina's nose would wrinkle.

'Well then how old do you think I am?'

Carmina paused, stared at her mother intently, searching for either stress or laughter lines on her face. Of these she had none, though on this occasion her translucent skin looked paler than usual. All this, together with a wraith thin body hidden under layers of clothing caused Carmina to exclaim, 'You're ageless.'

'Good. That's what I like to hear.'

'But why don't you want to celebrate your birthday?' Carmina always asked, though she well knew the response.

'I just don't.'

'There must be a reason.'

'Well if there is, I don't know it. So best you stop your nagging and accept it for what it is.'

'Well, then, I won't celebrate mine either,' Carmina threatened. But when her birthday came around, she entered into the spirit of it — for her mother went to great lengths to provide a truly happy and gift-filled event.

Though mid-summer, it was a cold, gray, and wet English morning. Heavy overnight dew glistened under the lamplights along the Thames Riverside Walk, which RosaMina and Carmina's Richmond apartment overlooked. Centre to the kitchen window view, remains a protected bird island supporting ancient willow trees. Swans and ducks began to wake, un-tucking their heads. They stretched their wings and shook out their tail feathers. They waddled to the edge before sliding into the barely moving water. After paddling around in a quick circle or two, reclaiming their water legs, they glided about, preparing to dive bottoms-up in search of breakfast.

A pair of athletic scullers slid into and out of the view framed by the kitchen window. But Carmina, seated at the high breakfast counter munching cereal, watched RosaMina move about the kitchen preparing Carmina's mid-morning snack to take to school.

In the background, a television announcer prattled about Princess Anne who was to marry a commoner, Mark Philips, in a few months time.

'Mum, please don't think you can hide it from me anymore,' Carmina suddenly yelled — all thoughts of her mother's steadfast refusal to acknowledge her birthday and age forgotten. For the third time in a quarter of an hour, she saw her mother wincing as her arm brushed across her left breast.

RosaMina responded in her monotone voice, 'Carmina, don't raise your voice like that. It's not ladylike.'

'I don't know how else to get your attention,' she responded, still yelling. 'I won't go to school until you've been to see the doctor. And that's that.'

Jumping down from the high counter chair, she charged into her bedroom and banged the door closed. She did not feel well either. Her final exams loomed ominously. But there could not be two sick people in the house at once. She fell face down onto her bed, pulled the pillow around her head.

'Oh Mum . . . you're so infuriating,' she screamed into the mattress, muffling her voice.

Her mother prided herself on never having been to a doctor or hospital except for the day she gave birth to her daughter. Yet, if Carmina sneezed, RosaMina was ready to rush her to the emergency room.

From as far back as Carmina could remember, her mother would tell her the story of her pregnancy; how the baby grew in her stomach and announced its presence by kicking little feet out to say hello. She knew about the birthing process having learned about it at school, but somehow her mother always skipped right over that part. But she never forgot to say how happy she was to leave the hospital and bring the precious newborn home. Carmina was around four-years old when she realized that she was the baby in the story.

Her mother rarely let Carmina from her sight. She grew up in an overprotective, almost stifling atmosphere. She did not always feel restricted though, unless without thinking, she asked questions. Soon Carmina learned which other subjects, aside of her mother's age and the reason for not celebrating her birthday, were taboo. Such as the day she asked without thinking, 'Mum, who is he? Where is he?'

The light in her mother's face went out — as if the sun had been swallowed. So shocked at this transformation she never asked again. And RosaMina never offered an answer. Carmina came to accept that her life consisted of her mother and herself. That was not strange. Several of her classmates at school had only mothers, and in one case, no mother, but two fathers.

In their apartment building lived a couple of elderly neighbours and Carmina's former baby sitter. All of whom had known her since her birth and doted on her. There was also Manuella, her mother's flamboyant spinster artist friend. Carmina regarded her as an aunt. They saw her twice a year for a couple of weeks at most. Then there was her beautiful, and very rich, widowed Spanish godmother. They saw Alejandra at odd intervals throughout the year.

Given one came from Spain and the other from Italy, it was not at all surprising to Carmina they never saw them together. Nevertheless, whenever either was about to put in an appearance or simply arrived unannounced, RosaMina would take Carmina aside. She'd hold Carmina tight. With her mouth close to Carmina's ear she'd whisper, 'Carmina, listen to me. Never under any circumstances tell Alejandra about Manuella.'

'Or Manuella about Alejandra?' Carmina asked, playing the innocent. Though she knew well her mother meant both of them. 'Why not?'

RosaMina responded in slow and controlled staccato, 'Because, Alejandra, is very old fashioned. It would offend her sensibilities. She would not approve knowing that I pose naked for Manuella. Or, that naked sketches of you were done too. She would be shocked rigid.'

'But mum, you and Manuella tell me there's nothing wrong with the naked form,' Carmina responded in a half serious, half teasing voice.

Humour was lost on her mother. If there was a competition for being being 'Seriously Serious', she would win it hands down. RosaMina's lips pressed into a thin line. It was Carmina's warning she was going too far. She had better drop the subject.

'That is correct. There is nothing wrong with the naked body. But you have to be sensitive of older people's views. Don't give Alejandra cause to become disillusioned. She may stop giving you all those gifts.'

The warning was not lost on her. But like most teenagers, Carmina tested how much was needed to rile her mother up.

'Manuella is very open. She wouldn't mind knowing about old fashioned Alejandra.'

Propelled by an unseen force RosaMina materialized next to Carmina. Behind slits, her eyes glittered. Even thin and frail, she gripped her daughter's forearm with surprising strength. She hauled Carmina up from the chair in which she was sprawled.

'I won't tell you again. Do you hear me?' Her voice had lowered.

Carmina nodded. But it was not good enough.

'Do you hear me?' Her grip tightened.

Carmina mumbled a yes.

'Louder. I want to know you understand me.'

'Yes,' Carmina managed to gasp more in utter surprise rather than pain, upon which her mother released her.

It was over in a few seconds. RosaMina's eyes returned to normal. But for Carmina, the memory of that episode remained long after the bruised finger marks on her forearm cleared. That was the only small, memorable deviation from the norm.

The rest of Carmina's childhood into young adulthood was unremarkable. She grew up in relatively privileged circumstances. Her mother never worked, except for the occasional part-time posing she did for Manuella. And volunteer work at one of the local charity clothes shops.

Mother and daughter lived comfortably, though nothing like Carmina's classmates. They lived in large grand houses dotted along the River Thames, or along the leafy suburban streets leading up into Richmond Park. In order to provide Carmina with what she needed, RosaMina was frugal. She rarely purchased anything for herself.

On balance, they got along very well. Carmina was her mother's whole world. There was nothing RosaMina would not do for her daughter.

Then, the night before RosaMina's birthday, mother and daughter had their most heated discussion.

On her last visit, Alejandra had invited Carmina to join her in Spain once she had written her final school exams. Carmina was overjoyed. Alejandra had often shown Carmina pictures of her house. Like her, it was grand and a bit old fashioned.

'I've not changed a thing in the house these last thirteen years,' she'd brag. 'Not since my dear darling José passed on. Everything is as it was on that day.'

Carmina's interest was piqued. On one hand, she shivered with the ghoulishness of it. On the other, she thought it romantic to turn one's home into a shrine dedicated to a dead, but not forgotten, person. At the telling of this, her mother's face remained impassive. RosaMina never commented either way. And ignored Carmina when once she said, 'Mmmm . . . I wonder what Alejandra's husband was like?'

Carmina reached bursting point. She wanted to see the house where time had stopped in honour of the dead. That, coupled with the fact that wherever they went, Alejandra turned heads. People wondered aloud as to which famous person she must be. This Alejandra bore with noticeable and practiced fortitude. Carmina suspected Alejandra enjoyed the disturbance she caused. And so did Carmina. She too got to bask in all the brouhaha. Once Carmina complimented her saying, 'Gosh, you managed that just like a princess.'

Chuffing her under the chin, Alejandra replied, 'That's not far off the truth.'

This set Carmina to thinking. She wondered if her mother was holding out on a secret. A secret in which she was connected to Alejandra. Because, if she was connected to her, and Alejandra was a princess, then so was she. In no time at all she'd convinced herself she was. One day, everything would be revealed — she would after all, be royal to the core. That would give her classmates something to think about, she thought with unrestrained delight.

For days, she had gone about in a state of excessive euphoria. Carmina was energized to the point where she could not sleep. RosaMina looked at Carmina's too bright eyes, raised her palm to her daughter's forehead, and asked, 'Are you feeling okay?'

'Great.'

As on other occasions, fantasies buzzed around Carmina's head, until they burnt out, leaving nothing but smoky cinders. Disillusioned, she accepted there was no likelihood of being a princess. She promptly fell into a wasteland of desolation. In contrast to her earlier behaviour, she became lethargic. She took no pleasure in anything at all. Not even the recent gift of jewellry Alejandra had given her. Again, RosaMina raised her palm to her daughter's forehead and asked if she were feeling okay.

'Horrible.'

'Don't worry. She's just suffering from normal teenage growing up pains,' Carmina's former babysitter was overheard explaining to RosaMina.

'She'll grow out of it. You'll see.'

But the cinders of this conspiracy theory refused to die. Despite accepting she could not possibly be a princess, Carmina lived with the nagging feeling she was connected to Alejandra. Connected in more ways than Alejandra simply being a friend from her mother's life, before her. Carmina had pieced together what she believed was the reason for all the secrecy cloaking her mother's former life.

It clearly had to do with the dire political situation that prevailed in Spain. That it had caused her parents to flee to England, her mother carrying her child in her belly. Her father rarely appeared. And on the few occasions he did, RosaMina left Carmina with their baby-sitting neighbour. Later, for all their safety, he never came again.

She knew the invitation was going to be a battle. Carmina waited for the right opportunity. Then, as lightly as she could, she presented it. She was met with RosaMina's immediate ironclad resistance. Carmina turned into a monster. She screamed and raged, berating her mother for her unfairness. But RosaMina did not budge. Usually she would give in just to keep the peace. But there were issues on which she would not. This was one of them.

Carmina knew her mother could, but would not, offer any valid explanation why she could not join Alejandra. And she could see no reason why she shouldn't.

That night they did not peacefully retire to their respective bedrooms. RosaMina wrote a letter. She declined Alejandra's invitation on Carmina's behalf. She woke Carmina from what Carmina called her hide-away sleep. The deep dreamless sleep she'd fall into when her questions begged answers. Under the light of the bedside lamp, RosaMina read the letter aloud. She handed Carmina a pen. Bleary eyed she was obliged to sign her name next to her mother's.

Carmina's misery was soon replaced. For the rest of the night she heard her mother move restlessly, stifling groans of pain.

Then, the following morning, lying on her bed face down, screaming into the mattress, Carmina underwent a weird experience. She found herself suspended from her bedroom ceiling. She looked down at another — her other self lay face down holding the pillow around her head. The pressure cooker of conflicting emotions built up, gathering a head of steam. It would have to be released or explode. But a crash coming from the kitchen brought Carmina down from the ceiling. The other her disappeared. Carmina returned to the kitchen.

She spoke to her mother in the quiet way that always received her mother's undivided attention. RosaMina promised that by the time Carmina returned from school, she would have either seen the doctor or made an appointment to see him. Mother and daughter hugged at the front door.

'Love you,' said RosaMina as she handed Carmina the packed snack box.

'Love you more.'

RosaMina then picked up the signed letter now sealed and stamped and handed it too, to her daughter.

Carmina jammed the letter into the mouth of the bright red letterbox. She hurt her fingers. Crying with pain and the frustration of the last twenty-four hours, she walked on to school.

Their local doctor, Dr Pratt, referred RosaMina to a specialist.

'It's advanced breast cancer,' he said a week later. His voice was quiet and his eyes focused on the reams of laboratory printed tests.

RosaMina ignored all practical advice and emotional pleading. She eschewed any notion of surgery or treatment. Carmina and RosaMina entered a new and the last phase of their relationship.

Carmina first gingerly tested the tightrope. It disappeared into the future without an end in sight. Dr Pratt said it could be a matter of weeks, a few months at best. Then Carmina stepped onto the rope. The path and responsibilities that lay before her were clear. Her mother grew sicker, weaker and though it seemed impossible, even thinner.

RosaMina had always been thin. Unlike Carmina, she did not enjoy food or eating. A holdover, she had said, from her deprived childhood. This was as much as Carmina knew about her mother's background.

Dr Pratt shook his head. He said there was nothing he could do. He could not force RosaMina into surgery or treatment. But he arranged specialist hospice nurses to come in and care for her.

Carmina was sitting her final exams at the local comprehensive school. She expected to achieve straight A's. She'd wanted to go to art school, following in Manuella's footsteps. But her mother overruled her. She had insisted Carmina do something that would hold her in good stead for the rest of her life.

'Specialist surgeons,' RosaMina had said many times, 'earn a lot of money, and, it's a kind of art.'

Carmina could never understand her mother's determination that she should go into specialist surgery. Her school aptitude tests showed she had a strong artistic side. It also showed she had a precise nature. To her chagrin, specialist surgery, among other academic and highly skilled vocations was purported to be a strong option.

'See,' her mother said, 'I told you, you would be a great specialist surgeon.'

Carmina rolled her eyes heavenward. 'Let me get started first, before you tell me how great I am.'

She often wondered at her mother's displays of naiveté. After some research, she came around to thinking that specialized surgery would not be such a bad thing. Projected earned income was on the high side. Her head buzzed with the thoughts of things she could buy as she applied to various medical universities.

Each day after school, Carmina went into her mother's bedroom to study. She had to prepare for her exams. At the same time, she wanted to be with and spend as much time as possible with her mother. It was the only way to combine both.

RosaMina perked up for a few minutes upon Carmina's arrival. After that she'd drift off, surfacing again every so often. Carmina's other self put in an appearance. Only this time, her other self was suspended from the ceiling watching over RosaMina while Carmina focused on her books.

In the late afternoon, there was a caregiver changeover. A new hospice nurse arrived. She moved about quietly preparing to settle her mother in for the night. Carmina was surprised: RosaMina struck up a conversation with the new nurse.

Just as her life was winding down, RosaMina's speech had wound down too. Carmina recalled her mother saying she only started talking when she was about twelve-years old. And when she did, it was monosyllabic. The nurse was fixing RosaMina's next shot.

'What a unique ring,' she said.

The nurse halted. 'It was my husband's,' she said.

'Was?'

'He . . . he's dead.' Her eyes glistened.

'I'm sorry,' RosaMina said. Instinctively she held out a tissue.

The nurse placed the injection needle in a metal basin and took the proffered tissue.

'I'm still not over his death. So silly of me. It was such a long time ago.'

'How long?'

'Sunday, April 28, 1958. Fourteen years ago.'

Carmina's fingers tapped out the years. She would have been three-years old.

'Were you married long?' RosaMina offered the nurse another tissue.

The nurse pulled up a chair close to the bed. She blew her nose.

Carmina watched from the chair in which she was sprawled. She had flung her left leg over an upholstered armrest, her foot dangled freely. She studied best in this position. Books around her, on the floor, opened face up over the armrest. She eased the book in her hands facedown upon her chest. Her head inclined slightly to one side.

'Tell me about him.'

The nurse blotted the corners of her eyes.

'He was a doctor training in specialized surgery for kids. I met him at the hospital where I, too, was training. What can I say. He fell in love with me.' She began to brighten, warming to her story.

'Was he handsome?'

'No. He was short and little on the fat side. We had running arguments about his weight. He hated exercise . . . well, no that's not quite true. He said he exercised enough . . . you know . . . .' She looked down at her hands embarrassed. She was spinning the family signet ring around on her finger.

RosaMina touched the nurse lightly on her hand indicating her understanding.

'He was attentive. Driven, almost. I mean, he pursued me. I wasn't the least attracted to him in the beginning. But he was so determined. Soon I couldn't help myself. And that was that. We got married soon after . . . oh dear,' she wailed, 'this is so unprofessional. You won't tell, will you?' She glanced around the room as if to make sure her supervisors weren't there, watching. Her glazed eyes slid right over Carmina who, immobile had become part of the furniture.

'Sorry to be such a ninny.'

'Please. Go on.'

This was more than Carmina had heard her mother speak in days. Her head inclined further.

'We married,' the nurse began again. 'A simple ceremony. Small. Just his parents and mine. His came from Spain. You're from Spain too, aren't you?'

RosaMina nodded.

'I noted that we have the same surname. It's quite a common one. You wouldn't have known him, would you? His name was Diego Rivas.'

RosaMina shook her head and said, 'No. Sorry. I did not know him.'

The nurse sniffed.

'But if you had known him, you would not have forgotten him.'

'I'm sure.'

The nurse sniffed again. 'Anyway we left the next day on honeymoon. Jamaica.'

'Why Jamaica?'

'Diego relaxed by reading James Bond novels. He liked the book, Dr No. It was set in Jamaica. We both wanted to go somewhere hot and a place neither of us had been to before.'

RosaMina waited for the nurse to speak again. Carmina's eyes slid down the bookshelves. On the bottom shelf tucked under a pile of her mother's trashy paperbacks was a well-thumbed copy of Dr No.

'The first day of our honeymoon, after a big breakfast and then an enormous lunch — he really liked to eat a lot . . . ,' another sniff, ' . . . it was hot, we went down to the beach. He went for a swim. I asked him to give it a little while longer. But no. He went. He never liked anyone to tell him what to do. When I woke up from dosing — he hadn't come back. I raised the alarm.' Her voice dropped. 'He was carried on a stretcher covered by a beach towel. He'd suffered a heart attack and drowned.'

'So, you were married for two days? I am so sorry for you.'

When the nurse sighed and stood up, Carmina caught her profile in the late afternoon sun slanting through the window. For a moment, Nurse Rivas looked like her mother before her illness. Only taller and fuller. She had the same kind of short curly hair framing her face and smattering of light brown sugar freckles across her nose.

'You'll find peace and happiness.'

'Yes. I think I'm almost ready. As Diego would have said, "Time for another go".'

Carmina did not understand it. RosaMina jerked as though a single volt of electricity passed through her body.

'Oh oh,' said the nurse becoming efficient again. 'It's time for your shot.'

Like an automaton, Carmina blew though her study schedule while her mother lay dying. She wrote her final exams. She assured her mother she had passed well. RosaMina insisted that she would hang on until Carmina's results had been posted.

'Just to make sure,' she said with a slight smile.

Carmina was sure this was her mother's first ever attempt at humour.

RosaMina did not make it to the results posting. With Dr Pratt and nurse Rivas present, Carmina held her mother until RosaMina breathed her last breath.

Several hours later with the afternoon mail, the letter bearing Carmina's results was delivered. It lay for weeks thereafter unopened on the entrance hall table.

Carmina catapulted into extreme efficiency. She felt strange, taut like an overwound spring. Above her head, her other self walked the tightrope.

A month before her mother's passing, Carmina had secretly written to Alejandra of RosaMina's illness. There had been no reply. She assumed Alejandra was on one of her travels. Carmina had no address for Manuella in Italy, but dropped a note through the mail slot in Manuella's front door. Carmina's neighbours, Dr Pratt, school friends and their parents, joined her in the small parish church, of St. Peter's, in Petersham, Richmond.

That it is a Church of England, she knew her mother did not care. For without fail, her mother attended service there each Sunday.

'I feel safe and cocooned sitting in its quaint ancient Georgian box pews,' she had said. 'And besides, it's in easy walking distance of our apartment.'

Carmina knew her mother loved the tranquil rural setting. Cows grazed in the meadow bordering the River Thames as it curved by. It was remarkable, given the hustle and bustle of Richmond was just a stone's throw away. Moreover, RosaMina had often told Carmina that it was the closest she would ever get to visiting St. Peter's in Rome. Not to see the church. But rather

the white marble carving of Mary holding her dead son's body draped in
her arms.

'Because you know,' she said, 'Mary never left her child's side. Not once.
From the day he was born and until he died. And even when he rose again, she
was at his side.'

Carmina did not miss that they had never spent a night apart.

And RosaMina had a surprising request. She had always dreamed of
visiting the macabre, Capuchin Crypt beneath the church of Santa Maria della
Concezione dei Cappuccini. This church in Rome, her mother had said con-
tained the skeletal remains of three thousand, seven hundred bodies. Because
of this, it was her wish to be cremated. She did not want the possibility of her
body being exhumed and any bones of hers' floating around earth for the rest
of time. Her desire was that her ashes were to be scattered in the small church-
yard of St. Peter's. Carmina was not ready to do this. Instead, when the box of
ashes was delivered she tucked it into the back of her wardrobe. She would deal
with it later.

After the memorial service, Carmina returned home to an empty
apartment. The exam results envelope still lay unopened on the entrance hall
table. Carmina did what she had been instructed by her mother before mor-
phine completely overpowered her. From her neck, she removed the chain
attached to a small solid key. It had been around her mother's neck for as long
as Carmina could remember. In her mother's wardrobe, at the back of one
of the shelves, was a fireproof box, twice the height of a shoebox. Carmina
removed the box. She placed it on the kitchen table.

Upon turning the key, the cylinders rolled back releasing the lock.
Lifting the lid, a stack of bank notes spilled out and slid, fanning out like a pack
of playing cards onto the table. Each note value was the highest The Treasury
issued. Carmina lost count after the first hundred or so. Easing out the rest of
the money she stacked it in three high piles to one side. Twelve dress pins fashioned in animals, insects and flowers set with coloured stones nestling under
the bank notes were revealed. Carmina had never seen her mother wear them.
Yet one, a hummingbird, was identical to the one Alejandra had given her for
her seventeenth birthday. Beneath the dress pins lay envelopes, upon which
were written in her mother's distinctive handwriting, titling their contents.

Carmina had access to their joint accounts. She rubbed her eyes and looked again at the current value of the savings account. Surprises did not stop there.

In the envelope below, lay the deeds to the apartment. She had always been under the impression they rented the apartment. But no, they were the rightful owners. Or at least, Carmina was. Her name was written in the deed owner's space. The next envelope held a document in Spanish. It was stamped with the Spanish London Consulate General insignia. This showed a change of surname from Expósito to her family surname, Rivas.

Pieces of a giant puzzle began to materialize. To be thrown into disarray again with the following single page letter.

It was written and signed by one, Maria Expósito. She claimed to be Carmina's maternal grandmother. She wrote saying first, apologies for the intrusion; she hoped that the letter would find both mother and daughter well; she stated she could never mend the past; nevertheless she wanted to ensure she could make a difference in her granddaughter's life. She'd purchased the rented apartment, and transferred ownership into Carmina's name. So, no matter what, her granddaughter would always have a home of her own. She wished both daughter and granddaughter the very best. Added at the bottom, was a postscript. Berta sends her fondest love.

So now Carmina understood her mother had family of her own. In a second, she had a grandmother and assumed Berta was her aunt. Given Carmina's family surname, it was no wonder that her mother refused to tell Carmina anything about her past. She had studied Spanish history and understood the significance of the surname Expósito. One train of thought followed another — if the woman claiming to be her grandmother was an Expósito, and her mother was an Expósito, then in reality so was she. She realized with finality how far she was from her years' earlier fantasy of being a princess.

In another envelope was a note. The ink had lost its colour but was still legible. The note was in the same handwriting as the single page letter from the woman, who claimed to be her grandmother. On the note, the name written was, RosaMina. The note was attached to a thin piece of fragile string. On the reverse side it was dated, *21 de Julio, 1939*. The date written was her mother's birthday, which RosaMina always refused to celebrate. Carmina inhaled sharply.

She had no idea her mother had been so young. It made her mother only eighteen-years older than she. Yet her mother had presented herself as much older. She wore demure and somewhat old-fashioned clothes, many of which had been purchased from the local charity shop where RosaMina had volunteered.

And her father? Was she about to have her belief confirmed? The last envelope trembled in her hands. She eased out a blood type report. It appeared that Carmina's blood type was O. Her mother's blood type was B. And Diego Rivas, had blood type B. Carmina did know enough about blood typing to know this proved nothing. She simply assumed that Diego Rivas was her father. And if he was the same Diego Rivas that Nurse Rivas had been married to, and though he was long dead, Carmina did not want to think about the relationship status between him and her mother. For nowhere could she see a marriage certificate.

Of its own volition, out slipped a Kew Gardens entry ticket attached to a clipped out newspaper article: 'Brilliant Young Specialist Surgeon Dies' read the faded headline. Carmina smoothed out the brittle piece of paper. She adjusted the lamp pulling it down closer over the newsprint. She began to read.

At that moment, nothing else in the world mattered. Or existed. Except for the faded article and the Kew Gardens entry ticket. Both of which shared the same date. Sunday, April 28, 1958.

After the three years it took to sort her father's life, Manuella joined a marble-sculpting studio.

In defiance against those who claimed sculpting a man's craft, The Studio had started with women only. As it evolved, men were permitted to work from there, too. An invitation to join The Studio was an honour. The tightly knit group of sculptors came from all corners of the globe. Few were recognized in Italy, though most were known in their home country.

No matter how good a sculptor, becoming known was hard. The next hurdle was to sell one's sculpture. This was where most artists, good and bad, fell down. Not all were blessed with the art of self-promotion. Being able to dip into the collective pool of The Studio's sculptors' experience was a gift, one Manuella grabbed with both hands.

Within weeks, all Manuella had learned during her three years of art school was wholly eclipsed, though the foundation of her sculpture education had been laid much earlier.

After the lands had been prepared for the winter fallow, her father, like his father before him, sculpted. They worked in the manner of generations' old, marble-sculpting artisans. They used manual tools. Each dedicated his sculpting life to perfecting a part of the human form. Manuella's grandfather specialized in hands and feet. Her father specialized in heads, torsos and drapery.

They never sold their work. There were no collectors then, for hands, feet, heads or torsos without the rest to go with it. On occasion they were asked to work on figurative pieces, so artisans like her father and grandfather, could add their specific carving skills to a piece of work. For this reason, and the availability of the finest white marble in the world, foreign sculptors flocked to Manuella's Italian hometown.

As a child, Manuella had never tired hearing her favourite bedtime story. Of her parents falling in love over a cone with a triple scoop of ice cream, in the square one hot summer's evening. During each telling, Manuella's mother changed the flavours and order of the ice-cream scoops. In a flash Manuella told her mother off. When she was not corrected, her mother knew Manuella had fallen asleep. And this is what she never told Manuella during story time.

That she too was a sculptor, English born, and on her first European tour when she met her father. For love, marriage, and children she gave up sculpting. That, against her parents' wishes, the marriage went ahead. Despite their misgivings, they shipped crates of family antiques to Italy by way of a wedding gift. On her wedding day, Manuella's mother received a letter by mail. Overjoyed, she tore open the envelope prepared to read her parents blessing and good wishes after all. Instead she read of her father's death and her punishment: banishment from her family home in England. Manuella's grandmother wrote, blaming her daughter for the death of the person with whom her life was entwined like a ball of wool. And to whom she clung for the living of her own life; for when he breathed she breathed. And when he no longer breathed, she tried to stop breathing too. Failing at the last attempt, she decided as long as fate would have her breathe, she would, if only to remember never to forgive her daughter. And in parallel, forget her daughter.

Manuella's surprises upon entering her mother's family home had been many; realizing then her mother was English and not Italian; hearing English coming from her mother's mouth; discovering an alive maternal grandmother. But, the greatest surprise was the glass conservatory at the back of the English house, which could have been substituted for the wooden barn at the back of her Italian house.

'Can I try too,' she had asked every time she saw her father and brother working with marble.

'Sculpting is a man's craft, not a woman's,' her father had growled.

Both conservatory and barn were filled with works. But — and here Manuella's heart skipped a beat — the glass conservatory was filled with sculpture produced by her mother. So, *Babbo* had been wrong after all, she thought. Not only did women sculpt, it appeared her mother must have been better than her father. For the conservatory was filled with wholes rather than pieces. Years later, when Manuella went through art school, she recognized her mother's sculptures indeed held merit — and far more so than her father's.

As a measure to counter her mother's spiralling drinking problem, Manuella encouraged her to take up sculpting again. She did. Producing one piece. It was the less than half-life size form of Giovanni. This she did from memory. She poured her energy into him. Her efforts did Giovanni proud. Down to the slightest and most obscure, she captured details of his entire body; his Peter Pan essence; his good-natured, mischievous innocence.

From what had started out as a cold block of marble, she rendered the stone, filling it with light and warmth. Giovanni was breathed back into life.

'There's no chance,' she had said, 'of forgetting a single thing about Giovanni. After all I gave birth to him. Through our connected fibres I know him as well as I know myself. Not even death can take that away.'

Manuella made no comment. But she wondered about the interconnected fibres between her and her mother. For as her grandmother had cut her mother off, so had her mother had cut them off from their former life in Italy. And she had cut herself off from Manuella.

Through Manuella's encouragement, which resulted in the single piece, fantastic as it was, it did not have the effect she had hoped. Her mother further drowned herself in alcohol.

The stuff nightmares are made of came true. Manuella found her mother dead in the conservatory, her body curled around the base of Giovanni, his stone feet pressed into her belly. She had tied her fringed shawl around them both ensuring their connection.

All of Manuella's past life events had been laid down solidly, one upon the other creating the foundation upon which her future rooted. Negative, pain-filled life events, lay loose. Every so often seeking attention, they rattled their presence, threatening the foundation with collapse. Ignoring the rattle calls for attention, her new life — she liked to call it — started with her joining The Studio.

Desire to create was an unstoppable geyser. She tried every genre. She took wrong turns and made many mistakes. But one day she would become known for the sculpting style aficionados would recognize as hers.

Her father grew older and slower. And as his life force shrunk so did he. Manuella saw him regularly for a shared meal or just a quick hello. Occasionally he'd drop by The Studio. Without comment he'd review her progress. If he found it difficult to accept his daughter was a sculptor he made no show of it. And if he suffered guilt or remorse from having stopped, first his wife, then his daughter, from sculpting, he did not show that either.

It was after the fortuitous meeting with RosaMina and her baby in Kew Gardens, that Manuella began to move away from abstract art forms. Through RosaMina's offered nakedness, she was able to concentrate on the body, in its whole, glorious, and natural state.

She'd sculpted RosaMina's headless body in the traditional way. She used manual tools. As her mother had done with Giovanni. And, as her father, grandfather and the artisans of Pietrasanta had done for hundreds of years. She would reveal this piece of work twice. The first, prematurely in England, and then again in Italy ten-years later as the centrepiece to her solo exhibition.

The period between the two exhibitions, the reclining figure of RosaMina was covered with a dustsheet and stored in the glass conservatory. Sketchpads filled with drawings of RosaMina and Carmina, she stowed and locked in a wardrobe including the stills and film.

Her father's silent visits to The Studio had increased, indicating his approval of the new direction Manuella had taken. After all, the human form was what he too knew best.

Manuella's life settled down in Italy. But she returned to the locked-up house in Kew for several weeks at a time. She was drawn to the house for many reasons: for her mother, who hovered over her as she worked; Manuella waited for those times when her mother's hands and fingers rested upon and guided hers.

And, she returned for peace and quiet, the likes of which she never found in Italy. The Studio was always noisy. Air compressors thumped dully against the pneumatic tools' high whine under the outdoor awnings protecting sculptors from the Tuscan sun. Most sculptors wore ear protectors. Those who did not — did not need to — they were already deaf. But above all, it was the silent noise of intense concentration that Manuella needed.

Meeting up with RosaMina, their on-going modelling sessions became her sole focus upon her returns to Kew. Less and less, she contacted the few remaining art school friends she had. They had gotten married and had children. Manuella was not fond of her friends' noisy children. More so when they constantly interrupted conversations, becoming even more demanding of their parents' attention when someone else was present.

It appeared to Manuella's father his daughter was destined to follow in the footsteps of his identical twin sisters — unmarried, and, more to the point, childless. But on this subject he kept quiet. Former unswerving loyalty to duty, desiring to pass on familial inheritance — shattering his family life — had fallen away. There was nothing left to pass on.

Manuella believed fulltime relationships were not necessary unless one planned to have children. And Manuella had chosen not to have children. Her mother's indoctrinated legacy and the pain of her father's rejection of her she never forgot.

The event in her life that often sought attention was her guilt being the surviving child. For her parents' lives would have continued into their golden years had Giovanni lived and she died instead. She took lovers where she could. And soon on left those who developed more than just a passing interest in her.

Despite her dismissive attitude towards children, she did take an interest in Carmina. She had noticed from an early age Carmina showed a flair for clay modelling. She bided her time waiting to see if Carmina was in possession of an ability worth cultivating, or if she'd received a God-given gift — one that set good sculptors apart from brilliant sculptors.

Playing the role of benevolent aunt was easy. Carmina had been a delightful, cuddlesome toddler. Then she grew up into a charming, sweet child. When Carmina hit her teenage years, she turned into a monster. RosaMina, in her unflappable manner, was always at hand to rein her daughter back. She'd explain Carmina's behaviour away as over exuberance.

At these times, Manuella saw RosaMina looking gaunt and not well. She thanked her lucky stars she had chosen not to have children and have to put up with an obnoxious teenager of her own.

As unflappable as RosaMina was, Manuella found her equally unfathomable — closed, quiet, and independent. Her daughter's exuberance had not come from RosaMina's character. It was a rare occasion to catch her smiling. Manuella recalled once when she heard RosaMina laugh out loud. It was embarrassing. It had sounded like a strangled hiccup. That said, RosaMina was an attentive mother, a dependable, though distant friend.

Upon first meeting, Manuella asked RosaMina in a roundabout fashion of her earlier life. RosaMina had simply said she had left Spain for England upon discovery of her pregnancy. Manuella curbed her tongue. If pressed too hard, she feared RosaMina might well simply leave her, too. But one small curiosity did get the better of her. She asked if Carmina's father had had a body as glorious as RosaMina's. Images of Alex's body came to mind while she asked. With quiet studied response RosaMina replied, 'Goodness no. He was a short roly-poly.' It was not the answer Manuella expected. After that, she asked no more questions.

She learned, though, that RosaMina came from rural Spain, a country where politics ended in more than lost blood. Somewhere hovering in the background was Carmina's godmother. These were the beginning bits of disjointed and confusing information coming together rattling their need to be heard. But Manuella ignored them all. Her geyser of unstoppable creativity made sure of that.

Manuella was not sure most days whether to call herself Italian or English. She had a foot in both places. But what she did know was, that to achieve recognition, she had to exhibit her art. To be successful, she had to sell her art. She had learned that lesson from sculptors at The Studio. She had a better chance of selling her work in England. So when invited to present at a group exhibition in The Orangery at Kew Gardens, she did.

A warning sounded. *Offering* was still too early for appreciation in prudish England. But she ignored it. She mounted four pieces demonstrating her evolutionary path from abstract to figurative realism. Other sculptors sold pieces. Manuella sold nothing. The following day, an article appeared entitled,

'The Show Stopper', with the subheading, 'The no-detailed-spared life size and headless *Offering*'. The article went on to say, 'In protest, a man's jacket draped over the private bits. Perhaps, in an attempt at chivalry, protecting the unknown woman's honour and modesty. In doing so, sadly, the exquisite skill with which this piece has been rendered was overlooked. The time will come when it will be viewed for what it is — a remarkable offering to the art of sculpting'.

At least her piece had created a stir, thought Manuella. But that was all. The mainly English art viewers thereafter studiously ignored it.

A week later, still nursing her wounded pride and disappointment at her no-sale show, Manuella popped into the Maids of Honour for afternoon tea. Maids of Honour was a traditional English teashop. It baked its own pastries and cakes. The most famous was a dainty and innocent looking custard tartlet. It was recorded the first tartlet was prepared in 1665.

The teashop, named after the tartlet, was a short walk from Manuella's home along Kew Road and can still be found today at Number 288-290 Kew Road, Richmond-Upon-Thames, England. All through her school years Manuella passed this shop twice daily. Her nose became well accustomed to the baking processes of the Maids of Honour. Through smell alone, she discerned each ingredient: ground almonds, grated lemon rind, castor sugar mixed together with butter and eggs. And the intense heady rush when warm cream was added and all ingredients were beaten together.

Dainty pie tins were lined with rich puff pastry, their hollows filled with the warm mixture and then baked. A few currants were sprinkled on top. A cloud of caramelized sugar turned the tartlets light golden brown. Their fragrance wafted out over the rooftops of Kew. Irrespective of age, mouths watered and stomachs ached in anticipation. The trays, removed from the ovens, were left to cool. After, the tartlets were turned out and then stacked in tall golden pyramids on glass counters or behind the tearoom's street-facing windows.

Manuella felt at home in The Maids of Honour like no other restaurant, café, bar or teashop. She sat facing the door. A tall and the handsomest young man walked in. For a heart stopping moment, Manuella believed it was Giovanni grown up.

The young man was intense. He had a sense of purpose. He chose a table, above which suspended a too bright light. The kind women of Manuella's age know to avoid. He glanced at the proffered menu. He placed an unheard of order, a cup of tea and a single Maids' of Honour. Unfolding one of the exhibition brochures he spread it out flat on the table. He examined it closely.

Manuella knew the exact position of the photographed sculptures on the brochure. She could tell from where she was sitting his index finger lightly rested on the photo of the *Offering*.

Having not been in a relationship for a while, Manuella was seized by the licking, burning flames of desire. Before she could stop herself, words fell from her lips.

'Which sculpture do you like best?'

Moments too long passed. He responded, 'this one.' His index finger moved over and jabbed at the amorphous ball.

He lied.

They may have both known it.

Manuella chose to ignore it. Out of the corner of her eye she saw a waitress whom she'd known for years advancing with his paupers tea.

'Here,' she commanded, 'set it down at my table.'

He probably realized he had no option but to join her.

Manuella was thankful she was wearing one of her eccentric Indian outfits. The reds and greens were good for her skin tone. Its voluminous coat hid lumps and bumps brought about by too many glasses of wine and plates of pasta eaten alone. She'd make an effort and get back into shape, she promised herself.

Close-up, he was jaw-dropping handsome, to the point of being beautiful. What was even more surprising, he seemed unaware of his incredible good looks. Manuella scrutinized him. A habit which made many squirm, but he held her gaze.

'Are you the artist?' he asked.

She laughed. Forgetting her gnarly, work-roughened hands, she waved them in perfect synchronicity through the air and said, 'Guilty.'

She held onto his interest for all she was worth. Like a spider, she put out her web. She began to draw him to her. Under the façade of intensity, he was lost and lonely. She invited him back home. She cooked him a great but simple meal. She relied on that old adage all women know — the one about paths, men's hearts, and stomachs.

Manuella was not disappointed with the outcome of her web. So much so, for a long while she forgot her mother's indoctrinated legacy.

She and Alex fell into an easy, warm, and comfortable relationship. Because of his quieter nature versus her more exuberant, energetic one, and ignoring their age difference, they were a well-suited couple.

Manuella's father loved Alex upon first clapping eyes on him. He believed Giovanni was returned to him. The Studio members, long acquainted hamlet friends and neighbours, welcomed him warmly, and more so when he worked his Chiropractic magic on them.

Like most new couples, they shared their past life stories. Manuella shared hers easily. By comparison, the same could not be said of Alex. There were many parts he held back. But Manuella chose not to let it concern her. After all, she too held back an event or two, which as time went by, became all the more necessary for her not to disclose.

Despite their mutual withholding some of the truth, each time she returned from London, they reunited with passion and joy. She took comfort in this. And her mother's legacy for a while longer remained in the background.

After Alex's return from his father's deathbed, he became even quieter. He began to write. From her experience, cathartic writing meant changes. Manuella did not like change. Slow growing apprehension, not dissimilar to the ivy creeping up through the boughs of the sour cherry tree, began to take hold of Manuella. She dreaded the day she'd wake choking.

Manuella was hesitant to read Alex's tome. She was sure he did not want her to read it either. Easing around the issue, they agreed Manuella would not read it, while it remained work-in-progress. She passed a flippant remark about reading it when it turned out to be a best seller, thus further delaying the inevitable. And the inevitable would be an earthquake, that, like it or not, was going to rock them.

One early summer morning, birds were coming to the end of their dawn chorus. Bees hummed between purple lavender spikes and pink climbing roses. A warming sun coaxed the Mediterranean into shimmering opalescence.

The hamlet residents were up, working in their vineyards, orchards or tending to vegetable gardens. Alex sat on the terrace. The typewriter clacked as his fingers pressed down on the keys. Manuella glanced over his shoulder. She read the words " . . . Rosa's *mons pubis* rose in a slight arch like an inverted sickle moon".

A tremor started underfoot rising through her calves and legs. It entered her belly and then vibrated its way through the rest of her body. She shook and almost toppled over. She was right to be afraid. She had never disclosed her relationship with RosaMina or Carmina to anyone. Let alone RosaMina's name or that she was her muse. And now staring at her typed in black ink was the first half of RosaMina's name along with the perfect description of her glorious body.

The following morning, Manuella woke to the sound of the rattles. They had been playing all night. She could not get out of bed. Her natural exuberance had deserted her leaving her feeling clingy and pathetic. A little like her mother's mother of her husband had been. The last thing she wanted was for Alex to see her in this light. She fled to Kew earlier than usual where another shock awaited her.

A single sheet of paper folded in half lay on the mat on top of the pile five months of accumulated mail. It was from Carmina, telling her of RosaMina's passing two weeks earlier. Manuella's hand flew to her throat. She had begun to choke. The wheels of change, like it or not, chugged into motion. Manuella telephoned Carmina. There was no answer. She went to the apartment in Richmond. Carmina answered the door.

Carmina was everything her mother was not. She was energetic, curious and emotional. She had no problem laughing or crying. But now, standing framed by the door, she looked just like her mother. And, she was reduced to a tearful and fearful mess.

Manuella bundled her up. Lugging several bags of clothes into a taxi they set off for Manuella's home in Kew. Of the luggage, Carmina insisted on carrying herself, as if her life depended upon it, was a largish metal security box. That box at that moment was her sole anchor and connection to reality.

Carmina remained with Manuella, trying to adjust to the loss of the person who had been her world. And who had made Carmina her only world.

Manuella realized Carmina's compass was well off. She vacillated between calm and hysteria, deep sleep and insomnia. Manuella's nerves were stretched taut until it was she who felt like the walking dead. She rustled around in medicine cabinet and discovered a bottle of old sleeping pills. They took two each.

Twenty-four hours later, Manuella could swallow easily again. Carmina claimed feeling better. But she was not. Manuella realized she'd have to continue caring for her. Until Carmina regained perspective and traction, she was in no fit state to be alone.

Italian food and several visits to The Maids of Honour, magically put meat back onto her bones. Fortunately, Carmina enjoyed eating. Unlike RosaMina, who as far as Manuella recalled, hardly ate at all.

By leaving Tuscany, Manuella had provided Alex with calm and quiet time to work through his issues by way of writing. In Kew, she was providing calm and quiet healing time for Carmina. No one helped Manuella. Foreboding tightened its grip and the rattles chattered incessantly in the background.

Of the metal security box, she saw no more. They had agreed Carmina should hide it somewhere about the house where only she knew its location. Had Manuella snooped, found it, and managed to open it, the rattles would have gone mad. She would have found more proof of the connection she had been too afraid of acknowledging. In the form of an art deco pin, an identical one of which, Alejandra had given her by way of a gift. When Alejandra had given it to her she'd said, 'I had this made up for you. There are only four in the world like it. I have one, my goddaughter has the second, her mother the third and now you have the fourth.'

Long ago, she'd had suspected that RosaMina and Carmina were connected to Alejandra and Alex. Instead of being the catalyst bringing change to all of them, Manuella had balanced the scales in her favour. She needed RosaMina for her art. She needed Alex for her heart.

While Manuella watched over Carmina, she decided to launch her first solo exhibition in the main square of Pietrasanta. The shippers arrived. In a morning, all her pieces were wrapped, packed, and stored in the back of a transport truck. It crossed the 'Atlantic Pond' by boat to France. From France, it would travel south into Italy. Manuella expected it to arrive in three days. From the back of the truck, along with Pietrasanta's town hall crane, her pieces would be assembled in the centre of the square along with other pieces stored at The Studio.

Pietrasanta's early morning denizens would bear witness to its assemblage. Her father would be one of them. He would stand along with his friends in the Bar Michelangelo and drink his first espresso of the day. Later rising residents would see the installation complete *in situ*. By lunchtime, through word of mouth, Manuella would know if she was to be regarded as a 'Daughter of Pietrasanta'. It is the title bestowed upon artists, local or foreign, whose work based on merit, sets a new benchmark for excellence.

Manuella realized a large part of her disquiet was knowing she could not leave Carmina in England. Against all her instincts screaming, Manuella made a decision. She would take Carmina with her. There was no telling the surprises in store or the resultant changes. But this much she knew — none of their lives' would ever be the same again.

For the first time in a long time, the rattles quieted down. The silence was sweet relief.

'Carmina,' Manuella called out as she walked through the house.

As she expected, she found Carmina bent over a piece of clay in the conservatory. The young woman had masses of talent. Carmina looked up.

'Surprise! You are coming with me to Italy. I am making good my promise I made you and your mother years ago. Guests of honour at my first solo exhibition.'

For the first time in a year, Carmina's face lit up.

anuella just called. She's on her way back to Pietrasanta. She's bring-ing a guest, the kid of a friend who is in some kind of trouble.

She asked would I mind if I moved in with Old Guy for a week or so. I'm relieved coz' aside of my feelings for Manuella it's time to move on.

I do not want to break it off with her just as she is opening her exhibition. So I'll hang until the frenetic activity is over and done. Then I'll do it.

Yes, Papa. I hear you. I'll be gentle. But like we both know, there is never the right time or a good time. It's going to be horrible and that's that.

So the sooner I pack up and get going the better. As for Old Guy, well, I'll miss him a lot.

To further break my balls, Alejandra also called. She arrives in Pietrasanta night after next, which is Manuella's opening night. Yup, that's right. With a new beau in tow. Holy crap. They get younger and younger. Sure she'll be the centre of attraction, just like always. Like you, I'm still not over the paternity question. Frankly, it's time for Alejandra to fess up. We both need answers. It will not be easy. She's more slippery than an eel — hell, I do not have to remind you. But, I am going to get to the bottom of the mystery of my paternity whether she likes it or not. So now I'm on a roll disclosing stuff, let me get this one out real quick. I'm done with being angry. You know. About you and me falling heads over with the same girl. I did not know and you did not know. Shit happens. It is what it is. There's nothing that can change that.

I cannot say I feel the same way about Diego. Whether he's dead or not. Never going to forget that one. Friend? My arse. But I'll say this. My guess is you'll understand. Hell, I miss the girl. Till later . . .

———— ◆ ————

*P*inch me, please. I feel I'm in a time warp. Years ago, Marco collected Alex and me. At my request, he drove by the Leaning Tower of Pisa. Here I am again. Being driven by Marco but this time, instead of our lover with me, it's your daughter Carmina and me. I can hardly believe my ears, but Marco has just told Carmina the same story about his Irish wife and kids. Some things change and others do not.

I am resigned to those changes that have already begun. You and I know there are even bigger ones waiting.

I cannot think about this right now, as I have the opening exhibition happening in two days time. Please God, the truck arrives.

To take Carmina's mind off you and other miseries, I have just explained to her, as I did to you so many years ago, of how this exhibition is going to be mounted. 'Life Changes but Sculpture Endures'. It'll be best shown at night, when the footage of everyday life in the square revolves around the buildings.

Oh, RosaMina. I am so very sorry you are not here. Without you, none of this would be happening. And I cannot begin to tell you how sorry I am for having kept you and Alex apart. I'm truly sorry.

But let me tell you this. Alex's time with me is done. It was good for a long time, but it's over. He's been treading water while concentrating on his book. Do you remember when I fell into a sobbing heap? You were so generous with your comfort. Thank you. Goodness knows how you would have felt knowing it was Alex I was crying over. I was so terrified. I was terrified of being without him. But I was equally terrified of losing you. I am so sorry for being so selfish.

I'm more sure of myself now, but oh how I miss you and I miss him already and we have not yet parted.

I'm going to pull the plug on Alex and me after the opening of the exhibition.

Having Carmina with me now is forcing me to keep myself together. It's a great help. You should be proud. You have a gorgeous daughter. Even if she still behaves like a monster teenager. (Ha, ha, that was a joke, no offence meant.) No, really. Her loveliness is because of you.

I wish now things could have been different. I wish you were here. I have been having these conversations with you since I learnt of your passing on. I'm so very sorry for blabbing on and on. RosaMina, please, forgive me . . .

◆

At Manuella's telephone request, I made sure Old Guy took a shower. He took his time and when he emerged from his bathroom, his wispy hair was slicked down. He had a few facial nicks stuck with bits of toilet paper blotting up the blood. After rummaging around in the back of the wardrobe, he pulled out a new shirt, still in its wrapping. He tore off the cellophane and pulled out the round-headed pins securing it to a piece of card around which the shirt was precisely folded. Then I understood why he rarely changed his shirts.

While he waged war on the buttons with his gnarly stiff fingers, I rummaged around in my holdall and pulled out three relatively new cotton shirts with green crocodile logos. The shirts sported two-button collars — the type that can be worn undone.

'Choose,' I said holding out all three shirts.

Old Guy did not talk much. He had claimed there was no point, when once, after two weeks' worth, it got him nowhere.

But his eyes sparked with amusement. All three shirts were the same dark blue colour.

'This one.'

His fixed-in-an-immovable-curve index finger stabbed at one of them. It slipped easily over his head — the buttons done up — and fit well, even though it was a little on the large side for him.

'Nice,' he said and gave me a light punch on the arm — his way of saying thanks, and then stuck an unlit cigarette in his mouth.

My turn in his bathroom took mere minutes. After pulling on clean clothes, (and leaving the other two shirts in his laundry basket for him — one of which he would soon be buried in), I ran a comb through my hair and tied it back without looking in the mirror. Then we left.

We walked through the narrow cobbled streets of the old town and headed for the square. As we turned the last corner and emerged into the square, Manuella's mounted exhibition appeared before us. Centre to the exhibition was the *Offering*. Like more than a decade before, my heart responded in recognition of it by thumping hard against my chest.

The usual suspects, being Pietrasanta's art crowd, the mayor, his entourage, and residents milled around. And groups of foreign tourists who flock to this town to soak up the magic of Pietrasanta's town square, its art — bronze and marble sculptures. Professional and local photographers snapped away. But everyone waited for the sun to set.

Then Manuella's film footage of everyday life would kick in and revolve around, glowing against the medieval buildings. It would create an old-fashioned outdoor movie theatre. But kids of today would liken it to an IMAX movie. While life continued and changed, Manuella's white marble sculptures would exist unchanged forever.

A wave rippled through the crowd. Without even looking, I knew my mother had made her entrance. All heads turned. Those less sophisticated, gawked at her. A moment later, she draped her arms around me. We embraced while camera flashes burst like fireworks around us. She looked marvelous. Cool and fresh. And like I'd written to my dead father hours' earlier, her new beau hovering in tow was younger than me.

'Álejo, my handsome boy,' she purred in my ear.

Trying not to be too brutal, I extricated myself from her embrace. Old Guy bent over her hand and kissed it with as much old-fashioned theatrical flair he could manage. I was further saved by those who came to greet her, and by others, hopeful to have their picture taken with her.

The sun set. Spotlights highlighting the medieval walls enclosing one side of the town got switched on. It was time for the show to begin.

The film footage depicted the townspeople. Twenty-four hours condensed into a two-minute clip, one clip for each season. The footage began to revolve. Like ribbons of silk, the images slid over the facades of buildings surrounding the square.

Everyone gasped with surprised pleasure, the locals more so when they saw themselves magnified ten times, living their daily lives on those walls. After each 365 degree rotation, indicating the end of a season, the footage halted upon the *Offering*. Then a new season of changes commenced. But the *Offering* remained the same.

It was a thought provoking presentation. Glancing around at Manuella's contemporaries' faces, I caught fleeting glances of covetousness or discontent perhaps. Those who may have felt that way would, the following day, decry it as a gimmick. But in truth, it was a creative platform highlighting the artistic flair and technical brilliance of the sculptor.

The buzz changed pitch. At the edge of the crowd, Manuella put in her appearance. She was wearing one of her inevitable Indian style outfits, trousers and long shift with a long flowing scarf. She'd lost weight. She was looking good.

Tightness around her eyes indicated control of inner turmoil — combat against looming change. I felt a twinge of guilt. I had contributed to her turmoil, as it would not have escaped Manuella's notice that I had removed my clothing, a couple of well-loved books, and typewriter. Leaving space free for her houseguest. But in reality, by doing so I had forewarned her I had vacated her little house on the hill. I had left her.

Manuella worked the crowd of well-wishers as she made her way up towards us. Old Guy had wandered off to join his cronies gawking at the *Offering*. Who knows whether they were viewing the piece for its sound sculpting technicalities or sumptuous naked visuals. I did not have to view Rosa close up. She remained etched in my memory.

Manuella reached us. She and Alejandra embraced warmly. As a mark of respect, Manuella wore the art deco hummingbird pin my mother had given her years before as a gift. It held the long flowing scarf draped over her shoulder in place. My mother too wore hers and maybe it was the fashion — both women wore them in exactly the same position. I could never look at those pins for being reminded of the blood dripping from my mother's stabbed fingertips.

And then there she was. Rosa. Standing behind Manuella. She too had a hummingbird pin attached to her white linen dress in the same position.

My head spun, memories accelerating backwards right to the moment I first saw Rosa in my father's studio standing in her silk sheath, fudge coloured curls dancing around her face. Over her shoulder, I could see the *Offering* but here right in front of me she stood and every bit alive as everyone else.

She opened her mouth. When she squealed with girlish delight the hairs on the back of my neck stood up. Her mouth formed the first letter of my name followed by the rest of it but for the last letter — she ended it instead with an *a*.

For the first time I saw my mother's composure fall apart.

'Carmina?' she responded to which Manuella said, 'Alejandra? Carmina?'

Then Manuella looked at me and said nothing.

Rosa flew into my mother's arms. They embraced with a warmth that had been there forever.

At that moment, I acknowledged total madness. Rosa was my mother's nemesis, the cause for the total disintegration of her and my father's lives. And in many respects the disintegration of mine, too. Yet here they were, hugging and clutching each other. Sheer joy blazed out of each other and for each other.

As if remembering me, my mother turned her head while still holding Rosa and using the diminutive of my given Spanish name Alejandro, for the second time in one evening, mouthed, 'Álejo.'

Then she turned her head and looked at Manuella and said, 'Manuella? Carmina?'

Sorry. I'm just a guy. I was lost. Who the hell was Carmina?

Rosa and my mother released their holds on each other. They drew Manuella to them, held hands with her, forming a closed circle. They began to laugh and cry at the same time and then, fell into hugging each other over and over again.

Old Guy appeared at my side. With a light tug, he led me away from the threesome. What was happening was for women only. Still watching from a distance and looking through the revolving film bouncing off the buildings, creating distortion of everything around us, I tried to take stock.

Conflicting emotions raced through my brain. For in my vision, I had three of the most important women in my life. None seemed what or who I had understood them to be.

But I remained rooted to the spot and continued to stare.

She was not Rosa, but such was her likeness I concluded it could be Rosa's sister. As said, I'm just an ordinary guy. Some things take me a little longer to go figure.

My mother and I are alike. Carmina and Alejandra were dissimilar. With Carmina being a ringer for Rosa, then just maybe Carmina was Rosa's daughter.

The penny had finally dropped. If Carmina was Rosa's daughter, where was Rosa?

No sooner did I think it, her voice from nowhere answered. She told me what I had long suspected, but had denied. Then, she shyly whispered, her warm breath caressing my ear, something I had had no inkling of.

I walked to the other side, crossing the subliminal bridge that separates men from women and joined Old Guy. And those who had the knack would have seen my father waiting for me there too.

The three of us walked back home through empty streets. Just like The Night That Changed Everything, so busy with our own thoughts, not a word exchanged between us.

And from the edges of outer space where reflections of fragmented, rainbow-coloured lights blend and merge — become whole — I knew then I was a father. RosaMina and I had had a daughter. Her name was Carmina. And I was going to claim her.

The morning after the exhibition, Manuella left Carmina at The Studio. She was to amuse herself modelling clay while Manuella went off to tie up loose ends. Or at least that was her excuse. Manuella's first stop was her father's apartment.

Bleary-eyed, an unlit cigarette stuck between his lips — he had been trying to give up smoking — he welcomed her in. No longer engaged in physical hard labour, his former strong stocky body had shrunk. Most noticeably his neck — now scrawny, like a plucked chicken's — and surrounded by a too-big neck collar. But this time, Manuella realized he was wearing one of Alex's signature dark blue shirts. It was a vast improvement on the greyed ones, he changed perhaps once a week, and, Manuella had realized, slept in too.

She was relieved, remembering the last time they had disagreed about his clothes.

'*Babbo*, there is no need for you to go around looking like a tramp,' Manuella argued as she tried to press new shirts upon him.

'Bah,' his voice rasped, 'I'm too old for new clothes.'

Manuella's face darkened. 'Humour me, please.'

'Okay, okay. I'll take one.'

Manuella's face brightened.

'Bury me in it.'

A sigh of exasperation escaped Manuella's lips.

Now she said with a ring of approval in her voice, 'Nice shirt,' and fingered the woven cotton. Her skin jumped at its feel — reminding her of Alex's skin against hers.

Manuella did not have to look around. Neither Alex nor his stuff was anywhere to be seen. He had moved on. And Manuella did not bother to ask her father Alex's whereabouts. Even if he knew, he would not say — it being a guy thing. As she left, her father awkwardly embraced her. She was not sure whether it was in sympathy for Alex leaving or congratulations on the exhibition.

'Manuella, don't become a stranger,' he said.

'I won't. Right now I've got things to do.'

'But don't go forgetting this old guy.' His voice quavered.

The memory of his voice, once strident and strong, shouting, 'get the useless girl away from me', returned in a flash. Manuella was not sure which made her sadder, his former strident voice demanding to be rid of her or, his now quavering voice begging not to be forgotten. Either way, she reassured him again.

Her next stop was Pietrasanta's best hotel, where Alejandra stayed when in town. Years ago, and a year before Alex's father José died, Alejandra had put in a surprise appearance. She was as shockingly beautiful then as she was now. Manuella had found they were similar in their outgoing personalities. And, she realized, their ages. So right from the outset, Manuella curbed her exuberance. There is nothing more pathetic than seeing two older women fawning over and competing for the affections of a younger man.

Alejandra was no fool. She had recognized Manuella's actions. Together they got along very well. As long as Alejandra was around, Manuella slid into third place. But as the years passed, they formed their own friendship that did not include Alex. They liked and respected each other. They had strong boundaries which neither crossed. Both had secrets. Neither pried the others' lest their own be revealed. But this was about to change.

In contrast to her father, Alejandra was clear-eyed and serene. She had been expecting Manuella as did somnolent revelations who roused themselves. They shuffled and straggled into a disorderly line, waiting their turn. Alejandra sliced through the heart of the matter.

'Why didn't you tell me you have known RosaMina and Carmina all these years, let alone RosaMina was your muse? Good gracious! Your sculpture of her, even headless, is a dead giveaway.'

'It never occurred to me.'

'But surely a muse is important in an artist's life?'

'To the artist. Not important to anyone else. And by the same token, why didn't you ever mention Carmina's name instead of always referring to her as your goddaughter? Maybe then we could have put two and two together.'

As Manuella said this, in her mind she crossed her fingers. She hoped her implication of withholding her understanding would remain only known to God. His punishment for this she could bear. Should Alejandra and Carmina ever come to know, she knew now they would possibly punish but ultimately forgive her.

For the night before, when Alejandra hugged Carmina tight and despite the distorting exhibition light, Manuella saw real warmth and care between them. The childhood pain she'd suffered being the odd person out struck her hard. Almost in the same moment, she found herself caught and pulled to form a close threesome circle — the women had neither abandoned nor forgotten her. Her childhood pain, cast out, vanished.

But once Alex realized her omission, she would never survive his punishment. He would never forgive her.

The first revelation shuffled forward.

'RosaMina was my husband's and Alex's lover.'

Manuella swallowed hard. Sharing the same woman. No wonder Alex was hung up about his father, she thought.

'How was that possible?'

'She was a local whore.'

'Then she must have been the least likely whore in the world.' Manuella surprised herself by rising swiftly to RosaMina's defence.

The next revelation shuffled forward.

'Carmina is Alex's and RosaMina's daughter.'

Now Manuella could not swallow. Her hand flew to her throat.

'I am her grandmother,' Alejandra said revealing her misrepresentation of the truth.

'Does Carmina know?' Manuella coughed out the question.

'That I am her grandmother? No.'

If Alejandra suffered regret or remorse for her duplicity, she did not show it. Except perhaps in the way her fingers strayed and fiddled with the jewelled pin attached to her dress.

Manuella's throat relaxed enough for her voice to squeak out, 'Alex has no idea he has a daughter.' This, she knew with certainty.

'I made sure of that,' said Alejandra. And so, another revelation slid out into the open.

Without realizing it, Alejandra unfastened the pin. And in doing so, stabbed her finger.

'But after last night, he should. If he doesn't, then he is a fool. And more like my husband than I thought,' came her surprising response. She was careful not to ruin her dress with the pinprick of blood that sprang up. She put the tip of her finger to her mouth.

Had she heard correctly? Had Alejandra just undermined her dead husband? wondered Manuella. For years, she had been subjected to hearing how wonderful José had been — such a saint, beloved by all. Now, he had been reduced to a philanderer and worse, stupid.

Both women sat in silent contemplation, perhaps each filtering the other's information. Letting it settle.

Another thought popped into Manuella's head which, under ordinary circumstances she would never have voiced aloud. But these were extraordinary circumstances — so she did.

'Carmina and Alex don't look alike. She looks only like RosaMina.'

'I know.'

'Then how do you know for sure Alex is Carmina's father?'

'A mother's intuition.' The images of the collision of two stars forming three, as only the heavens can conspire may have run through Alejandra's head.

For once, Manuella did not take Alejandra's comment as a snipe at her self-imposed childless state.

'Does Carmina know Alex is her father?'

'Absolutely not.' Alejandra knew she could have bet her life on this.

The glorious hand-painted frescos on the ceiling of the hotel suite filled with cherubs, wings and horns, and flowers and birds, was not an unpleasant canopy under which to fall back into contemplation.

'Did you have no idea about Alex and RosaMina?' Surely Alex must have told you something about her? After all, she was his first, you know.'

That Alex and RosaMina were connected was no surprise to Manuella. She'd known this for as long as the world was old. But it had completely escaped her that Carmina could be their daughter. RosaMina's long ago response regarding her lover's roly-poly body had thrown her off course. She'd assumed he was Carmina's father.

The shock of learning Alex was Carmina's father had led to small but still vibrating ripples moving through her body. Having rehearsed the answer a million times, it now stuck in her throat.

'Well?'

'No.'

And then words, she had so feared, for so long, fell from her lips.

'It's over.'

Alejandra took Manuella's hand. 'Really?' she asked.

'Yes really.' And you don't know the half of it, thought Manuella.

Through circumstance rather than choice, her father had welcomed her home and they were reunited. That he had never attempted to claim her prior to her mother's death was a chafing wound, resistant to healing.

She had been reunited with her dead brother — thanks to her lover. She had been reunited with her dead mother — thanks to her muse. Now that she had lost her lover and muse, she had lost her brother and mother for the second time.

Dare I finally admit it? she asked herself.

She reached down for the loudest rattle. Slipping and sliding she grasped it. Carefully she brought it from its dark hole into the light. Written as clear as day is separate from night — Alex was the man, to whom, despite her mother's legacy, she wanted to be married and with whom she had wanted a child.

◆

The two women collected Carmina from The Studio. They headed out to The Dune for lunch, an open-air restaurant on Pietrasanta's beach a few metres from where waves lap the shore. Here you can kick off your shoes and bury your feet in the warm sand. The beach is wedged between the sparkling Mediterranean and the base of the soaring Apuan Alps from which jagged white marble peaks pierce the blue sky. Carmina was animated.

'I have a confession to make.'

Both women held their breaths. They may have wondered if there was any space left for more revelations.

'I'm sure Mum won't mind. But I can't stop thinking of how silly she was,' she exclaimed. 'She had always warned me under threat of death, I must never tell either of you about the other's existence. Yet here I find you have both known each other for years. Mum would have been so surprised.'

Both women appeared to listen carefully.

'Did she ever say why?' Manuella asked.

'She thought you, Alejandra, were far too old fashioned. You would not be able to handle that Manuella sketched us both nude. At least, sketched me nude when I was a child. But she always sketched Mum nude. Isn't that so Manuella?'

Manuella nodded.

'But you aren't really so old fashioned, are you Alejandra?'

Contrary to expectations, Alejandra nodded her head.

'Your mother was right. I am nothing but an old-fashioned lady at heart,' she said.

Internally, she winced. But almost immediately set aside the beginning of a twinge of guilt for the lie she'd just told her granddaughter. And, it would be the first and last, she vowed to herself.

In the upheaval of the previous night, she had not introduced her new companion around. A man younger than her own son and better suited to Carmina's age than hers. She had realized then, lovely though he was, she no longer needed to provide herself with companionship of his sort.

Before Manuella's arrival that morning, and without a hint of regret, she'd said goodbye. She pressed into his hand a thin wad of cash. The hotel arranged for a local taxi driver to return him to Pisa airport.

Carmina wailed, 'Why did I have to lose my mother. We could have all been one family. Think what fun that would have been!'

All three women cried again, one in heartfelt regret, two in heartfelt relief. The waiter brought them menus, a basket of bread, and three glasses of cold prosecco.

'*Complimenti da tutti noi,* compliments from the management,' the waiter said, looking in Manuella's direction. He was referring to the exhibition, which she had forgotten about.

'A toast,' Alejandra cried. 'To RosaMina. And to you my dear, for a sensational exhibition. To Manuella. And, to us.'

'To us,' the women chorused. They clinked their flutes and sipped.

'Carmina,' began Alejandra. 'If it's not too difficult for you, I want to ask you a question.'

'Fire away.'

'Do you know who your father is?'

'Of course I do, silly. Only, you may really be too old-fashioned to hear this.'

Both women sat straighter. Each clenched their hands under the cloth hanging off the edge of the table.

'He was . . . ' she paused for effect, ' . . . a bigamist. Not by choice but circumstance,' she added quickly.

The women's jaws dropped.

'My parents married secretly and fled to England. You know politics. He was a Republican and my mother a Nationalist. One of Franco's men even came to England in search of us when I was still a baby — he asked all sorts of questions. Quite terrified our neighbours. Anyway, to protect us he never lived with us. He went to study medicine and then to throw Franco's men further off — from my mother and me — he married again.'

The two women glanced at each other, possibly trying to ascertain whether to laugh or cry. They did neither.

Mount Sagro, whose ridge was rounded like the smooth curve of a baby's buttocks, unlike its neighbours' soaring jagged peaks, appeared to grow higher.

'Did you know him?' asked Alejandra.

'I hardly remember him. Sometimes he'd call beforehand. But mostly he'd drop by unannounced. Mum would knock on my baby-sitter's door and ask her to take care of me.'

'Your baby-sitter. Take care of you. Why?' Manuella asked.

Though there were no other diners yet — they were unfashionably an hour too early for lunch — Carmina lowered her voice, 'so they could have sex of course.' She paused.

The women waited.

'But I did get to meet his second wife. Well, sort of.'

'How?' they blurted in unison.

The sea, the warm sand and Mount Sagro resuming its natural buttocks' curve, receded. Their attention appeared to be focused wholly on Carmina. She explained about the hospice nurse. Telling how similar she and RosaMina looked, and that she, too, had been present when RosaMina died. At which they all cried again. Without being asked, the waiter re-filled their glasses.

'But, she concluded, 'I did not think it right to tell her the truth.'

'Who is he?' asked Manuella.

'You mean, who was he. He's dead too. His name was Diego Rivas.'

'What happened?' Manuella asked.

Alejandra knew the story. She'd read it in the papers. Alex had called and asked, 'Did you contact Viola Flores?'

'I did the next right thing. I sent a beautiful funeral wreath from both of us.'

Carmina continued. 'He drowned in the Jamaican Sea while they were on honeymoon. Fish had had him for starters. All his soft bits were eaten before he was found. Ugh,' she exclaimed in ghoulish horror and wrinkled her nose.

'Carmina, don't do that. The creases will stay,' Alejandra warned as she pressed on. 'It's not that I don't believe you. But are you sure he was your father?'

'I have his surname. Though I guess for my protection they did not get round to filling out the space for his name on my birth certificate.' She slouched down, and under Alejandra's reproving gaze, sat up straight again. 'And, anyway Mum always wanted me to become a surgeon. Follow in his footsteps you know.'

To her mind, all Carmina's puzzle pieces had finally slotted together.

Possibly relieved, but perhaps daunted at the task of truth that still needed sorting and telling, the two women leant back into their chairs.

'But . . . ,' Carmina changed from the fount of all knowledge to a harbinger of different news. 'Did you see that handsome man at the exhibition last night? Long blonde hair tied back in a pony-tail? The one who was staring at me ever so intently? Well this morning he walked into The Studio.'

The buttocks curve of Mount Sagro leapt up once more. Both women removed their sunglasses. They raised their eyes and looked at Carmina over the tops of their menus.

'And,' she continued squealing in delight, 'he has invited me for an ice-cream in the square later.'

The climb up Mount Sagro would have to be carefully negotiated. For it was an awfully long way down to tumble.

Neither Alejandra nor Manuella said a word. They possibly realized that time for more truths to be told had arrived. Like old and weary war-horses, they mentally played out a variety of scenarios, which could have boiled down to two. The best, for telling the truth they would be forgiven. The worst, for their wrongs they would be forgotten.

With a light clap, the mail landed on the floor, inside the Salazar
Herrera family home.

'I'll get it,' Carmina sang.

The chair scraped against the tiled kitchen floor and almost toppled
over. Alex caught it and set it back on its legs. Moments later, clocks throughout
the house began to strike or chime. Alejandra, tired from broken sleep, halted
pouring coffee mid stream. Finally, the last dying vibration exited through the
walls of the house. After José's death, she had been happy to live with all the
clocks silent, their hands set to the hour of his passing. But when she and Alex
returned home with Carmina in tow, Alex had started them up.

'This way,' he said. 'Papa lives.'

Alejandra could not argue with her son's sentiment. Thus the clocks
chimed on time and in time once again.

Carmina returned. 'Papa, this one is for you. Alejandra — sorry,
nothing for you today,' she said. Carmina took her place at the breakfast table.
She held the bulk of the mail. Envelopes, some more weighty than others,
embossed with their university logos, were addressed to her.

Carmina sorted them into two piles. Heavy — acceptance. Light
— rejection.

It was clear, both Alejandra and Alex knew to keep quiet. Neither
pressed for information. Instead they quietly did everything to protect the
fragile equilibrium Carmina had reached. It had taken her a while to adjust,

one pain-filled step at a time, breaking and re-assembling, reconciling and accepting her new history. Finally, she had begun to think about her future. She returned to the promise she'd made to her mother. She would attend university. To make the application cut-off dates, she had, in a flurry and at random, applied to many universities. At the last count, she had been accepted by three. Yet Alejandra and Alex continued to despair. For Carmina could neither make up her mind where she wanted to study. Not being able to hold out any longer, Alejandra broke the silence.

'Aren't you going to open them?'

'After Papa has opened his letter.'

Alex was studying the official brown envelope addressed to him. The stamp was new, released for that year. It was the image of a bull outlined with a solid red line. On the inside, the bull was divided into sections by serrated lines showing the eleven primal cuts of Mexican beef. The black ink franked over the stamp showed it had come from the municipal hall in the town of Nuevo Laredo, Mexico, the place of his father's birth. Alejandra and Carmina watched Alex. He reached for the letter opener. It was encased in a leather sheaf and secured with a metal snap button. From the handle extended a stainless steel blade that was so sharp a man could shave with it.

It had belonged to Felipe Salazar and used by his wife to separate their son from her at birth. At their farewell, Felipe Salazar had gifted it to his son. José in turn had used it to slice open the blue, feather-light aerogram letters he received from his mother — one a week for as long as Maria Guadalupe Moreno had lived. And then it had passed to Alex. Of late, it was mainly in Carmina's possession. She had received more mail in a month than the letter-box had had pushed through it in the last five years.

Alex inserted the tip of the blade where the flap had been stuck. He sliced the narrow end of the envelope open then safely replaced the knife in its leather sheath.

It was a day of logos. The town's coat of arms emblazoned with the phrase, 'City with Courage', was embossed at the top of the page.

'What is it,' asked Alejandra.

'Good and bad news,' he replied from long habit. 'The good — my grandparents' graves have been located. Their bones have been exhumed.'

'The bad?' grandmother and granddaughter chorused.

'Their bones are to be cremated. New government rules don't allow human skeletons to be exported.'

'What are you going to do Papa?'

'Bring them home.'

————— ◆ —————

Two weeks later, Carmina found herself alone and on the way to Mexico. Alex had come down with a cold. Alejandra, who hated being alone, was quick to insist he remain behind.

'Carmina, it will be a rite of passage for you. It will solidify your roots,' was Dr Giulia Hernandez's parting remark to the young woman.

A few months before, Giulia had received an SOS. Alejandra Herrera requested she come out of retirement. And so she did. Not because of Alejandra's plea. Nor because of the envelope stuffed with cash, left on the office table, but in poignant memory of José Salazar Moreno.

It did not take long for Giulia to pick up the Salazar Herrera threads from where she had last left them after José's passing. But before she even started working with Carmina, she insisted Alejandra, Alex, and Carmina take a blood test. The results of the test proved their link. With that out of the way, she helped Carmina winch up her own sunken shipwreck, stuck fast to the seabed.

To keep Carmina occupied on the trip, Alex, a scarf wrapped around his sore throat, thrust a bundle of aerogram letters filed in chronological order into her hands.

'A years' worth,' his voice rasped, 'your great grandmother sent to your grandfather. Read. You'll learn about them. I am especially fond of her. When I sleep, she visits me.'

'Does she also speak to you?' she asked ready to laugh outright.

'Yes.'

Carmina swallowed her laugh.

Alejandra harrumphed, for until recently she had not believed any of it. Then, early one morning, she had passed Alex's bedroom door standing ajar.

She caught a whiff of the smell she'd hoped never to smell again. She pushed the door further open. Alex was in deep sleep unperturbed by the smell of rotten fish permeating the air. A smell so distinct and so acute she was immediately overcome with nausea.

The film reel of her life wound back. It paused at the moment when, clasped in her mother-in-law's farewell embrace, she smelt the rotten fish and heard once again the following words, 'May the Universe be with you and yours.'

Only then did she realize her mother-in-law had known she was already pregnant. For Maria Guadalupe Moreno could smell a pregnancy even before the mother, human or animal, knew it. As she did then, Alejandra fled to the bathroom and threw up.

That night, Maria Guadalupe Moreno paid a visit. She sat at the end of Alejandra's bed.

'My dear,' she began.

Alejandra shocked herself awake. 'It cannot be,' she said aloud to herself.

She slipped from her bed and opened the windows. A draught of cool night air entered reducing the acute smell. The next night, hesitant, and over-come with tiredness she fell asleep. This time Maria Guadalupe Moreno was waiting for her.

My dear,' she began again, 'unless you want your son to follow in your husband's footsteps, resolve the matter of paternity.'

So surprised were both women by Alejandra's meek acquiescent response, Alejandra woke and Maria Guadalupe Moreno disappeared. The film reel had been wound back to the beginning. All she had to do was press start. And this time there would be no skipping clips.

Without Carmina, the house turned quiet. Notwithstanding his current sore throat, making it difficult to speak, Alex had hardly spoken to his mother since their return to Spain from Italy. He had set aside his issues and focused his attention on helping his daughter. He was determined to make good and clear sense out of an endless string of wholly messy events, many of which remained in the shadows, waiting their turn. Alex found Alejandra at the breakfast table.

'How are you feeling,' she asked, placing the back of her hand upon his forehead as he sat down.

'Not great. But Alejandra,' (he had taken to calling his mother by her first name after José's death), 'no more escaping. Tell me the truth about my biological father.'

Alejandra gazed at her son. He was right. The time had come. And the time was now.

'Prepare yourself. It's a long story. But first, coffee.'

Alejandra used the time to prepare coffee as much as she needed time to prepare the telling of an unembellished or reduced account of her life for the first time.

She busied herself around the kitchen. A typical Spanish kitchen, with large square terracotta tiles under foot, it was long and rectangular, with windows on one side looking out onto a paved terrace, crowded with pots filled with herbs and flowers.

Coloured wall tiles in lavender blue and yellow rose from the floor to shoulder height. Above that, the walls were painted blue, matching the colour of the NorthStar three-door refridgerator that Alejandra had once set her heart on, and had, at great expense, imported from the United States of America. The rest of the walls were adorned with José's first collection of wall and floor standing clocks.

A fireplace in one corner had rarely been used to open-roast meat, given José had never been particularly fond of the smell. A slab of granite wedged against the wall served as a counter and the double sink dishwashing area.

Kitchen bric-a-brac filled the shelves below and were obscured by a yellow cotton curtain, embroidered with green stalks with lavender blossoms, running on a single metal rail.

Alejandra's precious gleaming copper pots and pans hung suspended from a curved rack above the six-burner gas stove. An oven that could roast the hind leg of a grown pig with ease sat below. To the side of that was a smaller oven, used for the delicate baking of bread and airy light custard tarts.

A gracious, wood-carved glassware and crockery cupboard, with hand-etched glass doors, filled to capacity stood close to the centre table. The table could fold out to seat eight, but for as long as Alex recalled, it had only ever been set for three places.

The kitchen soon filled with the aroma of fresh coffee. Believing she needed energy or courage, she was not sure which, Alejandra had prepared a stronger than usual brew.

Finally, she sat down with the coffee pot and placed two cups between them. She began to pour the coffee and mentally pressed the start button to the film reel of her life.

'I was five-years-old and with my mother on the edge of the wide open market square of Marrakesh . . . .'

If the clock collection did strike and chime on and in time, which it surely did, neither Alejandra nor Alex heard them. Nor did José, who took his place at the table and listened. As the telling unfolded, both José and Alex winced or flinched. Or released soft sighs of joy or sadness. And at the telling of some events, which were almost too much to bear, they were not ashamed to wipe away a tear or two.

'I had no idea I was pregnant at the time I left the *riad*. I learnt years later though, through Kamil, that everyone else knew. Do you remember him?' she asked.

Alex nodded. Like perfection, which is the meaning of the name Kamil, he was the man who did his best not to look like a eunuch and landed up looking perfectly like one.

'On my first journey alone, I returned to the compound. It was the last of a string of desert compounds where castrated slaves could rest. Put some meat on their bones before being sold at market. I found only Kamil. Never having had a home, he appointed himself janitor cum tour guide to the crumbling desert rest stop, which at the height of its use, supported up to three thousand souls. Today, the compound is a luxurious palm-dotted oasis for weekend getaways. The orange tree close to where Abd-al-Aziz was buried is now surrounded by an outdoor dining room. Kamil told me the swiftly received news of my banishment caused Abd-al-Aziz to have a heart attack. He also said if I wanted, he had the name of your father.

'Why then?'

'The princess had died and for two years I received no payment. A change of politics in Morocco caused the Princess's family to go broke. As we almost did. Your father, err . . . José took little money from his clients and . . . '

' . . . took up with RosaMina,' Alex finished his mother's sentence.

'And he paid a fortune for her. I could no longer keep us. So I found your father . . . .'

'You mean my biological father. Papa will always be my real father.'

Had mother and son glanced at José's place at the table, they would have seen a single tear splash onto the cloth, forming a fingertip sized damp spot.

Alejandra continued. 'Fortunately, he is the . . . '

'He is still alive?'

'Yes. And he is the only son of a wealthy English family.'

'Don't tell me. There is a fragrance house involved.'

'How on earth did you know?'

Alex looked at his mother carefully. 'From your first trip away alone, you changed your perfume to a light English floral scent. You have never stopped wearing it since.'

'Kamil called to make an appointment. And instead of Kamil arriving for the appointment, I did.'

'And he recognized you instantly. And you told him about me?'

'Yes.'

'He wanted to meet me?'

'Immediately. I refused. Saying, only once José had passed on. I did not want José to know you were not his son.'

'He knew. He had known from the beginning.'

It was Alejandra's turn to flinch so hard, the coffee pot grown cold, and the cup before her, flew off the table and shattered on the tiled floor.

'He knew?' she whispered, as the shards scattered all around them.

'All the time,' Alex repeated.

Alejandra looked as though she'd just had the stuffing knocked out of her.

'I'm just taking a minute,' she said. As Abd-al-Aziz had taught her so many years ago, she shut her eyes, breathed deeply, and counted to ten. When she was ready, she opened her eyes.

'Did he know about you and RosaMina?'

'I made sure he did not. It was difficult enough for me to face him while I knew. God knows it would have been impossible if he'd also known.'

Alejandra grabbed her son's hand. 'Thank you,' she said. 'I believe if he had found out, it would have destroyed the relationship between the two of you. He was totally in love with you and RosaMina.'

'That's where you are wrong. Papa adored you.'

Alejandra gulped. 'You think? He told you so?'

'On his death-bed. When he'd done telling me about him not being my father. Now back to my biological father. Does he still want to meet me?'

'Yes.'

'When?'

'Anytime you are ready.'

'Is he married? Does he have other children?'

'Widowed. No children.'

'I am his only child. Did he recompense you?'

'He wanted to. But I said no. Having you was recompense enough.'

This did not ring true. Alex knew his mother was shrewd when it came to money.

'But I did accept shares in his company. In my name and yours. Lucky for us they have done very well.'

'So that's how we get along.'

'We get along on my share. Yours is banked.' Alex looked at his mother.

'Is that what you meant before I left, when you said, the money was mine too?'

'Yes. And, I'll tell you something else: I also took care of RosaMina and Carmina.'

'You did?' Alex was flummoxed.

'Though RosaMina's mother did the largest part.'

'RosaMina's mother?'

'Maria Expósito. You probably remember her as Madam.'

'Madam. Of, The House, Madam?' Alex's eyes opened wide. 'So RosaMina had a mother after all,' he said, hardly believing what he had just learned.

'This may come as surprise to you, Álejo, but all of us have mothers. Maybe just not the mothers we would like them to be.'

Memory of the shadows in RosaMina's eyes rose up to haunt him again. But that was in the past. Now he was in the present. He looked at his mother clearly for the first time in years. He stood up from the table. He grabbed her into a standing position and hugged her. He hugged her and he hugged her until he thought his heart would burst.

'You are the only mother I would ever want,' he said.

Unseen, José stood alongside them.

'I wish your father were here now.'

'He is. Can't you feel him?' said Alex as José's arms embraced them.

And so the threesome stood clasped in a hug while Felipe Salazar and Maria Guadalupe Moreno stood to one side, smiled and nodded.

But then they turned away. They had another matter to attend. Their granddaughter was on her way to Mexico.

And if one listened hard enough, you may have heard the single command Felipe Salazar gave. Furry-mounded sentinels, indistinguishable one from the other, uncurled their bodies and rose up. Loping around and ahead of their leader, they darted off to flush out imaginary quails, returned, and took up their flanking positions again.

Carmina flew from Madrid to Mexico City, then to Quetzalcóatl Airport. From there, she boarded a bus heading to the city centre of Nuevo Laredo, Mexico.

Zipped into one of the pockets of her holdall was the letter her father had received. In another was a battered travel-size Spanish-English dictionary. On the inside cover, barely legible was the name, Raul Perez. She was a long way off from speaking fluent Spanish, although after the last nine months she could string more than just two words together.

'You'll be fine,' Alejandra had said. 'You're not my granddaughter for nothing.'

But it was Giulia Hernandez who gave her the real confidence to undertake the journey.

'Time and space away will be good,' she said. 'It will put all you have been exposed to into perspective. Remember, it is after all only history. Albeit, yours, and truly it is a rich one. But, one lives in the present. Not the past. Hold up your head. Be proud of who you are.'

Learning about her mother had been hard. She had cried unrestrainedly. Alex had spared her nothing. He felt she ought to know all of the truth, for it was the lack of it that had so shattered José and almost brought him to his knees.

Carmina reconciled herself to her mother's past. She took comfort in knowing she had been a victim of circumstance. She could not blame her grandmother, Maria Expósito either. She had proof of her maternal grand-mother's ample amends; through the letter she'd written RosaMina; and, through the purchase of the apartment in Richmond, of which Carmina was the sole owner. This was compounded by Giulia's comment claiming her grandmother to be unique, and that the world would be a better place if there were more like her. For a moment, Carmina speculated where her grand-mother was. And if she might still be alive.

Alejandra was not used to explaining herself or her actions. But this time she did, and in infinite detail. To her relief, Carmina accepted her explanation. In return, she received a long and silent bear hug. For there, too, was plenty of evidence that Alejandra had more than made up for her divi-sive actions.

Alex held Manuella responsible for 'knowing the truth', but never letting on. He could not forgive her for what he called, 'her totally selfish reasons'. After all, starting with Maria Guadalupe Moreno, who selflessly sent her only beloved son away to a better life, Maria Expósito took care vicariously of her absconded daughter and grandchild, Alejandra Herrera paved the way financially for her son, while RosaMina Rivas took her unborn child to a new country. They all did what they possibly could to protect and help advance their offspring. At their last meeting, Alex had unkindly said to Manuella, 'It's because you have never been a mother. Mother's just don't behave like that.'

'Bah,' Giulia said. 'Don't take on board your father's unresolved issues with Manuella. Those are his problems — not yours.'

'Manuella is too much part of our lives for us never to have anything to do with her,' Alejandra had said. 'Your father, just like everyone else, needs time to process. Just some of us take longer than others. Besides, his pride has been hurt. And that will take him more time to get over it and come to his senses.'

To his annoyance, Alex found his sins of omissions creep unexpectedly upon his waking and sleeping moments. Against his will, he came to realize he was not entirely blameless for where he found himself.

Having read a year's worth of the bundled letters during the flight to Mexico, Carmina learned more about the couple her father considered his grandparents. One of whom he conversed with in his dreams. Carmina was intrigued by both grandparents and looked forward to finding out more. She felt honoured to bring Felipe Salazar and Maria Guadalupe Moreno home.

The bus pulled up at the terminus just across from the imposing building of the city hall. Her curly hair was matted and her eyes grainy. But a shower and sleep could wait. She had an appointment with one Teo Perez. Preparing to meet him, she took out the small, battered dictionary. It felt snug and warm in her hand, perhaps it was the heat, Carmina thought.

She exited the bus. Checking the letter addressed to Alex with detailed directions in her other hand, she crossed the road. She stepped into the revolving front door and entered the quiet and cool City Hall.

⎯⎯⎯⎯ ◆ ⎯⎯⎯⎯

The midday bus from Quetzalcóatl Airport was almost always on time. Even bus drivers wanted to get home for lunch. Then, abandon themselves' to a few hours' worth of siesta. Today was no different.

Teo Perez had seen the bus pull into the station almost dead on time. He had left his office — he called it that but in reality it was a desk squashed into the unclaimed artifacts storage room — and was now standing on the top step of the sweeping staircase. Looking down, he wondered what the great granddaughter of Felipe Salazar would look like.

His great grandfather, Raul Perez, had told him the story of the miracle cure that was Felipe Salazar's so many times he could recite it word for word. The bit about the mild earthquake, Teo scoffed at only once. So great was Raul Perez's annoyance that Teo never dared scoff aloud at the telling of it again.

He saw a young woman enter the building. While he had no idea if it indeed was Carmina Salazar Rivas, a voice from deep within said. 'That is she.'

⎯⎯⎯⎯ ◆ ⎯⎯⎯⎯

Consulting the letter once again for directions, Carmina turned left and started the climb up the staircase. Rounding the curve, she caught sight of a young man standing on the top step.

He stood upright. He wore a cotton open-necked shirt and mustard-yellow cotton chinos. He was neat. His dark straight hair was cut short. He had thick eyebrows and almost black eyes. His skin was clear and he had a strong jawline. All in all he was a perfect example of his mixed Mestizo ancestry.

'Carmina Salazar Rivas,' he said, stepping down, outstretching both hands to clasp hers. His hands were clean and fingernails cut short and square. 'Welcome to Nuevo Laredo.'

It did not matter that he had climbed the same steps several times a day for the last four years. His body simply forgot. And his coordination behaved as if it had never existed. Or perhaps it was, as the newspapers would report the following day, Mother Earth, giving a single violent jolt around mid-day — a firm reminder to all of who really was in charge.

Either way, Teo Perez, to his great consternation, disbelief and acute embarrassment missed the step. He fell forward, crashing headlong into Carmina. Weighed down with her backpack, gravity tipped the scales. Clutching each other they tumbled and bumped their way down each step in a flurry of flailing arms and legs. The letter and dictionary followed suit.

'You okay?' Teo asked in English, his arm pinned down by Carmina lying over it. For a moment longer neither moved. They were not sure which legs belonged to whom. And anyway, they fit so well, it seemed a pity to separate.

'I guess,' she said.

But when Teo looked again, her right eye was already beginning to close and swell. They disentangled. With caution they stood holding onto each other for support. For the first time in what seemed like a century to her, Carmina giggled. And then laughed. Teo was astonished at the lovely bells sound of her voice. Still perplexed at his momentary clumsiness, but forgetting his embarrassment, he imagined the comical sight they must have presented — clutching each other for dear life as they rolled their way down the steps. He began to laugh, too.

And if you listened hard enough, you may have heard Raul Perez laugh. Mother Earth had taught Teo a long overdue lesson — she did not take kindly to being scoffed at, neither aloud nor in silence.

But Teo would regale his children and grandchildren to be with another story. Mother Earth, making sure he would realize Carmina was 'the one', gave a single quake, catapulting him right into her arms.

At the strike of midday, City Hall workers streamed out of their offices, down the staircase, heading home for lunch. They by-passed the laughing couple, who, despite clearly having had taken a tumble, appeared to be all right. In a matter of minutes the City Hall had emptied. The revolving door turned for the last time.

'Let me try again. Carmina Salazar Rivas,' he said still holding her, 'Welcome to Nuevo Laredo. I am . . . '

' . . . Teo Perez,' Carmina finished his sentence.

If their bodies were made up of a million small distinct dots, akin to the painting method, Pointillism, each dot searched its corresponding, equal opposite in the other, connected, and fused together.

'You need some ice on that bump,' he said. 'Come with me.'

He grabbed her backpack, gathered up the letter and dictionary, whose cover lay open, exposing his grandfather's barely legible signature, and taking her by the hand they passed through the revolving door into bright sunlight. Carmina held a hand over her eye, which had begun to throb.

He lived a few minutes walk from the City Hall in a studio apartment on the third floor. He opened the front door, which entered directly into a small compact kitchen.

'Sit,' he said.

Removing an ice tray from the freezer he fashioned an icepack in a teacloth. 'Hold this over your eye.'

She winced at the coldness. He held out a glass of water and two tablets. 'Drink these.'

Travel, the shock of the fall, and her throbbing eye caused her to shiver.

'Come.'

Carmina rose. Like a sleepwalker she moved into the next room, sank down onto the narrow bed and passed out. Teo removed her shoes and covered her with a light blanket. He placed the backpack close to her and left her to sleep.

Carmina dreamt. And in her dream, her mother stood on one side of the bed. Dr Raul Perez, Felipe Salazar, Maria Guadalupe Moreno, and Dr José Salazar Moreno, stood on the opposite. Consuelo the bitch lay at the bottom of the bed. A skeleton suspended in a corner of the room glowed luminously. It made its presence known to her in order that upon waking she would not take fright. All watched over her.

Carmina made a mental note during her dream: she was to remember, when she woke up, there was a person missing — Maria Expósito. And her missing told Carmina her grandmother was still alive.

Hours later, she woke. It was dark outside. Dull traffic sounds came through the window. A small table lamp shone alongside her. On the reverse side of the letter, Teo had written, 'Back around nine with dinner. Clean towels in the bathroom'. He had weighted it down with the dictionary.

She eased herself off the bed. She felt like she'd been run over by a bus. Finding her balance she moved to the only other door, leading into the small bathroom. She stripped and stood under a torrent of hot water. The heat seeped into her sore and bruised body. After, she dried herself. Brushed her teeth and hair. Pulled on a pair of loose trousers and an oversized T-shirt.

Teo returned with dinner. She was ravenous.

'Hey. You're up. Let me take a look at you.'

She stood while he, standing a few feet away, assessed her. 'Turn around. All's, well. You haven't suffered any permanent damage.'

'Ah,' Carmina said making the connection helped by the glowing skeleton. 'You are a chiropractor.'

'Getting there. I still have to write my finals.'

'My father is one. As was his father.'

'José Salazar Moreno. I knew about. But I did not know his son, Alex Salazar Herrera, is one, too.

Sitting on the floor, and using the coffee table as their dining table, Teo and Carmina shared their dinner. While it was a new experience to both of them, it was an experience so old that almost everyone, more or less, gets to live it. And old as it is, it feels natural. And right. Just as it was meant to be.

The following morning, Teo produced an eye patch for Carmina. It stopped her eyeball rolling around as the lid involuntarily tried to slide open.

'Much better, thank you,' she exclaimed.

They headed off to the City Hall. This time when they walked up the curving staircase each tread remained fixed in place. But just in case, they held hands. So they were ready, should either miss a step and slip.

They entered the storage room. Teo produced three metal canisters with screw on lids. And sheet upon sheet of well-stamped and signed official documentation.

'The two larger canisters are the ashes of Felipe Salazar and Maria Guadalupe Moreno,' he said, consulting the documents. 'The smaller one contains the ashes of a dog.'

'Her name is Consuelo,' Carmina said. She recalled her feet being warmed by the old, yellow dog that had crawled up onto the bed and lay at the foot of it. She'd read about Consuelo's death in one of Maria Guadalupe Moreno's letters. Where, against all religious beliefs, she had been buried in the piece of land set aside for the human members of the Salazar Moreno family. And she'd read how Felipe Salazar had ordered the blacksmith to fashion a metal cross, inscribed upon which was her name.

But that was not all.

She read how Consuelo had died. It caused Carmina to cry so much, she heard Alejandra's alarmed voice in her head, warning of the permanent injury she'd suffer to her eyes.

— ◆ —

Consuelo had outlived most of her offspring. In her last years she had claimed one of the whelping boxes as her space, in which she lay corkscrew curled most of the time.

Maria Guadalupe Moreno coaxed her from this position at meal times. The bitch struggled to her feet and tottered on her spindly legs outdoors. Her patchy yellow coat revealed a network of old hunting scars. Maria Guadalupe Moreno hand fed her the choicest bits of meat. Including, sometimes, the placenta — being rich in iron and protein taken directly from Consuelo's birthing great-great-great granddaughters. Once Consuelo had eaten, Maria Guadalupe Moreno scooped her up in her arms. She caressed the bitch and like she'd done once before to Felipe Salazar's forehead, placed gentle kisses upon hers. She returned Consuelo to her box bed and tucked the old bitch under the cover of a blanket.

Consuelo's eyesight and hearing had failed. Yet each time Felipe Salazar entered or left the kitchen, she raised her head, sensing movement through vibration and smell. From the time she was a puppy she had singled out Felipe Salazar. She adored him. She became his shadow. He was the God of her life.

On the last day of Consuelo's life, both Felipe Salazar and Maria Guadalupe Moreno had been out of the house for longer than usual. Consuelo left her bed. On unsteady, stiff legs she went in search of Felipe Salazar. Her nose pressed as close to the dusty earth as she could get it. She followed his scent to the corral where a *sorteo* was taking place.

All eyes were on the young bull being put through his potential fighting test. Consuelo slipped under the horizontal corral pole, not into the practice ring, but into the corral where *Toro de Semillas* was grazing.

In his peripheral vision, the old bull must have caught sight of a moving shadow. He trundled around. With slow plods he advanced upon Consuelo. She halted. Her body shivered in apparent confusion. Danger warned in the form of vibration — from the young bull being put through his paces in the coral alongside her and from the heavy steps coming inexorably and directly towards her. Confused, her compass switched off. She did not know which way to turn out of harm's way.

But Felipe Salazar turned. The film reel that was Consuelo's life slowed. Felipe Salazar was not able to reach her in time. *Toro de Semillas'* massive head dipped. With the slightest, almost imperceptible turn of his head, the tip of his right horn sliced Consuelo open from her sternum to her crotch.

At Felipe Salazar's warning shout, *toreros* jumped into the corral, drawing away *Toro de Semillas'* attention. At the moment of being sliced open, shock caused Consuelo's sight to reverse. As Felipe Salazar reached her, catching her just as her legs buckled, she looked up.

As it had been from when she had been a puppy, bright-eyed adoration blazed from her eyes into his. He carried her home in his arms. His hands held closed the wound from which her intestines threatened to spill. All the while, her tail thumped against his ribs. She nudged his arm with her wet nose. She licked him. By the time he had reached the house, the thumping tail and licking tongue had ceased.

A week later, the Mexican veterinary surgeon confirmed *Toro de Semillas* had ingested the poisonous plant, whitesnake root. He had died after suffering tremendous muscle tremors. He was gutted. His organs burned to cinders. A fire was built on the inside of his stomach cavity. There his body burned for several days, until only charred remains of his hooves and horns remained.

'I'd like to visit the ranch.'

Teo looked at Carmina. 'The ranch no longer exists. It's currently a building site. Didn't you know that?'

'My father told me the ranch had been sold to the city for development. But I had no idea building was already underway.'

Teo placed a cardboard box on his desk and lifted the lid. Inside lay three metal crosses, all the same size and design. Each had a name cut into the horizontal bar. They were rusted, their edges uneven and encrusted with dirt.

'You can take these back with you to Spain, too, if you like.'

'I will. But I'd still like to go and visit the ranch. Even if it is a building site.'

The new low cost houses appeared to be only incomplete shells. Yet inhabitants had already moved into them. All around construction continued. Row upon row of identical houses, built to a grid, had sprung up from the dusty earth. Electricity poles had yet to be connected to each other, as were the telephone poles and streetlights. Huge cement blocks standing over five metres high rimmed the border.

'What's on the other side of cement barrier?'

'No-man's-land, and then the Rio Bravo. Beyond the river lies our sister city in the U.S. Together, both cities are referred to as Los Dos Laredos.'

'Maria Guadalupe Moreno wrote of mesquite trees, cacti, bees, and hummingbirds with orange throats. And owls. Do any still exist?'

'Come.'

Carmina followed Teo and in turn, a ragged group of children followed Carmina. Notwithstanding her eye patch, she was something of an oddity. Her hair compared to theirs was light and curly versus their dark and straight. And even stranger to them, it appeared a teaspoon of light brown sugar had been spilled and stuck to her nose.

Teo flashed his official city hall badge at a guard. He opened the metal gate crisscrossed with steel gauge wire set between two concrete boulders. They walked along a path that took them towards the river. The further they walked, scrub vegetation increased, and the noise of the building site behind them decreased. The sun was at its peak. Dotted between the mesquite trees at various heights stood columns of thorny cacti. The Rio Grande came into view. It flowed like a sparkling silver ribbon.

'Take a seat.' Teo indicated to the earth under the shade of a stocky mesquite tree. 'Listen.'

Carmina became aware of constant hum. She followed Teo's gaze and looked up into the branches of the tree. Even with the use of one eye, she saw a mass of bees collecting nectar. She had never witnessed so many and such busy-ness. When Teo changed his gaze direction, so did she. Clumps of bright-coloured plants with red stalks for flowers were scattered around and in front of them.

'Stay still,' he whispered.

The first rufous hummingbird appeared, then another, and another. Bright sunlight set fire to the iridescent orange spot on their throats, as they hovered and darted from one flower to another. It became clear why a hummingbird is called a hummingbird. Their wings beat so fast as to be invisible but the sound that they make is a hum. And another curiosity: hummingbirds can fly upside down. At least rufous hummingbirds can.

Viewing the bees and hummers through her good eye caused it to throb. But Carmina was enchanted.

'Ready?' Teo gave her his hand and helped her up from the ground.

They walked back in the direction of the building site. He had one more surprise in store for her.

'Stand here,' he said. He walked towards a cactus. Using his knuckles he rapped upon its trunk. He pointed to a small hole. He rapped again.

An elf owl popped its head through the hole. Its yellow eyes were highlighted by a pair of perfectly tweaked white eyebrows.

'It's so tiny.'

'Smallest owl in the world.'

Carmina and Teo enjoyed another three nights of each other's company, and sharing dinner over the coffee table. On the fourth day, she repacked her backpack, making space for the three metal canisters and three worn and rusted crosses.

'Do you have space for this too?' Teo handed her a manila envelope.

Inside, neatly tied in bundles, were blue aerogram letters. The letters José Salazar Moreno had written to his mother.

'I found them among other documents taken out of the adobe house before it was pulled down.'

She laughed gaily, releasing the lovely bells sound of her voice. 'Papa is going to be thrilled. He thought they had been forgotten.'

W ith a light clap, the mail landed on the floor, inside the Salazar Herrera family home.

'I'll get it,' Carmina sang out. The chair scraped against the tiled kitchen floor and almost toppled over. Alex, already prepared, caught and set it back on its legs. Alejandra and Alex glanced at each other.

For months since Carmina's return from Mexico, her day had not gotten off to a good start until after the mail had been delivered. More to the point, until after she had received and read a letter from Teo Perez. The young man was attending the Palmer School of Chiropractic in Davenport, Iowa. He would complete his course in June. Then he was coming to Medina del Campo.

Clocks throughout the house chimed. Alejandra rejoiced at their sound. For she now believed, as her son did, their sound meant José remained close. Carmina returned.

'We are all in luck today. There's mail for each of us,' she said gaily. 'Alejandra, this one is for you. Papa, these are yours.' Carmina took her place at the breakfast table. She held a single blue aerogram letter in her hand. Reaching for the leather sheath, she snapped it open and the awfully sharp and slender Bowie knife slid out.

So intent on slicing opening her letter, Carmina did not notice her grandmother's actions. She'd slid her letter under her plate. When no one was about, Alejandra would open and read it. Meanwhile she hoped the contents would tell her what she wanted. Nor did Carmina see her father shuffle through his mail. He paused for a moment longer on a particular envelope. He, too, would read its contents when neither his mother nor daughter were around.

Usually, while Alejandra served coffee, Carmina scanned Teo's letter. Then, starting at the top, she'd read out aloud those bits she did not mind sharing with her family.

Alex was always interested in hearing Teo's experiences from the college where José Salazar Moreno had graduated. And Alex compared his experiences from The London College of Chiropractic where he had graduated to Teo's. Given there was more or less sixty year's worth between the three of them, Alex could not help but marvel at the level to which, in leaps and bounds, the profession of Chiropractic had risen. A beguilingly simple, drug-free, hands-on process focusing on the health and function of the musculoskeletal system facilitated by the 'Chiropractic adjustment'.

Alex made a mental note to attend the next Chiropractic refresher workshop as soon as possible.

Alejandra and Alex waited patiently for Carmina to begin reading from her letter. That day things were different. She grew pale.

'He's arriving tomorrow afternoon,' she announced, checking the postmarked date. 'It's too soon. The piece is nowhere close to being finished.'

Months before, to Alejandra and Alex's dismay, Carmina had decided not to attend university after all. Her artistic calling had been far stronger. Begging her mother's forgiveness by burning too many candles and almost setting San Antolín's altar alight, she hijacked her father's oldest jeans and shirts. She fashioned headscarves from Alejandra's cotton teacloths. Once dressed — much to Alex's shock — she looked not dissimilar to Manuella. He found himself missing Manuella. He had begun to wonder if he'd been too hasty in wholly breaking off their relationship.

To Alejandra's surprise, Carmina reopened the garden shed where she'd once painted. Carmina persuaded Alex to remove large sections of the roof. It had been replaced with clear glass, flooding the old shed in bright light.

She clapped her hands. 'It looks just a little bit like The Palm House at Kew Gardens. Have you ever been there?' she asked her father.

The lid of that particular memory box blew off. 'Yes. Just once.'

Carmina turned facing him. 'Don't tell me. I know when. I was three-years old. It was . . . ' here Alex's voice joined his daughter's, ' . . . Sunday, April 28, 1958.'

A lejandra's dried-out paints and brushes were tossed. Carmina sorted through her grandmother's canvases. Some had been left unfinished. She cleaned and stacked them on the floor lining the walls facing inwards. Alejandra had had a preference for colourful exotic flowers.

'A holdover,' she said,' from having lived in the desert, where flowers only exist in dreams.'

The first thing that found a new home in the shed was the delicate and glowing Chōtē haḍḍiyōṁ. Carmina suspended her from a hook in one cor-ner. The three rusted metal crosses got tacked to one wall. Photos — Teo had gone back to no-man's-land and taken many — had been blown up into glossy prints. In glorious colour, swarms of bees in mesquite trees, orange-throated hummingbirds, an elf owl poking his head out of a hole in a cactus and the sil-ver ribbon flow of the Rio Grande, were tacked to the opposite wall. A tattered magenta and gold bullfighting cape hooked over the horns of a bull skull she'd found at the Medina del Campo's flea market. A single one hundred pesetas note bearing the image of Maria Teresa Lopez González lay on the table face up. Carmina was ready to get to work.

Over the following weeks, Alejandra and Alex had gone down to the shed to view the work in progress.

Strewn about were cut-outs of Alejandra's oversized painted flow-ers; threads from the magenta cape each painstakingly removed by means of eyebrow tweezers; an assortment of containers (raided from under Alejandra's bric-a-brac shelves in the kitchen) holding sheets of paper soaking in glue stiff-ened water; an easel upon which stood a canvas deeply grooved with wax lines, being the beginnings of a woman's face and bare shoulders; pots of paint and brushes; a miniature cross — a copy of the original — with three capital letters, in the process of being hammered flat and encrusted with viciously sharp shards of antique mirror glass; vivid blown up photos, cut and pasted to form a three-dimensional, background collage.

Alejandra wondered if perhaps they should have pressed harder on the university issue.

While Carmina worked on her piece, Alex sorted and matched the letters his father and grandmother had written each other. It was not difficult, given they had neatly filed their letters. Alex pulled out the manuscript he'd started in Italy. He found the typewriter, removed the grey plastic dust cover and changed the ribbon. He set to work.

'Papa, what are you typing?'

'My grandparents and father's story,' he said. 'And mine. Maybe, one day you can add to it by including yours and your mother's.'

'I'll start today. Alejandra, please write all of yours too. Combined, we'll have one family history.'

For a moment, denial clouded Alejandra's face. Midway she had a change of mind.

'Okay,' she said. To herself she said, 'Maybe not all of it. But, then again, maybe all of it.'

Abd-al-Aziz's stern lesson of always keeping one's cards close to one's chest was hard to let go.

Alex reviewed his previously typed notes. He found himself thinking about Manuella again. The first time he'd seen her in the English teashop, when his head and heart was so full of RosaMina.

Alejandra returned to her box of trinkets. She picked up a pen and began to record the memory each one held for her. This time she did not stab her fingers.

Carmina sorted through the items in her metal box. She placed it all out in chronological order. There were several large gaps which needed filling. But she set about writing that which was hers.

The following morning, before the mail's arrival, the doorbell rang. Alex answered. Teo Perez stood on the doorstep.

The men liked each other instantly. Just as Alex and Old Guy had, when they first met. Alejandra, despite the earliness of the hour, arrived minutes later enveloped in a cloud of light floral fragrance. She looked lovely and fresh, as she always did. Graciously, she made Teo welcome.

'Carmina?' Teo asked after polite necessities were completed.

Alex pointed him in the direction of the shed and disappeared back to his study. There was the matter of yesterday's letter to attend to.

Alejandra retired to her private sitting room. She drew out a sheet of paper. This time, instead of drawing up a list of suitable families in the region, she wrote an invitation list for a wedding. The first person on the list was the writer of the letter she'd received the day before.

When they all assembled for breakfast, the young couple's faces said it all. The table had been laid, including champagne flutes. Across each woman's plate lay a single rose. Alex popped the cork of a bottle of champagne he'd found in the refrigerator. He made a toast. The date was set for one month hence.

The couple left. They went in search of wedding rings along Padilla Street, where all the jewellry stores of Medina del Campo are to be found. Alejandra and Alex cleared the breakfast table.

'Thank you,' she said.

'What for?'

'The champagne and roses. It was a thoughtful touch.'

'I'd like to take the credit. But I can't. It wasn't me.'

◆

The day of the wedding dawned fresh and clear. Carmina had had little to do with the preparations. Alejandra had arranged everything. When she had proposed Carmina look at Alejandra's wedding dress, there was not the slightest hesitation in Carmina's mind. She would wear it with joy.

To the plain silk dress, Alejandra added a layer of tulle. Pinned at strategic points holding the tulle in place, was the entire collection of jewelled pins, Alejandra's and RosaMina's.

Secretly, Carmina felt she would finally become the princess she'd dreamed of being — if only for one day. And Alejandra finally got to dress up the girl child she had always wanted.

Carmina went down to the shed. She viewed the separate pieces of her sculpture once more. It was a mix of stone, metal, paper maché.

On an easel stood her version, in oil, of Maria Teresa Lopez González. When she had begun first sketching the image, she noticed a curious thing. Flashbacks of how her mother and Manuella looked, and the wonderful beauty of Alejandra all came crowding on the canvas.

'It's a fine painting,' her father came up behind her. 'You've captured your mother's quiet mystery.'

'It also looks quite a lot like Manuella. Her open face and direct eye contact. Don't you think?' asked Alejandra as she walked into the shed.

'Alejandra, go and stand next to it, won't you?' asked her granddaughter.

'See, Papa. It also looks like Alejandra.'

'Now you go and stand next to your grandmother.'

As impossible as it may seem, the women past and present, blended, and reflected back as one.

'Are you ready to see the finished piece?' she asked.

Methodically Carmina, who had assembled the sculpture a hundred times in her head, began to slot the pieces together, starting from the stone base. First, centre to the base of stone, was the paper maché human skull, festooned with her grandmother's flowers. A bull's skull, complete with horns, sat to the left of the human skull. On the opposite side, a wrought iron cross with the first three letters C O N, stuck with glittering Venetian mirror shards. Behind the bull's skull and iron cross rose a human skeleton. Darting and hovering between the skeleton bones were hummingbirds — one flying upside down. Rising still higher, and centre right a glowing heart made of magenta cloth. And above the heart, the face of all women descended from Eve crowned with a halo of golden bees. Alejandra and Alex stood speechless.

'Enough gawping. Off you go and get dressed,' she said.

———— ◆ ————

And then, for the third time in her life, Alejandra entered the Church of San Antolín where the wedding service was to be held. The front pews were reserved for the Salazar Herrera and Perez families, and their closest friends. The rest of the church was packed with the townspeople of Medina del Campo. This was one event they would not miss for anything in the world. Those elderly folks, who had been patiently waiting in God's waiting room, gave up their turn in the queue and attended the service. And if they could make it to the church service, they would, with God's help, make it to the reception too, they declared.

The reception was held in the square around the town's fountain. Long rows of tables and benches had been set up. Blazing fires had been started at dawn and tended until a mass of glowing embers slowly roasted full carcasses of sheep and pigs. Townswomen, fiercely competitive of their culinary abilities, had prepared the rest of the feast. The local vineyard had set up wooden barrels of corn-yellow and blood-orange red wine.

The mayor, dressed in his official regalia, gave a long speech honouring the Salazar Herrera family. José's kindness was lauded, for he still lived in many hearts.

The Perez family was welcomed and embraced as one of the town's own. A former judge, who had given up his queue in God's waiting room, had to be helped to the microphone, whereupon he promptly sat down, for he could not speak and stand at the same time. Yet another town official had something to say, and so speeches ran on, matching the flow of wine.

But when the roasted meats were cooked to perfection and the air was thick with their fragrances, running like knives through everyone's bellies, the speeches came to a halt. Finally after a great carve up, platters were passed along the tables. Praises were sung to the town's womenfolk, meat roasters and wine maker.

And as most brides and grooms come to understand, getting married is not just their day. Rather, it is an opportunity for everyone to look back at where they were at this event in their own lives. And memories — sad, happy, buried or forgotten — are lived once more.

'Alejandra, Papa, come. I have a surprise for you,' called Carmina.

The event that refused to go away in Alex's memory bobbed to the surface. Berta, looking even more like a Valkyrie than he last recalled, came forward. She was pushing a wheelchair.

'Alejandra, this is my other grandmother.'

Alejandra bent down. Despite the awkwardness of the wheelchair, she gave the frail Maria Expósito an enveloping hug.

'Welcome, welcome,' she said, smiling.

Alex adopted Manuella's father — Old Guy's — romantic mannerisms. He bent over Maria Expósito's hand and kissed it. Like his mother, he said, 'Welcome.'

When he bent over Berta's hand — his head directly opposite her breasts — his ears burned red hot. Nevertheless, he did not embarrass himself and warmly welcomed her too.

A sleek black car with a chrome jaguar leaping off the bonnet pulled into the square. With difficulty, an elderly man emerged from the back passenger door, held open by a chauffeur. The man had been tall once. Now he was stooped. His face, despite loose flesh that comes with age, was smooth planed. His nose, however, still held its curved and well-defined nostrils. His knees were stiff and he walked with the aid of a stick. A classic English pinstripe suit that was too hot for Spain in June sagged, now too big for the man's slender frame. Alex searched his mother's face. She smiled slightly.

'We've been in contact for a while. He wanted to see you, to make his personal amends. Try to be nice. He is a dying man.'

Alejandra took her son's proffered arm. Together they walked towards the man standing at the periphery, looking anxiously into the celebrating crowd.

And yet another car pulled up. A cherry red convertible with its top down.

This time Alejandra searched her son's face.

Mother and son separated.

From the sports car emerged a woman dressed in an Indian outfit. Its green and red hues suited the tone of her skin. A jewelled pin attached a long flowing scarf to her shoulder. In one hand, she carried an artist's portfolio case. It was filled with sketches done long ago of a mother and her child.

The sun had set and the lanterns — the Town Hall usually only hung them out for great feasts — got switched on. A light breeze caused them to bounce, casting dancing shadows on the stone paved square. A gramophone started up. Strains of the town's music, 'La cumparsita', drifted over the crowd.

Before minds remembered, bodies did. Ears caught the dear familiar rhythm. Hearts gave a trill of joy and beat a little faster. Toes and feet began to twitch, then tap in time.

Fausto drew Giulia to him, the light between their bodies closed. His cheek rested against hers. The crowd hushed. The past rushed forward. For a moment each entered their own dream of love. Perhaps found, lost, regretted or joyfully recalled.

The dancing couple glided, twisted and turned, inspiring all those around them. Men and women, old and young, turned to each other. Putting the past behind, grateful for the present partner in their arms, they took to the square's stone pavings. Until dawn, they attacked, repelled and enticed their partners with vigour.

On the edges of the dancing mass, out of harms way, children attempted copying the complicated and simple kicking up of feet, stiff quick and slow walking, and fast twists.

It was a night neither past, present, nor future would ever forget.

THE END

If you'd like to share your thoughts with me, I'd really like that! Please visit my website at www.jacquelinefalcomer.com to contact me.

About The Author

Jacqueline Falcomer was born in Natal, South Africa, and grew up between Johannesburg and Durban. She has travelled extensively, living in the UK as  well as the USA, twice, and dreams of returning. Perhaps one day . . . For the last decade she has lived in a small hilltop house in Italy, with a splendid view of the Mediterranean.

She still travels, including to new places likely to be used as a backdrop in future books.

Forget Me Not features locations in Mexico, the United States, Spain, the United Kingdom, Morocco, and Italy. The second book in her trilogy of memories, *Memento Mori* (Remember Death), is set primarily in the Italian Alps and Salzburg, Austria.

More information about Jacqueline, her inspirations, audio versions, and first chapters of upcoming books may be at www.jacquelinefalcomer.com.

The Journey to *Forget Me Not*

I am still not sure how this happened, but writing *Forget Me Not* started in February 2013. My fingers flew over the keyboard with places and characters materializing out of thin air and cramming my brain. I hung on and went for the ride . . . never knowing which shore I was going to land upon.

I do hope you enjoyed *Forget Me Not*'s characters and their stories as much as I did writing them.

The second novel in this trilogy, *Memento Mori* (Remember Death), is a work in progress.

Publication updates will be found on www.jacquelinefalcomer.com.